Praise for Kerry Barrett

'Heart-breaking but so uplifting – Kerry really is a hugely talented voice.' Nicola Cornick, author of *The Forgotten Sister*

'Wonderful … Both heart-warming and heart-breaking … Unputdownable.' Kathleen McGurl, author of *The Girl from Bletchley Park*

'Poignant and full of heart, this is a beautiful read about love, kindness and impossible choices … Heart-breaking but ultimately uplifting.' Annie Lyons, author of *Eudora Honeysett Is Quite Well, Thank You*

KERRY BARRETT was a bookworm from a very early age and did a degree in English Literature, then trained as a journalist, writing about everything from pub grub to *EastEnders*. Her first novel, *Bewitched, Bothered and Bewildered*, took six years to finish and was mostly written in longhand on her commute to work, giving her a very good reason to buy beautiful notebooks. Kerry lives in London with her husband and two sons, and Noel Streatfeild's *Ballet Shoes* is still her favourite novel.

Also by Kerry Barrett

The Could It Be Magic? Series

The Missing Wife

KERRY BARRETT

ONE PLACE. MANY STORIES

HQ
An imprint of HarperCollins*Publishers* Ltd
1 London Bridge Street
London SE1 9GF

www.harpercollins.co.uk

HarperCollins*Publishers*
Macken House,
39/40 Mayor Street Upper,
Dublin 1
D01 C9W8

This paperback edition 2023

1
First published in Great Britain by
HQ, an imprint of HarperCollins*Publishers* Ltd 2022

ISBN: 9780008481131

*For my son Sam, whose determination
to visit 'the Loch Ness' led to our trip
and the inspiration for this story.*

Chapter 1

Hannah

1933

'You look beautiful.' Aunt Beatrice took me by the shoulders and turned me so I could see my reflection. 'A beautiful bride.'

I stared at myself in the mirror. I was wearing the Snow family veil and a headdress that was too big for my small face. I looked like a little girl playing dressing-up. Which, in a way, I was.

'I don't look like me.'

'Nonsense,' she said briskly. 'Lawrie will be thrilled when he sees you walk down the aisle.'

I doubted that very much, but I didn't say so. I simply bit my lip and nodded, feeling nerves churning in my stomach.

Sensing my reluctance, Aunt Beatrice met my gaze in the mirror.

'Hannah,' she began.

I stared steadily into her eyes and she looked away.

'Hannah, this is a good thing you're doing, for the family.'

I nodded again.

'And Lawrie, of course, will benefit too. The terms of his inheritance …'

'I know,' I said quickly. 'Don't make it sound like this is a business agreement.'

Aunt Beatrice looked like she was about to say something and I had a horrible feeling she might point out that a business agreement was what this was, more or less. I didn't want to think that way. I didn't love Lawrie, because I really didn't know him that well. But he was kind and handsome and he listened when I talked and I couldn't help but hope that perhaps one day our "business agreement" of a marriage would turn into something more like the romances I liked to read or watch at the pictures. I looked away from my aunt and smoothed down the front of my gown.

'Everyone wins,' I said, trying to sound cheerful.

With a sigh, Aunt Beatrice shook her head. 'Hannah, I understand this isn't what you planned for your life. But we've been through this. There is no money left. What other option do we have?'

'I could get a job. I could work for a living instead of marrying a man I hardly know, for money. Plenty of women have jobs.' I turned back towards Aunt Beatrice and looked at her in defiance while she pulled her shoulders back and stood up a little straighter.

'That may be the case,' she said, as she did every time I brought up the subject of getting a job. 'But not Snow women.'

'Well, I won't be a Snow woman much longer, will I? I'll be Hannah Wetherby.'

'You'll be Mrs Lawrence Wetherby,' Aunt Beatrice said. 'And Lawrie will get his inheritance, and secure his position in the government, and your future will be safe.'

'Lawrie says he'll help me find a job.'

Aunt Beatrice raised one neat eyebrow. 'Help you find a job?'

'He said I could become a journalist.'

'Oh, Hannah, really?'

'Women can do anything nowadays,' I said. 'We can be journalists if we want.'

Aunt Beatrice looked amused, which was unusual for her. 'Right.'

'Lawrie knows everyone. He said he'll put a word in for me.'

This time Aunt Beatrice actually laughed. It was an unfamiliar sound and I wasn't sure I liked it.

'Then I look forward to reading your articles in *The Times*,' she said, making it perfectly clear that she didn't think that would ever happen. She tapped my arm. 'Come on. Let's go.'

I took a deep breath. More than anything I wanted to rip the veil from my head and run down the stairs, out of the front door and never return. But instead, I looked at my reflection again. 'Goodbye, Hannah Snow,' I said.

*

The wedding was brief and business-like. I had no bridesmaids and we had few guests. Aunt Beatrice sat on my side of the church, straight-backed and unsmiling. On Lawrie's side, his brother Simon sat in the front pew looking disgruntled. But as Simon always looked disgruntled I didn't give him much thought.

The rest of our guests were people I didn't know. A handful of Lawrie's fellow MPs, staff from his constituency office, perhaps. I wasn't sure. I didn't care.

When the vicar pronounced us man and wife, Lawrie kissed me on the forehead like a friendly uncle and threaded his arm through mine. Relief shone from his face, like the sun breaking through a cloud. Aunt Beatrice's expression was the same. I was off her hands. No longer a problem for her to deal with.

Afterwards we had a wedding breakfast in the Royal Hotel in Westminster and to my surprise, I found myself beginning to enjoy the afternoon. Lawrie was full of bonhomie, introducing me to his friends and colleagues and buying drinks. Simon, who was unpredictable and unpleasant when alcohol was involved, seemed to be behaving. Even Aunt Beatrice seemed to relax a little. I saw her smile as she chatted to an MP's wife and accept a glass of sherry from a waitress. Wonders would never cease.

'Hannah?' I turned to see Lawrie next to me. He was older than me – in his mid-thirties while I was only 19 – but he was handsome and charming. And very clever. He was already making a name for himself in the government as a junior minister in the Treasury, and he was tipped for great things.

'Come and meet some people,' he said now.

Obediently, I let him lead me over to where three men in suits stood. I recognised them all from the newspapers. One was Lawrie's boss at the Treasury, Neville Chamberlain. I could see Lawrie was brimming with pride that he'd come along today, and it made me smile. The other chap was from the Foreign Office I thought.

'Gentlemen, may I introduce my wife, Hannah Wetherby,' Lawrie said.

Mr Chamberlain took my outstretched hand. 'Delighted,' he said. He had a twinkle in his eye that I rather liked. The other man looked less pleased to meet me.

'I'm sorry, are we interrupting some important government business?' I said. I held my hand out to the man from the Foreign Office and he gave my fingers the briefest shake without bothering to introduce himself.

'Wetherby, I was just filling in Chamberlain on the latest from Germany,' he said, speaking to Lawrie over the top of my head as though I wasn't there.

'Tsk, Mr Bishop,' Mr Chamberlain said in a warning tone. 'Mrs Wetherby doesn't want to hear such boring dispatches on her wedding day. Tell me, have you read the latest Agatha Christie novel? I hear it's marvellous …'

'I'm not much of a one for books,' I lied, because I did enjoy detective novels but I didn't want to talk about that right now. 'I

4

actually prefer newspapers. In fact, I'm desperate to hear everything you've got to say. Is it true that the prime minister is keen to continue with disarmament in Europe despite the German election? Is that wise?'

Mr Chamberlain looked slightly taken aback. 'Well, erm, I …' he stammered. I didn't let his lack of response slow me down. I had so many questions.

'And what of the prime minister's health?' I went on. 'Is he well enough to travel? I've heard he's not up to the task. Will his doctor be accompanying him to Geneva?'

Mr Bishop frowned. 'Wetherby?'

Lawrie glanced at me and then at Mr Bishop.

I carried on: 'I really think that if Germany is intent on rearmament, then the prime minister needs to stand firm …'

'Wetherby,' Mr Bishop said, spitting Lawrie's name out. I stopped talking and looked at him in surprise, while Lawrie put a hand on my arm.

'Wetherby, this simply will not do,' Mr Bishop said. His face had gone quite red. 'Please control your wife, and may I remind you that affairs of state are not to be discussed in the bedroom.' He looked at me in disgust.

I turned to Lawrie, expecting him to tell Mr Bishop that I was well versed in politics. That I read the newspapers every day. That sometimes, if I was at a loose end, I would take myself off to the Commons and watch debates. That Lawrie enjoyed – or at least he said he enjoyed – hearing my opinion on his work.

But instead, he squeezed my arm slightly in what was obviously a warning. He looked round at the other men with an indulgent smile. 'I'm so sorry, gentlemen. My wife has a keen interest in politics and occasionally jokes that she would like to be a member of the press.' He let out a hearty laugh as I stared at him, furious.

'She'd keep us on our toes and no mistake, wouldn't she?' he went on. He was speaking in an odd way. Louder and more self-consciously jovial than usual. 'Lucky for us, she's chosen married life instead, eh?'

Mr Chamberlain chuckled and clucked at me, and for a horrifying moment I thought he might pinch my cheek like a proud grandfather. But then Mr Bishop tutted – I wasn't sure if he was showing his displeasure at Mr Chamberlain, or Lawrie, or me, or all three of us.

'Keep her in check, Wetherby,' he said.

Lawrie turned to me. 'Run along and speak to your aunt, darling,' he said. 'I'll be there shortly.'

I shook Lawrie's hand off my arm in fury.

'Tell me, what do you think of Mr Roosevelt?' I asked Bishop, drawing myself up so I was almost at his eye level. 'Do you think his plan for economic recovery has legs?'

Lawrie took my elbow, gripping more tightly than was comfortable. 'Let me help you find Beatrice,' he said. 'Would you excuse me for a moment please, gentlemen?'

He steered me through the few guests to the edge of the room, ruffled and annoyed that I'd talked about politics instead of detective stories. Though he wasn't nearly as cross as I was.

'Stop it,' I said sulkily, pulling my arm away from his hand. 'Don't push me around.'

'You can't fire questions at those men in that way,' Lawrie hissed. 'It's not …'

'What?' I stared at him in defiance.

'It's not seemly.'

'Seemly?'

'You're not a journalist, Hannah.'

'No.' I met his gaze. 'More's the pity. But I thought now we're married, you could perhaps—'

'Hannah,' he interrupted with a sigh. 'My job is very important to me. To us. I need to be respectable.'

'You need to be respectable,' I pointed out. 'But do I?'

Lawrie lifted his chin. 'You know I enjoy your interest in my work. I am more than happy to discuss current affairs at the breakfast table or over pre-dinner drinks.' He looked round. 'But you are my wife,' he continued in a low, urgent voice. 'You stand at my side and you laugh at my jokes and you nod at my suggestions. And when you are among my colleagues, you do not talk about politics or speculate about the health of the prime minister, for heaven's sake.' He sounded slightly incredulous.

'Why not?' I felt as though I was being scolded by a strict schoolmaster. 'I wanted to know.'

Lawrie looked up at the ceiling in despair. 'Because you're my wife now,' he said. He threw his hands out, at a loss for words. 'You are part of something bigger than you or me.'

We looked at each other for a moment, and then feeling a flash of sympathy for him, much to my annoyance, I backed down, dropping my gaze from his. 'Sorry,' I muttered.

He put his hand on the back of my head and pulled me towards him so he could give me that fatherly kiss on the forehead again. 'It's been a long day,' he said. 'We're both tired. I know I'm almost ready for bed.'

I wondered if he was suggesting what I thought. He'd never seemed overly interested in me that way before, but perhaps he had been waiting until we were married? A little flutter of nerves and – I admitted – excitement swirled in my stomach. Lawrie and I may have been thrown together by a determined Aunt Beatrice, but there was no denying he was handsome. Perhaps tonight I would discover what all the fuss was about …

'Get a drink,' Lawrie said. 'I need to talk to Neville.'

Perhaps not. I forced a smile. 'And then perhaps we could go to our room?'

Lawrie nodded vigorously in a way that suggested his enthusiasm was entirely false.

'Absolutely,' he said. 'Abso-blooming-lutely.'

Confused and still a little annoyed at the way he'd spoken to me, I stood for a moment watching him walk back to his colleagues, and then I turned on my heel and headed to the bar.

'What can I get you, madam?' the barman asked.

With some difficulty, thanks to the skirt on my wedding dress, I hoisted myself up on to a stool. 'What's the strongest drink you've got?'

'Old-Fashioned?'

I glanced over at my new husband. 'Perfect.'

While I watched the barman pour whisky into my glass, someone sat down beside me.

'Congratulations.'

I turned to see a young man – closer to my own age than Lawrie's. He was languid and long-legged and very good-looking. He draped himself over the bar.

'Scotch,' he said. 'No ice.' He looked up at me through dark eyes. 'So you married Lawrie.'

'I did.' I wondered who he was. He was too young to be an MP and he wasn't a relative. 'I married Lawrie.'

'He's a shit.'

Startled, I let out a little bark of laughter. I looked at him but he didn't look annoyed despite his harsh words. He looked sad.

'Lawrie can be a little pompous,' I said as the barman put my drink in front of me. I took a swig, feeling the whisky burn my throat. 'But he is marvellous company.'

'He was annoyed with you. I could tell.'

I felt my cheeks flush. 'I went too far with his friends.' I sighed. 'I talk a lot.'

'He upset you?'

'A bit,' I admitted. 'It's been a long day.'

'He will always put his career first.' He picked up his drink and took a huge gulp. 'His reputation,' he said in a way that made it sound like a dirty word.

Across the room, Lawrie guffawed with laughter at something one of the other men had said. I shifted on the bar stool, feeling uncomfortable. 'I'm not sure that's true,' I said, uncertainly.

The young man swallowed the rest of his drink in one mouthful. 'He expects things to go his way,' he said.

I looked at him carefully, impressed at his insight. Because that was exactly what Lawrie did. It wasn't his fault. He'd been brought up that way and he had enough charm that he got away with it. I thought that underneath it all he meant well, but he often just expected things to work out in a way that I – who'd lost both my parents when I was still at school and been thrown into a frightening cold life of funerals and Aunt Beatrice – did not.

As I glanced over at Lawrie, movement by the door of the function room caught my eye. My new brother-in-law Simon was standing, watching Lawrie with contempt, as he chatted to the other MPs.

Simon was furious that Lawrie and I had got married. Their father had died just a couple of months before I had met Lawrie and left a clause in his will saying Lawrie would only inherit his estate if he married before he was 35. If Lawrie had remained a bachelor, Simon would have been treated as the older son and heir. Lawrie always said his father had cared little for either of his sons. I didn't know if that was true but I did think dangling an inheritance in front of a younger brother, knowing it could be taken away at any time, was rather cruel.

Lawrie said Simon was a typical younger brother – a little wild, more than a little reckless. That was him being generous, in my opinion. Simon was a gambler, and I knew Lawrie was always bailing him out to pay his debts. Simon borrowed money from his friends and when they stopped lending to him, he borrowed from the sort of people who weren't so forgiving when he didn't pay them back.

He drank too much. He was lazy … he had few redeeming qualities and he certainly hadn't inherited the easy charm that Lawrie had. He was surly and sulky and I didn't like him much, though the feeling was definitely mutual. Lawrie and I saying our vows today had cheated poor Simon out of his fortune and he was furious about it. I couldn't blame him, really. I'd tried to speak to Lawrie, and suggest we gave something to Simon, just to smooth the waters over. An allowance, perhaps? But he'd laughed.

'Simon will have enough to live on,' he'd said. 'He can't be trusted with any more than that. My father knew what he was doing. Believe me, there would be little inheritance left if Simon were to get his grubby hands on it.'

And he'd refused to discuss it any further.

Now I watched as Simon looked at his brother through narrowed eyes, and I wondered if I should try to convince him again. Simon, I thought, could be trouble if he was angry.

'Simon is worse than Lawrie,' the young man next to me said, following my gaze. 'Lawrie is careless, but Simon is cruel.'

'Who are you?' I said to the young man. 'How do you know Lawrie?'

He sat up, unfurling himself from his slump across the bar. 'I'm Freddie,' he said. 'I'm …' He paused. 'I'm an old friend.'

'Lawrie's never mentioned you.' There was something about this young man that put me on edge.

'No?' he gave me a slow smile. 'Funny.'

'What did you mean? About Lawrie being careless?'

'You don't agree?'

'No, I do in a way.' I looked over at Lawrie again as he took a drink from a tray without even turning to acknowledge the waitress who held it. 'I just wondered what made you say it.'

'He crashed his car, you know?'

'I know.'

'But it doesn't matter. He'll just buy another.'

'He is careless with his belongings,' I said. 'He breaks things.'

'He breaks people,' Freddie said. He sounded bleak. 'And hearts.'

I rolled my eyes. I wasn't stupid. I knew a man of Lawrie's age and looks would have a past. But whatever liaisons he'd had before we met, well, they were none of my business.

'Did he have a fling with your sister?' I asked pointedly. 'Or steal your girlfriend?'

Freddie leaned close to me and I smelled the whisky on his breath. 'He breaks things,' he said again. More barbed this time.

Awkwardly I took a mouthful of my drink. I wasn't enjoying this conversation anymore. But Freddie hadn't finished. He leaned closer. 'Lawrie and his friends were the Bright Young Things, weren't they?' he said bitterly. 'Not caring who they hurt.'

'They lived through the Great War.'

Freddie shrugged, his face still close. I wanted to move but I didn't want to seem rude.

'They didn't care,' he said. 'They were blazing a trail with the parties and the drink and the drugs.' He put his forehead against mine. 'And the sex.'

I reared away from him, almost losing my balance on the high stool. 'Stop it.'

He reached out to steady me and gave me that odd smile again. 'Do you ever wonder where Lawrie goes when he's not with you?'

'No.'

'When he's working late at night?'

'He's an MP,' I said. 'He keeps strange hours.'

'Right. You just tell yourself that.'

I'd heard enough. I slid off the stool awkwardly and turned to go. Freddie reached out and took my hand in his. He had long, elegant fingers.

'I'll be here,' he said. 'Here in the bar. If you want to talk.'

'I don't.'

'You might.'

I stared at him for a moment and he stared back, then he spun round on the stool and turned his attention to the barman. Feeling slightly silly and unsettled, I turned to see where Lawrie was. He was alone now, standing to the side of the room and watching Freddie too, his lips pinched together in what seemed to be disapproval.

'Old friend,' I muttered. I took a deep breath, forced a smile onto my face, and went to find my husband.

Chapter 2

Scarlett

Present day

'You look great,' my best friend Robyn said. 'Chic. Award-winning.'

'I look ridiculous.' I balanced my phone on the sink and adjusted my cleavage. I was wearing a wiggle dress with a tight skirt and deep heart-shaped neckline. It was very 1950s so I'd done my hair in the same style and added thick winged eyeliner. I'd liked how I looked when I left home but lost my nerve when I'd arrived and ducked into the loo to call Robyn instead.

'Everyone here is in suits,' I said to her little face on my phone screen.

'Bet they're not. It's an event for podcasters, Scarlett. You're all weirdos.'

'Thanks.'

Robyn chuckled. 'Is it Charlie?' she said softly. 'Are you worried about seeing him?'

'I see him all the time.'

'Not in real life.'

I picked up my phone and went into one of the cubicles, sitting down on the closed loo seat.

'Are you having a wee?' Robyn shrieked. 'Do not keep talking to me while you're weeing.'

'I'm not weeing, I'm sitting,' I said.

She narrowed her eyes at me. 'If I hear trickling, I'm ending the call.'

I laughed, but my heart wasn't in it.

'I just want him to be sorry,' I said.

'I know, sweetie.'

'See what he's missing.'

'He will.'

I shook my head. 'He's bringing Astrid,' I said. 'I saw her name on the table plan.'

'What?' Robyn sounded furious. 'How did he pitch that one? Hey, babe, want to come with me to an awards ceremony celebrating the podcast I do with my ex?'

'Well, she's coming.'

'So what? You don't want Charlie back anyway.'

'I definitely don't want him back,' I said, more certainly than I felt.

'And you're going to win this award, and get loads of attention and listeners, and you can quit your job and do the podcast full-time.'

'Fingers crossed.'

'And your dad will be like "ohmygod, I can't believe my daughter is an award-winning podcaster. I'm going to boast about her to all my old man mates and stop trying to get her jobs elsewhere".'

'Chance would be a fine thing.' But I laughed because somehow when Robyn took the piss out of my father it unknotted the tightness in my stomach I always felt when I thought about him.

'And then you can ditch Charlie.'

'I need Charlie.'

Robyn snorted. 'Not now you don't. He might have been useful at the start with getting contacts, but you know everyone now and you do all the work.'

'The podcast is literally named after him.'

'So make a new podcast and name it after you. I always thought *Cold Cases with Burns* was a stupid name anyway.'

I laughed again. 'Thank you for making me feel better.'

'Any time.' She blew me a kiss. 'I'm going to bed because this blooming baby is exhausting me.' She pointed downwards towards her tiny pregnancy bump. 'But tell me when you win.'

'I will.' I ended the call, flushed the loo even though I'd not been for a wee, and went out of the cubicle, giving my cleavage a final hoick as I went.

The venue for the podcasting awards was one of those slightly down-at-heel London hotels that always look like they'd been terribly glamorous five years ago. I took a glass of fizz from a tray held by a bored waiter, breathed in deeply and then went into the function room.

It was buzzing with people and conversation. I scanned the room for Charlie but I couldn't see him – thank goodness. Hovering by the door, I felt a bit like a spare part. I knew lots of other podcasters because I worked at a radio station where just about everyone did a podcast, but for a second I couldn't spot anyone familiar. I felt a lurch of nerves. Maybe I should just go home?

Then a group of people at one side of the room moved slightly, and there, in the corner just behind them, I saw Charlie. He was tall, so he was easy to spot now I knew where to look. He was laughing and he looked annoyingly good in his open-necked shirt. I knew he'd have worn a tie for about three seconds then taken it off and put it in his pocket. That's what he always did. Next to him was an actual goddess. A blonde, athletic-looking woman with sculpted shoulders who was as tall as Charlie and seemed to glow with health and vitality. Astrid, I assumed. Great.

I looked down at my wobbly bosom, drained my drink and turned to leave. I couldn't handle this.

'Scarlett, you're on my table, I believe.'

I closed my eyes briefly then opened them to see an older man heading towards me, carrying two drinks.

'Gervase,' I said, forcing a smile. 'We're sitting together are we? How funny.'

He handed me a drink and gave me a kiss on the cheek, taking the opportunity to have a good look down my top as he did. I moved away deliberately.

'Professional rivals we may be,' he said sounding as though he was introducing us to an invisible audience. 'But we are firm friends away from the microphone.'

'Aren't we just.'

'And of course your father and I go way back. Waaaay back. How is the old sod?'

'He's really well, thank you.' My dad, who was regarded as a bit of a national treasure thanks to his days fronting the ten o'clock news, had very little time for Gervase. It was one of the few things we agreed on.

Gervase Desmond was a retired radio presenter who had a true-crime podcast, just like ours. Except he'd worked for the BBC, and he knew everyone, could call in favours at the drop of a hat, had thousands of listeners, and definitely didn't record his podcast wedged into his airing cupboard with old duvets pinned to the wall. He was nominated for the big award – Podcast of the Year. Charlie and I were up for Best Episode. We'd been nominated for our investigation into a case from the 1980s where thousands of pounds had gone missing from a company's accounts.

Charlie and I had solved the case accidentally really. Our podcast wasn't supposed to be about finding answers, it was just reporting unsolved mysteries. But we had solved this one. Well, if I was being big-headed, I'd solved it.

Charlie – who was an actual detective for the actual police – had been convinced one of the employees, a softly spoken woman called Shirley Pilgrim, was guilty. She'd been accused at the time but never charged, though the rumours followed her for decades. But I'd managed to find the real culprit – an anticlimactic and slightly silly accounting error made by an apprentice bookkeeper with terrible handwriting, just like me.

We got quite a lot of attention for cracking the case and the podcast really took off. But Charlie, who loved attention, took all the credit, and it annoyed me so much that our relationship, which had been on shaky ground before if I was honest, fell apart.

Sick of being taken for granted, I'd asked him for some time to think about what we both wanted. We were living together then of course. Had been for years. We weren't married and that was fine with me. I wasn't sure I wanted to get married. I wasn't even sure I wanted kids any time soon, or ever, even though my friends were all popping babies out left, right and centre, and every time I went to renew my pill prescription the nurse would remind me that there was an over-35s fertility clinic at the surgery if I was interested.

But it would have been nice to think we weren't just bumbling along, with Charlie paying me no attention, and life just happening to us instead of being planned.

So when I'd asked for time out, he'd been shocked and upset and promised he'd change, but I'd put my foot down. We needed the space, I said. We needed to decide what our priorities were.

It was Charlie's house so I moved into a flat-share, absolutely confident I'd only be there for a little while.

And then about five minutes later Charlie had met Astrid and before I'd even had a chance to rethink how hasty I'd been, they were an item, and we were recording the podcast over Zoom because he didn't think it was appropriate for us to spend too much time together.

So, I didn't feel much like celebrating Shirley Pilgrim's exoneration, even though an award was an award.

I took a swig of my drink and followed Gervase to the table, keeping my eyes away from Charlie and Astrid, who were taking their seats close to the stage.

*

It was a long evening but fortunately Gervase loved to tell a story and he kept everyone at our table entertained. I sat quietly, playing with my food, and drinking too much, and occasionally watching Charlie gazing at Astrid with adoration. He'd never looked at me in that way. He sat with his arm draped along the back of her chair, occasionally grazing her bare arm with his thumb and she leaned towards him slightly. They made a handsome pair. I felt tears of self-pity well up, and I rubbed my eyes with my fingertip to stop them falling.

'You've smudged your eyeliner,' Gervase said to me, topping up my glass. I knew I'd had more than enough to drink, but I didn't stop him.

'Oh bugger, have I?' I tried to see my reflection in the back of a spoon on the table, but I just looked like a Moomin whose hair was escaping from its carefully tousled beehive. 'I'll go and sort it in the loo.'

'Not now,' Gervase said. 'Your category is next.'

'And the winner is,' said the presenter on stage. 'Charlie Burns and Scarlett Simpson for *Cold Cases with Burns*, episode 5. The Innocence of Shirley Pilgrim.'

'Oh shit,' I said, rubbing underneath my eyes in a panic. 'Do I look awful? I have to go on stage.'

Behind me, a waitress was clearing the table. As I jerked upwards in a flap, I knocked the tray from her hand and two half-full coffee cups, and a wineglass with a centimetre of red left in the bottom, upended on to my lap. I gasped in shock,

17

sitting back down with a thump as wine and coffee splattered all over me. It was astonishing really just how far a little bit of wine could spread.

The waitress looked horrified. Gervase was delighted.

'Let me help you,' he purred, patting my damp chest with a napkin.

'I can do it.' I snatched the serviette from his hands and watched as Charlie took to the stage. I couldn't go up there now, could I? With eyeliner all over my face and wine dripping down my boobs.

Resigned to simply watching, I sat back in my chair, waving the mortified waitress away with an "it's fine, honestly" and dabbing at the coffee dribbling down my arms.

'We're so chuffed to receive this,' Charlie was saying. He looked good up there, confident and proud. I felt a flush of happiness. All those hours I'd spent researching the mysteries, interviewing people, and editing the podcast, staying up until the early hours then heading to work in time for the *Breakfast Show*, on my knees with tiredness, had all been worthwhile.

Charlie was still talking. 'I know podcasting seems frivolous, at least compared with my day job in the Met.' I rolled my eyes. Charlie was obsessed with how important being in the police made him. He sometimes introduced himself as DC Burns at parties and then laughed and pretended he'd said it by mistake when he clearly hadn't. And he'd always made it very clear that being a broadcast assistant at Britain Live, as I was, wasn't nearly as worthy as his job.

'... like to think we make a difference,' Charlie finished. Had he mentioned me? I'd not been paying attention. I looked at the stage where Charlie, grasping the award in his hand, turned away from the lectern and then back again.

'Lord, I forgot to do the "thank you"s,' he said, slapping his forehead. A ripple of laughter spread around the room and I smiled. This was my bit.

'Obviously we need to thank Shirley Pilgrim who let us rake

through her memories to make the episode,' Charlie said. 'And I'd like to say a massive thanks to my colleagues in the Met …'

'Oh, are you in the Met?' I muttered scornfully under my breath. 'You've never mentioned it.'

'… sharing contacts,' Charlie was saying. 'And of course, I can't forget one other very important person.'

I sat up straighter, hoping I'd wiped all the wine from my arms. Gervase gave me a little nod, acknowledging my part in the podcast's success and I glowed with pride.

'My gorgeous girlfriend, Astrid Nilsen,' Charlie said. He blew a kiss to Astrid who was gazing up at him. 'She's the reason I get up every day and she's the best person I know. Thank you.'

He waved his award at the crowd, jumped off the stage and pulled Astrid into an embrace. The audience all "ahhhed" at his sweet gesture, and I wanted to slide under the table and disappear.

'Well, this is awkward,' said Gervase with a certain amount of glee. 'I thought you did most of the work on your podcast.'

'I do.'

'All the research and the techy stuff – the recording, the editing – do you write the scripts, too?'

'Oh yes,' I said through gritted teeth.

'And what does Charlie boy do?'

'Charlie boy,' I said, feeling a rush of rage, 'gets right on my wick.'

I pushed my chair back from the table, picked up my bag, and wishing I could walk more quickly in my wiggle skirt, headed for the door. It was definitely time to go home.

'Scarlett?'

Knowing it was Charlie, I kept walking.

'Scar, stop.'

I turned.

'Oh, you remember my name, do you?'

He managed to look ashamed. 'Where were you?' he asked,

looking confused. 'I thought you'd get up on stage with me.'

'A waitress spilled wine on me.' I showed him my speckled arms. The corners of his mouth twitched and I glowered at him to stop his laugh before it started. I was not in the mood.

'I should have thanked you. I was caught up in all the excitement.' He paused. 'I'm sorry.'

'It's fine.' I shrugged, suddenly feeling very tired and very sober. 'I'm going home.'

'No, wait a minute.'

'What do you want, Charlie?'

'There's a case that's come up. The chap wants to meet us tomorrow. You need to be there.'

'Do I need to be there, or do you need me to be there?' I said pointedly. I knew Charlie wouldn't want to do a meeting on his own.

'Scar, please. I said sorry. Don't be funny with me. You have to come.'

'Don't call me Scar. And don't tell me what to do.'

Charlie looked exasperated. 'Are you free?'

'No, I'm busy,' I lied.

'Can you move stuff around? This bloke is really posh and he says he'll pay us to investigate.'

'Pay us?' I frowned. 'That's weird. We're not private investigators. What if we found something out he didn't like? How would that work? Anyway, are you even allowed to get paid to investigate something?'

Charlie screwed his nose up. 'Not sure,' he admitted. 'But he could pay you and then you could pay me.'

'Right, that's totally ethical.' For the gazillionth time I thought how lucky it was that Charlie was so good-looking, because he definitely wasn't the sharpest tool in the box.

'Let's just meet him and find out more, shall we? Honestly, he was talking thousands.'

'Thousands?'

'Enough for you to quit work, I reckon. Or at least enough for you to get your own place.'

He looked at me and I sighed.

'I'm off tomorrow, but I'm not committing. I'll decide in the morning.'

'Great, see you then,' he said cheerfully. 'Scar.'

I stuck two fingers up at him, and headed to the lift.

Chapter 3

Hannah

1933

I thought we'd go to bed, Lawrie and me. In my head, I thought we'd go to the honeymoon suite in the hotel and I'd get changed into the slippery satin nightgown I'd packed for the occasion.

I imagined appearing at the door of the bathroom, perhaps one arm stretched up on the frame to look more inviting.

'Will I do?' I'd say. And Lawrie would take my hand and spin me around, and then he'd kiss me so thoroughly, I'd have to bend backwards ... but perhaps I had spent too many long Saturday afternoons at the pictures.

Because what actually happened was very different.

I went to say goodbye to Aunt Beatrice, expecting Lawrie to wait for me in the ballroom. But when I'd waved her off into a cab, Beatrice slightly tipsy and more emotional than was normal, Lawrie was nowhere to be seen.

'Mr Wetherby has gone upstairs, madam,' the concierge said as I stood in the foyer, clearly looking confused. He handed me a room key on a large wooden fob. 'He said he'd see you in your room.'

'Thank you.'

Slightly put out that I was leaving my own wedding alone, I went up in the lift to our room. The bridal suite. It was a large room. It had a sort of sitting area with a sofa and two squidgy armchairs, and then two doors – one led to the bathroom and the other opened on to the bedroom.

I found Lawrie sitting on the side of the bed, his shirt open at the neck and his hair ruffled. He looked very handsome and very, very miserable.

'Hannah,' he said as I went into the bedroom, looking up at me but staying where he was. 'Oh, Hannah.'

'What's wrong?' I was alarmed. His eyes were red and I wondered if he'd been crying, though he did have a whisky glass in his hand. 'What is it?'

I went to him, standing slightly awkwardly in front of him where he sat.

'I'm fine,' Lawrie said, visibly gathering himself. 'Just drunk and emotional, that's all.'

He reached out to me, putting his arms round my waist and pulling me close to him, then he rested his head on my chest, and I stroked his hair.

'Thank you,' he muttered.

'Whatever for?'

'For marrying me.'

I let out a little laugh. 'I think I should be thanking you.' I kept my voice light, though I was worried by his gloomy tone. 'I've been told you're the most eligible bachelor in London.'

Lawrie sat back, his arms still around my waist. 'Not anymore,' he said.

I pushed his hair off his forehead and kissed the top of his head. 'There's no need to sound so glum about it. You're not the only one who's eligible, you know. I could have my pick of the men in town.'

23

I was joking, trying to lighten the mood, but Lawrie didn't laugh.

Not sure what to do, I sat down next to him and put my hand on his leg, wondering if I should kiss him. He looked round at me and, feeling a little self-conscious, I took my hand off his thigh and put it behind his neck, pulling his head towards me. But when I touched his lips with mine, he pulled away.

'Hannah,' he said, with a groan.

Thinking about Norma Shearer, whose films I adored, I got to my feet, in rather ungainly fashion because I'd had one of my legs tucked under me and my toes had gone to sleep. Lawrie looked up at me as I reached round and tried to unlace my wedding dress at the back. Aunt Beatrice had wanted me to change after the church ceremony, but I'd been quite adamant I wanted to stay in my gown, though I'd ditched the Snow veil as soon as I could. Now, struggling with the fastenings, I regretted my decision.

With my cheeks burning, I turned round. 'Could you …'

Lawrie didn't move.

I looked over my shoulder at him.

'I've got a nightgown,' I said awkwardly. 'I was going to …'

He took a deep breath and stood up. But instead of undoing my dress as I'd expected, he fastened it up again. Then he stood behind me, close but not touching. I could feel his breath on the back of my neck.

'What are you doing?' I asked, humiliation flooding my body. 'Don't you like me?'

'No,' Lawrie said. 'No, that's not what it's about, Hannah.'

I whirled round to face him. He looked awful. His expression bleak and his eyes bloodshot.

'Then what is it about?'

He held out his hands in despair. 'It's practical,' he said.

The word hit me like a punch to my gut. 'Practical?'

'We both benefit. The money from my inheritance …'

'I don't care about the money. That's not what this is.' I swallowed. 'That's not all it is.'

'It is,' Lawrie said softly. 'It's just a way of both of us getting what we need. I needed to be married in order to inherit and you needed financial security.' He breathed out. 'I can't be the sort of husband you thought I would be.'

Annoyingly, I felt close to tears. Ashamed and embarrassed that I'd got this so wrong. And then suddenly, filled with rage. With the palms of my hands I pushed his chest so he took a stumbling step backwards.

'I don't need financial security,' I hissed. 'I don't care about financial security.'

'Beatrice was quite clear …'

'Beatrice is only concerned about her own affairs,' I said, my voice louder now as everything became horribly clear. 'Beatrice has sold me to the highest bidder, with no regard for my feelings or my future.'

'That's not quite true,' Lawrie said. 'I admire you a great deal.'

'Admire me?' I shrieked. 'What does that mean?' I took a deep, shuddering breath. 'I knew this was an arrangement, but I thought we could become a couple. I thought we'd be together. Properly.'

Lawrie shook his head. 'I'm sorry if that's the impression I gave you. But I never intended it to be that way.'

'Then what?' I said, feeling sick with embarrassment. 'You thought I would move to your house in Sussex and stay there, while you carried on as before?'

Lawrie's expression told me that was exactly what he'd thought.

'I wanted to be a journalist,' I said in a small voice. 'I wanted to join in the chat about politics, and be asked my opinion on world affairs. I wanted people to think of us as a team. A force to be reckoned with. "The Wetherbys," they'd say. "They're such a clever couple. He's an MP you know. And she writes for *The Times*." And I'd be so proud of us.'

Lawrie was staring at me in astonishment.

'I never said that's how it would be,' he said. 'I didn't know that's what you were thinking ...'

With a start I realised that all those conversations, all those plans and pondering about the future, had only taken place in my imagination. I put my hands on my head in despair. 'What next?' I said. 'What happens now?'

'Now?'

'Now I understand this isn't what I expected. What shall we do?'

Lawrie shuffled his feet. 'Nothing.'

My heart thumped and I felt a vein in my temple begin to pound. I was embarrassed and upset and absolutely furious all of a sudden.

'Nothing?' I snapped. 'What do you mean, nothing?'

'We're married now. What is there to do?'

'This is my life, Lawrie.' I clenched my hands into fists to stop them shaking. 'I'm only 19 years old. This is my life.' My voice was loud and shrill.

'Shhh,' said Lawrie. 'Someone will hear.'

'I don't care,' I shrieked. 'Let them hear. Let them hear how you tricked me into this sham of a marriage and took away my future.'

'Calm down,' said Lawrie, holding his hands out to me. 'Don't get hysterical.'

With a rush of red-hot fury, I grabbed his empty glass and the whisky bottle and marched into the sitting area.

Lawrie followed. 'Hannah, I really don't think that's a good idea ...'

'Don't tell me what to do,' I growled. Instead of filling the glass, I flung it at him where he stood in the doorway of the bedroom. He ducked out of the way and the glass hit the wall and shattered with a satisfying crack.

'Hannah, bloody hell,' Lawrie gasped. 'Stop this.'

'I won't.' This time I swung the bottle of whisky by its neck, and threw that too. It exploded against the wall, spraying both of us with alcohol and tiny bits of glass. Lawrie winced as a shard hit him on the cheek.

'Christ, Hannah, stop.' He ran towards me, grabbed my hands in his, and held them above my head. I struggled to get free, watching a trickle of blood dribble down his cheek and feeling no remorse.

'Let me go.' I kicked out at him but he moved, so instead I just overbalanced and Lawrie tightened his grip on my wrists. 'Get off me.'

And then there was a knock on the hotel room door. Still holding my wrists above my head, Lawrie froze.

'Mr Wetherby, sir?' a voice called. 'Is everything all right. Someone reported hearing a breakage.'

Lawrie's eyes widened as he looked at me. He let go of my hands and I fell back onto a chair, rubbing my wrists where he'd held them.

'Stay there,' he hissed.

He went to the door and opened it a small way. Through the gap I could see a member of the hotel staff.

'Mr Wetherby,' he said. 'Are you hurt?'

Lawrie put his hand to his cheek and then looked at the blood on his fingers. 'This?' he said. 'It's nothing. I'm afraid I broke a glass.' He laughed. It sounded fake to my ears but the bellboy laughed too, looking relieved. 'One too many at the wedding breakfast, I'm afraid. And when I was clearing up, I must have cut myself.'

'Shall I come in and help clear the mess?' the bellboy said.

'No,' Lawrie said quickly. 'It's all done now and my wife is tired.'

'So everything is all right?'

'Quite all right,' Lawrie said.

'Thank you so much,' I called. 'Goodnight.'

Looking reassured, the bellboy went off down the corridor. Lawrie shut the door behind him and leaned against it.

'Let's hope he doesn't tell the papers,' he said.

I winced at the mention of newspapers, but the anger had gone out of me. And from Lawrie, too, by the look of him.

'I'm so sorry, Hannah,' he said. 'I thought you understood.'

I felt like the ground was shifting beneath my feet. I didn't understand. I didn't understand anything except that married life was so far entirely unlike how I'd imagined it.

'I don't,' I said. 'But I can try.'

Looking wretched, Lawrie walked away from me, sitting down on the other chair at the side of the room. He didn't meet my gaze. Instead he lit a cigarette and smoked for a few minutes, looking out of the window, while I watched from where I sat.

'I didn't think it would be this hard,' he said. He sounded so sad, that I felt desperately sorry for him suddenly. And for me, too.

'You should have been honest with me,' I said. 'Is there someone else? Are you in love with another woman?'

Slowly, he shook his head. 'It's not that.'

I wanted to shake him and ask him then what was it. What meant that instead of the loving wedding night I'd imagined, we were in this awful room together with broken glass on the floor, and blood on his face, and bruises on my wrist, and me bewildered and confused.

But Lawrie gave me a small smile. 'I bought you a present.'

I wasn't expecting that. 'Really? I didn't get you anything.'

He shrugged. He put out his cigarette and slid off the chair. On the desk in the room was a square box, which he picked up now and handed to me.

'I realise this won't make up for ... for everything,' he said. 'But I think you'll like it.'

Intrigued, I sat on the bed cross-legged and opened it.

'Oh heavens,' I breathed in delight. 'Oh, Lawrie.'

Inside was a camera – a Kodak Brownie.

'It's nothing fancy,' he said. He went into the bathroom and came out again dabbing his cut cheek with a flannel. 'But if you get the hang of it, we'll get you something better.'

'I do like it,' I said, still cautious but pleased all the same.

'It'll give you something to do while I'm at work. Keep you busy.'

'In a way that's more seemly than asking questions of your colleagues?' I said sharply and Lawrie had the grace to look slightly sheepish.

'I never meant to mislead you,' he said. He was straightening his hair in the mirror but now he turned and looked at me. 'I honestly thought you understood.'

'Aunt Beatrice says I shouldn't let my imagination run away with me,' I said. 'Now I see why.'

Lawrie gave me a small sad smile. 'We'll work things out,' he said. 'I don't want you to be unhappy.'

I looked down at myself, still wearing my wedding gown.

'Can you unfasten my dress please?' Lawrie looked alarmed briefly and I sighed. 'I need to get changed.'

'Here.' He gestured for me to go to him and obediently I did, turning my back for him to loosen the ties.

'I meant it when I said I admire you.' He undid the final fastening and I put my arms up to my chest to hold the dress in place. 'You are clever and funny, and I enjoy your company. I think …' He paused. 'In time, perhaps, we could be good friends.'

I turned to look at him. He seemed more than a little defeated. I put my hand to his cut cheek.

'I'm sorry I hurt you,' I said.

'I'm sorry too.'

There was a brief moment when we both looked at one another, sad and confused, and then I took a deep breath.

'I'm going to go,' I said.

'Go?' Lawrie looked worried.

'Just for tonight. I'll go to Aunt Beatrice's. I'll tell her you've been called in to work. She won't question it.' I bit my lip. 'I just need a bit of time, Lawrie.'

He leaned forward, resting his forehead against mine, and I

felt a rush of unexpected affection for him. Kinship, almost. Like we were both fighting an unknown enemy. 'You will come back?'

'I will.' I wasn't lying.

I put the camera on the side table and went into the bathroom to get changed. Lawrie and I weren't going on honeymoon – but I had a smart tweed suit with a matching hat hanging on the back of the door.

When I came out again, my wedding dress in my arms, Lawrie was fiddling with the camera.

'I put some film in it,' he said. 'You have to do it in the dark. I got inside the wardrobe.'

I smiled briefly. 'I wish I'd seen.'

He handed me the camera and I put it round my neck.

'Please don't go,' he said.

I glanced at my watch. It was only just after nine o'clock yet I felt like days had passed since the wedding.

'Just for tonight,' I promised. 'I'll come back in the morning and we can go to Sussex, like we planned.' I felt I needed time away from him, from the room, from my life falling apart, just to get things straight in my head.

'Then don't go to Beatrice's. Go to the flat in Westminster,' he said. Lawrie had a house in Sussex and a small place where he stayed when he was working. 'It's closer than your aunt's and there's no one there who will ask questions.'

He took his jacket from the back of a chair and felt in the pocket for his keys. I held my hand out and he dropped them into my palm.

'What will you do?'

'I've got work to do. There's so much happening with Roosevelt's inauguration, and the PM not being well …'

'Ha!' I said in triumph. 'I knew he was ill.'

'Hannah,' Lawrie said, holding one finger out in warning. 'This goes no further.'

I rolled my eyes. 'Who would I tell?' I said. 'You may have

bought me a camera, but I'm not actually a journalist, am I? I don't even know any journalists.'

'I'll come and meet you at the flat in the morning.' Lawrie ignored my ranting. 'The front door is stiff to open. You have to wiggle the key and then give it a bit of a shove.'

'All right,' I said. I dropped my wedding dress onto the bed, and picked up my overnight bag. 'I'll see you tomorrow.'

*

I went to the flat, which was only five minutes away from the hotel. And perhaps it was because my hands were freezing cold from the stiff early March wind. Or perhaps I was just too shaky. But whatever the reason, I couldn't open the door. Lawrie had said it needed a wiggle and a good shove, but I couldn't even get the key to turn.

Eventually, shivering because I didn't have a proper coat and the hallway in the block was draughty, I gave up. I'd have to swallow my pride and go back to the honeymoon suite.

After picking up my bag, I dragged myself out into the quiet Westminster streets and back to the hotel.

'Good evening, Mrs Wetherby,' the concierge said as I went past. I nodded to him, not in the mood for a chat.

I walked past the entrance to the hotel bar and my thoughts turned to the man I'd met at the wedding – Freddie – and what he'd said about where Lawrie really was when he said he was working. Lawrie was working now. Or so he said. He was a dedicated public servant.

Wasn't he?

Was Lawrie spending time with another woman? That certainly seemed to be what Freddie had implied, and the way Lawrie had rejected my advances – I shuddered at the thought – seemed to back it up.

But if so, why marry me? He could have just married her

31

instead – his inheritance didn't rest on him marrying anyone in particular. Unless she was already married?

I changed course, walking away from the lifts and instead heading into the bar. Freddie had said to come and see him if I wanted to talk. Well, now I wanted to talk.

I wanted to know the truth.

The bar though, was empty. Deflated and exhausted, I ordered a drink and slumped into a booth.

My new camera was still around my neck, but now I took it off and looked at it. It was something rather special and I couldn't understand how Lawrie knew me well enough to give me something he knew I'd love so much, and destroy my dreams all on the same day.

I doubted real journalists had little Brownie cameras like this, but perhaps it was a start.

I turned to the mirror on the wall of the bar where I stood with my camera at my chest, and took a photograph of myself. My eyes were sad and ringed with dark circles. I didn't look remotely like a blushing newlywed, full of joy for the life that awaited her. I looked gaunt and unhappy. It didn't surprise me, really.

I drained my drink and with my camera slung around my neck again, I picked up my bag and went upstairs to our room. The so-called bridal suite.

As I approached our room, feeling in my pocket for the key and realising I'd left it behind, the lift doors opened again and a bellboy with a trolley emerged – a different lad from the one who'd come when I smashed the glass. He nodded at me as he came towards me, and I smiled politely.

'Taking some pictures?' he said.

I looked down at the camera. 'It was a present.'

'Nice.'

We were standing outside our room and we both raised our hands to knock at the same time. The bellboy laughed. 'After you, miss.'

I knocked and he called: 'Room service,' as he opened the door with his master key and let us both in.

For the first time, I noticed his trolley had a bottle of whisky on it. Lawrie obviously wanted to replace the one I'd broken.

'Leave it just inside the door,' Lawrie called from inside the room. The bellboy took out his key, opened the door and pushed his trolley in. I followed.

The bellboy took the whisky bottle off the trolley and put it on to a silver tray, followed by two glasses. He refilled the ice bucket and wiped the surface with cloth. Tucked under the tray was some money, which he pocketed deftly.

'All done, sir,' he called. He turned to go and gave me a little cheeky wink. 'Have a good night, miss.'

Quite offended that he clearly thought Lawrie had ordered me to go along with his whisky – there were two glasses on the tray with the whisky after all – I gave him a humourless smile and headed to the bedroom, looking for my husband.

*

It wasn't that I'd caught them doing anything. They weren't kissing, or even touching really, but I knew I'd stumbled upon something intimate. Lawrie was in bed. But he wasn't alone.

Instead, there with him was Freddie, the man from the bar. His naked torso was half covered with a sheet and his long bare legs were sprawled on top of the bedclothes. He was propped on his elbow, gazing down at Lawrie.

My husband.

Lawrie was also naked, with just a little of the sheet protecting his modesty. He had his hands behind his head, and he was smiling up at Freddie. I'd never seen him look so relaxed, or so happy. The room was dimly lit – the large window had a streetlamp outside, which was shining through – and actually the two men together, both so handsome in different ways – looked rather beautiful in the orange light.

Without thinking, almost as if I was dreaming, I raised my camera, peered down into the viewfinder and took a picture. I wound the film on and snapped another.

But the click of the shutter startled Freddie and Lawrie and they both looked up as I took one more photograph. Then another. And another. It was like I couldn't stop because if I stopped, I'd have to think about what I was seeing here. What was happening in front of my eyes.

'Hannah?' I heard Lawrie gasp in shock. 'Hannah, stop. This isn't …'

Much to my surprise, Freddie laughed. It was a triumphant sort of laugh, and I knew with absolute certainty that he was pleased I'd found them there, together. Perhaps he'd wanted me to find them together. Perhaps that's what he meant when he said I should ask questions about where Lawrie was when he said he was working – because Lawrie was with him.

I took another photograph.

Lawrie was struggling upright now, holding the sheet on his groin so it didn't slip when he moved. I wanted to remind him that I was his wife and that any modesty was misplaced. But instead, in an icy voice, I said: 'How are your preparations for Roosevelt's inauguration coming along? All going well is it?'

'Hannah …' Still clutching the sheet, Lawrie jumped out of bed, leaving Freddie exposed. Not remotely embarrassed he settled himself against the pillows, watching the show. I averted my eyes from Freddie's nakedness, as Lawrie approached me. He held one hand out towards me, as though I were a skittish cat that might scratch. 'Hannah, this isn't what it looks like.'

'Oh silly me,' I said. 'I thought it looked like you two discussing the PM's health? Is that not what you were doing? Am I confused?' I brandished the camera. 'Still, I can always have a look back and see what you were really doing, can't I?'

Lawrie's face was turning puce. 'Hannah, there's film in

your camera. I know there is – I put it in myself. Did you take photographs?'

'Photographs?' I smiled. 'Like a journalist would, you mean? Perhaps.'

'Did you take photographs?' He spoke slowly and deliberately.

'You were the one who bought me my camera.' I stared at him, defiance hiding my humiliation and shock. 'It's a distraction.'

'I'm an MP,' Lawrie hissed. 'My career would be over. I could go to prison.'

'You could,' I agreed. Then suddenly as I stared at my new husband, the enormity of what had happened overwhelmed me and all my bravado faded away.

'You're in love with Freddie,' I said, my brow furrowed with bewilderment. 'You like men?'

Freddie grinned at me from where he lay on the bed. 'Why do you think his father wanted him to get married, darling? He thought he could bribe him to be normal.'

I looked at Lawrie, whose expression had gone from anger to sadness. 'I'm sorry,' he said. 'I should have been honest with you from the start. Perhaps we could have come to some arrangement.'

'But it's illegal.' My thoughts were racing and my cheeks were on fire. I'd never seen a man and woman together, let alone two men. I felt as though I'd stumbled into some sort of seedy nightclub in Soho and I didn't like it. 'It's wrong.'

'It's illegal,' Lawrie said, holding his hand out again. 'But it's not wrong. It's just … love.'

I took a step away from him. 'You're both men.'

'Yes,' Lawrie said simply. 'We are.'

I stared at him, horrified by his admission, but strangely touched by his acceptance of his feelings.

'You love him?'

'I do.' He winced. 'And I'm so sorry I didn't tell you.'

'You're my husband,' I said in a very small voice.

35

'I know.'

'You're cheating.'

'Strictly speaking, I'm the one being cheated on,' Freddie pointed out, adjusting how he lay on the bed to get more comfortable. 'He was mine first.'

'Shut up,' I said, anger overtaking confusion again as I looked at him, lying on my honeymoon bed, so sure of himself. 'Shut up, Freddie. This is all your fault.'

I whirled back round to face Lawrie.

'He told me I should think about where you went when you said you were working,' I said, spitting the words out, wanting to punish Freddie for having Lawrie's affection. 'He wanted me to find out.'

I thought Lawrie would be angry as I was, but actually he looked as though his heart had shattered into pieces.

'You did this?' he said to Freddie in a small voice that made me want to cry. 'Why? Why would you?'

'Because I love you,' Freddie said like a petulant child, but his voice cracked on the words. 'And I don't want to share you.'

I wanted to get away from this. From them. With their attention on each other I saw my chance, but Lawrie spotted me moving.

'Hannah, wait,' he said, grabbing my hand. 'Take the film out of the camera.'

'No.'

I yanked my hand away and rushed out of the bedroom. Lawrie tried to follow me, but the long sheet he'd draped round himself was tangled and as I pulled away from him, he overbalanced, tripped and fell heavily, hitting his head on the bedroom doorframe.

In horror, I froze as Lawrie slumped to the floor and was still.

'Lawrie,' Freddie gasped. He leapt off the bed and crouched over my husband, stroking his face and holding his hand. 'Lawrie?' he said softly. Then louder and more panicked, he said: 'Lawrie? Can you hear me? Wake up, Lawrie.'

I looked on, hugging myself tightly, trying to stop myself from shaking. 'Is he all right?' I said over and over. 'Is Lawrie all right?'

Freddie looked up at me, his eyes huge and filled with tears. 'He's dead,' he wailed. 'You've killed him.'

Chapter 4

Scarlett

Present day

Hungover and grumpy the next day, I dragged myself out of bed and into the kitchen to make coffee.

I lived in a sort of house-share with two other women. They were best friends, at least ten years younger than me, and one of them, Anita, owned the South London maisonette we all called home.

I had thought it would be a good idea to live with the owner. Much better than having an absentee landlord like ones I'd had in the past, who wouldn't fix the boiler or mend a broken window.

Oh how wrong I'd been.

Anita was finicky and fussy and very, very bossy. She knew what she liked – me paying my rent on time, me staying out of her way, me not bothering her and Maddy, our other housemate, when they were watching *Love Island* – and what she didn't like – me. Basically.

But this morning Anita and Maddy were both at work so I

could relax a bit. With my head banging, I filled the kettle and went to the fridge to get the milk. There was a full carton in the door with a Post-it Note stuck to it saying *A & M* with a little smiley face underneath. I rolled my eyes and used it anyway.

Next to the kettle, stuck on the wall, was a small, laminated piece of card. Laminated. It said: *Scarlett! Please remember to put your teabags in the food-waste bin!*

Once, a few months ago, I'd been making a cup of tea when I'd discovered the waste caddy was full. I'd taken the bag out to the bin in the front yard, got chatting to the postman who was delivering a parcel and forgotten to put a new bag in the caddy, or throw my used teabag away.

It was one time. But Anita had not reacted well. The laminated reminder appeared the next day. There was a similar card on the food-waste caddy that said: *Scarlett! If you empty the caddy, please remember to replace the bag!*

I hated living here.

My phone had gone flat and I'd forgotten to charge it overnight, so now I plugged it in and immediately it buzzed with messages. I glanced at the screen. It was my dad.

Is this your chap? he'd written. He'd attached a link to a story from the *Broadcast Journal* daily newsletter about last night's awards, showing a picture of Charlie holding the award aloft.

Ex-chap, I replied, feeling prickly. I deleted the message so I didn't have to look at Charlie's smug face, then read the next one, leaning against the counter to wait for the kettle to boil.

This one was from Anita, asking me to keep the noise down when I came home from late-night parties. The noisiest thing I'd done last night was to shut the front door. I deleted that message too, as my phone buzzed again. This time it was Charlie.

You are coming today, right? he had written.

My thumb hovered over the delete button. But then another message arrived from Anita.

Please don't make a mess in the kitchen, she'd added.

I deleted that message instead, and – hating myself and my life a little bit – I replied to Charlie.

Tell me where and when.

Once I'd finished my coffee and washed up the mug and put it back in the cupboard, so I'd left no evidence that I'd ever been in the kitchen, I had a shower. Charlie had messaged me the address of a pub in Covent Garden where we were meeting the "posh bloke" at midday. I really wasn't in the mood, but I kept hearing Charlie's voice in my head saying it would pay enough for me to get my own place, so I dressed in my only proper work outfit – a suit I'd bought on Vinted. The trousers were too long for me, and I had no idea how to take up the hems, which meant I could only wear it with heels. So even though my feet were still aching from last night, I shoved a pair of smart boots in my bag, put my trainers on and tucked my trailing trouser legs into my socks for the journey.

'Very chic, Scarlett, well done,' I muttered to myself as I checked my reflection. 'Way to wow the posh bloke.'

Normally, before we talked to someone about the podcast, whether over the phone, or Zoom, or in person, I did my homework. I'd know all about the story we were telling, I'd know everything there was to know about the people involved, I'd have a clear idea of the timeline – you get the picture. Charlie called me a girly swot. I just thought if people were giving up their time to talk to us, then we owed it to them to put in the groundwork.

But this time, I was going in blind. And deaf. I didn't have a clue about who we were meeting, which made me antsy.

I was so desperate to get out of the house that I left too much time for the journey and got to the pub about fifteen minutes early. I was pleased to have a chance to check it out, find a good table and get settled. I paused outside to gather my thoughts and change my shoes. Resting against the pub's window ledge, I reached into my bag for one of my boots. As I leaned down, I glanced through the leaded window and there, sitting in the corner, right on the other side of the glass from where I stood, was Charlie with another man. He was an older gent with a good head of hair and smart glasses. He was talking fervently, pointing to something on the table, and Charlie was nodding. They'd bloody well started without me.

Fuming, I shoved my boot back into my tote bag, and marched into the pub.

'Hi,' I said, interrupting Charlie, who was in full flow talking about some "misper" case he was working, which I was ninety-nine per cent sure he shouldn't have been sharing. 'I'm Scarlett.'

Charlie had his back to me, and he jumped as I spoke and looked over his shoulder.

'Scar,' he said. 'You made it.'

I flashed the other man my best, most winning smile. 'So sorry I'm late,' I said, reaching over Charlie to shake hands with him, and noticing he'd stood up when I arrived – lovely manners, my gran would say. 'Bit of confusion over the timings.'

'Not a problem,' said the man. 'Can I get you a drink?'

'Just a latte, thanks.'

'Feeling delicate?' Charlie said.

I glowered at him. 'It's not even midday,' I pointed out, letting him know I was still annoyed he'd started the meeting early.

There was a bit of flurry of activity as the man got up to go to the bar, and I took off my coat, and found my notepad and pen, and tried to curl my feet under my seat and pretend I wasn't wearing trainers with my trousers tucked into my socks. Perhaps no one would notice.

'Interesting outfit,' Charlie said with a smirk as I sat down. I ignored him.

'I'm afraid I don't know much about your story,' I said as the man put a coffee in front of me and sat down. 'Nothing at all in fact.'

The man nodded. 'Then let me explain. I'm Quentin Wetherby.'

He said his name like I should know who he was, but I was

clueless, so I just took a sip of my coffee, then opened my note-book at a clean page.

I wrote down his name and looked at him expectantly.

'I'm an MP,' he said.

'Lovely.' I wrote that down too. Charlie looked impressed.

'My uncle was called Lawrence Wetherby,' Quentin went on. 'He was also an MP – in Ramsay Macdonald's government before the war. In May 1933 he disappeared.'

'Like Lord Lucan,' said Charlie, looking pleased with himself.

'Well, sort of.' Quentin frowned. 'Without the murder bit. But with the media attention. It was all over the papers at the time.'

'So your uncle just vanished?' I said, feeling a glimmer of interest. 'No body? He never turned up?'

'Nope. There was no body found.'

'How awful for your family.'

'Yes,' said Quentin without sounding like he really meant it. I felt that flicker again. There was clearly more to this than myste-rious disappearance.

'Could he have been in an accident?' I said. 'Or taken his own life?'

'Well,' said Quentin, and I sat up a little bit straighter, 'it's my belief that my uncle was murdered.'

Across the table, Charlie breathed in sharply.

'Why do you think that?'

'My father was Lawrence's younger brother,' Quentin said. 'Simon Wetherby.'

Again he spoke as if I should know who he was but I didn't. I nodded, pretending I knew the name.

'Back then, the older brother inherited everything. The family home, the wealth ...'

Charlie gave me a little knowing eyebrow raise at the mention of money. I ignored him.

'So your Uncle Lawrence was rich, and your father wasn't?'

'Actually, my father did all right. He started a business, importing wine.'

'Nice.'

Quentin grimaced. 'Less nice now. I sold most of my shares in the business years ago, but it's been a good side-line until recently.'

'Brexit?' Charlie asked.

'Brexit. Pandemic. Ukraine. You know. But anyway—' Quentin clearly didn't want to discuss his troubles. 'Dad was doing all right, but by all accounts he really had to work hard to get the business up and running. Times were tough. And he could have done with a bit of a hand, you know?'

'But Lawrence didn't share his inheritance?'

'Lawrence didn't inherit. He couldn't have inherited – because he was dead.'

I frowned. 'So where did the money go? Did someone steal it? Is that why you think Lawrence was murdered?'

Quentin picked up a beer mat and began rotating it in his fingers.

'My grandfather left a condition in his will that Lawrence would only inherit if he married before he was 35. If he reached 35 and was unmarried, my father would inherit.'

'Odd, but okay,' I said, scribbling furiously in my notebook. 'So he didn't marry? But your dad still didn't get the money?'

'Lawrence did marry, shortly before he vanished. A woman called Hannah Snow. She was much younger than him, from a good family but one that had fallen on hard times.'

'God it's like a film,' Charlie said. 'So Hannah's the murderer, right? She bumped him off and took the cash?'

Quentin looked a bit disappointed that Charlie had worked it out. 'Well, yes, that's what I think.'

'Do you have any proof? If there was no body, then surely Lawrence might not even have died, let alone been murdered,' I said.

'Well, no. But this all happened a long time before I was even born. But believe me, I'm absolutely sure that my uncle didn't just disappear. I know he died.'

'How do you know?' I stared at him.

'My father told me that he'd always believed Hannah killed him,' Quentin said.

I watched him look down at the table, not convinced he had told me the truth.

'Why did he think she'd killed him?' Charlie asked.

'For the money, obviously.' I wasn't sure that was what Charlie had been asking, but it was what Quentin chose to answer. That interested me too. I wrote down a question mark next to Hannah's name.

'I believe she took my father's inheritance and that's not all she took.'

'What else?' Charlie's eyes were gleaming.

'I don't know.'

'Oh.' Charlie looked deflated.

'Apparently there were rumours at the time that Hannah had taken something precious from my uncle. Priceless, even.'

'Treasure?' I said, half-mocking, half-serious.

'Perhaps. I don't know.'

I shook my head. 'This isn't really our sort of thing, Mr Wetherby.'

Quentin lowered his voice so no one on the table next to us could hear. 'I'm willing to pay handsomely for your time.'

'That's neither here nor there. We don't work for a fee. We're not private detectives. Ouch.' Charlie kicked me under the table and I glowered at him.

'We can discuss payment,' he said.

I was feeling a little uneasy about this.

'What if it wasn't Hannah who took the money and the treasure?'

'Who else could it be?'

'Normally we do a bit of research first and see if the mystery has enough legs for an episode, or even a couple of episodes,' I said. 'We couldn't commit straightaway.'

'Ah,' said Quentin.

'What does "ah" mean?' I was beginning to feel prickly and annoyed. This man was clearly not telling us the full story and it was getting my back up.

'I don't want you to make a podcast about this. It's family business, not entertainment.'

I stared at him, open-mouthed. 'That is literally what we do. Like I say, I think it's a private investigator you want.'

I shut my notebook with a thwack but Charlie put his hand on mine, stopping me from getting up.

'Why us?' he asked. 'Scar's right. We're not investigators. Well, obviously, I am in my day job …'

'Yes,' I interrupted. 'Why us?'

Quentin shrugged. 'My son Felix likes your podcast. He suggested it. He said you made a programme about a woman who had been accused of stealing from a company and that it reminded him of our mystery. He made me listen and he was right. All the evidence pointed to her being guilty, but she'd never been charged or convicted. Just like Hannah.'

'Shirley Pilgrim was innocent,' I pointed out.

Quentin waved his hand as though to say that was totally not the point.

'There are a lot of similarities,' he said firmly.

'But you don't want us to make a podcast?'

'No.'

I looked straight at him. 'Why not?'

'I'm led to believe that my uncle may have been …' He shifted on his chair, looking uncomfortable. 'He may have been gay.'

I looked at Charlie, who raised an eyebrow. 'So?' I said.

'So that's not really in keeping with … his reputation. He was quite the shining star, you know? In politics. Neville Chamberlain's right-hand man at the Treasury in the aftermath of the Depression.'

Charlie shrugged. He wasn't interested in present-day politics, let alone those of ninety years ago. 'No one would care.'

45

'I would care,' Quentin said firmly. 'And it would change things. Change how his disappearance was viewed. People would look at it in a different way.'

'It might be relevant,' I pointed out. 'Certainly gives his wife a motive for murder.'

'The money was her motive.'

Realising I was getting nowhere with this I changed tack. 'So why now? It's ninety years since your uncle disappeared. Why do you want to solve the mystery now?'

'Because,' said Quentin, 'if Hannah stole that money, then legally it belongs to me. My grandfather was a very wealthy man and if Hannah inherited his entire estate, as I believe, then she would have been extremely well off. I want you to find out what happened to the money.'

'You want your inheritance?' I said. 'And the treasure? Whatever it is.'

'I do.' Quentin looked defiant. 'Times are hard,' he added. 'You know how it is?'

Charlie and I looked at each other again. He widened his eyes, pleading with me, and I turned away.

'I can pay you £10,000 now and another £50,000 when I get the cash,' Quentin said.

I almost fell off my chair. 'I'm sorry?'

'I said £10,000 now and ...'

'I heard,' I said faintly. 'But tempting as it is, I'm afraid we can't accept.'

'Scarlett,' Charlie said. 'What are you doing?'

'We can't take money for this, Charlie.'

I looked at Quentin. 'What if we discovered something you didn't like? What if we can't find any evidence of Hannah's guilt? Perhaps someone else murdered your uncle. Or what if she didn't have any descendants for you to claim the money from? Maybe she spent all the money. Or gave it all to a donkey sanctuary. You can spend a lot of cash in ninety years.'

'Well, obviously the payment would depend on a satisfactory outcome.'

'What does that mean?'

'I mean, I'm sure you could …' Quentin paused. 'Find enough evidence to prove Hannah's guilt.'

'Find?' I said. 'Do you mean make up?'

'I'd expect you to do whatever you needed to do.'

'No,' I said. 'That's not how it works. I expect that's really why you came to us, isn't it? Did all the proper PIs you approached tell you where to go?'

Quentin looked sheepish and I knew I was right.

I shook my head. 'No,' I said. 'That's not happening. Charlie could even lose his job.'

Charlie opened his mouth to argue but I stood up, knowing I had to get out of there before I caved. We couldn't take this money – our podcast relied on us being impartial. I was a journalist, for heaven's sake. I had to stay neutral. And on top of all that was the fact that I didn't trust Quentin Wetherby one tiny iota. He was entitled, and prickly, and very probably homophobic, and I didn't like him.

'I'm really, really sorry,' I said. 'Believe me, I'm sorry. But we can't take your money.'

Chapter 5

Hannah

1933

I couldn't believe this was happening. Lawrie – slumped to the floor, horribly still; and Freddie – still completely naked as the day he was born, crouched over him.

'Get away from him,' I said frantically, looking round as though hordes of policemen could come crashing through the door at any moment. I lurched towards him, wanting to pull him away from Lawrie, then retreated because I didn't want to touch his bare skin.

'Get off him. We need help. We need to help Lawrie.' I dragged a bathrobe from where it was hanging on the back of the bedroom door and shoved it at Freddie. 'Cover yourself up,' I hissed, fear making me sharp-tongued.

He stood up and painfully, excruciatingly slowly, he shrugged on the robe and tied the belt. I didn't want to look but to avert my eyes from Freddie's body would be to look at Lawrie on the carpet, and I didn't want to do that either.

Freddie crouched back down at Lawrie's side, blocking him from my view.

'We can't help him,' Freddie said. 'It's too late.'

'What do you mean it's too late? What are you doing?' I shrieked. My voice was shrill and my breaths were shallow and gasping.

Freddie paused for a second, like he was gathering himself, and then he threw his head back and wailed: 'He's dead!'

My stomach heaved and I thought I was going to be sick. I steadied myself on the doorframe, then heaved again as I noticed a smear of blood on the bright white paintwork, presumably from Lawrie's head.

'He's not dead,' I said shrilly. 'He's not. He can't be. Check his pulse. Do something, Freddie.'

I tried to see past him to where Lawrie lay, but all I could see was his hand. Which was moving.

'He's alive,' I gasped, trying to get closer. 'He moved, Freddie. He's alive. Oh thank God. I'll get someone. Call for help.'

Freddie stood up. Despite him looking faintly ridiculous in the too-small dressing gown, he was intimidating as he towered over me, and I took a step backwards.

'Are you going to get help?' I said.

'Lawrie's not moving,' he said. He put a hand to his forehead dramatically. 'He's not moving. He's dead, Hannah.'

He took a step towards me, his expression hard.

'And you killed him,' he said. 'You killed Lawrie.'

He was much taller than me and as he approached, he blocked the light from the window. I felt a rush of fear. Would he hurt me?

'I didn't kill him,' I stammered. 'Check again. I saw him move. He's alive. I saw his hand move …'

'It was just a trick of the light,' Freddie said, ashen-faced. 'He's dead.'

I began to cry. 'I didn't mean to hurt him,' I said. 'He … he fell. You saw. The sheet, the sheet got caught and he fell.'

For a second, Freddie just looked at me. Then his face softened. 'I know that, Hannah. I know you didn't mean to hurt him and everyone else will realise that too. They'll know you didn't hurt him on purpose.'

Weak with relief I swayed slightly. 'We need to tell someone,' I whispered. 'We need to get help.'

As if I'd not spoken, Freddie carried on. 'Of course, they'll know you didn't hurt him on purpose. Not this time.'

'What?' I felt an icy chill down my spine. 'What do you mean?'

'You threw a glass at him, didn't you? He was bleeding.' Freddie clutched his heart. 'You smashed a glass and it made him bleed.'

'No,' I said. 'No, that's not what happened.'

'Isn't it?' Freddie gazed at me, wide-eyed. 'That's what Lawrie told me. He said you were arguing and you smashed a glass and he was hurt.'

'Well, yes, that's true, but I didn't mean ...' My head was spinning. 'We need to get help, Freddie. We should call the police.'

'All right, if that's what you want,' he said. 'After all, no one else knows about your argument earlier. Or Lawrie being hurt. Do they?'

I stared at him.

'And no one knows you were here, do they? Lawrie said you'd gone to the flat. It's late. Surely no one saw you come back to the hotel?'

'Well ...' I began, my voice thick with tears. 'There was a bellboy who heard the glass smash. He saw that Lawrie's face was bleeding. And then there was room service, when I came back ...'

'Hmm,' said Freddie. 'A violent argument? And then a tragic accident?' He emphasised the last two words in a way that made me feel sick. 'You can see how it looks, darling?'

I tried to lean round so I could see past him again to where Lawrie still lay, and once more he blocked my view.

'It looks like I hurt him on purpose.'

'It does.'

'What are we going to do?' I was panicking now, my breath jagged and shallow. 'I didn't mean it. I didn't mean to hurt him. What should we do?'

Freddie took me by the shoulders and steered me into the lounge area of the room, pulling the door to behind him so Lawrie was hidden. He pushed me down onto the sofa and poured a whisky from the bottle the bellboy had brought.

'Drink,' he said.

'I don't want it.'

'Drink it.'

He handed me the glass and I sipped. The whisky burned my throat, but it was oddly comforting. Freddie poured himself a glass and drank it in one gulp, then he poured another.

'You need to go,' he said.

'Back to the flat?'

'Oh no, darling. You need to run.'

I stared at him. 'Run? Where?'

'As far as you can go. Do you have a passport?'

I shook my head. I'd barely left London, let alone Great Britain, since my parents died more than five years ago.

'Well, go somewhere quiet. Where no one knows you.'

'But …' My head was spinning. 'But why? I didn't kill him. I know it looks bad, with the row and the glass, but you saw what happened. It was an accident.' I was shrill again, my voice sounding squeaky and pained to my own ears. 'You can tell the police what you saw.'

Freddie looked genuinely sad. 'I can't.'

'Yes, you can. You saw Lawrie trip. Just tell the police.'

'They can't know I was here.'

I drained my glass and stood up, suddenly furious. 'What? What do you mean they can't know? How dare you? How dare you protect yourself?'

'I'm protecting Lawrie,' Freddie said.

I scowled at him. 'Like hell you are.' I stalked to the bottle of

51

whisky and poured myself another stiff measure. 'You're afraid you'll get into trouble for being homosexual.'

'Darling, I'm not afraid of the police,' Freddie said. 'I've been arrested more times than you've had hot dinners.'

'Then why?'

'Because Lawrie has a reputation and a career and a family. Can you imagine the papers if it got out that we'd been involved in this …' he paused '… confrontation.'

I sat back down again, all bravado gone. 'Oh Lord,' I said, picturing Aunt Beatrice's face if I was slapped across the news with my new politician husband and his lover. 'Lord.'

'Do you understand?'

I nodded. 'I should go?' I said. 'But not forever?'

Freddie didn't speak. So I carried on. 'Just for a few weeks, perhaps? Find a quiet spot and hide out until the dust settles. Then I can come back.'

'Absolutely.'

'Right.'

I finished my drink and stood up. 'But what should we do about …' I took a step towards the room where Lawrie lay and Freddie stopped me with an outstretched arm.

'I'll sort it.'

'But, Freddie …'

'I'll get him dressed and make the bed, and make it look as though he tripped on the rug or something. Someone will find him in the morning. A chambermaid, most likely.'

'But he'll be all alone, all night.'

Freddie bit his lip. 'It's the only way.'

I swallowed a sob. Poor Lawrie. What an awful end.

A noise from the bedroom made me gasp. 'What was that? Is it Lawrie? I knew I'd seen him move. We should check.'

Freddie suddenly pulled me into a hug, wrapping me in his dressing-gown-clad arms tightly. 'Hannah, he's dead. That was just the floorboards creaking in this old building. He's dead. And

I'm so very sorry.'

'You told him you loved him,' I said, disentangling myself and staring at him in disgust.

'I do.' He grimaced. 'I did.'

'This is on you,' I hissed, jabbing him with my finger. He didn't flinch. 'It's all your fault.'

'Is it? You took the photographs. You made him fall.'

'Can't you see? This only happened because you were here with him. You've got Lawrie's blood on your hands.'

'No one knows I was here,' Freddie said. He sounded almost gleeful. 'The only person anyone saw coming into this room was you. The only person with blood on their hands, is you. The new Mrs Wetherby. Heir to the Wetherby fortune. You're going to be a rich woman, Hannah.' He sighed. 'Looks like you've got the means and the motive to do away with your husband.'

'This isn't a bloody Agatha Christie mystery,' I spat at him. 'This is my life.'

Freddie shrugged. 'I can leave if you want,' he said. 'Let you get on with it. You'd just have to take your chances and hope that London's policemen are a little less clever than Monsieur Poirot.'

With sudden, awful, horrible clarity I saw he was right. Of course I would be blamed for this. Of course I would. The bellboy who came when the glass smashed would remember Lawrie's bleeding face. And he'd know I was here because I'd called out. And the lad who delivered the whisky would remember me because we knocked on the door at the same time. And I would, indeed, be a wealthy woman. Or at least I would be when Lawrie's 35th birthday came around in October.

Freddie was watching me intently.

'You need to go,' he said again. 'It's the only way.'

I looked from him to the door to the room where I knew Lawrie lay. And then back to Freddie. And then I nodded.

'Pack a bag and go,' Freddie said. 'Go.'

Bewildered, I rubbed my head, wondering how everything had

53

changed so completely in such a short space of time.

'I don't have any money,' I said, practical as ever.

Freddie went to a bag that was at the side of the room and dug about inside.

'Take this,' he said, shoving me a handful of notes. 'That's enough for a while.'

'Where did you get this?'

'Lawrie.'

I wanted to thrust it back at him, but I knew I needed it.

'Is this really the only way?' I whispered.

'You killed Lawrie,' Freddie said. 'Deep down, you know you're to blame. It's really the only way.'

With the money clutched in my hand, I nodded. 'Will you look after him? Lawrie? And tell him …' My voice caught in my throat. 'Tell him I'm sorry.'

'It's too late,' Freddie said. 'Go.'

Ridiculously, I was still wearing my coat and hat, though I'd dropped my overnight bag by the hotel room door. So now, trying to seem calm, which was the opposite of how I felt, I walked over and picked it up, then I went to the door and opened it a fraction. The corridor was quiet and empty. Without even glancing back at Freddie, I slid outside and walked quickly to the stairs.

In the stairwell I paused for a second to tuck the money Freddie had given me into the side pocket of my bag. For the briefest moment I thought about leaving the camera behind, unspooling the film and destroying the pictures of Freddie and Lawrie together. But then I unhooked it from round my neck and put it inside the bag too. Then I made my way downstairs. I'd go to Euston, I thought. Head up north somewhere. Just for a while.

It was after ten o'clock now and the hotel was quiet. My footsteps echoed through the tiled foyer as I went out into the chilly night air.

'Can I get you a cab, miss?' the doorman said.

I kept my face away from him so he couldn't identify me later.

'Yes please,' I said. 'I'm going to Gower Street.'

That was a lie, of course, but it was vaguely in the right direction.

A cab pulled up and I got inside. And when the driver had turned the corner away from the hotel, I said: 'I'm sorry, I was mistaken. Could you take me to Euston instead?'

The cabbie tipped his hat to me and I sat back in my seat, feeling my heart thump.

'Not many trains this time of night,' he said.

'No.'

'Except the sleeper of course. Headed north are you?'

'Yes.' I hadn't thought about where I'd go. I simply intended to get on the next train and go wherever it took me.

'The wife's always wanted to do that trip. Go to sleep in London, wake up in Inverness. It's like magic. Where is it you're going?'

'Inverness,' I said, feeling the unfamiliar name stick in my mouth. 'I'm going to Inverness.'

Chapter 6

I met Lawrie at a benefit. Some charity dinner for retired gentle-women, or former soldiers, or ageing racehorses – I was hazy on the details.

It seemed to be part of my arrangement with Aunt Beatrice that every now and then, I'd dress up and accompany her to one of these charitable occasions. I thought she liked how caring my presence made her appear.

'My niece, Hannah,' she would say. And then I'd hear her murmur: 'My brother Jeremy's girl. Tragic.'

She would give a shrug, and a tiny saintly shake of her head to show that taking in her orphaned niece had been no hardship.

'Well of course, I had to take her,' she would say. 'What else could I do? Poor mite.'

I'd been 14 when my parents died in a car accident in India and, in actual fact, after the crash, I'd spent most of my time at school, where I'd stayed for the holidays too with only brief visits to Beatrice at Christmas and occasionally when she wanted to show me off.

I had suspicions that my aunt had offered herself as my guardian because she thought my father had money and she would – finally – be financially secure thanks to his death. By the time she discovered his bank account had been emptied due to his tendency to make very bad business decisions – the same trait that had led my grandfather – Beatrice's father – to lose his money – it was too late.

But the fact remained, Beatrice had given me a home, of sorts, and welcomed me into it when I'd left school. So I accompanied her to her benefits. And I smiled gratefully as she told my tragic story.

Until the day of the benefit for the retired gentle racehorses, or whatever it was, when Lawrie caught me rolling my eyes at Beatrice's chatter.

'Poor girl was devastated,' she was saying to a gaggle of clucking women. 'What choice did I have?'

'You don't look devastated,' someone said. I turned to see Lawrie – though of course I didn't know he was Lawrie then.

'How do I look?'

He studied me carefully. 'Bored.'

'Nonsense,' I said. 'I care deeply for the cause.'

'And the cause would be?'

I screwed my nose up. 'Racehorses?' I ventured.

Lawrie shook his head, looking disappointed. 'Orphans.'

Oh, now I understood why Beatrice had been so keen for me to accompany her.

'Oops,' I muttered, feeling slightly guilty. 'Should have known that.'

'Given your own tragedy.' He touched my arm gently. 'It can't have been easy for you.'

I looked at him, wondering if he was mocking me, but actually I saw sympathy in his eyes.

'Thank you.' I tried to smile but found it was easier to frown. My parents had been distant but I'd loved them and he was right

– it hadn't been easy. 'I miss them.'

'Fancy a drink?' he said.

And that was that really.

I liked Lawrie. He was funny and kind and interesting. I loved to hear his stories about politics and his tales of dinners with ambassadors and other bigwigs. And Lawrie liked my interest. I think it fed his ego – which wasn't a bad thing, really, because he was rather quiet and prone to being self-deprecating.

Flattered by him wanting to get to know me better, I told myself he'd seen something in me. Of course, now I knew he'd seen a naïve, impoverished young woman, ripe for the picking. With the countdown on to his 35th birthday, he'd needed to act. And he'd found me. Someone he could marry to secure his inheritance, someone with whom he could rub along nicely, and who wouldn't question his … I breathed in sharply … indiscretions.

*

I bought a ticket for a shared cabin on the sleeper to Inverness. I hadn't been keen to share with a stranger, but double cabins were all that was left. I was hoping the exhaustion of the day would mean I dropped off as soon as my head hit the pillow and I could avoid any small talk.

But actually, when I clambered aboard the train, just minutes before it steamed out of the station, it was my cabin-mate who was already in bed and fast asleep. And instead of sleeping myself, I lay on top of the hard, narrow bed, thinking about Lawrie and trying to make sense of everything that had happened.

How could my life have changed so completely in just a few hours? The sheer speed of it all made my head spin. I was exhausted but every time I closed my eyes, I saw Lawrie slumped on the floor. And the knowledge that I'd done this, that it was all because of me – even though I told myself I'd not hit him or pushed him, I knew it was because of me – made me feel sick.

I swung my legs off the bunk and, swaying with the movement of the train, I left the cabin and headed to the bar. In normal times this would have been thrilling. The little wooden tables with their amber lights glowing were cosy and welcoming, and the barman nodded to me as he wiped down the surface. It was like being in a rather smart, rather narrow hotel bar.

Not wanting to be alone, I perched on a stool at the bar.

'What can I get you, miss?' the barman asked. Then, as I steadied myself with a hand on the bar, he said. 'Oh, I'm sorry, madam?'

I glanced down at my wedding ring, shiny and new on my left hand. 'Whisky,' I said, thinking I'd never drunk as much whisky in my whole life as I had that day.

He pushed the drink towards me, and I took a sip.

'Husband joining you, is he?'

I looked round at the door to the carriage, as though Lawrie might walk through any moment. And I wished with every bone in my body that he would.

'No,' I said. 'He's ... asleep.'

'It's the movement.' The barman leaned against the back of the bar and crossed his arms.

'Pardon?'

'The movement of the train, sends some people straight off.'

I thought of the woman asleep in my shared cabin and nodded. 'Yes, I can see that.'

'Doesn't work for everyone, mind you.'

'No.' I gave him a small smile.

'On holiday?'

I shook my head. 'My husband has business,' I said vaguely, kicking myself for not sitting at a table after all, where I would have been anonymous and ignored.

'What line of business is he in?'

I looked down at my glass. 'Whisky,' I muttered, hoping he

wouldn't ask me any more questions about myself. To change the subject I asked: 'Do you work all night?'

'Until the morning. Then I hand over to the breakfast crew at Edinburgh. Back to London tomorrow night.'

'You must meet all manner of interesting people.'

He grinned. 'You wouldn't believe the stories I've heard.'

I wondered how he would react if I told him my story. He began to tell me a complicated tale of a married couple who he reckoned were bank robbers, and I half-listened as I sipped my drink, letting the words wash over me. What on earth was I doing here? I wondered. It had all happened so fast. I closed my eyes briefly, then opened them again as pictures of Lawrie and Freddie on the bed, and Lawrie on the floor, filled my head.

Perhaps all this was a bad dream. Perhaps I'd wake up in our hotel room in London, and everything would be all right.

'... well, it was obvious he'd done him in,' the barman said. I looked up from the bottom of my glass in horror, my stomach lurching.

'What?'

'The posh bloke. He killed the woman's husband.'

I'd not been following his story. I stared at him and he chuckled.

'Well, it's obvious, isn't it?' he said. 'If he hadn't done it, why would he run?'

'He killed someone's husband?'

'Well, that's what I reckon.' He lowered his voice. 'Only guilty people run.'

The whisky was burning my throat. I pushed it away, feeling sick, his words ringing in my ears.

To my absolute relief, a group of four men arrived in the bar carriage, already looking three sheets to the wind, and demanding more drinks. I saw my chance, so I thanked the barman, slid off my stool and went to sit at a table at the far end of the carriage.

'Only guilty people run,' I muttered. What on earth had I done? I'd been so shocked by everything that had happened, that I'd let

Freddie take charge. Freddie. He was hardly trustworthy, was he? And he was almost definitely not a doctor. I'd seen Lawrie's hand move – I was sure of it. Perhaps it had been a trick of the light, as Freddie said. But perhaps it hadn't. Perhaps Lawrie had still been alive. Though there was always the possibility that he wasn't now. But then maybe he could have been saved if we'd acted faster. If I'd stayed in the hotel room, called for help, explained what had happened, then maybe everything would have been all right.

My thoughts swirled round my mind, making me grip my head in despair.

What had I done?

Now everyone would think I'd attacked Lawrie. Aunt Beatrice would think that the niece she had welcomed into her home was a violent criminal. That would ruin her tales of tragedy, I thought uncharitably.

I put my hand over my mouth to stop a sob and stared out of the window into the dark countryside. I could see my own reflection in the glass, ethereal and pale, like a spirit, my eyes hollow shadows.

I stayed in the carriage all night, as the train steamed north. I didn't want to talk to anyone and I didn't want to be alone. So I huddled in the corner booth, turning everything over and over in my head.

Eventually, after we'd stopped at Edinburgh, and I'd caught a glimpse of the castle in the dim early morning light, I made a decision.

By now, I thought, Lawrie would have been found – alive or dead. And I didn't trust Freddie to speak up for me. Far better for him to let the finger of suspicion fall on me than risk anyone thinking he was in Lawrie's hotel room, despite his bravado about being arrested. In fact, could it be that the police were already looking for me? Perhaps they'd even told the newspapers.

I slumped down in the seat, knowing I'd made the worst mistake of my life, running away. And as the train puffed across the Forth Bridge, I made up my mind. I would hand myself in at Inverness. I would find a policeman and tell him the truth: I had hurt my husband – I might even have killed him – and I needed to pay.

Chapter 7

Scarlett

Present day

Once I'd marched out of the pub, I didn't go back towards the tube station. Instead I walked all the way down to the Strand, then down the side of the Savoy to the river where I sat on a bench and tried to collect my thoughts. I liked being by the water normally, but today my mind was racing.

It's such a lot of money, a little voice in my head said. *You could get your own place where no one will leave you laminated instructions.*

Shush, I said to myself. Stop it.

You could leave work. Do your own thing.

You love your job, I told myself. Love it.

Except, the trouble was I didn't. I had loved my job until a few months ago when the station we worked for – Britain Live – had been taken over by a huge company and we'd been swallowed up. Suddenly we'd lost half our team, and we had a new boss – a micromanager called Kevin who had been over-promoted much to our bewilderment and who liked to keep secrets from us all simply to make himself feel important.

'Keep it on the down-low,' he was fond of saying about inconsequential things like the exact week Robyn was planning to go on maternity leave – as if she hadn't already told me – or whether or not there would be a summer party this year.

And he really loved to check up on us. To offer us solutions to problems that didn't exist. To get us to change guests on our shows, or the running order, or rewrite a script, just to make us change it back again. It was soul-destroying and exhausting and I envied Robyn's pregnancy that was going to get her out of the place, even for a few months. The only saving grace was that Robyn herself produced the shows we worked on, and she acted as an effective buffer between us and Kevin. Most of the time. But I was dreading her going off on maternity leave and leaving me to deal with Kevin on my own.

Of course, the takeover had happened almost exactly the same time as Charlie and I had broken up and I'd moved out of the house Charlie and I had lived in – and into Anita's where I felt uncomfortably like a silly schoolgirl and a grandma at the same time.

I'd felt as though my whole life had fallen apart, so the lure of the money offered by Quentin Wetherby was strong. It could help me put my life back together.

But.

We'd only get the money if we proved Hannah Snow was guilty, whether or not that was the truth. I pushed away the thoughts of not having to share a kitchen with Anita anymore.

Even £10,000 would be enough to get your own place, the voice said. *It would easily cover the deposit and help with the rent.*

'Shut up,' I said aloud. A man walking past glanced at me and I shrank back against the bench, hoping he didn't realise it was me who'd spoken.

No harm in looking into it, is there? A quick google, perhaps …

It's ten grand, Scarlett. Ten grand.

Realising I'd not be able to let it go, I stood up. I needed a second opinion.

*

'Why are you here?' Robyn said as I went into the office and dumped my bag on my desk. 'Not that it's not nice to see you, but isn't it your day off?'

'Is Kevin here?'

She shook her head. 'He went off somewhere about ten minutes ago. Obviously far too important to tell us where he was going.'

Relieved, I sat down. 'I'm not here to work, I just wanted to check something.'

'Something to do with Charlie's meeting?'

I eyed her suspiciously. 'How did you know about that?'

'You sent me a voice note last night on your way home.'

I winced. 'Oh yes. Bit of a drunken rant that, sorry.'

She chuckled. 'You told me three times that Charlie called you Scar. What was the meeting with this posh bloke, then?'

'It's a long story.'

Robyn pushed her chair away from her desk. 'Tea?'

'I'll make it.'

'It's fine.'

'How are you feeling?' I looked at her carefully, noticing she wasn't as pale as she'd been lately. 'Are those iron tablets kicking in?'

'Seem to be. I've definitely got more energy.' She smiled proudly. 'I watched a whole episode of *Drag Race* last night without falling asleep.'

'Well done,' I said, pleased for her, though her obsession with RuPaul left me slightly bewildered. 'But I'll still make the tea.'

*

65

When I got back to my desk, Robyn was on the phone, talking to someone who was going to be a guest on the drive-time show later. We worked across three newsy programmes, at breakfast, lunchtime and early evening. My job paid peanuts, involved lots of early starts, and took up every other weekend too, but I'd never minded until now.

I knew there would be no career progression while Kevin was keeping us in our places. I'd raised the possibility of presenting my own segment – after all, I did it all the time with the podcast – or even my own series. In fact, I'd pitched Shirley Pilgrim's story as a stand-alone documentary for an evening slot. Robyn had backed me. But Kevin had laughed. Laughed. And I couldn't even rub his face in the fact that it had won an award, because all the stories about it online – like the one my dad had sent me – only mentioned Charlie.

So now I thought leaving and going it alone was the only way to get my voice heard.

While I waited for Robyn to finish her call, I woke up my computer. There really was no harm in a quick google.

I typed in Lawrence Wetherby MP and hit return. There were a lot of results. The top ones were mostly mentions of him as "the inter-war MP who disappeared", in relation to Quentin when he was first elected.

I scrolled down to find a story about Lawrence's disappearance in a feature about unsolved mysteries. There wasn't much information – just that he had disappeared in May 1933 when he was newly married and was presumed dead, though no body had been found. I knew all that already.

I deleted Lawrence's name and typed in Hannah Snow instead. This time the results were all about an American soccer player who'd scored a goal at the weekend. I clicked on one of the videos at the top and watched her score, even though I had very little interest in football. She was very good, and I liked her bouncy ponytail, but she was definitely not the Hannah Snow I was looking for.

Disappointed, I swapped Snow for Wetherby and added Lawrence. Then I hit return again.

This time I had one result, another unsolved mysteries website – old and neglected as far as I could see – but it had a page about "the missing British MP and his wife". I scanned the text, which gave me all the same information as I'd known before, except it added that Hannah had also disappeared around the same time.

'What?' I muttered in confusion. Was that a mistake or had Hannah vanished too? If so, surely there was no mystery. Surely they'd just gone off somewhere together?

'What?' asked Robyn, who'd finished her call.

Quickly I filled her in on Quentin Wetherby's request.

'And he wants to pay you to do a podcast about this missing MP?' she said, frowning.

'No. He wants to pay us not to do a podcast.'

'Now you're making no sense.'

'He wants us to find Hannah Snow's descendants, if she has them, because he says she killed the MP – his great uncle – and pocketed the inheritance and stole some sort of treasure, but he doesn't know what the treasure was. And he doesn't want us to feature the story on a podcast.'

'Now he's making no sense.'

I shrugged. 'I know.'

'So how much does he want to pay?'

'Guess. No don't guess. You won't guess.'

Robyn gave me a stern look. 'Just tell me.'

'It's £10,000 now and £50,000 if we get a successful result.'

'Shut up.'

'It's true.'

'Fifty bloody grand?' Then her brow furrowed. 'Hang on, what does he mean by a successful result?'

'Proof that Hannah was the murderer.'

'What if she wasn't?'

I rolled my eyes. 'Exactly. We only get paid if we give him the result he wants. Plus, this is all arse about tit. We don't solve mysteries, we just consider the evidence and tell the story. And we really don't get paid to make the mystery fit the answer that someone wants it to fit.' I sighed. 'Charlie wants to do it.'

'Of course he does. Can he even be a PI at the same time as being a serving police officer?'

'Not a clue. I doubt it. The whole thing just seems …'

'Dodgy?'

'Totally.' I tapped my keyboard. 'It was making me feel uneasy anyway, and then I found this.' I turned my screen so she could read the extract. 'Look, it says that Hannah disappeared at the same time.'

'This same Hannah who supposedly murdered the MP?'

'Yes.'

'So actually she could have died too in a tragic double accident. Or they could have just sodded off to the Caribbean or somewhere.'

'Except … Quentin was absolutely adamant his uncle had died, and that Hannah killed him.'

Robyn pulled her chair closer to mine. 'This just got interesting.'

I gave her a sideways glance. 'What are you saying?'

'Do more googling.'

'Don't you have work to do?'

'I do, yes. But you don't. It's your day off.'

Casually, as though I wasn't really interested, I turned back to my computer and searched for "Hannah Wetherby disappearance". The first page of results were all about Lawrence vanishing – results I'd missed first time round, making me snort about the patriarchy, and also my own rubbish skills at internet searches.

Grudgingly I thought Charlie had been right when he said it was like Lord Lucan – because Lawrence seemed to have just vanished into thin air. Or actually, thin water because for some reason there were mentions of him disappearing in Loch Ness.

Even though he worked in London. It made no sense.

I pulled up Wiki and searched for Lawrence. There was a short page about his disappearance. Apparently, he had been a junior minister at the Treasury when he went missing. He'd last been seen in London one afternoon, then not turned up at work the next day when he'd been expected to. But there were rumours that he and his bride had been seen in Loch Ness around the same time before they both disappeared.

'What have you found?' Robyn asked. 'Anything useful?'

'The Wiki page says Lawrence left work one day and was never seen again. Or at least, nothing concrete – just rumours that he'd been seen in Loch Ness.'

'Loch Ness?'

'That's what it says. But there were no clues. No evidence. No body.'

'What about Hannah? She definitely disappeared too?'

'Erm, not sure. There's only that one reference to her going missing.' I frowned. 'Maybe Hannah did kill him and then she went on the run.'

'He's just as likely to have killed her,' Robyn pointed out. 'More likely, probably. Men are more violent than women.'

'Or maybe they ran off to a commune together to live a simpler life.'

Robyn chuckled. 'When did they vanish?'

'In 1933.'

'So the MP went missing in London, then turned up in Loch Ness?'

'Well London was where he was last seen.' I frowned. 'I suppose he'd have been in Westminster.'

'Maybe he was MP for Loch Ness?' Robyn opened her notebook and wrote down Lawrence Wetherby. Then she turned to her own computer and googled. 'Nope. West Sussex,' she said, adding that to her notes. 'About as far away from Loch Ness as you can be.'

'You're supposed to be working,' I pointed out.

She stuck her tongue out at me in a very childish fashion. 'It's fine, I'm friends with the producer.'

We both laughed, pleased with her extremely funny joke that she cracked at least once a day, possibly more.

'So there's nothing about Hannah?' she said to me. 'Was she in Loch Ness too?'

'The only mentions of her are in relation to Lawrence.' I shook my head. 'I'm as confused as you are, Rob. I don't understand why were they in Loch Ness if they lived and worked in London or where did you say his constituency was? Sussex?'

'Yes, Sussex.' Robyn shrugged. 'Did you say they were newly-weds? Could they have been on honeymoon?'

'That's an idea. But wouldn't he have said so when he left work that last day. "Bye, all, I'm off to Scotland for a holiday. See you in a week." And then no one would have worried when he didn't turn up the next day.'

'You're right. So why would they go to Loch Ness?'

'Absolutely no idea. Monster hunting?'

Robyn laughed. 'It's a mystery.' She raised an eyebrow at me. 'It's a really good story.'

'I know.' I groaned. 'It would make a great podcast.'

'You're not tempted by the money?'

'So tempted, but there's something not right about it, Rob.'

'You didn't trust him?'

I thought for a moment. 'Not at all. He was ... entitled.'

'Entitled?'

'Yes, like he expected us to fall at his feet and do his bidding.'

'For fifty grand.'

'Don't,' I said.

'And he's an MP, too?'

'He is.'

'So he's probably used to people doing what he tells them to do.'

'Probably,' I said glumly.

'Google him,' Robyn said.

70

'Now who's expecting people to do what they tell them to do,' I said. But I typed in Quentin's name anyway.

There were pages of results. I clicked on the "news" tab and the most recent story was about a drinks reception at the House of Commons for Pride.

'That's him,' I said, showing Robyn the photograph of a smiling Quentin, under a rainbow flag, and flanked by two younger men. Intrigued, I read the caption. 'Huh.'

'What?'

'Quentin told us he didn't want us to do the podcast because there were rumours Lawrence was gay and he didn't want it getting out. I assumed he was homophobic as well as bossy and entitled. But here he is, celebrating Pride with his son Felix, and Felix's husband, Declan.'

'He looks pretty happy to be there,' Robyn said. I nodded, taking in Quentin's arms looped round both younger men and his broad smile.

'That's most definitely not the face of a homophobe,' I said. 'Though he's still bossy and entitled.'

'And a liar,' Robyn pointed out. 'Because there must be another reason for him not to want you to do the podcast.'

I sighed. 'Even more intriguing.'

'It is,' Robyn said.

I groaned again. 'A brilliant story and loads of money.'

Robyn gave me a pitying look. 'I can see why Charlie wants to do it, to be fair.'

'He can't do it. He'd lose his job,' I said. 'And we know how much Charlie loves his job.'

'Rick?' Robyn raised her voice and shouted over to our colleague who worked on police and crime stories. 'Can police officers work on other stuff on the side?'

'What sort of stuff?'

'Like being a private investigator.'

Rick laughed loudly. 'Nope. They have to declare everything.

71

Even if they have a lodger, they have to tell professional standards.'

'See,' I said. 'It's not happening.'

'Well, not officially. But Charlie's sneaky.'

'Sneaky?'

'Not trustworthy.' Robyn had never liked Charlie. She made a face. 'I bet he'd find a way round it. Put the money in your name or something.'

'That's exactly what he suggested,' I said.

Robyn looked smug.

'I suppose ...' I began as my phone buzzed with a notification. *Cold Cases with Burns is going live*, it said.

'Charlie's doing a live stream,' I told Robyn. 'What's he doing? He's rubbish at this stuff. He normally leaves the social media to me.'

'Probably boasting about this job.' Robyn shifted closer. 'Let me see.'

I tapped on the notification and opened the live stream, putting the phone on my desk so Robyn could see. It took me a minute to work out what was on the screen because it was just a light fitting with brass details and a green glass shade. Where had I seen that recently? Then I remembered.

'He's still in the pub. He's put the live stream on by mistake and now he's showing all our followers a lovely view of the ceiling.' I shook my head. 'He's such an idiot. He did that a while ago – accidentally live-streamed when he'd been showing someone our feed.'

'It's not exactly making the podcast look professional,' Robyn pointed out. 'Message him and tell him what he's done.'

I picked up my phone but as I did so, I heard my name.

'Scarlett isn't interested,' Charlie was saying.

I stiffened, turning the volume up on my phone and exchanging a glance with Robyn.

'What's he talking about?' Robyn asked. I shushed her, trying to listen to what was being said. I could hear a man's voice – not

Charlie – but I couldn't make out the words. Then Charlie spoke again, clearer because the phone was obviously right next to him.

'I'm definitely in,' he said. 'Just me alone.'

This time, I heard what the other man – it had to be Quentin Wetherby – said. 'Are you up to it?'

Charlie laughed. 'I'm the detective,' he said. 'Scarlett does the tech stuff. No podcast, no need for Scarlett.'

I stared at Robyn, hardly able to believe what I was hearing. Charlie was talking again, something about expenses. Then he said: 'I'll have to arrange some leave from work so it'll be a week or so before I can get up there.'

Up where? I thought wildly. Loch Ness?

'He's bloody well taken the job on his own,' I said.

'Oh bugger, I'm streaming,' Charlie said suddenly, and his face loomed up on the screen. He'd clearly picked up the phone.

I froze, feeling like I'd been caught out. Would he notice the little avatar that would tell him that I was watching?

'Shit,' said Charlie, with a chuckle. 'Bloody social media, am I right? I'll delete it.' I saw his face more clearly as he lifted the phone and then the stream ended abruptly.

'I hate him,' said Robyn with real venom. 'Did he seriously just agree to do this without you?'

Tears sprang into my eyes. This felt like even more of a betrayal than Charlie moving on with Astrid so fast. 'He said he didn't need me. "No podcast, no need for Scarlett," he said. You heard him.'

'He's such a shit.' Robyn leaned back in her chair. 'So what do you reckon he's doing? Heading off to Loch Ness right now?'

'I don't know.' Anger was growing inside me. 'He didn't say Loch Ness specifically. He just said "up there".'

'Has to be Loch Ness, though, right?' Robyn said. 'If that's where Lawrence disappeared.'

'I suppose so. But he said it would be a while before he went up there, so I guess he's not going right now.' I looked up at the ceiling, trying not to cry. 'How could he do that, Rob? How could he go to Loch Ness?'

Robyn put her hand on my arm in sympathy. 'I expect he'll get the train to Gatwick and then the plane.'

'I didn't mean how would he get there,' I said.

'I know, I just wanted to make you laugh.'

But suddenly, I had a thought. A ridiculous, stupid, brilliant thought. I looked at Robyn. 'A train and a plane?'

'Or maybe a train all the way? I don't know, I've never been there.'

'I could go first.' I stood up, not really sure what I was saying. 'I could go to Loch Ness and find out what happened to Hannah, before Charlie does.'

'You could go,' said Robyn in delight. 'Do a podcast on your own. Pull the rug out from under Charlie's traitorous feet.'

And then just as suddenly as I'd stood up, I sat down again.

'I can't go. I've barely got enough annual leave left, and I've got no money. I can't afford to take time off and go swanning away on a plane to the other end of the country.'

Deflated, I leaned my elbows on the desk and put my head in my hands. 'This is Charlie's gig now.'

There was a pause and then Robyn said: 'What if it was work?'

'What?'

'Your podcast.'

'It's not work,' I said.

'Not up until now.' Robyn turned to her computer and pulled up BBC news on her screen. 'Look,' she said.

There was a story about Louis Nardini, a cerebral, rather serious TV presenter, who'd been accused of sexually assaulting several of his female staff going back decades. I rolled my eyes. 'Filthy,' I said.

'We've pulled his programme about mineral water.'

'I can't believe we ever commissioned him to do a programme about mineral water.'

Robyn rubbed her nose. 'Kevin commissioned him. And even as far as his ideas go, it wasn't the best.' Then she grinned at me.

'But it means there's a slot. What if you go to Loch Ness and make a programme to fill the gap?'

I stared at her. 'Are you serious?'

'Totally. I'll come too and produce it.'

'Kevin would never agree to that.'

'He might. If I tell him there's nothing else for that empty slot.'

'He could just drop in a repeat.'

'He could, but listener numbers are down. It's risky.'

'You really think he'll go for it?'

'I think he might have to even if it's only out of desperation.' Then she groaned. 'But I've got my scan on Monday. I could see if I can change it, put it off until we get back …'

'Doesn't your scan have to be done at a certain time?' I was vague about the details of pregnancy.

'Pretty much.'

'So why don't you stay here and produce the programme? I can go alone and you can always pretend that you'll let Kevin have oversight of what we're doing.'

Robyn did a little Andy-Murray-style air punch. 'Yes! That's what I'll do.'

'What will you do, Robyn?' Kevin walked past our desks wearing his jacket – obviously on his way back from wherever he'd been.

'I'll fill the gap left by us pulling Louis Nardini's programme.'

Kevin looked weary. 'I can't believe the bigwigs are forcing us to drop that,' he said. 'Just because a few women got a bit lippy.'

'Could I have a quick word about it all?' Robyn said through gritted teeth.

'Come,' Kevin said, like Lord Muck, gesturing for her to follow.

'Want me to come?' I said as she got up.

'Nah,' she said in a quiet voice. 'I'll stick my bump out – I think he's a bit scared of my unborn child.'

I watched as she followed Kevin into his office, which had glass walls so I could see her. I couldn't hear what she was saying, obviously, but she seemed very earnest. Kevin looked stern. 'He's going to say no,' I mumbled to myself, disappointed.

But then Robyn stroked her bump and Kevin looked a little alarmed. Robyn was making sort of wavy gestures with her hands that I thought might have been related to the Loch Ness monster, and Kevin was nodding, though not with a great deal of enthusiasm. Maybe it was going to work?

Eventually, Robyn came out into the office, wearing a wide smile.

'Three half-hour episodes. First one on Monday evening, then Wednesday and Friday. And they'll put it out as a podcast too. I said you'll go tonight, to give you more time to research and to give Kevin less time to object. Apparently, you can get a sleeper train but he said get a seat not a room, because the rooms are really expensive. And you need to make a trailer before you go. I'm producing.'

I stared at her.

'What?' she said. 'Charlie's a shit and Kevin's one too and this is the best way to get one over on them both. We just need to make sure it's really, really good and gets a million more listeners than Louis Nardini would have.'

'Only a million?' I said, suddenly absolutely terrified. 'This is amazing.'

'I know, right?' Robyn said, doing a little bounce of excitement on her toes. 'Your first official presenting gig, and a chance to smash the bloody patriarchy at the same time.'

'What more could a girl want?' I said. 'What time is this sleeper train?'

'Not sure? Maybe around 11 p.m.?'

I looked at my watch. 'Best get cracking, then.'

Chapter 8

Hannah

1933

By the time I got to Inverness I was almost cross-eyed with tiredness. I was hungry and dirty and barely able to think straight.

The train had taken longer than I had expected. Inverness, it turned out, was much further north than I'd realised. When the train finally shuddered to a halt at our final destination, it was teatime, and I'd barely eaten since our wedding breakfast, which seemed days and days ago. I'd also hardly slept, and the combination of no food and no rest made me light-headed.

As I clambered down from the train, I half expected to see a band of policemen waiting for me. But there was no sign of any uniforms.

Feeling an odd mix of relief and disappointment, I followed the other weary travellers along the platform to the main concourse of the station, where I stood for a moment, unsure where to go next.

'Can I help you, miss?' I turned to see a man in a railway uniform, smiling kindly at me.

I meant to ask for directions to the police station, but as I glanced down at my grubby coat, and caught a whiff of food on the cold air blowing in from outside, I changed my mind.

'Is there a hotel nearby?' I asked, adding hurriedly: 'Nothing fancy. I'm on quite a strict budget.'

The man gave me a slightly curious glance and I kicked myself for speaking to him. Perhaps he'd remember me if someone came looking. Though, I reminded myself, that was of no consequence if I was going to confess to my crime.

The man said something, so fast that I didn't understand a word, and then chuckled as he saw my wide eyes.

'First time in the Highlands?' he said, slower this time and I nodded.

'Welcome,' he said. 'It's a wonderful part of the world.'

I tried to smile, wishing I was here on holiday. Honeymoon, even. But my lips stayed firmly turned down as he gave me directions to the Royal Hotel where, he assured me, there was hot and cold water in each room.

Thanking him, I hurried outside where the rain was lashing down and an icy wind took my breath away. I hunched down in my coat and, with no energy to run, trudged on towards the hotel the stationmaster had recommended, desperate for a wash in that hot water.

Inverness was a pretty city, or at least I could see it would be pretty if the rain stopped. It felt grand and proud, sitting astride the river. In the distance were dark hills, taller than I'd ever seen before, and up ahead was a large castle overlooking the houses. Safe, I thought. It felt safe. Like a fortress, holding its position against invading troops.

My tired legs protested as I climbed the few stairs up to the hotel entrance, but they didn't totally give in until I'd paid for one night – wincing at how depleted the stack of notes Freddie had given me was – and let myself into the room on the first floor. Once I was inside though, glad to be out of the rain and off the street, my knees buckled beneath me and I threw myself onto the bed. On the table next to where I lay there was a jug of water. I shifted across the counterpane, hoping I wasn't leaving grubby smudges, and poured myself a glass, which I drank in one gulp, then another, washing away the taste of the whisky from the train.

I would lie here for five minutes, I thought, and then have a wash and go in search of food. And once I was clean and rested, I could think about what to do next.

But maybe I'd close my eyes, just for a second …

*

I awoke with a start to the clanging of church bells and for a moment I didn't know where I was.

I lay there for a minute, staring at the white ceiling, then it all came back to me in a rush – Lawrie, Freddie, Lawrie lying on the floor, so terribly, terribly still.

Sitting up, I looked at the clock on the bedside table. Goodness, it was seven o'clock in the morning. I'd slept right through the night, still wearing my dirty travelling clothes and without even taking off my shoes. Aunt Beatrice would be horrified.

I rubbed my forehead, thinking carefully. I couldn't possibly go to the police station looking like this, so I'd have to have a proper wash, and do my hair, which was a tangled bird's nest, and change my clothes.

My stomach growled so loudly I thought the people in the next room would be able to hear it.

'Food,' I said aloud. I'd get washed and dressed, have breakfast, and then find the police station.

I was so dirty that I really could have done with a bath, but that wasn't an option so I stripped off and had a good wash in the hot water the stationmaster had boasted about. Though lukewarm would have been a more accurate description.

The receptionist had told me breakfast was included in the

price of the room, and when I went downstairs and smelled toast and sausages and other tasty aromas, I was glad. The dining room was quiet. Just a well-dressed couple at one end, engrossed in one another, and a young woman – maybe around my own age, who was sitting alone at a table right in the middle of the room. I chose a small table in the corner and sat down, hoping I'd be tucked away enough that no one would pay me much attention.

I asked the waitress for porridge – I was in Scotland after all – and a pot of tea, and then added with a certain amount of trepidation: 'And a newspaper, if you have one?' I wanted to know if there were any reports of Lawrie's … Even in the safety of my own thoughts, I shied away from the word. Lawrie's accident.

She nodded and hurried off. I sat back, watching the woman at the centre table, who was wolfing down an enormous plate of breakfast with gusto.

'Davina, I'm glad you've left,' my waitress said to her as she walked past with a tray of tea and my newspaper. 'Our profits went up when we stopped having to feed you. I don't know where you put it all.'

The woman – Davina – stuck out her tongue at the waitress. 'Hollow legs,' she declared cheerfully.

I couldn't help smiling at their exchange. Davina was so full of life and energy. She was positively fizzing with it as she sat there, one leg tucked up under her, gobbling down her breakfast.

'Your newspaper, miss,' said the waitress, handing it to me.

'Thank you.'

She put down the tray and unloaded the teapot and cup and saucer, plus a little jug of milk that I thought Aunt Beatrice would have approved of, though she most definitely wouldn't have approved of me breakfasting alone, and neither she nor Lawrie would have liked me reading the newspaper.

To my disappointment, it wasn't *The Times* that the waitress passed me, but the local *Inverness Herald*. Nevertheless, once I'd got past the adverts on the front, I found an account of President

Roosevelt's plans for the banks.

I poured myself a cup of tea, and settled back in my chair to read. Even with the guilt about what had happened to Lawrie weighing heavily on me, it felt good to be alone. I felt grown up and independent.

I turned the page as the waitress asked Davina how her breakfast was.

'It was good, but the sausages at the Drum are better,' she said. She had short, curled hair tucked behind one ear and, as I watched her over the top of my newspaper, one curl came loose and she pushed it back in exasperation. 'You should come and work with me, Mary. Mrs McEwan's wanting more staff.'

'Och, I'm no going all the way out there,' said Mary in a much broader accent than she'd had when she spoke to me. 'I'm a city girl.'

I turned my attention back to the newspaper, reading about the elections in Germany. And there, at the bottom of the page was a photograph that made me start in fear and my stomach lurch.

It was a picture of me in my wedding gown. I was gazing to the side, my hair tumbling over my shoulders. I frowned at my own image in front of me. I looked demure and innocent, and I barely recognised myself. How was it possible that was only two days ago?

Still holding my teacup in a slightly trembling hand, I took a deep breath, readying myself to read the accompanying story.

'Your porridge,' said the waitress, making me jump as she put the bowl down in front of me. In surprise, I dropped my teacup and the newspaper, spilling liquid all over the page.

'Oh, I'm so sorry, I didn't mean to give you a fright,' she said. 'Let me move you to another table and get that cleaned up for you. Davina, give me a hand?'

She bustled me over to another table, closer to where the couple were sitting, while Davina bounced to her feet and cleared the table, whisking away the sodden newspaper.

Still shocked about the story in the paper, and more than a little soggy myself, I let Mary sit me down and put the porridge bowl in front of me.

'I'll get you more tea,' she said, hurrying away.

I picked up the spoon, but I didn't eat anything. My mind was racing. People must be looking for me. Why else would my photograph have been in the newspaper? Was I being hunted? The word conjured up images of hounds tearing through the countryside. At this very moment, were detectives studying train timetables or interviewing the taxi driver who had driven me to Euston? I shook myself, slightly disgusted at the way my mind had got lost in the excitement of it all. Lawrie was dead, I reminded myself.

Perhaps.

I thought again of his hand moving when he lay on the hotel room floor, and the way Freddie had stopped me seeing him properly.

I knew, of course, that the right thing to do would be to go straight to the police station and hand myself in.

And yet …

Hadn't Lawrie been living a double life? Hadn't he done exactly what he wanted, in his own best interest, no matter the consequence for me, his oblivious bride?

Suddenly, beneath the guilt, and the nerves, I felt something else. Something a little like … excitement? Because finally, I was alone. With no Aunt Beatrice telling me what to do or how to be. No Lawrie telling me not to ask questions or show an interest in politics.

*

I knew I'd done wrong by hurting Lawrie, and perhaps I was indeed a wanted criminal. I thought, rather bleakly, that for the rest of my life, the way he'd slumped to the floor would haunt my dreams. There was no doubt that I'd reacted badly. No doubt at all. Though frankly, I was sure any bride in my position would have been just as shocked to discover what I had about her groom.

My mother had always told me that when God closed one door, he opened another. Was this my door? My chance to change the life that had been mapped out for me?

What if they're looking for you? a voice in my head taunted me.

But what if they were? They were looking for demure Hannah Wetherby. That wasn't me. She didn't even really look like me. Maybe she'd never been me.

Unconsciously, I put my hand up and smoothed my hair in the bun I'd tucked it into when I got dressed as I watched the couple on the table close to mine clasp hands over the salt and pepper cruets and gaze into one another's eyes. To the side of the room, another waitress was arranging daffodils in a vase, snipping the stems as she worked. I felt like all my senses were on high alert as I took in the room. And then, without thinking too much about it, I got up from the table.

'Just popping to the ladies', I said as Mary darted forward to tend to me. 'I think that gentleman wanted something though.'

I nodded towards the couple who were still gazing at each other, and Mary went over to them. With her attention diverted, I walked briskly to the side of the room and swiftly pocketed the scissors the other waitress had been using to cut the flowers. Then, on my way out of the dining room, I swiped a hat that was hanging on the coat rack and which I suspected belonged to the love-sick woman on the other table and, without pausing, I hurried out into the main part of the hotel and into the lavatory.

There was no one around, thankfully. But I knew I had to be quick. I unwound my hair from its grips and let it hang around my shoulders. And then, taking a deep breath, I began to cut.

The scissors weren't really sharp enough, but my hair was thin and they did the job. Strands fell into the basin as I hacked away until I had chin-length hair.

'Golly,' I said aloud as I looked at my reflection. It made my eyes look enormous, and I seemed older suddenly. I was quite pleased.

I smoothed it out, thinking I'd have to get a proper hairdresser to tidy it up soon enough, tucked it behind my ears, and pulled on the hat I'd stolen. It was dusky pink, with a brim that tilted down and I thought it would do a good job of hiding my face.

I wasn't sure what I was doing. I didn't have a plan. But I knew now that I wasn't going to be handing myself in at the police station. I had a little bit of money left and I was resourceful and hard-working. I could find a job. There were lots of options here in Inverness. I could work in a shop, or a café, or a hotel like Davina and Mary. The world was my oyster.

I took a last look at myself in the mirror, straightened my blouse, and threw back my shoulders. I wasn't Hannah Wetherby. I was Hannah Snow. And I was starting a whole new life.

With my chin lifted, I pushed open the door to the toilet and walked through the hotel foyer, heading for the lift. I'd fetch my bag and make a plan, I thought. A plan that involved food, because I'd still not eaten anything.

I strode towards the lift, and there, leaning against the wall, and looking for all the world as though she'd been waiting for me – was Davina.

'Hello,' she said, straightening up.

'Hello.'

I reached past her to press the call button and she put her hand out to stop me.

'What are you doing?' I said, alarmed.

'I saw you take that hat.'

I put my hand up to the tilted brim. 'Don't be ridiculous,' I said in my best clipped tones. 'How dare you.'

Davina smiled at me. 'And you cut your hair.'

'No.' Again I reached for the call button and again she stopped me. 'Don't,' I warned. 'I'll call someone.'

'Go on then.'

At a loss I stared at her. And then, to my horror, from behind her back she produced the soggy newspaper, still open at the photograph of me, though the story was impossible to read and the ink had run on the picture.

'Is this you?'

I couldn't deny it. Instead, I shrugged. 'What do you want? Money?'

She laughed. 'Got any?'

'No.'

'That's what I thought.' She nudged me. 'Have you run away?'

'Did you not read the story?' My heart was beating fast, as I wondered if the article said I was wanted for murder.

Davina looked a little embarrassed. 'Some of it.' Then she gave me a defiant stare. 'None of it. It's all splattered with tea, anyway. Can't see the words properly.' She turned and dumped the soggy pages into a nearby bin. 'I just saw the way you reacted when you spotted yourself in the photograph.'

I made a face. 'It was a bit of a shock,' I admitted.

'So what are you running away from?'

Weak with relief, I leaned against the wall. 'My husband,' I said. 'I ran away from my wedding.'

Chapter 9

Davina came up to my room with me. I didn't ask her. She just sort of invited herself along and, to my surprise, I found I didn't really mind. I quite liked her. She wasn't like anyone I'd ever met before.

'What's your name?' she asked as I unlocked my door and I realised she'd been telling the truth when she said she hadn't been able to read the newspaper story.

I paused. 'Hannah,' I said. 'Hannah Snow.'

Davina stuck her hand out for me to shake. 'Davina Campbell,' she said.

Inside the room, Davina prowled round straightening things and plumping the pillows and rearranging the bedding. I put my meagre belongings back into my bag and checked my unfamiliar reflection in the mirror.

'Do you work here?' I said. 'I thought you said to the waitress that you'd left?'

'Used to,' she said. 'I was a chambermaid.'

'Where do you work now?'

Davina sat down on the bed with a contented sigh. 'Drumnadrochit.'

I blinked at her. 'Drumna … what?'

'Drumnadrochit. It's a wee place beside Loch Ness.'

'Where's Loch Ness?'

'Where are you from?' she said, looking at me with her brow furrowed.

'London.'

She nodded, as if to say that was a reasonable explanation for my lack of local knowledge. 'Not too far.'

'You like it?'

'I love it.' She lay back on the counterpane, making herself at home, and put her hands behind her head. 'Listen.'

I listened, but I couldn't hear anything. 'It's quiet,' I said.

Davina sat up again. 'It's not. Listen properly.'

I listened. I could hear a car engine outside of my window, and seagulls shrieking, and church bells clanging.

'In Drum, it's properly quiet,' Davina said. She flipped over so she was lying on her tummy and looked straight at me. 'My mind is busy all the time. All my thoughts buzzing around like bees. So it's nice being somewhere quiet.'

'I understand that,' I said, fastening my bag. 'It makes sense.'

'Was he bad, your husband?'

Goodness, her thoughts really did buzz around like bees.

'Not bad,' I said carefully. 'Not really.'

'Then why did you run?'

I glanced at where she'd left the soggy newspaper on the side. 'He didn't love me.'

'Do you love him?'

'No.'

'So why did you marry him?'

'My family has no money. Marrying well was my only option.'

Davina made a face. 'Except you didn't.'

'Didn't what?'

'Marry well. Not if he didn't love you.'

I couldn't argue with that. 'I suppose not.'

'So, if you're so poor …' The way Davina looked at me suggested she thought I was lying about my family's finances, but I couldn't begin to explain that now. 'Why did he marry you?'

What could I say to that? My husband preferred the company of other men to women, and marrying me would have been a smokescreen for him and allowed him to claim his inheritance? That was the truth, but it still felt so shocking to me that I didn't think I could say the words. Instead, I shrugged. 'He needed a wife and I suited him.'

'Romantic,' said Davina drily.

She slid off the bed and clapped her hands together.

'Are you coming, then?'

'Where?'

Davina tutted. 'Drumnadrochit.'

'Buzzing like bees,' I said. 'Why would I come to Drumnadrochit?'

'You need a job, right?'

'I suppose.'

'And somewhere to live?'

'Yes.'

'Will your husband come looking for you?'

I shook my head. 'Not him,' I said. 'But someone might.'

'Then Drum's perfect. You can work at the hotel, and we can stay there too. It's quiet and no one will look for you there.' Once more, Davina looked me up and down with a slightly quizzical expression. 'It's not fancy, mind …'

'I don't want fancy,' I said hurriedly. 'What would I have to do?'

'Chambermaid, most probably,' said Davina. 'Maybe some waitressing. We all do a bit of everything. Mrs McEwan, she's the boss, she's so kind. She calls us her girls.' As she said the word "girls" she adopted a rather well-to-do accent and rolled the R dramatically. 'But Mildred went to live in Aberdeen when she got wed, and then Dougie moved to Glasgow to work in a big hotel and I said he'd be back within a month, because he's not nearly as bold as he thinks he is, but Mrs McEwan said he was ambitious and that I shouldn't underestimate him, and it seems she was right because he's not come back.'

She paused to take a breath and I couldn't help noticing she looked a little sad. 'Anyway, when I came here to pick up some wages I was owed from before, Mrs McEwan said I should see if anyone wanted a job and that she'd give me a bonus if I could get them to come and work at Drum. And Mary said no, but here you are and you need a job ...'

She stopped again and looked straight at me. 'Are you coming then?'

'It's quiet?'

'So quiet.'

'Who comes to the hotel?'

'Ladies and gentlemen who want a peaceful stay on the shores of the impressive loch,' Davina parroted. 'And some folk come for afternoon tea, or dinner. Older people mostly.'

I took a deep breath, feeling a weight lift – just a little – from my shoulders.

'I'd have somewhere to live?'

'We all have our own rooms,' Davina said dreamily. 'They're not big, but we don't have to share.'

'And I'd get paid?'

'What sort of odd job would it be if you didn't?'

I thought about the feeling that had come over me at breakfast, when I'd realised I was all alone and beholden to no one.

'All right,' I said. 'I'll come.'

Davina gave me a triumphant smile. 'Knew you would.'

'But before we go, can we get something to eat? I'm absolutely starving.'

*

We took the bus to Drumnadrochit, Davina jabbering all the way, telling me about the other staff at the hotel, and what everyone's jobs were. I knew I wouldn't remember, but I let her talk because it was distracting me from the guilt I was feeling about not handing myself in. Guilt and a sort of shocked exhilaration about what I was doing. I kept putting my hand to my neck, feeling my short hair and marvelling at what a turn my life had taken. And yet, it felt so right. The thought of being Lawrence's wife, holed up in Sussex while he worked all hours in London, seemed completely alien to me now.

After we'd been in the bus for almost an hour, a huge body of water opened up on either side of us. I could see a large house on the far side and boats bobbing about on the waves.

'Oh, heavens,' I said in delight. 'Is this it? Is this Loch Ness?'

Davina hooted with laughter. 'This is Loch Dochfour,' she said. 'This is a wee puddle compared with Loch Ness.'

And sure enough, a little while later, the road wound round again and once more we were travelling alongside water. Dark, inky black water, that stretched as far as I could see into the distance.

'This,' said Davina proudly, 'is Loch Ness.'

I had no words. I'd never seen anything like it.

'It's so big,' I said stupidly.

'Aye, well, it's long,' Davina said. 'It's not wide.'

I couldn't tear my eyes away from the scenery. The trees alongside the road were budding bright green, and some were beginning to blossom in pinks and whites, and the hills on the far side of the loch itself were dark khaki and brown, and the colours dazzled my eyes. I drank it in, unsure how this view, this wonderful riot of nature, could exist in the same world – in the same country even – as London with its grey river and its grey buildings and its grey skies.

And in the middle of it all, was the loch. Its dark waters reflected the clouds above and made me feel dizzy as I tried to work out what was sky and what was the land.

'I love it,' I breathed. 'It's the most beautiful thing I've ever seen. I can't believe I've never been here before.'

'People don't know about it,' Davina said, shoving me over a bit so she could see out of the window of the bus, too. 'But it's wonderful.'

'It really is.'

I gazed out of the window until, to my disappointment, the road swung away from the water's edge and Davina nudged me. 'This is us.'

'I can't see the loch,' I said, gathering my belongings as the bus slowed down. 'I thought you said the hotel was on the shore.'

'Well, almost,' she said with a shrug. 'You can see it from some of the bedrooms. Come on. Hurry up.'

Obediently, with my bag banging against my legs, I followed her off the bus and out into the street.

The hotel was a rather grand building made from grey- and sandy-coloured stones with bay windows and iron railings. It looked quite imposing there on the roadside. Outside, two very well-dressed elderly ladies were getting out of a car. They both looked a little like Aunt Beatrice. The thought unsettled me and my stomach twisted with nerves. I slowed down as we approached.

'Davina?' I said. 'I'm not sure this is a good idea.'

She turned to me, and to my surprise, she wasn't smiling. 'Come ON,' she urged. Her voice was cold. 'Mrs McEwan promised me a bonus for finding more staff. Come on.'

For the first time, I realised her urging me to come and work at the hotel wasn't entirely altruistic. Mind you, I thought, I was hardly in a position to judge. Recruiting a new chambermaid for money was far less extreme than marrying for money.

I adjusted my bag and hurried after her.

Inside the hotel was a large mahogany reception desk, manned by a woman with dark hair peppered with silver, and a pair of pince-nez perched on her nose.

'Mrs McEwan,' Davina said, pushing through the doors and not bothering to hold them open for me. 'I've found someone to replace Mildred. Or Dougie. Either.'

Mrs McEwan stood up, peering at me through her glasses.

'And your name is?'

'Hannah,' I said, slightly out of breath from carrying my bag. I hoped she wouldn't want to shake my hand because my palms were clammy. 'Hannah Snow.'

'English?' She sounded disapproving.

'Yes, ma'am.'

'For heaven's sake, call me Mrs McEwan,' she said. 'Can you read and write?'

'Yes, Mrs McEwan.'

'Well, that's something.' She ran her eye over me. 'Nice coat.'

'Thank you.' I resisted the urge to curtsey.

She nodded. 'Yes, you'll do very well.' She reached over and picked a key from a peg board behind her. 'Room 25,' she said. 'Top floor. Be back down here in an hour and I'll take you through how it all works.'

I took the key, noticing my hands were rather shaky, and with a thumping heart, I followed Davina up the stairs.

Chapter 10

Scarlett

Present day

The sleeper train really ought to be renamed as the no-sleeper train, I thought as I trudged along the road almost twenty-four hours later. I'd slept a bit, snatching an hour or so, then waking up as the train rattled over a bridge, or another train passed us with a whoosh of air.

I'd spent the hours I was awake listening to many podcasts discussing the theories about the Loch Ness monster. It was all quite fun, though not relevant to my own hunt for Hannah Snow. I kept nodding off and missing bits so my knowledge was a bit patchy and I'd had several odd dreams when I did sleep. Still, it kept me amused as the train rumbled north, until I arrived in Inverness. I wasn't a very good traveller, so when I finally clambered down from the train, I was tired and dirty and very grumpy. And even more so when I realised my destination – a small town on the shores of the loch called Drumnadrochit – was a bus ride away.

I toyed with the idea of getting an Uber, but thought about Kevin's face when I tried to expense the journey and instead I stomped along the road a little way, found the bus stop, and after an infuriatingly long wait, eventually climbed aboard the little green single-decker that pulled up. I settled down with my bag on my lap to stew about the events that had led me to this smelly bus, carrying the strangest mix of people I'd ever seen.

There were some normal types – a young couple with their arms wound round each other, a woman with a baby strapped to her chest, a man in paint-splattered trousers carrying a hold-all – but there were also a lot of oddballs, to put it politely.

There were a lot of binoculars slung around necks, some rather questionable shorts and cagoule combos, one or two of those tartan hats with the ginger hair attached … I guessed these were the people on the hunt for Nessie.

The bus trundled down the road, across a low bridge over a small lake – which I knew from following our progress on my phone was called Loch Dochfour – and then suddenly the bus hummed with excitement as a huge body of water opened up in front of us. Loch Ness.

I'd chosen a seat on the wrong side of the bus to properly admire the view. Or perhaps, I thought, as my travelling companions adjusted their tam-o'-shanters and rushed to the windows, I had chosen the right side of the bus.

There was a flurry of activity as one by one they all got out their phones.

'Hi, guys,' one said, then another, then another, holding out their cameras to film themselves, rather than the view. 'I'm here at Loch Ness on the trail of Nessie herself …'

'I'm here at Loch Ness …'

'Here I am at the site of the famous Loch Ness …'

Surreptitiously I got out my own phone and snapped a photo of the eager monster hunters to send to Robyn, wondering if everyone here would be hunting for Nessie or if anyone else would want to find Hannah Snow.

When the bus arrived at Drumnadrochit, where I was booked into the only hotel with a vacancy, I gathered my belongings and jumped off the bus with a certain amount of relief. Though, to my dismay, all the monster hunters disembarked too. I supposed it was the obvious choice, for them. This was where the Loch Ness monster had first been spotted, after all, as I'd learned from my research overnight.

I hoisted my backpack on to my shoulders and followed the gaggle of YouTubers into the hostel. It was a lovely building, standing proud, set back from the road. Outside was a sign bearing a cartoon of the monster wearing a rucksack, saying Drum Backpackers Hostel.

'Bloody hell,' I muttered. I wasn't exactly used to swanky hotels but I thought the radio station's budget could have stretched to something a bit more upmarket. I just hoped I wouldn't have to share a room.

I fished out my phone and found the email Robyn had sent me with all the booking details.

Ask for Joyce, she'd written. *She's expecting you and she said she might be able to help with your research.*

Despite my tiredness and my lack of a comedy tartan hat, I felt that flutter of excitement again. This was a good story – I could feel it in my bones. And I knew it would make a good podcast too. I would go for a wander later, I thought, and record some background stuff. It made sense to get started as soon as possible. After all, Charlie could already be on his way up north.

Inside the hostel was a large reception desk with a stand next to it stuffed with leaflets about monster-spotting boat trips. There was a woman who I thought had to be in her seventies, but looking good on it, behind the desk, cheerfully checking in the queue of tourists that had formed ahead of me, handing out keys and giving directions to the nearest cafés.

When it was my turn, I gave her my most winning smile.

'Hello,' I said. 'I'm Scarlett from Britain Live. I'm to ask for Joyce.'

'I'm Joyce.' She stuck her hand out and I shook it. 'How was your journey?'

'Long,' I admitted. 'But now I'm here I see that it was worth it. It's so beautiful.'

'Isn't it?' She tapped a few keys on her keyboard. 'I've put you right up in the attic. It gets a good strong Wi-Fi and phone signal up there. It'll help with your recording.'

'Thank you.' I was a bit surprised but I supposed when you ran a hostel frequented by broadcasters you got the hang of catering for their needs.

'Is Britain Live doing something about the Loch Ness monster then?' For the first time I noticed a teenage girl – maybe around 14 – wearing denim dungarees and Converse, with a cloud of dark curls around her face, sitting behind the desk reading a Colleen Hoover novel.

'Nope,' I said.

She frowned, her dark eyes regarding me sharply. 'Then why are you even here?'

'Different mystery.'

'This is my granddaughter Bonnie,' Joyce said. 'She's supposed to be helping me today, but Bonnie's idea of helping is to sit with her nose in a story.'

I grinned at Bonnie. 'You've got the right idea. That's a great book.'

'Ohmygod,' she sighed. 'Have you read it? It's amazing. I've read it like four times already.'

'I've only read it once but I enjoyed it.'

Bonnie regarded me again, with more warmth this time. 'What mystery?'

'Pardon?'

'You said you're doing a podcast about a different mystery. What mystery?'

'Oh, an MP who went missing.'

Joyce nodded slowly. 'Lawrence Wetherby?'

'That's the one.'

'Nothing to do with the monster?' Bonnie said.

'Nothing.'

'Weird.'

I chuckled. 'I guess most people come here to spot Nessie.'

Bonnie rolled her eyes. 'Everyone comes here to spot Nessie.'

'I can't deny it's nice to have something different to think about,' said Joyce. She handed me my room key. 'Right up on the top floor.'

I swayed slightly on my feet, suddenly feeling the after-effects of my overnight journey. 'Thank you.'

'There's a lift round the corner. Why not have a wee rest and when you're ready come down and we can have a cup of tea and a biscuit, and you can tell me all about it.'

*

My room was the only one on the top floor. It was tiny, tucked into the eaves, with a sloping ceiling and a double bed in the middle. On the opposite wall to the bed was a large fireplace. It was a lovely room. I was a shortie, so it was perfect for me and I chuckled at the idea of Charlie, who was well over six foot tall, and Amazonian goddess Astrid in here. It had an equally small en-suite shower room, where I stripped off the clothes I'd been wearing all night and let the water wash away all the travelling dirt.

Clean and with my wet hair wrapped in a towel, I put on joggers and a T-shirt and lay down on the bed. I'd just close my eyes for a minute, I thought, and then get to work.

*

When I woke up a couple of hours later it was past lunchtime and I was starving. But I felt much better than I had done before I slept. Rested and ready for action. Or ready for a sandwich, at least. Then action.

My hair had dried in a very odd shape under the towel, so I brushed it through and twisted it up into a bun, while I sent Robyn a voice note telling her I'd arrived.

'I've got the best room,' I said. 'Right up in the roof of the hotel.'

As I sent the message I realised I'd not even looked out of the window properly. The curtains on the small gable windows were closed, but now I opened them up, letting the spring sunshine in.

'Oh my,' I said in amazement.

My room looked out over the road in front of the hotel, and beyond that – over some trees – I could see the loch. Its pewter water was shimmering darkly in the weak sunlight and I could see several boats skimming over the surface. It was so big I couldn't see either end of the loch itself, as it stretched out in both directions as far as my eyes could see. But I could see the opposite shore, where there were more trees stretching up on to green-purple hills.

It would be easy to go missing here, I thought.

A shout from below made me look down. The car park at the front of the hostel was filled with people. They were dotted about, reminding me of the days of social distancing, and every one of them was posing for a selfie or recording a video. Two young women in matching outfits were doing a TikTok dance balanced on the wall at the front of the hostel. It was impressive, though slightly bewildering.

'Bloody hell,' I said aloud. 'Literally everyone here is a podcaster or a YouTuber.'

I watched as one man emerged from the hostel entrance, paused to look at the people in the car park and then walked with determination across the road, where he stopped by a tree and began fixing his phone to a selfie stick. He was wearing ripped black jeans, battered DM boots and a *Red Dwarf* T-shirt that was so faded I thought it had to date back to when *Red Dwarf* was an exciting new television show. He had long hair tied back in a ponytail and a beard.

He looked, I thought with a grin, exactly how you'd expect a Nessie hunter to look. He sat down, holding his phone out and began talking.

'Clever,' I murmured. I thought him sitting down would make the woods look thicker and more mysterious as they loomed over him. A nice touch.

At that moment he looked up, as if he knew I was watching, and I shrank back behind the curtain, even though I knew I was too high up and the window was too small for him to see me.

'Come on, Scarlett,' I told myself firmly. 'Stop spying, start working.'

I picked up my laptop bag, checked my handheld recorder was in there, and headed off downstairs to find Joyce. It was time to discover more about Lawrence Wetherby.

Chapter 11

Hannah

1933, Six weeks later

I was happy in Drumnadrochit. Really happy. Perhaps it was the happiest I'd ever been, which was odd when you thought about it, so I tried not to think about it.

The hotel was quiet and refined. It was full of elderly ladies from Edinburgh or Dundee, who came for afternoon tea or to spend a week getting some fresh air. Sometimes some older gents came to play golf or go fishing in the loch.

We had a string quartet that played in the dinner hall. The lounge bar only really served whisky and sherry, and we staff were expected to be immaculately turned out and perfectly polite at all times.

I was surprised by how much I enjoyed it. I enjoyed being useful – having proper jobs to do. And I enjoyed getting my little brown envelope each Friday with my wages in it. Davina huffed and puffed about how much we were paid, and kept saying she was going to ask for more, but I'd never had a job before and I was astonished to be earning.

The biggest surprise, though, was Mrs McEwan.

I'd been intimidated by her when I first met her. She was brusque and efficient, and ran the hotel with an attention to detail that was impressive but also a little scary. Davina and I knew if we left the corner of a bedsheet untucked, or a pillow unplumped, we'd be in trouble.

'She's divorced,' Davina had whispered to me as we cleaned a bedroom one day not long after I arrived. 'This hotel was her husband's but he's gone back to Glasgow to live with his fancy woman.'

Once upon a time, I'd have been shocked that Mrs McEwan was divorced. Aunt Beatrice always said "divorce" in a hushed tone with a raised eyebrow and a knowing nod. But not anymore. Not after everything that had happened. I was far more worldly than I'd been two months ago.

'So her husband gave her the hotel?' I asked.

'She took it.' Davina looked thrilled. 'Apparently, he wanted to sell because it wasn't making much money, but Mrs M was furious with him and she got a solicitor and everything, and in the end he signed over the whole lot to her. It's why she's so determined to make it work.'

'It must be making money now,' I pointed out, pummelling a pillow so it met Mrs McEwan's high standards. 'We're pretty busy.'

'Mrs M always thinks we could be busier.'

But ferocious and focused as Mrs M was, she also – unexpectedly – turned out to be a hoot.

She was very protective of her staff. I liked that she called us all "doll" and how she praised us when we'd done something well.

And best of all were our Sunday night "staff soirées" as Mrs M called them. Once the guests were settled for the evening, we'd all gather in the lounge bar and chat over drinks. It had turned into something of a storytelling session recently, with my fellow maids and waitresses sharing tales that were funny or shocking or sad. Sometimes they were even scary. I liked the spooky stories best of all.

I never said much, because obviously I didn't want to draw attention to myself. But I liked sitting at the side of the room, hearing all the stories from the other staff. Everyone seemed to have led such interesting lives. Often there would be guests in the bar too and they'd join in the chat and tell their own stories. I liked that too. Especially the older people who would share anecdotes from the Great War, or the turn of the century.

Sometimes I'd rush back to my tiny room in the attic and write down everything I'd heard in a notebook I'd bought with my first week's wages. I longed for a typewriter but I knew it would be months before I'd squirrelled away enough money for that. Instead, I lay on my narrow bed, and jotted down the anecdotes I'd heard, as though I were reporting on them for a newspaper or a news bulletin on the wireless. It was good practice, I thought, though my Kodak Brownie sat gathering dust on my bedside cabinet and my dreams of being a journalist were further away than ever before. And let's face it, they'd hardly been within touching distance before.

This Sunday it was my turn to get the bar ready for our soirée. It wasn't a hard job. I just had to make sure the guests who were sitting in the lounge were warned that the staff would be joining them, and I had to get the drinks and glasses ready.

It was quiet in the lounge this evening. Just two ladies – elderly sisters both called Miss James – sitting chatting beside the unlit fire with a glass each of sherry. And behind the bar was Tobias, who served drinks and waited on tables and carried guests' luggage and had even been known to mend a motor car that had broken down. Davina, I thought, rather liked him. She had a tendency to appear wherever he was and her eyes sparkled when he came up in conversation.

'You're on drinks tonight are you?' Tobias said with a grin as I came into the lounge, nodding to the Misses James. 'You know Mrs M's not here?'

'She's not?'

'She's away to Inverness to see some chap from a golf course about offering a deal to his golfers. She'll be back soon.'

'Will we still have the soirée without her?' I asked uncertainly. Even though I'd settled in to the hotel life, I sometimes felt like the new girl, still.

'Certainly we will,' said Tobias. 'We'll have the good stuff.'

He reached under the counter and pulled out a bottle of gin, and what I thought was port, and several bottles of beer.

'Let's get cracking.'

Amused, I helped him set out some glasses as the rest of the staff wandered in.

'Gin for you, Hannah?'

'Please.'

Tobias poured me a large measure and I settled down next to Davina who had rosy cheeks already. Perhaps it was being close to Tobias or perhaps she'd had a sneaky swig of something while she was finishing clearing away dinner.

It was a raucous evening. The drinks flowed, thanks to Tobias keeping everyone topped up. Miss James and Miss James proved to have some excellent anecdotes to share about their time driving ambulances at the front during the war, and I made a mental note to write down everything they'd said before I went to bed. The way my head was spinning, thanks to Tobias's overgenerous drinks, made me worry I would forget everything I'd heard if I wasn't careful.

'Hannah,' said Davina, when there was a lull in conversation. 'We don't know anything about you. Why don't you tell us a story?'

'I don't have anything to tell,' I said, trying to keep my voice light. 'I'm terribly dull.'

'Doesn't have to be about you,' Tobias pointed out. 'What about a friend?'

Perhaps it was the drink that had made me reckless. Or perhaps it was the eager faces all looking up at me. Maybe it was my own arrogance that made me fancy myself as a storyteller. Whatever it was, I nodded.

'This happened to a friend of mine,' I began. 'It was her wedding day and she'd just exchanged vows with her new husband ...'

Rapt, my audience hung on every word as I spun my tale. Because of course it was my story really. I changed the names, of course, and I substituted a beautiful young woman for beautiful young Freddie. I hadn't completely taken leave of my senses.

'And what happened then?' said Marjorie, one of the kitchen hands, as I paused in my storytelling. 'When she walked in and saw him with this woman?'

'Well,' I said. 'She was heartbroken, as you can imagine. She let out a sorrowful wail ...'

At that moment, the quiet in the lounge was broken by something that sounded very close to a sorrowful wail.

All of us jumped in fright. The two Misses James grasped each other's hands, and Marjorie put her hands to her cheeks. 'What's that?' she gasped.

The door to the lounge bar was thrown open, and there stood Mrs McEwan, her hair escaping from its usual immaculate chignon, and her lipstick smudged. Her face was pale and her eyes wide.

'Oh, Mrs M,' said Davina, jumping to her feet and going to the door. 'Whatever's the matter?'

Out of the corner of my eye, I saw Tobias hide the bottle of gin under the counter and pull out some sherry. He poured a small glass and held it out to Davina, who hustled Mrs M into a chair and gave her the drink.

'Here,' Davina said. 'Drink this. What's happened?'

Mrs M took a large slug of her sherry. 'You'll never believe me.'

Intrigued, I edged my chair slightly closer. 'Try us,' I said.

Mrs M pushed a stray strand of hair from her face. 'I was driving home,' she began. 'It's not dark yet, not properly ...'

I looked out of the window. She was right – the sun hadn't

long set. It got darker much later here than in London.

'Did you see something frightening?' Davina said, and I swallowed my exasperation. I wanted Mrs M to tell the story, not Davina.

'I did.' Mrs M looked around at all of us, looking for all the world like she was enjoying the drama of this.

'What did you see?' asked one of the Misses James.

Mrs M took a deep breath. 'I was driving alongside the loch. Same as I always do. And I glanced over at the water, same as I always do.'

'You do,' Davina said. 'You love the water.'

Again I wanted to shush Davina, but I bit my tongue.

'I love the way it looks when the sun's setting,' said Mrs McEwan. 'The way the water is so flat and still as evening comes.'

Very poetic, I thought.

'But not tonight,' Mrs M went on. She drained her sherry glass and held it out for Tobias to refill. 'Tonight, the water wasn't flat. Tonight, the waves were turning and churning.'

Was it windy? I glanced out of the window again, where the trees were standing still. There wasn't so much as a breeze.

'I stopped the car,' Mrs McEwan said. 'Because I couldn't believe my eyes, and I didn't want to drive off the road. I got out and went over to the banks of the loch so I could see properly.'

'What was making the waves, Mrs M?' Davina breathed. 'What was it?'

Mrs M sat up a little straighter. 'A gigantic beast!' she declared. 'And the water around it bubbling like a witch's cauldron.'

'A beast?' Marjorie said. 'Like King Kong?'

'No, not a monkey. This was more like a whale with a huge, humped back,' Mrs McEwan said.

'How big was it?' I asked. 'Could it have been a fish?'

Mrs M snorted. 'No. This was no fish. This was a monster.'

There was a stunned silence. And then from the corner where the Misses James were sitting, came a small, stifled snigger.

'A … monster?' Marjorie said, her lips twitching. 'Like a dragon?'

'It wasn't a dragon.' Mrs M sounded injured.

'Of course it wasn't a dragon,' said Davina mock-sternly. 'This is Scotland, not Wales. We have our own monsters.' She began to giggle. 'Mrs M, did you have some sherries at the golf club?'

Everyone laughed, except Mrs McEwan. But even she was looking less sure now.

'I had one or two drinks,' she said. 'But I had my wits about me. I'd driven all the way home for heaven's sake. I got such a fright, I abandoned the car. It's still out there on the road.'

Tobias sighed. 'I'll go and get it.' He stood up. 'You know the story, right? About the beast that lives deep below the water?'

I felt a little shiver of excitement. 'There's a beast?'

'Oh aye, every child in Drumnadrochit knows the story.'

'Tell it,' Davina said, her eyes fixed on Tobias. 'Tell the story.'

Tobias pulled up a chair and sat down again.

'Way back, when the Picts still lived in Scotland, a monk called Columba came across a group of men burying a body at the side of the loch. When Columba asked how their friend had died, they said he'd been attacked by a gigantic beast.'

Marjorie gave an overexaggerated sigh. 'Oh it's this story. I know this story.' She sounded disappointed.

'I told you everyone knows it,' said Tobias, standing up. 'I'll go and get the car.'

'I don't know the story,' I said quickly. 'What happened? Did the beast attack Columba?'

Marjorie rolled her eyes. 'The beast came out of the water, and Columba made the sign of the cross and it ran away.'

'Swam away,' said Davina. 'It couldn't run. It was in the water.'

'Ran, swam, who cares?' said Marjorie. 'I'm off to my bed. I'm on breakfast in the morning.'

'Maybe you imagined it?' I suggested gently to Mrs M. 'Maybe it was a boat, or a piece of wood in the water, and it reminded you of the story of Columba?'

She shrugged. 'Maybe,' she said. She took out her powder compact and flipped it open so she could see in the mirror. Then she smoothed her hair down, wiped her smudged lipstick, and I watched in awe as she visibly gathered herself.

'Right then,' she said, standing up. 'While Tobias is fetching my car, who's for another drink?'

Chapter 12

'Do you believe what Mrs McEwan said?' I asked Davina the next morning. 'She looked genuinely scared.'

Davina shrugged. 'Corner,' she said, coming towards me with the ends of the sheet we were folding. 'I've only known her a wee bit longer than you have, but Mrs M doesn't seem the type to get rattled for no reason.'

We walked away from each other, backwards, to stretch the sheet out again. We were outside the hotel, taking in the laundry. It was a brisk, breezy, spring day and Avril, who did the hotel's washing, was on a mission to get everything clean and dry as soon as possible.

'It'll rain again tomorrow so let's crack on,' she'd said, hurrying Davina and me outside. 'Go on.'

Now I looked round the corner of the building to where I could just catch a glimpse of the loch through the trees.

'A beast, though,' I said as we folded the sheet once more and I took it, smoothing it flat into the laundry hamper. 'It can't be true. I don't believe it.'

'It doesn't matter whether you believe in it,' Davina said, screwing her nose up. 'If there's a beast in the loch, it'll be there whether or not you believe in it.' She grinned at me. 'And just because you don't believe in something, doesn't mean it's not true.'

'If there's a beast in the loch I'll be very surprised.'

'Aye, well, I've been surprised by things that have happened in my life, more times than I can count.' Davina looked at me out of the side of her eyes. 'Like your story last night, for example.'

My stomach twisted. I'd woken up with a pounding headache thanks to the gin, and with a horrible feeling of dread that I'd given myself away.

'What story?' I said casually, turning away from Davina so she couldn't see my face, and putting the pegs into the bag that hung from the line.

'About your friend …' Davina said, putting a lot of emphasis on the word "friend". 'The one who walked in on her new husband doing the dirty on her.'

'What about her?' I studied the peg bag carefully.

'It's you, isn't it?'

'What's me?'

Davina gave an overdramatic sigh. She ducked under the washing line and came to stand in front of me, her face close to mine. 'You walked out on your husband on your wedding day?'

Knowing she wouldn't stop asking until I'd told her the truth, I nodded. 'That was me.'

'Why didn't you tell me?' Davina looked positively thrilled at the scandal. 'No wonder you ran away if you caught him with another woman.'

Thinking that she didn't know the half of it, I gave a little smile, hoping that was the end of it. But no. Davina's cogs were whirring.

'Why did you have to run, though?' she said, almost to herself. 'Surely no one would have blamed you for leaving? And why did you run so far?' She ran her eyes over me, like she was seeing me for the first time. 'And why change your hair?'

I grimaced. But Davina was sharp-eyed and quick-minded and she saw my reaction.

'What?' she said. 'What else aren't you telling me?'

'Leave me alone, Davina,' I snapped.

Davina, though, looked giddy with the excitement of it all. 'I will not leave you alone. Not when you've got a story to tell.'

In despair I threw my head back and looked at the little clouds scudding across the sky.

'Ohhh,' Davina said. 'Did you take terrible revenge? Criminal revenge?' She put her hands to her mouth in gleeful shock. 'Did you kill him?'

Horrified, I stared at her, not sure what to say.

'You did.' Davina stared back at me, her eyes wide. 'You bloody killed him.'

'It … he … I didn't mean to.'

Davina pushed the lid on the laundry hamper down so it shut with a snap and sat down on top.

'Tell me everything.'

'Davina, no …'

She leaned forward with her elbows on her scrawny knees. 'Tell me,' she said. 'Or I'll tell everyone else what you did.'

I tried to laugh, but Davina wasn't smiling anymore.

'You wouldn't,' I said uncertainly.

'Wouldn't I?'

With a heavy heart, I sat down on the hamper next to her.

'It really was an accident,' I said. 'He fell and hit his head. And I don't know if he was dead. I thought he moved. But I wasn't sure …'

'So why did you run?'

'Because I was scared.' I paused. 'But now it makes me look guilty.'

'Was he rich, your husband?'

I shrugged. 'Quite rich before we got married. He'd have been richer soon. He would have inherited his father's estate on his

35th birthday in October.'

'His father's estate,' Davina said in an affected posh voice. 'Oooh. Was he a bigwig?'

'He was an MP.'

'An MP? Fancy. What was his name?'

'Lawrence.'

'Lawrence what?'

'Lawrence Wetherby.'

In the same silly cut-glass accent, Davina said: 'Air hillair, I'm Lawrence Wetherby. I'm an MP, don't you know.'

'Why are you talking about Lawrence Wetherby?'

Davina and I both shrieked in surprise as Tobias pushed aside one of the sheets still flapping on the washing line like a curtain.

'I've come to collect the linen for Avril,' he said with an amused frown. 'She said you'd be done.'

'We got chatting,' Davina said jumping off the hamper.

'I heard.'

I went cold. What exactly had he heard?

'I didn't have you girls down as political types.'

'Well, no, we're erm, we're not really …' I stammered getting off the hamper.

'But you were talking about Lawrence Wetherby?'

'Have you heard of him?' Davina said, her bright eyes fixed on Tobias.

'I was just reading the newspaper five minutes ago and there was a story about him.'

I felt the ground beneath my feet sway, and I put my hand on the hamper to steady myself. I'd not so much as glanced at a paper since the one I'd seen in Inverness the day I'd decided not to turn myself in. I left the room if a bulletin came on the wireless. I'd even avoided going to the pictures, because I didn't want to see any newsreels. It hadn't been easy for me, given I was a committed devourer of current affairs. Sometimes I found myself wondering what was happening in Germany, or whether

Roosevelt's New Deal ideas were being well received. But the fear of seeing news confirming Lawrie's death had stopped me every time I was tempted to pick up one of papers. And now here was Tobias, confirming my worst fears.

I swallowed. 'What sort of story?'

'He's been talking about Roosevelt's plan for recovery.'

'I'm sorry, what?' I said weakly. 'He's what?'

'He's been talking about Roosevelt. You know? The new American president? Are you all right, Hannah?'

Davina gave me a disdainful glance. 'He's not dead then? Or in hospital?'

'Roosevelt?'

'No, Wetherby.'

'Lawrence Wetherby?' Tobias shook his head. 'No. Why?'

'You're sure?' I said. I felt sick suddenly. 'You're absolutely sure he's alive?'

'I just read his response to Roosevelt's speech,' Tobias said slowly.

'It wasn't an old article?' Davina said.

'No, definitely not. Roosevelt only just made that speech the other day.' He looked from Davina to me. 'Why do you think he's dead?'

I opened my mouth and no sound came out.

'No reason.' Davina gave me a nudge with her elbow. 'Must have got him mixed up with someone else.'

Tobias looked a little confused and I couldn't blame him. But he waited for us to take down the final sheet and then he lifted the hamper on to his broad shoulders – Davina looked on approvingly – and he hurried off to take the linen to Avril.

'We should get going on the bedrooms,' I said, when he'd gone. I turned to walk away, still struggling to take in what he'd said. Lawrence really was alive, just as I'd hoped? I was relieved. And confused. But I had too many chores to do to think about what it meant.

Davina grabbed my hand. 'Wait,' she said. 'He's not dead. Your husband is alive?'

The image of Lawrence lying slumped on the floor flashed before me once again, Freddie bent over him, feeling for a pulse and then wailing in dramatic fashion. This was what he had wanted. Freddie had wanted to get rid of me. He'd seen a chance and he'd taken it. He must have known all along that Lawrie wasn't dead. Had he even whispered to Lawrie to lie still, as he bent over him? Told him to play dead just to fool me? I felt very stupid all of a sudden.

I rubbed my forehead. 'I don't understand.'

Davina tugged my arm gently. 'Let's go and see the newspaper. See for yourself that he's alive.'

'I don't want to,' I said. But she tugged my hand.

'Come on. Let's get the newspaper and see if Tobias is right.'

Numbly, I let her lead me through the garden of the hotel, in through the side door and to the lounge where the day's papers were stacked at the end of the bar. One of them was folded less neatly than the others, and Davina picked it up.

'Must have been this one he was reading.' She unfolded it and shook it out, peering at the page. I held my breath as she scanned the articles. But then she shrugged.

'I'm not clever with words,' she said, looking a little defensive. 'I can read but it takes me a while. You do it.'

With trembling hands, I took the newspaper from her.

'We should give President Roosevelt our full support, Treasury minister Lawrence Wetherby has told parliament …' I read aloud. 'Mr Wetherby was responding to a speech made by the US president on Tuesday (April 18).'

My legs went weak beneath me and I slumped down on to one of the red chairs in the lounge.

'He's alive,' I whispered. 'Lawrence is alive.'

'This is good news,' Davina said, sitting down opposite me. 'You're not a murderer.'

My head was a whirling mess of questions and emotions, happiness, relief and anger. 'Freddie,' I hissed. 'Blasted Freddie.'

'Who's Freddie?' Davina frowned.

'No one.' I shook my head. 'How is this possible?'

With a slightly disgruntled expression, Davina pushed her hair out of her eyes. 'Will you go back then? Back to London.'

'I'd not thought …'

'Because you don't need to be here, now, do you?' She sounded cross. 'You don't need to be working here, changing bedding and serving breakfasts, and telling stories at the staff soirées every week. You can go back to London and your fancy life.'

I stared at her, knowing she was right. In theory, I could go back. I could leave the hotel right now, head to Inverness and get on a train back to London. I could apologise to Lawrence, hope he'd forgive me, then move to Sussex and live out my life as an MP's wife.

But I didn't want to. And besides, it was a bit more complicated than that, wasn't it? How could I go back to Lawrence knowing what I knew about him? He wasn't who I thought he was when I agreed to marry him. I thought of him and Freddie gazing at each other as they lay on the bed and how far Freddie had gone to keep Lawrie for himself. And for the first time, I wondered if, perhaps, this wasn't so much shocking or disgusting as very sad.

'Are you going?' Davina interrupted my thoughts.

'I don't think so.'

She scratched her head, a tiny smile on her lips. 'You're staying?'

'I like it here.'

'But you'd be a rich posh lady back in London.'

'I'd be miserable.'

'You'd rather be here than there? Really?'

'I would.'

Davina shook her head. 'When I was wee, we had nothing. No money. Sometimes no food. My ma …' She took a breath. 'She tried her best, but every time she thought things were going to be all right, something happened, you know? She'd lose her job, or we'd get thrown out of the place we'd been living, or she'd get pregnant, or one of us would get sick. Things were always changing. There was no …' She looked up at the ceiling, grasping for the word.

'Security?' I said. 'There was no security.'

'Yes.' She nodded. 'And I promised myself I'd never live like that. So I got out as soon as I could. Chose a job where I'd have a roof over my head from the off. Now I've got savings. And I work hard. I take on extra jobs. I'll do anything to make sure I'm all right, you know? I left my job in Inverness to come here because Mrs M pays better, even though I didn't know anyone and I'd never been to Loch Ness.'

'I understand,' I said.

'Do you?' Davina looked fierce. 'Do you really?'

'I do.' I took a breath. 'You can't rely on anyone except yourself.'

'So why won't you go back?'

'Because there I'd be relying on Lawrence. And …' I took a breath. 'I don't want to.'

'Because he cheated.'

'Yes,' I said. 'And here I can do whatever I want. In London, I'd have people telling me what to do the whole time. Stopping me doing what I want.'

'What if he wants you to go back?' Davina said. 'What if he makes you?'

'I'm not sure he would. And anyway …' I trailed off, thinking of the photographs I'd taken. Perhaps they would offer me some protection – I could tell Lawrie that I'd destroy them if he let me live my life alone. But then again, could they make me vulnerable? He knew I had them and they could put him behind bars if anyone saw them. Lawrence was a good man, but I wasn't sure how far he'd go to save his own skin.

'Anyway?' Davina prompted.

'I took something from him when I left. From Lawrence.'

'You stole something?' Davina's eyes gleamed.

'Not exactly.'

'What did you take? Is it something valuable? Will he want it back?'

I held up my hands to ward off her questions, but she was still going. 'You could send him a telegram. Say you'll give it back if he gives you some money – if he sees you right.'

'No,' I said firmly. 'No.'

'What is it? Is it treasure? Is it in that box you had with you when you arrived? That square box? I saw how carefully you looked after it, cradling it like it was a baby.'

I started in surprise. She was astute, Davina – there was no doubt about that.

'It's a camera,' I said. 'Lawrence bought me it as a wedding gift.'

She made a face. 'That's it?'

I didn't want to lie to her, but I wasn't about to tell her the truth either, so I shrugged. 'Sort of.'

'Well, you make sure you look after whatever it is,' she said. 'Because if people realise it's valuable, who knows what could happen.'

She smiled at me as she spoke, but I couldn't help thinking her words sounded like a threat.

Chapter 13

Scarlett

Present day

I found Joyce and Bonnie in the hostel's lounge. It was a nice room with large windows and framed photographs of the Loch Ness monster on its walls. There were a couple of overstuffed comfy sofas, where a few guests were chatting or reading or scrolling through their phones. Bonnie was curled up at one end of the biggest sofa, still engrossed in her book.

I thought it would be a good place to record some background. Seeing all the other podcasters here in the hostel had been unexpected but they would add lots of colour to my own programme and they might even have some knowledge to share.

In the corner there was a small counter where Joyce was filling the fridge with soft drinks. There was a display of home-made sandwiches and cakes that made my mouth water, and some crisps and other snacks for sale. I sat down on one of the bar stools, putting the trusty notebook I carried everywhere with me on the counter, and she smiled at me.

'Cup of tea?'

'Yes please,' I said. 'And a sandwich please.' I leaned over to see what was on offer. 'Chicken salad.'

Joyce put the plate in front of me and set about making tea, waving off my attempts to pay. 'Welcome gift,' she said. 'It's nice to have something to talk about that isn't Nessie.'

'Are you fed up with monsters?'

She shrugged. 'Not at all. After all, I make a good living from this hostel and the guests are always a hoot. But it's good to have a break sometimes.'

I chuckled. 'I understand that.'

'So tell me what you're up to.'

'I have a podcast,' I began. Behind her book, Bonnie snorted. I ignored her. 'I'm a broadcast assistant at Britain Live and I have a podcast on the side. *Cold Cases with Burns*?'

Joyce nodded, the vague smile on her face telling me she'd never heard of us.

'Anyway, we – that's Charlie, my erm, ex-boyfriend, and me, we investigate unsolved mysteries.'

'Like Nessie?'

'Not really.' I made a face. 'Smaller things like unsolved thefts, or unexplained deaths. Not supernatural. Charlie's in the police.'

'And now you're trying to find the missing MP?' Joyce looked round. 'So where's Charlie?'

'Dur, Gran,' said Bonnie, not lowering her book. 'She said he was her EX-boyfriend.'

I winced. 'Yes, he is. Though we still do the podcast together. But this is different. This is for my day job at Britain Live.'

'Even though it's a cold case?' Joyce frowned.

'Well, yes.'

Joyce looked as though she was going to ask more questions, so I jumped in.

'Lawrence Wetherby went missing here and I would like to find out more about him definitely. But it's really his wife, Hannah, who I'm interested in.'

'What about her?'

'She went missing too, apparently.'

Joyce made a face. 'I've never heard about his wife going missing. Did they go off somewhere together?'

'There is some suggestion she might have been involved in his disappearance.'

'It's always the spouse, isn't it?' said Joyce with glee. 'Remind me when this happened? I've run this place since the 1980s, so it must have been before that.'

'Early May 1933,' I said.

Joyce looked at me in surprise. 'No,' she said. 'When did the MP and his wife go missing?'

'In 1933,' I repeated.

'But that's around the time when the monster was spotted.'

'So? Isn't it being spotted all the time?'

'Yes and no,' Joyce said.

'Riiiight. So do you believe in Nessie?'

'Yes and no,' she said again and I laughed.

'What does that mean?'

'When anyone asked my mother if she believed, she always said …'

'Just because you don't believe in something, doesn't mean it's not real,' Bonnie finished.

I chuckled again. 'I suppose she's right,' I said. 'So, what happened here in 1933?'

'Joyce? Sorry to interrupt.'

We all looked round as the bearded man I'd seen earlier in the faded *Red Dwarf* T-shirt came into the bar.

'There's a delivery for you in reception,' he said to Joyce. 'They need you to sign something.'

'Heavens.' Joyce looked at her watch. 'They're early. I'd better go and sort it out. Why don't you two have a chat in the meantime? This young lady is interested in 1933.'

She bustled off and the man sat down next to me.

'Good sandwich?'

'Amazing,' I said honestly. 'I'd not realised how hungry I was.'

He stuck his hand out for me to shake. 'I'm Lucas, as in George.'

I frowned, not following. 'Hi … Lucas?' He nodded. 'I'm Scarlett. As in O'Hara.'

He chuckled. He had a nice laugh, low and rich, which seemed at odds with his appearance. I wasn't completely sure how I'd amused him but I smiled at him anyway.

'So you want to know about 1933?'

'I do.' I put the last bit of sandwich into my mouth and opened my notebook to a blank page.

'Are you doing a podcast?'

I made a face. 'Sort of. I work for Britain Live,' I went on. 'I'm doing a programme, but it'll go out as a podcast, too. I do podcasts on the side as well.' I paused, not knowing whether he'd be like Joyce and politely make it clear he'd never heard of us. '*Cold Cases with Burns*?'

Lucas looked impressed. 'That's you? Unexplained mysteries, right?'

'Right.'

'So what's the mystery?'

I leaned towards him and lowered my voice. 'Apparently, some people have seen something in the water. I've heard it's some kind of monster …'

He laughed again, loudly and heartily. 'Not the monster, then?'

'Not the monster. There was an MP who went missing up here in May 1933.'

'In May 1933?' He raised an eyebrow. 'That's interesting.'

'That's what Joyce said. Why? What can you tell me?'

Lucas rested his forearms on the countertop and I couldn't help noticing he had rather bulging biceps. If Charlie was here, he'd be all intimidated and start asking him what he bench-pressed.

'May 1933,' Lucas said, shifting slightly, which made me realise

I was still staring at his arms.

'That's right.' I picked up my pen. 'Fire away.'

'So, 1933 is when the story of the Loch Ness monster really took off. Before then, the story was just that – a tall tale local people told each other. It goes back to before the Romans when a monk supposedly encountered a beast in the water. Though I think that was actually the River Ness, rather than the loch. But it wasn't a big thing back then, just a local legend.'

'Stop!' I said, pulling out my recorder. 'Can I record this? Do you mind?'

'Not at all,' Lucas said. He had a nice voice. Deep and rhythmic like his laugh, with a Scottish accent, which was always good for Britain Live listeners who often complained we were too London-focused.

I pressed record.

Lucas grinned at me. 'Back in 1933, this hostel was a rather posh hotel. Refined, you know? Genteel. The story goes that one evening in April, the owner of the hotel, a lady called Mrs McEwan, was driving home when she saw a huge beast in the water.'

'Would she have known the story?'

'Undoubtedly.'

'So she could have seen something else, a big fish or a boat maybe, and just put two and two together and made five?'

'That would be possible, if it wasn't for one thing,' Lucas said. I could tell he was used to telling stories himself. He had a definite flair for the dramatic. 'Just a few days later, two guests at the hotel saw an enormous creature on the shore of the loch.'

'But did they know what Mrs McEwan had seen?'

Lucas looked triumphant. 'They did not.'

'Really?' I was doubtful.

'Well, it's possible they'd heard the staff talking about it, but at the time no one admitted to telling them.'

'What happened then?'

'Things went crazy,' said Lucas. 'Bonkers. The nation's press descended on this wee hotel and the legend of the Loch Ness monster was born. By May 1933 – when your man disappeared – there were photographers and journalists everywhere. Amateur monster hunters. The whole shebang.'

'Good news for Mrs McEwan,' I said drily.

'Indeed.'

'And this all started when in 1933?'

'It kicked off in the April of that year, but it carried on for months.'

I wrote down April 1933. 'Is that what you do?' I asked. 'Do you look into mysteries like the Loch Ness monster?'

'Ish,' said Lucas. 'I've got a YouTube channel called *The Other One*. It's not the stories themselves I'm focused on, but the interest. I like knowing why some stories grab the public's attention, and others don't.'

'Like *The Matrix*,' said Bonnie. I'd almost forgotten she was there, but she'd clearly been listening the whole time. She put her book down on the sofa next to her. 'There are loads of stories about "what if the world we know is really a dream or a TV show or a video game or whatever?" We learned about it at school. It's called the Simulation Hypothesis. But *The Matrix* is the one we all use as a shorthand for that stuff. Like saying something's a glitch in the Matrix, you know? Or taking the red pill.'

Lucas and I both stared at her. I wasn't sure I'd been so sharp when I was a teenager.

'Exactly that,' said Lucas, sounding a little put out. 'Why *The Matrix* and not *The Truman Show*? Why the Loch Ness monster, but not the one that's been spotted in Loch Lochy?'

'There's another monster?'

'Apparently.'

'In Loch Lochy?'

'Loch Lochy.'

'And that's a real place, is it?'

He grinned. 'It is.'

'Huh,' I said. 'Who knew?'

'I rest my case.'

'That's really interesting. I suppose it's a bit like my missing MP. It was big news at the time, but he's no Lord Lucan.'

'Tell me about his story,' said Lucas.

I rubbed my nose. 'I am woefully under-researched,' I admitted. 'I'm never usually this unprepared. But from the little I know, this MP also went missing in May 1933.'

'Here at the hotel?'

I shrugged. 'Here or hereabouts.'

Lucas's eyes gleamed beneath his bushy eyebrows.

'And you want to find him?'

'No.'

With a slump of his shoulders, Lucas gave me a sad stare. 'Really?'

'I want to find his wife. She went missing too. Or at least, I think she did.'

Lucas sat up again. 'Excellent.'

'I think it's a good story,' I said. 'But like I say, I've not properly looked into it. I came up here in a bit of a hurry.'

'Which also sounds like a good story.'

I looked away from his curious stare, because I found I really didn't want to talk about Charlie right now. 'For another time.'

'Fair enough,' he said with a good-natured nod. He slid off the stool. 'I'm here for a week, so give me a shout if you need anything.'

I bristled a little bit. I didn't need help. And I certainly didn't need Lucas doing his own investigation into "the other Lord Lucan". I was already kicking myself for putting that idea into his head.

'Thanks,' I said, abruptly. 'But I'm fine.'

He paused for a second but I turned my attention to my notebook and when I looked up again, he was gone. I hoped he wasn't offended. I hadn't meant to be rude, but this was my project. I didn't want anyone else's help, and nice as Lucas seemed to be, I didn't know him from Adam. Perhaps he wasn't the type to nick someone else's research, but I didn't know that and I wasn't about to risk it. I was doing this alone. No Lucas. No Charlie.

Thinking of Charlie made me wonder whether he was on his way up to Scotland. I opened Find Friends on my phone. I could still see Charlie's location because he was rubbish with even basic techy stuff and he'd not turned it off since we split. I waited for the little icon to pop up and sighed in relief to see him still in London. I had time then.

'Is that your ex?' Bonnie plonked herself on the stool where Lucas had been sitting. 'Are you stalking him?'

'No,' I said defensively. Then I grinned. 'A little bit. But not because I want to get back together.'

'You don't want to get back with him?'

'No,' I said. 'Definitely not. I did, for a while, but not now.'

She looked dubious. 'Really?'

'He's got another girlfriend.'

'Is it like a dagger in your heart?' she said, clutching her chest dramatically. 'Are you devastated.'

'Noooo,' I said. 'Though I was gutted at first.'

Bonnie slumped over the counter. 'But is he your soulmate?'

'He's an idiot,' I said. 'And I don't believe in soulmates.'

She fixed me with a steely glare. 'Just because you don't believe in something, doesn't mean it doesn't exist.'

I laughed. 'He's not my soulmate,' I said.

'So why are you stalking him?'

'For work. Sort of.'

Bonnie twirled one of her curls round her finger. 'I googled you,' she said.

'Now who's the stalker?'

'Are you trying to beat him to this story about the missing MP?'

Crikey, she really was sharp. 'Sort of.' I sighed. 'Someone asked

124

us to find out what happened, but I didn't like their …'

'Attitude? That's what my mum always says to me: that she doesn't like my attitude.'

I laughed. 'Yes, I didn't like their attitude. But Charlie did and he decided to go on without me.'

'What an arsehole.'

I laughed again. I liked Bonnie. 'Totally. So I want to find everything out before he gets a chance.'

Bonnie looked thrilled. 'It's a competition, like *The Hunger Games*.'

'I really hope not.'

'Can I help with your research?'

'No,' I said.

'You don't like people offering to help, do you?' she said, her sharp eyes studying my face and making me feel self-conscious. 'You don't have to beat me to the story, you know. I'm just bored and when I'm bored my gran gives me chores to do.'

I felt a bit ashamed of myself. She was only a kid, for all her smarts.

'Is there anything else you should be doing? Schoolwork or anything?'

'No.'

'Then yes please,' I said. 'I could really use some help.'

Bonnie jumped down from the stool. 'I'm ready. Just tell me what to do.'

Chapter 14

Hannah

1933

Davina asking about my camera made me think about the photographs I'd taken. I had no way of developing them, of course, but I wanted to make sure the film was safe. When I had a break, I went up to my little room in the eaves of the hotel, locked the door and shut the curtains.

Then I took out my camera, and in the dim light, I wound the film on to the spool, took it out of the camera and popped it into the cardboard box it had come in. With it safely stowed away, I opened my curtains again and looked around the room for somewhere to hide it. I liked Davina, but I wasn't sure I entirely trusted her.

My room had a fireplace, which was empty because it was actually warm and cosy up there in the roof and, with spring on its way, I'd not had cause to light a fire. I remembered Aunt Beatrice's house had an enormous fireplace that I could stand up in. It had a sort of shelf on the inside and Aunt Beatrice had once told me it was to give the boys who'd cleaned the chimneys back in Victorian times a foothold to start shimmying their way up. The thought had made me shudder, but now I wondered if there was a similar protruding brick inside my fireplace here.

Holding my precious box, I went over to the grate, kneeled down and peered upwards. I could see daylight not far above me and, sure enough, there was a brick sticking out just up from where I crouched. I stretched up my arm, but I couldn't reach it.

Luckily the hearth was clean, so I shuffled over a bit, still on my knees, so I could stretch further. But no, I still couldn't reach it. Thinking of the poor young lads who'd been forced into chimneys a hundred years earlier, I took a deep breath and with a wiggle of my shoulders, managed to squeeze myself right inside the fireplace. It took a bit of manoeuvring to raise my arm but this time when I reached up, I could touch the brick. I pushed the cardboard box on top of it and then backed out again, rolling my eyes as I realised I was covered in soot. I'd have to have a wash and change my dress before I went back downstairs. I just hoped Mrs McEwan wouldn't notice how long I'd been away.

*

When I'd finally brushed the soot from my hair and washed it from my face and arms, I slipped down the back stairs and into the kitchen, pretending I'd come in from outside so I could say I'd been speaking to a guest in the garden if anyone asked.

But the kitchen was deserted.

Thanking my lucky stars, I wandered out towards the dining room, ready to help set tables, but that was empty too. Where was everyone?

I heard a burst of laughter from the lounge that answered my question. What was going on? Intrigued, I slid in the door and found just about all the hotel staff, and some of the guests, too, sitting watching Mrs McEwan talking to an earnest-looking young man. He had slicked-back hair and little round glasses and he was scribbling furiously in a notebook as Mrs McEwan talked. On the table next to him was a camera – much fancier than my Box Brownie – and I felt a thrill of excitement tinged with nerves. Was this man a journalist?

'What's going on?' I whispered to Tobias, who was cleaning glasses at the bar with a pained expression on his face.

'Mrs M told the papers about the beast she saw,' he said, holding up a sherry glass to check it was clean. Our residents were very particular about their sherry glasses. 'This one's from the *Inverness Herald* or something. He's writing a story.'

'How exciting,' I said.

Tobias shrugged. 'If you like that sort of thing.'

'I do.'

He gave me a disdainful glance and turned his attention back to the glasses. I left him to it, weaving through the gathered staff until I was closer to the front and could hear what Mrs McEwan was saying.

'It was huge,' she said, gesturing with her arms.

The journalist leaned forward, a glint of mischief in his eyes. 'What would you say to people who don't believe you?'

He was younger than I'd first thought, I realised. A little older than me, perhaps. Mid-twenties? I liked the flash of fun in his otherwise serious face. And so, it seemed, did Mrs M. She leaned forward too.

'If someone didn't believe me, I'd tell them to come and see it for themselves.'

I smiled to myself. Mrs McEwan was a clever one, there was no mistake. I wasn't sure how much an advert in the Inverness paper would cost, but this story would be free. And it was bound to attract more guests.

The interview over, the journalist started packing up his bag, and saying his goodbyes to Mrs McEwan. I was disappointed I'd missed it and wondered if I dared go and speak to him, perhaps ask if there were any women who worked on the newspaper with him.

'You should speak to him.' Davina appeared beside me, echoing my thoughts so precisely that I jumped.

'What? Why?'

'About Lawrence.'

I looked at the journalist. 'What if he realises who I am?'

'He won't see you,' Davina said, a sharp tone to her voice. 'He'll see your cap and your apron, that's all.'

I touched my head, where the little cap all the maids wore rested on my newly short hair. 'Do you think so?'

Davina gave me a nudge in the small of my back in response and without stopping to think any more, I took the few steps to where the journalist was doing up the strap on his bag.

'Hello,' I said.

He looked up and smiled, showing a dimple in his left cheek. 'Hello.'

'You're a journalist?'

'Yes.' He stood up a bit straighter, then deflated again. 'Well, I'm just starting out really. I'm hoping to get a job on a paper in Edinburgh soon. Inverness is great but I'm a bit fed up now. I just need a big story – one to really cement my reputation.'

'You think this could be it?'

'Maybe. I hope so.' He pinched his lips together, as though he hadn't meant to say so much, while I sighed at the thought of being fed up with a job on any newspaper. He didn't realise how lucky he was.

I glanced at Davina, who gave me an encouraging nod.

'I want to be a journalist,' I said. He looked at me again, his eyes narrowed behind his glasses and I thought that Davina was wrong. He saw me.

'Do you?'

'More than anything.'

He gave me a small smile. 'Do you write?'

'Sometimes.'

'What sort of things?'

'I keep a diary.'

'Of course. What else.'

'We tell each other stories,' I said.

'We?'

'The staff here.' I felt a bit silly, but I carried on. 'And sometimes I write them up afterwards. I'm saving up for a typewriter.'

'Good for you,' he said. He looked like he was wanting to leave so I added quickly, 'And sometimes I write stories based on what I've read in the newspapers.'

'Do you?' He smiled. 'Maybe you should write about Mrs McEwan's beast?'

'I should,' I said. 'I will.'

'I'd like to read it, when it's done.'

I glanced at him, wondering if he was mocking me, but he looked back, his expression nothing but interested and suddenly I found I wanted to write something for him to read.

'Do you take photographs as well?' I asked him, wanting to keep talking.

'I do.'

'I have a camera but it's very new. I'm still learning.' I wasn't sure why I was telling him all this, but I felt that speaking to this man was a chance for me to one day follow my ambition to be a journalist.

'Photography is a lot of fun. You should come to the newspaper office and see the darkroom.'

'I'd love that,' I said, dreamily. 'I'd love to learn how to develop photographs.'

'What's your name?' he said.

'Hannah,' I said, wondering if I'd regret telling him my name. 'Hannah Snow.'

'I shall look out for your by-line, Miss Snow. But now I must go. Sorry.'

'I wrote something about an MP,' I said quickly. 'Lawrence Wetherby? Apparently he'd like to be prime minister one day.'

The journalist raised an eyebrow. 'Is that right?'

I kicked myself mentally, because though Lawrie had often told me about his ambition, I wasn't sure he'd ever shared it publicly.

'I wondered if you knew what he's doing?' I said casually, leaning on the table. 'I read what he thinks of Roosevelt's New Deal.'

'I read that too,' the journalist said. 'You probably know as much as I do.'

'No new story then?'

'No new story.' He looked at me oddly. 'I don't do many political stories, though. That's my colleague's territory.'

'The article I read mentioned that his wife went off somewhere. That's a good story.' I was pushing my luck, I knew. The last thing I wanted was for him to recognise me and for me to become the story.

But the journalist frowned. 'Now that I do know about. We were talking about it at work the other day. It was all a misunderstanding apparently.'

I stared at him, surprised. 'What?'

'A few days after there was that first report that she was missing, he said it was all fine.'

'Fine?' I repeated, bewildered. 'How was it fine?'

'Apparently, he fell and bumped his head, and he said that was what caused him to be confused.'

'But he wasn't badly hurt?' I said. 'When he fell?'

The journalist gave me a sharp glance. 'I don't think so. He's been in the Commons so it can't have been a bad bump. Just enough to make him a little confused.'

I nodded. 'I guess.'

'But it's strange though,' he added.

'Very strange.'

He gave me that same curious look again, then he picked up

his bag and put it on his shoulder.

'Nice to meet you, Miss Snow.'

'And you …'

'Angus,' he said. 'Angus Reid.'

His eyes met mine and I felt a little pull of attraction towards him that made my cheeks flush.

'Keep writing,' he said. 'I'll see you.'

He walked out of the lounge, and I stared after him.

'What did he say?' Davina dashed to my side and clutched my arm. 'You're white as a sheet. What did he tell you?'

Wide-eyed, I looked at her. 'Lawrence told the newspapers that it was all a misunderstanding and that I am not missing.'

'But you are missing. Aren't you?'

I shook my head, still trying to work it all out. 'I don't understand.'

'What about the thing you took? Maybe he decided you can keep it?'

I gave her a small smile. 'Maybe.'

'Or maybe he doesn't know you took it?' Davina sounded suspicious. 'Does he?'

'It doesn't matter now.' A rush of relief flooded me and with a sudden burst of excitement I grinned at Davina. 'It's all fine. Lawrence isn't looking for me. No one knows I'm here. I'm safe.'

'Why would he lie and say it was a misunderstanding?'

I had an idea that Lawrence didn't want the newspapers digging about in his personal life, and that was why he'd put them off the scent, but I tried to look like I didn't have a clue.

'No idea.' I frowned as a thought struck me. 'I wonder, though, what he told Aunt Beatrice.'

'Would she be worried about you?'

Slowly I shook my head. 'I doubt it. She'd believe whatever Lawrie told her. If he said I was in Sussex, she wouldn't question it. She's glad I'm off her hands.'

'And there's no one else who'd worry you weren't around? No

brothers or sisters?'

I eyed Davina carefully, wondering what she was up to. But perhaps she was simply nosy.

'No, no siblings.' I gave a little chuckle. 'Lawrie's got a brother – Simon. Mind you, like Aunt Beatrice, he'd probably rather I disappeared forever.'

'You don't get on?'

'Lawrie and I getting married meant he wouldn't inherit.' I chewed my lip feeling the familiar prickle of guilt that always arrived whenever I thought about Simon.

Davina looked thrilled. 'Perhaps that's why Lawrie's pretending you're there. To get the money?'

I rolled my eyes. 'I don't think so.' But maybe she was right, in a way. A wife was a convenient way of hiding his true feelings, whether I was there or not. I didn't think he'd planned this – but I suspected once he'd recovered from what had clearly not been a serious bump on his head, he'd seen an opportunity and taken it. Thanks to a bit of play-acting from Freddie. Because the fact was, it didn't matter where I was – Lawrie and I were married now and we'd stay that way. And in the meantime, Lawrie could live his life the way he wanted. It had worked out perfectly. Sort of.

'So you're definitely staying?'

'Where else would I go?'

Davina beamed at me. 'That's good, because Mrs M reckons we're going to be busy with people wanting to see the beast of Loch Ness.'

'Tsk,' I said. 'No one will be interested in that silly story.'

'You'd be surprised. Did you see the queues at the picture house when King Kong was showing? Everyone loves a monster.'

I laughed, feeling lighter now I knew Lawrence was alive and no one was looking for me, and I had met an interesting man who had offered to teach me about photography. 'It'll be forgotten about by the weekend.'

Chapter 15

Scarlett

Present day

Bonnie and I started with the newspaper archive. She was amazed when I showed her how many old papers were listed and how to search.

'We can narrow the date range, you see?' I said, setting it to 1933. 'So could you perhaps search for Lawrence Wetherby and see what comes up? I'm going to start making some notes about what I know already. I'm going to have to record something today – an introductory episode – if I'm going to hit my deadlines. I'm on a tight schedule.'

Bonnie nodded eagerly, scrolling through the results like a pro.

I sat down at a table in the quiet lounge, with my notebook in front of me, and leafed through the pages. What did I know? Not much. The thought made me nervous. I understood it was a big thing that Robyn had done, talking Kevin into giving me this opportunity. I didn't want to let her down. Or let myself down, actually. And I definitely didn't want to let Charlie win.

I stared at my notes. All I knew for sure was that Lawrence Wetherby had disappeared in 1933 and had been spotted in Loch Ness. And that Hannah Snow had possibly vanished in 1933, too.

And someone – Hannah or Lawrence, or perhaps someone else entirely – had claimed Lawrence's inheritance and diddled Quentin's dad ... I checked my notes for his name – Simon – out of what he thought he was due.

I shook my head. Nothing about this made any sense. There was nothing to research. Just an absence of people. I needed to write a script and there was nothing to say.

My phone rang and I groaned as I saw my dad's name on the screen. I braced myself, then answered the call with a cheery – and totally fake – "Hi, Dad!"

'Where are you?' he said.

'Hi, Scarlett, how are things?'

To give him his due, he laughed.

'Sorry, darling. I was just worried. I rang you at work and they said you'd gone to Scotland.'

'I did. I have.' Then I frowned. 'Who did you speak to?'

'Someone with a man's name, but who sounded like a woman.'

'Robyn,' I said. 'You know Robyn. You've met her.'

I was relieved Dad hadn't spoken to anyone else. He had a very recognisable voice, and I didn't want anyone to know he was my father. He'd been delighted when I'd first shown an interest in broadcasting, but his delight had faded away very quickly when I'd opted for radio instead of television, and even quicker when I'd chosen to use my mother's maiden name – Simpson – instead of my actual surname, which was Newton and – thanks to Dad's many years presenting the news – somewhat legendary in the television business.

'I want to get jobs on my own merits,' I'd told Dad. He'd looked at me in amazement.

'I could introduce you to Greg,' he said, naming an old friend who just happened to be controller of Radio 4.

But though I'd been tempted, I shook my head. I'd always suffered with low self-confidence and awful imposter syndrome, and I absolutely knew I had to get a job by myself if I wanted it to work.

Since then, Dad had regarded my career with a slightly affected, befuddled air, as if he couldn't quite understand what it was I did. We had a few presenters at Britain Live who were outspoken and got a lot of attention, but Dad always pretended not to know who they were. I was fairly sure he'd never listened to our podcast either.

'Robyn,' he said now. 'Yes, that's it. She said you were on an assignment.'

'I am. I'm doing an investigation. It's my first presenter gig for Britain Live.'

'Oh well done, darling,' my dad said in the tone parents normally used when their toddler had used a potty for the first time.

'I'm actually just about to do some recording, Dad, so …'

'Oh yes, I won't keep you. I just wanted to let you know, your chap called me.'

'Charlie?' Charlie was awful around my father. He acted as though they were best friends and did mortifying things like slap him on the back and suggest they played a round of golf. My dad didn't play golf, but that didn't stop Charlie. Who also didn't play golf. In my more charitable moments, I understood that Charlie was nervous when he was with my father, but it was still annoying. 'Why did he call you?'

'No idea. I didn't speak to him – he left a message. I just wanted to see if you thought I should call him back?'

'Dad, do you know someone called Quentin Wetherby?' I knew how Charlie's mind worked and I was fairly sure he'd think Quentin was a posh white bloke, and so was my dad so they were bound to move in the same circles. I had to admit, he wasn't completely wide of the mark. Perhaps he wanted to pick

Dad's brains about his new employer.

'Name rings a bell. MP is he? Don't know much about him. Should I?'

'No. I was just wondering.' I paused. 'Don't bother ringing Charlie back. I'll speak to him.' I had no intention of speaking to Charlie, but I didn't want my dad to be involved in this investigation. He had a habit of taking over.

'No skin off my nose,' said Dad, who wasn't hugely keen on Charlie anyway. 'Let me know if I can help with your little programme, darling. Lots of love.'

He ended the call and I put my phone down with a sigh. At this rate the programme was going to be very little.

I looked at my notes again. I literally had nothing to say.

'Huh,' said Bonnie.

'What?'

'I started at the beginning of 1933 and there's loads of stuff about Lawrence being an MP and stuff about Britain having talks with Hitler …'

'Nice.'

'I know,' said Bonnie raising an eyebrow. 'And he was working with President Roosevelt who had some big plan to save America from the Depression.'

'Oh right,' I said. I'd not really twigged that there was other stuff going on in 1933 besides monsters and missing persons. I made a note of that. It was good background.

'And then I found a couple of articles about a hunt for Lawrence's wife. She went missing on their wedding day, it says. March 1933.'

'In March? Are you sure?'

'Totally sure.'

'So she went missing in March, and Lawrence disappeared in May? How odd. Still, at least she really did go missing. That at least gives me something to say.'

'Yes, but it's weird because look. A couple of weeks later, there's this tiny article here, see?' She turned the screen of my laptop round so I could see it. 'That says it was all a misunderstanding and Lawrence's wife isn't missing at all.'

'You have got to be kidding me.'

'That's what it says.'

'So she was missing for what? A fortnight?'

'Or not missing at all.'

I put my head in my hands. 'Why am I here?'

'I can't hear you because you're talking into your fingers,' said Bonnie.

With considerable effort, I lifted my head.

'I've got no programme,' I said. 'There is nothing to say.'

Bonnie shrugged. 'Why are you here?'

'Exactly.'

'No, I didn't mean like in an angsty way. I meant, why did you come to Loch Ness?'

'Oh, yes. I saw something that said Lawrence was last spotted here.'

'Where did you see that?'

I made a face. 'Wiki.'

'And you didn't check it?' Bonnie sounded stern.

'I was in a bit of a hurry,' I admitted, shamefaced. 'I'll look now, hang on.'

I found the page on my phone, and scrolled down to where the references were listed.

'It was in an interview with Simon Wetherby,' I said, sitting up a bit straighter. 'He's the dad of the man with the attitude – Quentin. The interview was in *The Telegraph* business section in May 1933. Can you find it?'

'Two ticks,' said Bonnie, who was clearly loving every minute of this. She typed furiously and then sat back in satisfaction.

'Oooh here we go,' she said.

'What is it?'

'It's like a profile of this Simon Wetherby.' She tilted her head to look at the picture. 'He wasn't as handsome as his brother was. Shall I read it out?'

'Go on.'

Bonnie cleared her throat. 'Wetherby brushes off questions about his sister-in-law, who was reported missing, only for his brother, MP Lawrence Wetherby, to claim her disappearance had been a misunderstanding. Is she in West Sussex? I ask. Wetherby raises an eyebrow and tells me he thinks she is in Loch Ness. Is Lawrence with her? I ask and he shakes his head, not willing to confirm or deny. When I laugh at the idea of an MP and his wife joining the hordes of monster hunters heading north, he refuses to comment further and instead brings the conversation back to his new business …'

'Bonnie, you're a bloody genius,' I said. 'Thank God you're here.'

She looked chuffed with herself and I beamed at her.

'That's so strange though – that this Simon was behind the rumours that they were in Loch Ness. I wonder why he thought they were here? It's so random, there had to be a reason.'

'Maybe Hannah did come to look for the monster. My gran tells stories about it to the guests. Her mum – my great-gran – worked here then. Apparently people were coming from all over Britain.'

'But the monster was first seen in April 1933, right?'

'Right.'

'And Hannah's misunderstood disappearance was in March.'

Bonnie deflated. 'Oh. I thought we'd solved it. Like a couple of Miss Marples.'

I laughed and then stopped as a thought struck me. 'Miss Marple,' I said.

'She's like this old lady who solves mysteries. My gran loves the TV show.'

I waved my hand. 'Agatha Christie went missing in the 1920s for something like ten days. Then she came back again.'

'Like Hannah.'

'Like Hannah. If Hannah did disappear, that is.'

'Where did Agatha Christie go?'

'Some hotel in Yorkshire, I think?' I frowned, trying to remember. 'Her mum had just died, and then her husband cheated on her with her mate.'

'Rude,' said Bonnie.

'So rude. She clearly had a breakdown of sorts.'

'Maybe that's what happened to Hannah. Maybe she found out her husband was cheating on their wedding day and she ran away.' Bonnie wiped away imaginary tears. 'Maybe her heart was broken. And then Lawrence tracked her down and came after her, and he disappeared instead.'

'Poor Hannah.'

'Poor, tragic, betrayed Hannah. How awful for her.'

'But how lucky for me because now, thank goodness, I've got something to talk about.' I checked the time. 'Speaking of which, I'm going to have to record something. I need to send Robyn the whole episode a day ahead of when it'll go out.'

Bonnie got to her feet. 'My dad's here anyway.' She pointed out of the window, where a man and a little girl, who was a smaller duplicate of Bonnie, were walking towards the hostel's back door. 'Can I help you again?'

'Of course.'

'Will you mention me on your show?'

I laughed. 'Perhaps.'

'Cool.' She skipped off and I pulled my laptop towards me and opened a blank page. It was time to write a script.

In 1933, the world was changing. As Britain emerged from the Depression, there was a new president – Franklin D Roosevelt – in America, and a new chancellor – Adolf Hitler – in Germany.

In London, an up-and-coming MP – tipped to be prime minister one day – called Lawrence Wetherby, married his young bride Hannah Snow.

But by the end of their wedding day, Hannah had vanished. And 500 miles north, in the murky waters of Loch Ness, a monster was stirring.

I sat back and looked at my screen. Was it too dramatic? It was important to grab my listeners' attention from the off.

I'd record some background bits, I thought. Perhaps chat to some of the people staying at the hostel. Then I'd talk about Hannah going missing, or perhaps not, and Simon saying she was in Loch Ness. I could include the story Lucas told about the monster, and hopefully no one would realise that I actually had very little to say.

My phone beeped with a message. It was my dad again.

Darling, just had a thought, he wrote. *Should I speak to someone at* Newsnight *about getting you some work experience? Might help if you're dabbling in presenting.*

I threw my head back in despair. I had been working in broadcasting for well over a decade now and my father still looked on me as a newcomer. Work experience? Was he serious? How old did he think I was exactly?

Thanks but I've missed the deadline for work experience placements, I typed furiously in response. *They had to be confirmed by June 2003.*

Wishing I had the guts to send it, I instead deleted it all and wrote: *Thanks, but no need. I know what I'm doing.*

Did I though? I knew I was horribly unprepared for this. If it was a *Cold Cases* podcast I'd feel nervous about trying to make something out of the little information I'd found out so far, but it wasn't. It was my big chance to make something of my career. To drag it out of the doldrums where it had been languishing. And to get one over on Charlie, of course. But I had a horrible nagging feeling that I was about to totally blow it.

In my hand, my phone rang.

'I don't need work experience, Dad,' I said as I answered

141

without bothering to look at the screen.

'I wasn't going to offer you work experience,' Charlie replied. 'Unless you want to come and work in CID with me?'

'Hi, Charlie,' I said flatly. 'What do you want?'

'I wanted to tell you something but I think I should do it face-to-face. Could we meet?'

Mt stomach lurched. 'Are you and Astrid getting married?'

'No,' he said, sounding slightly confused. 'Why would you think that?'

'Oh my God, is she pregnant?'

'No, she's not pregnant. Scar, are you okay?'

'I'm fine,' I muttered. 'What is it then?'

'Are you at the office? Fancy a quick drink?'

'I can't,' I said. 'I'm out on a job.'

'When will you be back?'

'It's an overnight,' I said, bending the truth as much as I could. 'Just tell me now.'

'Remember Quentin Wetherby?'

'Who wanted us to find evidence that doesn't exist proving a woman diddled his rich dad out of his even richer inheritance, even though she could be totally innocent?'

There was a pause at the end of the line. 'Yes,' said Charlie cautiously. 'The thing is, Scar. The thing is …'

'What is the thing, Charlie?' I snapped, even though I knew what he was going to say.

'I took the job,' Charlie said in a hurry. 'I'm going to find out how Hannah Snow stole the money.'

'How are you going to do that?'

'Well, that's also the thing.'

I sighed. 'No, I won't help you. And neither will my dad if that's what you phoned him for.'

'I just wanted to check out Quentin,' Charlie said sounding a little sulky. 'I thought your dad might know him.'

'He doesn't.'

'Fine.'

'Good.'

'It's a lot of money, Scar.'

'It's not right, Char,' I said, my voice dripping with ice. 'You're the bloody detective. Why can't you see that there's something off about this? Or are you as completely crap at your job as I've always suspected?'

There was another pause.

'You know what, Scarlett?' Charlie said eventually. 'I don't actually need your help. You're not nearly as good as you think you are. I can find someone else to help with the tech stuff. Robyn, perhaps.'

'Robyn won't help you.' I was outraged.

'Someone else then. You are …' he took a breath '… replace-able. You're nothing special.'

I felt a jab of pain as he hit me right in my weak spot. Charlie had replaced me once, and he'd do it again. Maybe Kevin would too, if my programme was as disastrous as it was shaping up to be.

'And also …' Charlie began, but I ended the call and turned off my phone. I was done with him and my dad.

With dread gnawing at my stomach, I read through my notes again. Charlie was right. I wasn't anything special. I'd messed everything up and I was going to mess this up too. I had half an hour to fill with nothing to say. I knew nothing about Hannah Snow, next to nothing about Lawrence Wetherby and really very little about the Loch Ness monster. It was going to be a total disaster.

Chapter 16

Hannah

1933

Of course I was completely wrong.

The interest in the beast Mrs McEwan had seen did not die down by the weekend. In fact, by the weekend the hotel was busier than it had ever been.

The day before Angus's article appeared in the newspaper, a couple who had been staying in the hotel for a few days arrived back from an evening walk, white-faced.

'We saw a great beast in the loch,' the husband – a Mr Fanshaw, who had a ruddy face thanks to his whisky habit – declared. 'It was an enormous thing, rising up out of the water.'

'A beast?' Mrs McEwan said, a tremor of excitement in her voice. I stood where I was, polishing the reception desk, but my ears pricked, waiting to hear what the Fanshaws said. 'What did it look like?'

'A huge, black hump, like a whale,' Mr Fanshaw said. 'A terrible, terrifying sight to see.'

I glanced at Mrs Fanshaw who was nodding along. 'Terrifying,' she said. 'My hands are still trembling, see?' She held out her fingers to show Mrs McEwan how shaken she was. 'I thought it would come for us.'

'No, no,' said Mrs McEwan hurriedly. 'I'm sure we are quite safe. Come and have a drink, calm your nerves. Hannah, can you help Mr and Mrs Fanshaw?'

I thought Mr Fanshaw was more in need of a strong coffee than strong liquor but I tucked away my duster beneath the desk and smiled. 'Right this way.'

I led them into the lounge, with Mrs McEwan cooing calming reassurances as she followed. 'It must have been quite a shock for you both,' she said, settling them down at a table, and sitting opposite. There was no sign of Tobias, so I went behind the bar and poured a whisky for Mr Fanshaw, and a sherry each for his wife and Mrs M.

'I thought I was losing my mind,' Mrs Fanshaw wailed. 'I thought I was imagining it. But then Desmond said he saw it too.' She looked at her husband. 'Or did you see it first? I can't remember now. But oh, Mrs McEwan, it was quite a shock I can tell you.'

Mrs M leaned forward as though sharing a secret. 'I myself saw a similar beast some nights ago.'

Mr Fanshaw let out a sigh of relief and I smelled the Scotch on his breath, even though I was some distance away from him. 'You did?'

'I did.'

'Then you believe us?'

'Of course. And with your testimony so similar to mine, the whole of Scotland will believe you too.'

I vaguely remembered the Fanshaws being in the lounge when Mrs McEwan had been interviewed by Angus from the *Inverness Herald*. I was sure Mrs Fanshaw had dropped her scarf and I'd picked it up. Or perhaps I was getting muddled. There was so much going on, it was hard to remember who had been where and when.

'Perhaps you should call your friend at the newspaper?' said Mr Fanshaw. 'Tell him there has been another sighting.'

I stood up a little straighter. I couldn't deny I'd like to see Angus again. Just to talk about journalism, of course. No other reason.

Mrs McEwan looked thrilled. 'I should indeed. Would you be willing to talk about your experiences?'

'Well, I'm not sure I'd want the attention ...' said Mr Fanshaw and Mrs McEwan's face fell. But he hadn't finished. 'Though it strikes me that the public should know what's happening.'

'Indeed,' said Mrs M, perking up.

'In fact, I'd say it's our duty to talk about it.'

'Quite.'

'In that case, I would say I'm more than happy to be interviewed,' said Mr Fanshaw, puffing his chest out. 'Perhaps you could mention that I myself run Fanshaw's Gentleman's Outfitters in Penrith? It might prove my credentials as someone to be trusted.'

Might give your business a plug, more like, I thought to myself.

'I will go and telephone the *Herald* now,' said Mrs McEwan. 'Hannah, you hold the fort.'

*

Later Angus would tell me it was a combination of what he called a "slow news day", Mrs McEwan's engaging interview, and – yes – Mr Fanshaw's position as a well-regarded businessman, which meant the story about the beast in Loch Ness hit the front page of the newspaper the following day.

Or perhaps it was just that, like Davina had said, everyone loved a story about a monster.

But whatever the reason, a rather smashing picture of Mrs McEwan, looking pensively out across the loch, accompanied

Angus's piece about the sightings of the beast, and Drumnadrochit was buzzing with people talking about the monster.

By the Sunday, the story was in the national newspapers too and I wondered if this would be the thing that got Angus his big break.

'Our government is busy trying to keep Adolf Hitler happy, and the Americans are trying to make sure everyone has food to eat and shoes to wear, and we're all talking about a monster?' Tobias said, shaking his head as he arranged the newspapers on the reception desk. 'Is this what counts as journalism, these days? Surely there are more important things to be concerned about?'

'Perhaps folk just want a distraction,' said Davina. 'Too much doom and gloom isn't good for anyone.'

'Couldn't agree more.' Mrs McEwan held up *Sunday in Scotland*, which had used the photograph of her right across the top of the front page to great effect. 'Perhaps we should find a frame for this, Tobias? What do you think?'

Tobias rolled his eyes, but in a good-natured fashion, and headed off to find a suitably ornate frame for the front page.

By the afternoon, the phone at the hotel was ringing off the hook and Mrs M took me off chambermaid duties to take bookings, while Davina and another maid called Milly were given the task of moving our belongings out of our rooms. We'd been asked – bribed, I supposed would be a more accurate way to describe it – to give up our rooms for guests and sleep in an outhouse. It was basic but it was cosy. With four beds lined up inside it reminded me of boarding school. I hoped if any of these extra guests Mrs M was expecting went into my room, they didn't feel the need to search up the chimney. I didn't want anyone to find my hidden film.

Despite the flurry of activity, though, I didn't really believe that our sleepy wee corner of the Highlands would attract any interest. A part of me still thought that it would blow over. That Tobias was right, and everyone would realise there were more important things to worry about.

Until, I was out the front of the hotel late on the Monday morning, polishing the brass plaque on the porch, when I heard what sounded like several motor cars.

I stopped polishing and stared in amazement as a cavalcade of vehicles – mostly cars but also the bus from Inverness, which had clearly been held up in the unexpected traffic, and one rather noisy motorcycle – came hurtling down the main road towards the hotel and one by one they all turned into the entrance where I stood.

'Monster hunters?' I muttered. Surely not?

Car doors banged as people – mostly men, though there were a couple of women – emerged. There were a lot of pairs of binoculars slung round Tweed-clad necks, and lots of cameras. There were shouts and waves as the men recognised friends and slapped one another on the back.

And with a sudden lurch of trepidation, I realised these weren't all monster hunters at all. Some of them – a lot of them, judging by how well they all seemed to know each other – were journalists. Already one gentleman had raised his camera and was snapping shots of the entrance to the hotel, where I stood.

'Oh no,' I breathed. 'No.'

Slowly, I backed away, ducking inside the hotel's porch. My heart was pounding and all the excitement I'd felt when Angus first came to the hotel just a few days ago had vanished. Because my hideaway had been uncovered.

Of course these journalists weren't looking for me. No one was looking for Hannah Wetherby anymore – Lawrie had told everyone I was in Sussex. But even though they'd not intended to, they'd found me. I was already in their photographs. All it took was for Aunt Beatrice, or any of the girls I'd gone to school with, or one of Lawrie's friends – or worse, one of his political rivals – to pick up the *Daily Mail* or the *Telegraph* and spot me lurking in the background of a picture and suddenly I'd be the talk of the town again. Or, more accurately, Lawrie would be. My new life – my independence – would be threatened, and as for Lawrie – well, he had even more to lose. His freedom. His reputation. Perhaps even his life.

I peeked outside. The journalists were all gathering in groups, chatting and laughing and looking for all the world like they were at a garden party.

As I stood there, Mrs McEwan came rushing past, dolled up to the nines and looking extremely glamorous.

'Welcome to the Drum Hotel,' she declared leaving a cloud of eau de parfum hanging in the porch where I stood. 'Home of the Loch Ness monster!'

My hands were beginning to sweat.

'Come on in,' called Mrs M, throwing her arms out wide. 'Come on in and Hannah will help you get settled.'

As the journalists picked up their bags and started heading up the steps to where I stood, I turned on my heels and fled, not even caring what Mrs McEwan would think.

'I don't feel well,' I said to Davina as I hurried past her. 'Please help Mrs M check everyone in.'

Mrs McEwan didn't like Davina being on reception because she was inclined to make rude jokes or inappropriate comments, but I couldn't do it. I had to get out of there.

I scuttled past the entrance to the lounge, and out into the garden where I slumped down on a bench to catch my breath.

'Had enough?'

I turned to see Angus, sitting on another bench a little way along from where I sat. I was, I found, surprisingly pleased to see him.

'It's crazy out there.'

He grinned. 'May I?' He gestured to the bench where I was and I nodded, shifting along a bit so he could come and sit next to me. When he sat down he made a little "oof" noise like I remembered my dad making years ago and the thought made me smile.

'What's the collective noun for journalists?' He looked up into the grey sky, thinking. 'A scribble?'

'A press?'

'Ooh nice one. So, a press of journalists is advancing on the hotel, and you're ...' He looked at me carefully. 'You're not happy about it? Even though you yourself want to be a journalist?'

I shook my head. 'It's just a little overwhelming. There are a lot of cameras. I don't want to see myself on all the front pages tomorrow.'

'No,' said Angus. 'Me neither. Myself I mean. You'd look a lot nicer on the front pages than I would.' He stopped talking abruptly and I saw two pink spots appear on his cheeks. 'I mean ...'

I felt an odd rush of affection for him, this stranger who'd brought the press of journalists to our door. He was so confident in some ways, and yet a little ungainly.

'You did this,' I said. 'You've put the Drum Hotel on the map. Mrs M is completely beside herself.'

'I suppose I did.' He looked pleased.

'It could help you get that big job you're after.'

'I hope so.' He pushed his glasses up his nose. 'But you don't like it? This attention from the press?'

I shrugged. 'I'd rather be watching it all than be in it. Does that make sense?'

'It makes absolute sense,' Angus said. 'You're an observer. And in my humble opinion that means you're already halfway to being a journalist.'

I was absurdly pleased. 'Do you think so?'

'I do.' Angus picked up his camera, which he had slung round his neck. 'I'm never in photographs because I'm always taking them,' he said. 'You've got a camera, right?'

'I have.'

'So why not use it? Document everything that's going on. You said you keep a diary – keep one about this.'

'Everyone will be gone in a few days,' I said. 'This will all have blown over.'

'I've heard someone is going to offer a reward. Some industrialist chap in London.'

I raised an eyebrow. 'A reward?'

'Twenty thousand pounds for the first person who catches the monster.'

I almost fell off the bench. 'Twenty thousand pounds? Are you serious?'

'Apparently so.'

I stared at him in astonishment. 'That's such a lot of money.'

'Small beans compared with how much Mrs M's going to be making when the monster hunters arrive. Those journalists outside and the people with their binoculars, they're just the beginning.'

I breathed out slowly, my head spinning as I thought about what that would mean. 'You think so?'

'The hotel is going to be full for weeks. Good news for Mrs M.' Angus rubbed his fingers and thumb together to signify money.

I knew the sensible thing would be to leave. To head off somewhere far away where there was no risk of me being spotted by Simon – or Lawrie. But I didn't want to. This was exciting. It could be a chance for me to finally have a go at being a journalist.

'I could take photographs of the monster hunters?' I said almost to myself. 'And if I'm taking pictures, no one will be photographing me?'

'Exactly.'

'And I could keep a journal of everything that's happening.'

Angus pointed at me. 'You could write a column for the *Herald*,' he said. 'An insider's view of the hunt for the Loch Ness monster.'

'Are you serious? I could write a column?'

'Totally serious. It would be great. Like "our man in Drumnadrochit".'

'Your woman,' I said.

'Our woman.' Angus smiled at me and it was like the sun

151

coming out to warm me on a cold day. 'What do you think?'

'I think yes please,' I said, resisting the urge to jump to my feet and run around squealing in excitement. 'Yes please.'

'You can give us all the insider gossip.'

'Mrs M might not like me giving all the insider gossip,' I said, feeling the thrill subside a little bit. 'She might sack me.'

'You could write under another name.'

'You think?'

'It'll give you the freedom to say what you want to say.' He looked earnest. 'Because in the end, the story is what matters isn't it?'

I wasn't sure I agreed with that, but perhaps he knew better than me, being as he was a proper journalist and I wasn't.

'A pen name?' I said thoughtfully.

'Yes.' Angus pulled his notebook from his inside pocket and found a stubby pencil in another. He found a clean page.

'You're Hannah Snow, right?'

I nodded, pleased that he'd remembered but slightly nervous that he'd put two and two together and realise I was Lawrence Wetherby's sort-of-missing wife.

'Hannah Snow,' Angus wrote. He held the page out and tapped it with the end of his pencil. 'We could call you … Anna Frost?'

I shook my head. 'Too obvious.'

'We could mix up the letters? Make an anagram.' He began writing down letters, and crossing them out again. 'How about this?'

He'd written *Ann O'Shawn*.

'I like it.'

'Words and pictures by Ann O'Shawn,' Angus said. 'How does that sound?'

'I love it.' I clasped my hands together. 'Do you really mean it? Really?'

'Well, I need to check with my editor but I really can't see him saying no. This is the biggest story the *Herald*'s ever broken,

I think, and having you writing for us will give us something different that the nationals don't have.'

I grinned at him, and he smiled back at me, and I thought again how nice he was.

'So, what do you think? Will you write for us, Ann?'

'That's Miss O'Shawn to you.'

Chapter 17

Scarlett

Present day

Like a grumpy, overtired toddler, I felt much better once I'd had a good night's sleep. So it was with a new rush of determination that I started the following day. I'd decided the key to this whole thing was the Loch Ness monster. After all, everyone loved a monster, didn't they? I'd fill my airtime with tales of Nessie and build an atmosphere, and hope that by the time I was due to record episode two, I'd have more to say.

Trying not to think about the fact that I was on very shaky ground with this approach, I decided to head outside and into the car park. I would grab a willing podcaster or YouTuber and interview them, and then maybe record some background sounds of the waves crashing on the shore. Did loch waves crash? I hoped so. I was feeling slightly more frantic than I had done the day before as I hurried across the car park, my eyes fixed on the distant loch. If the waves didn't crash, then I'd take my shoes and socks off and paddle or do something that would make the water splash. Would it be cold? It looked cold. But anyway, I'd walk down to the shore ... OOF.

I walked straight into something large and firm and, winded, sort of ricocheted off and sat down with a thump on my bottom in the middle of the tarmac. My papers scattered around me and I only just managed to keep hold of my laptop.

Above me, silhouetted against the white sky, loomed a figure.

'Shit, sorry,' it said. A large hand reached out to help me to my feet and I realised it was Lucas. As in George. 'I must have reversed into you.'

I knew he was just being kind and I'd clearly walked straight into his back as I dashed towards the loch.

'Are you okay?' he asked as I got to my feet and looked in dismay at my notes blowing across the car park in the breeze.

'Absolutely fine.' I nodded vigorously. 'Absolutely top notch.'

And then I burst into tears.

'Oh flipping heck,' said Lucas, hoisting me up to my feet and staring at me in concern. 'Are you hurt? Did I hurt you?'

I breathed in, a huge shuddering gulp of air, and tried very hard to sound normal. 'Noooo,' I said, wiping away the tears that were snaking down my cheeks. 'I'm fine. It was just a shock.'

'You don't look fine.'

'Thanks.'

'Well, you know, the tears, and the panicky look were a bit of a clue,' he said.

I glanced at him, wondering if he was being serious and caught the flash of mischief in his eye. I found myself smiling, which was quite surprising.

'I think I'm just stressed,' I admitted. 'I'm on a deadline.'

'For your podcast?'

'No, for my radio programme. If it was the podcast, I'd just delay putting the episode out.' I dug about in my pocket for a tissue and wiped my nose. 'But the first episode's going out tomorrow and the only content I've got is you telling the story of Nessie.'

Lucas bent down to pick up a piece of paper I'd dropped and handed it to me. 'Want a hand?'

'With?'

He shrugged. 'Research? I'm quite good at digging into things.'

'Because of your podcast?'

'Well, that and for work.'

I narrowed my eyes at him. 'You're not a detective, are you?'

He laughed in a very hearty way that I quite liked. 'No, I'm an accountant.'

'Right. But you want to help me?'

'A forensic accountant.'

'What like dead bodies and fingerprints and stuff?' Lucas laughed again and I realised I was being stupid and laughed too. 'God, no, ignore me. It's investigating fraud and whatnot, isn't it?'

'That's it,' he said. 'But I'm quite good at finding little irregularities that could mean something's not right.'

I was so stressed that I almost caved, but then I thought about how being here, doing this programme on my own, would prove something to myself and Charlie and my father, and even Kevin, and I shook my head.

'I'm good, thanks.'

'Oh come on, I've got days and days to kill up here and there's literally nothing to find out about the mysterious Beast of Loch Lochy.'

'Beasty McBeast Face,' I said.

'Exactly.'

'It's kind of you to offer, but I'm really fine,' I said.

'Fair enough,' said Lucas.

'I'll get on then,' I said.

'Right you are.'

I shifted my laptop in my arms because I was in danger of dropping everything again. 'Thanks for picking me up,' I said, a little awkwardly.

'No problem.'

There was a pause while neither of us moved.

'I don't suppose you fancy going to the pub?' Lucas said. 'I personally always feel research goes more smoothly when I have a pint in my hand and it might help you. I promise not to talk at you while you're working.'

'Oh go on then,' I said.

*

We went to a pub called the Black Friar, which was quiet but not deserted and had a large table in the corner free. Lucas bought the drinks and I settled down with the laptop and spread out my notes.

'What have you got so far?' Lucas asked, putting a beer in front of me. He'd screwed his nose up when I'd asked for a bottle of Italian lager, but he'd not argued. 'Tell me the story from the start.'

I picked up my notes, and he put his hand on mine, stopping me. 'No, just tell me. Don't look at what you've written.'

I looked at him in surprise.

'It's a tactic I use at work,' he said. 'Gets straight to the heart of the story because you automatically filter out what's not important without thinking about it.'

'Really?'

'Worth a go?'

'Okay, then.' I took a mouthful of beer. 'Hannah and Lawrence – he was an MP – got married in March 1933. And according to a couple of newspaper reports, she went missing on their wedding day.'

'She just vanished?'

'No. That's the thing. A few weeks later, it was reported that she was actually fine and it had all been a misunderstanding. But Lawrence's brother, Simon, said he thought she was really in Loch Ness despite what Lawrence had said.'

'Why?'

'No idea.'

Lucas frowned. 'But it was Lawrence who actually went missing, right?'

I nodded. 'Yes. But a bit later in 1933, which is weird too.'

'Where?'

'If we knew where he went, then he wouldn't have been missing.' I watched hopefully to see if Lucas laughed, and I was rewarded with a small chuckle.

'Where was he when he went missing?'

'London. He was in the House of Commons one day, then he didn't show up again. But then there were rumours he was in Loch Ness, too.'

'What else?'

I thought. 'Erm, Lawrence had an inheritance that was due to pay out on his 35th birthday in October of that year, and he claimed it. Or someone did.'

'Anything else?'

I made a face. 'Simon's son is a man called Quentin Wetherby.'

'The MP?'

'You've heard of him?'

'Well, him not so much. His family business, yes. They're struggling a bit, I think.'

'Brexit, apparently.'

Lucas raised an eyebrow. 'And the rest.'

'Quentin thinks his father should have inherited.'

'Presumably he would have if Lawrence had died.'

'Well, that's why ...' I drank some more beer as Lucas looked at me curiously. 'That's why Quentin asked us to investigate.'

'You're working for Quentin Wetherby?'

'No, I'm not.' I hit my hand on the table to make my point and regretted it as a couple of other drinkers looked round at me. 'He wants to prove Hannah killed Lawrence and claimed the inheritance, and I want to prove she didn't.'

Lucas's eyes gleamed. 'This is good stuff,' he said.

I sat up a bit straighter, because he was right, actually. It was good. I felt a bit more hopeful.

'I thought for my first episode I'd just set the scene really. Like we said, it all happened around the time the monster was spotted, when everyone came to Loch Ness to hunt for it. I even wondered if that's why Hannah had come up here – to find the monster. But the dates don't work.'

'God, that's brilliant.' Lucas sounded a bit envious. 'Better than the untold story of Loch Lochy, in any case.'

I chuckled. 'Bonnie was looking at newspapers for me, but maybe I should look at some more. The local Inverness paper, perhaps? Really get a feel for the time?'

'Good plan,' said Lucas. 'Why don't I see if I can have a root about and find out anything about Lawrence going missing?'

'No,' I said, a little bit louder than I'd intended.

He looked put out. 'Sorry. I wouldn't steal your research, if that's what you're worried about.'

'No, it's not that.' I sighed. 'I didn't mean to be rude. This is just my thing, you know?'

Lucas looked as if he didn't know but he nodded. 'Fair enough. Shall I leave you to it?'

'If you don't mind.' I thought I was actually being a bit rude, even if I didn't mean it, but I was not going to let some Viking-esque YouTuber take over.

'Not at all.'

'If you get stuck, have a look on here,' he said. He picked up a beer mat and wrote on it. 'Might help.'

Then he drained his pint and wandered off, without even looking round. For a tiny second I thought about calling to him and getting him to come back, but then I thought better of it. Working with Charlie had always been pretty stressful. He would always make me look at what he was doing, and often expect me to do his tasks too. Then I'd somehow end up doing the research he'd started, and not my own, and having to squeeze in my own work at odd hours of the day – or night. It was easier just to do this alone.

I picked up the beer mat Lucas had scribbled on. He'd written a web address, a username – Obiwankenobi – and a password. One of the proper ones with a mix of letters and symbols and numbers rather than my too-easy-to-crack Scar!ett.

Intrigued, I put in the address and logged on. It was a Metropolitan Police site – staff records as far as I could see – with a similar search function to the newspaper archive I was familiar with. I supposed Lucas, being a forensic accountant, used these records to check pensions and payouts and stuff like that. I couldn't quite see how it would help me, but nothing ventured … I typed in Lawrence Wetherby and up came one result.

I put my beer bottle down on the table with a triumphant thud and clicked on the link. It was the staff record belonging to a police officer called Sergeant Vassily. I scanned the information. He'd retired in 1938 but had come back to work during the war and won an award in 1945.

'Good on you, Sarge,' I muttered to myself. My mum was a retired teacher who'd gone back to work during the pandemic to help in a local school, much to my pride.

I read on further. There was a report of the award ceremony, which talked about air raids, blackouts, saving someone's life in the Blitz, and then there it was. In 1933, Sergeant Vassily had been part of the investigation into the disappearance of MP Lawrence Wetherby.

I breathed in sharply, but that wasn't all. Because the brilliant Sergeant Vassily had, according to this, "liaised with officers in Inverness as part of the investigation".

'Oh my God,' I said out loud. 'Lawrence was definitely here.'

Filled with new enthusiasm, I sent a quick message to Robyn, asking how she was, and telling her I'd have the first episode to her tomorrow. *It's good stuff*, I wrote. *Lots of monster hunters and people looking for things that might not exist.*

Well done, she replied immediately. *How did you get so much info so fast?*

I didn't want to say I'd had help, so instead I just replied: *Hard work, man.*

I spent the rest of the afternoon adding to my notes and writing the beginning of a script, and I felt brilliant. I was doing my job, and I was doing it well, and for once self-doubt had left me alone.

So when I got back to the hostel later on, I was delighted to see Lucas sitting in the lounge, chatting to Bonnie and Joyce.

'Lucas, it's no exaggeration to say you might have saved my career.' I beamed at him, plonking myself down on a chair next to him. 'And probably my best friend's too.'

Lucas looked very pleased. 'Really? That's unusual for me. Normally I ruin people's careers.'

'Ah well the good thing about having no money is I can't do anything dodgy with it,' I said cheerfully. 'Except buy you a coffee to say thank you? Or another beer?'

Lucas grinned. 'Coffee would be lovely.'

Joyce busied herself with the coffee machine and I shot a glance at Lucas who was looking at his phone, resting his chin in his hands. His long hair was tied back in a ponytail. He definitely reminded me of a Viking. Though, actually was it Vikings who had ponytails? Or was it them who had the pigtails? I couldn't remember. Either way, Lucas reminded me of one. Uncharitably, I thought how Charlie would look next to him. He was fit, Charlie, and he went to the gym all the time but he was tall and sort of stringy and lean. Lucas was more … what was it Anita always said? Hench. Lucas was hench.

'So what did you find out?' he said, glancing up from his phone as Joyce put the coffees in front of us.

I filled him in on finding Sergeant Vassily's staff record and how it confirmed that Lawrence had definitely been up here.

'He was here before he vanished, and I know that his brother thought Hannah was up here. And I know that Hannah went missing but then Lawrence claimed she was fine. So perhaps he knew where she was all along – Loch Ness – and came up to see her?'

'And she bumped him off.'

'No!' I looked at my notes. 'Well, perhaps.'

'It's not looking good for Hannah, guilt-wise,' Lucas pointed out.

'Shush.'

He grinned. 'And all this was happening while Drumnadrochit was full of monster hunters.'

'Yes, it seems to match up with the sightings of the monster you told me about. It's brilliantly atmospheric. I thought I'd focus on that for the first episode really. Just the background stuff. I found this column in the *Inverness Herald* that's all about what it was like here at the time. I can use that. It seems all the monster hunters stayed here at the hostel.' I looked at Joyce for confirmation and she nodded.

'It was a hotel back then,' she said. 'Quite posh, I believe. Though my mother worked here and she was most definitely not posh.'

'Maybe Lawrence and Hannah stayed here too,' I said, feeling that tingle of excitement again. 'Maybe your mum met them?'

'She probably did,' Joyce said. 'It was only a wee village back then and this was the only hotel. Before monster mania struck.'

'How exciting.'

'Show me this column, then,' said Lucas. 'What does it say?'

Chapter 18

Inverness Herald
Friday April 28, 1933
Hordes of monster hunters descend on Drumnadrochit
Words and pictures by the Herald's Loch Ness correspondent,
Ann O'Shawn

Just a few weeks ago, the little village of Drumnadrochit –
no more than a handful of houses, a few shops and the Drum
Hotel – was a sleepy place. A sanctuary for holidaymakers and
day trippers away from the hubbub of life in a city or town.
There are plenty of good spots here for boat trips. There are
many beautiful places to walk. The air is clean and the wind
bracing. There's no doubt it's a lovely place to spend a few days.

But now the quiet stillness of the Drum Hotel has been
shattered and the village is full of people.

Not just people.

Monster hunters!

Last week, as you surely know, Mrs Aileen McEwan, the
proprietor of the Drum Hotel, spotted an enormous beast

writing in the dark waters of Loch Ness, quickly followed by another sighting by Mr Desmond Fanshaw, of Fanshaw's Gentleman's Outfitters in Penrith.

And now the hotel is full of monster hunters – and newspaper reporters, of course – from all over Scotland, England and further afield, desperate to see the beast that lives in the murky loch.

The Drum Hotel is a sleepy sanctuary no more. Instead, the lights blaze until the wee small hours, and the bar is never shut. The guests spend their days taking boats out on to the loch and their evenings discussing what they did – or didn't – see over a stiff drink.

And I'm there too, right in the thick of the action. I'm going to be bringing you all the news from the Drum Hotel, dear readers.

We've heard rumours that a wealthy industrialist is planning to offer an enormous reward to anyone who manages to catch the monster. So many more people are expected to arrive in Drum that the enterprising Mrs McEwan is busy turning outbuildings into sleeping quarters for her staff, in order to free up rooms for more guests.

In the meantime, we'd love to know what you, our readers, think about the Loch Ness monster. Will you be joining the hordes swarming onto the shores of the water at Drumnadrochit, with one eye on the reward? Or will you be staying away? Let us know!

Chapter 19

Hannah

1933

I was having enormous fun, which was, I had to admit, surprising. It seemed that overnight, the hotel had gone from being a quiet, genteel place to a glittering palace of parties and fun.

The day before, I'd gone with Tobias to pick up some extra bottles of whisky from a supplier in Inverness and I'd taken the chance to pop in at the *Herald* offices to sign my contract. My contract! I was being paid actual money – though I hadn't yet received my first paycheque – to write columns for the paper, and take photographs, while the hunt for the monster continued.

I didn't tell Tobias where I was going. Instead I fibbed and said I needed a new hat – because I wanted to keep Ann O'Shawn's identity a secret, of course.

Angus hadn't been there when the editor's secretary showed me into the editor's office. I was disappointed not to see him, but even that couldn't dampen the thrill I felt to be in a real live newspaper office.

I looked round the newsroom, enthralled by the hubbub and noise and clatter of typewriters. There was a fug of cigarette smoke in the air and two men were having a noisy discussion about the headline on page 5.

'Is it what you were expecting?' the secretary asked. She was tall and willowy and looked so exactly how I imagined a newspaper editor's secretary to look that I had been startled when she came to fetch me from reception.

'It's even better than I was expecting,' I breathed.

She gave me an amused glance. 'Really?'

'It's wonderful.'

She laughed but as she showed me into the editor's office, she put her hand on my arm.

'Nice to see more women on the paper. There aren't many of us.' She glanced over her shoulder at where the two men were still shouting even though they were standing right next to one another now. 'More's the pity.'

I'd left with an armful of paper, rolls of film, instructions for phoning in my stories – I crossed my fingers and hoped Mrs McEwan would let me use the telephone in the office – a list of deadlines that "absolutely had to be met" and a spring in my step. What a chance this was. What an opportunity to make something of myself – to be a journalist at last. And perhaps I wasn't an international correspondent, whizzing across Europe to report on talks with Adolf Hitler, or writing about Roosevelt's plan for economic recovery. But I was writing. I was being paid to write. This was my job now.

Well, this and cleaning the lavatories at the Drum Hotel.

As Tobias and I drove home, the sun was setting.

'Did you not get a hat?' he asked, glancing over at me from the driver's seat.

'Pardon?'

'You went to buy a hat, but all you have is a bundle of paper.'

'Oh,' I said. 'Yes.' I thought desperately for an explanation and couldn't come up with anything. But fortunately at that moment, we rounded the corner on the approach to the hotel, and Tobias let out a bark of delight.

'Would you look at that?'

Ahead of us, the hotel sparkled with light, every window glowing in the dim evening gloom.

'It's like a fairy castle,' I said in glee.

'This is brilliant,' Tobias said, putting his foot down and driving a little faster. 'Brilliant!'

As we pulled up to the front of the hotel, we could see people on the terrace and silhouetted in the windows. Music was playing and when we got out of the car, I could hear a buzz of laughter and conversation.

'Mrs McEwan is a very clever woman,' said Tobias, half to me, half to himself. 'A very clever woman.'

'You're going to have to learn how to make cocktails,' I said. 'These people won't be happy with a glass of sherry before dinner.'

He opened the boot of the car and there were several boxes of whisky and gin and other spirits. 'I'm ahead of you there, girl,' he said. He sounded absolutely thrilled to bits and I couldn't blame him, because lovely as the Drum Hotel was, it was verging on boring. 'What's your favourite?'

'Old-Fashioned.' I said it without thinking, then shuddered as I remembered asking for one at my wedding.

'I'll make you one later.'

'It's a deal.'

He handed me one of the boxes, and I balanced my film and paper on top, then together we walked into the hotel, eager to join the fun.

Inverness Herald
Friday May 5, 1933

Drumnadrochit thrums to the beat of monster hunters' drums

Words and pictures by our Loch Ness monster correspondent, Ann O'Shawn

Since the announcement of a £20,000 reward to the first person to catch the Loch Ness monster, the Drum Hotel has become the place to be.

Dear readers, it seems to us that many of the guests at the Drum are doing less monster hunting and more drinking and dancing. But that's just fine. The hotel staff are enjoying it as much as the guests and embracing the new challenges this exciting adventure is bringing. We even heard whispers that the staff themselves have responded to this new liberal atmosphere by getting rather more friendly with each other than they had been. Is it true that a handsome male member of staff has been entertaining a female member of staff after hours?

We hope so!

But what then of the hunt for the monster itself? We watch the hunters head off each day, eagerly snapping photographs with their cameras and clambering into boats. Sometimes, dear readers, your correspondent fears they will tumble into the murky depths themselves, as they tussle for the best spot in the boat or rush to the side of the vessel in order to get the best shot – sending waves slapping over the side.

Despite their enthusiasm, though, we can't help thinking some hunters aren't playing by the rules when it comes to getting proof of the monster's existence. Word has it that one of the hotel's chambermaids spotted someone faking footprints on the loch shore using an ashtray made from an elephant's foot, which they'd pilfered from the lounge bar.

How far will they go to get their monstrous mitts on the reward?

'Have you read the *Herald*?' Tobias asked me the following morning as I helped him restock the bar.

Mrs M was giddy with delight at how much money was being spent on drinks each evening, and I wasn't surprised. Those monster hunters – and the reporters – seemed to be treating this like one enormous party, and quaffing food and drink accordingly.

'Today's *Herald*?' I said, trying to sound casual.

'Yes, have you read it?'

Had I read it? I'd read it over and over again. I'd had two columns published now, and I thought I'd never get over the thrill of seeing my name in print. Even if it wasn't actually my name.

'Glanced at it,' I said with a shrug.

'Which one is Ann O'Shawn?' Tobias asked. He leaned over the bar towards me, and lowered his voice. 'She knows everything.'

'Ann O'Shawn? No idea,' I lied.

Tobias glanced round, as though Ann might be lurking behind him. Which, in a way, she was. The thought made me smile.

'She knows all sorts,' Tobias hissed urgently. 'How did she know about ...' He looked round again. 'About what the staff are up to?'

I stared at him with wide, innocent eyes. 'I have no idea.'

'She could be watching us now.' He sounded a bit cross, which annoyed me. Hadn't Angus said that the story was the most important thing? Even if I hadn't believed it at first, it was rather thrilling to be the person in the thick of all the action.

'Perhaps she is watching,' I said. 'Listening to our conversations wherever we go.'

Tobias looked alarmed. He backed away from me, his eyes darting from side to side, and he began polishing the beer pumps with vigour. I laughed and raised my camera to my chest. I'd taken to carrying it around with me, snapping photos whenever I could.

'Hey,' Tobias said. 'How do I know you're not Ann O'Shawn? Taking photos on the sly and selling them to the *Herald*?'

My palms felt sweaty suddenly on the edges of my camera. 'Well, my name's Hannah for a start,' I said. 'Gosh, I'm only learning photography. These pictures are just for me, and Mrs M, of course. She asked me to take some photos of everything that's going on.'

'What's this?'

I turned to see Davina loitering by the door of the bar. It was her who'd seen the men faking the footprints on the beach while she was changing the beds in an upstairs room. She didn't miss much, Davina. For a second she looked at me, and I thought the game was up. But instead, her sharp eyes fell on to my camera. Davina loved the camera.

'Take one of me,' she said. She positioned herself looking out of the window towards the loch, and grinned at me. I raised the camera but she shouted, 'Wait!'

'What?'

'I need to look like I've spotted something.'

She arranged her face into a shocked expression, pointed out of the window towards the loch and, giggling, I snapped a photo.

'Aye aye,' Davina said, dropping her arm and giving me a knowing glance. 'Your man's here. He's walking up from the loch.'

'What man?' I asked, though I knew.

'That Angus from the *Herald*.'

'Maybe he's Ann O'Shawn,' said Tobias to himself.

'Give it a rest, Tobe,' Davina said with a tut. 'No one cares.'

I grinned at Davina, glad she was there. 'Is he coming in? Angus?'

'Looks like it.' She came over to me and smoothed down my hair, tucking a stray strand under the little caps we wore. 'There. You look pretty.'

'Can you cover my shift?' I said. 'Angus promised to take me to the darkroom at the newspaper and show me how to develop the photos I've taken.'

'All right,' Davina said. 'But only as long as you tell me everything after.'

'There won't be anything to tell,' I said, half-hoping that I was wrong.

I gave her a quick hug, waved to Tobias, who was still poring over Ann O'Shawn's article, and dashed out of the lounge.

'Hannah?' Davina called after me. 'You owe me one!'

Chapter 20

Scarlett

Present day

In the middle of the night I woke up thinking about Hannah. These nocturnal awakenings quite often happened to me when I was in the middle of a busy time at work – it was as though I slept but my mind kept going.

I'd wake with a start, realising I'd forgotten something important about an episode, or a guest on the radio show. Sometimes – not often enough – it was an idea about where to take the programme, or a question to put to the guest. And that night, it was a thought about how Hannah could afford to live while she was in Loch Ness. Did she have money in a bank account or a chequebook she could use? Would that have shown everyone where she was – I wasn't sure if transactions could be traced to locations back in 1933 like they could be now.

Or did she have a job?

I lay in bed, listening to the distant sound of the waves on the loch and tried to leaf back through the thoughts that had woken me.

In the lounge the previous evening, I'd had a cup of tea with Joyce and a lovely long chat about the hotel and its history.

She had told me that the room where I was sleeping now had once been staff quarters, but that during the monster-hunting frenzy the poor chambermaids and waitresses had been forced out of their rooms and into an outbuilding to make space for more guests.

'It was where our glamping site is now,' she'd said, pointing out into the grounds of the hostel, where I could just see the tops of the tepees. 'They had a lot of live-in staff back then. I've got a photograph somewhere. There are quite a few pictures from that time, actually, if you'd like to see them? My mother kept them all. There was nothing she liked better than talking about her time here when the monster hunters arrived. And one of the maids was a photography enthusiast apparently.'

'I'd love to see them, if you don't mind digging them out?'

'Not at all.'

After spending the day researching, writing the script for the episode, and then chatting with Joyce, I'd gone to bed for the first time since this whole ridiculous escapade began, feeling positive.

I'd read over my script and sent it to Robyn to check and I was planning to record the final bits tomorrow, then get it all edited. I had that little flutter of excitement deep within me that told me this was good radio. It was the same way I'd felt when we recorded the Shirley Pilgrim episode that won us the award, though I also had a slight – okay, massive – anxiousness about how Charlie would react when he heard it. If he heard it. And Quentin Wetherby too of course. Would he listen? Would he be annoyed?

I turned over in bed and rearranged my pillows to get comfortable. Mind you, it didn't really matter how Charlie or Quentin Wetherby reacted. There was nothing they could do.

But that wasn't what had woken me. No, not worries about the reaction to the first episode. It was Hannah who'd roused me. Hannah and her money.

I sat up suddenly, making my head spin.

'Did she work here?' I said aloud, my voice croaky with sleep. Did Hannah work in the hotel?

Hadn't Joyce said there had hardly been anything in the town before monster mania hit? Surely there weren't a lot of jobs on offer. And she had to support herself somehow, didn't she?

I stretched out my legs under the duvet, pleased with my revelation. Would Joyce have old staff records? I hoped so. She seemed to have a lot of things left over from those times, which wasn't a surprise really, given how important 1933 was in putting the hotel on the map and her mum's eagerness to remember it.

I looked over to the window, where I could see the sky starting to lighten round the edges of the blind. Perhaps I'd get up now, I thought. Get a good start on the day. Maybe go for a run, get my blood pumping before I started recording.

I felt my eyelids drooping and forced myself to sit up. I had lots to do.

Slowly, I dragged myself out of bed and with a distinct lack of enthusiasm, pulled on my running gear. I knew I might not feel like it now, but once it was done I'd feel better and have more energy for what was bound to be a busy day.

I opened the blind and looked out at the loch. Could I run round it? I couldn't remember how big it was but it looked pretty long. Long and narrow.

'Siri,' I said to my phone. 'How far is a circuit of Loch Ness?'

'The walk around Loch Ness is 80 miles,' my phone told me.

I laughed. Perhaps a quick 2.5 kilometres out and the same back would have to do.

*

174

I was running back towards the hostel, red-faced, sweaty and out of breath because it was ages since I'd done a proper run, when I saw someone running towards me. Someone tall and broad, with his long hair tied back under a baseball cap, looking very unlike the geeky Viking I was used to and more like … well, more like that hot Aussie bloke from those Marvel films. That was a surprise.

'Bugger,' I muttered to myself, looking round for an escape route. Could I duck into the woods at the edge of the path? Nope, too late. He was waving at me.

I wiped the sweat from my forehead as Lucas approached, and hoped my face wasn't as tomato-like as I feared.

'Morning!' he called. 'You're an early bird.'

We both stopped running as we got close to one another and I checked my watch to see if I could consider my run done: 4.91 kilometres. That would do.

'Things … to … do,' I panted, wondering how exactly he looked so good in his workout gear when I was fairly sure I looked like a small, sweaty sausage in a skin. And then wondering why I cared.

'Sets you up for the day, doesn't it?' Lucas said. 'How far did you go?'

Bent over, trying to catch my breath, I showed him my watch and he grinned. 'If you go round the side of the hostel, past the wonky tree and back, you'll get to 5km exactly.'

I blinked at him.

'Got to get it exact, right?'

'Right,' I said, even though I'd been planning a shower, a coffee and perhaps a pastry from Joyce's selection. 'Definitely.'

'See you later?'

My heart gave a bit of an unexpected thump – must have just been because of the exercise. 'Great,' I said.

Lucas gave me a cheery thumbs up. 'Wonky tree and back,' he said, as he ran towards the loch.

I thought about waiting for him to disappear out of sight and then legging it into the hostel, but – I realised, with a certain

175

amount of disbelief – I wanted to impress him.

I remembered when I'd wanted to impress Charlie, he was himself trying to impress his new team in CID who were all a bit "lads, lads, lads" and spent a lot of time in the pub. I'd trained myself to drink a whole pint of lager in one just to see the pride in Charlie's eyes when he introduced me to his colleagues. It had taken me ages to get rid of the beer gut I'd developed.

But this was completely different to that fairly shameful incident. I'd been head over heels for Charlie back then. This was just about proving myself as a presenter and podcaster and general all-round capable human being.

So just in case Lucas was watching, and wondering how capable I really was, I set off to the wonky tree, watching the numbers on my wrist change the whole way.

*

When I was showered, coffeed and pastried, I found Joyce in reception.

'Did you manage to find those photographs?' I asked. 'I think Hannah – the woman I'm looking for – might have worked here. She might be in some of the pics. Not that I know what she looked like, but …'

'It's definitely worth a look,' Joyce finished for me, smiling. 'If only my mother was here to ask, eh? I did find the photographs, but Bonnie pilfered them. She's taken them into the lounge, I think. Shall we go and find her? I'm done here.'

Bonnie had spread out the photo albums across the sofa by the window.

'These are so funny,' she said as we joined her. 'Look at them all wading out into the loch with their binoculars.'

I looked at the photograph she was holding, which showed a group of men in huge wellies and those massive trousers people wear for fishing, knee-deep in the water. To the side of them were three more men in a little wooden rowing boat looking out into the centre of the loch with binoculars.

'I suspect that if there was a monster in the water back then, it would have stayed very far away from that lot,' I said and Bonnie laughed.

Joyce was looking through another of the albums. 'We're so lucky to have all these pictures,' she said.

'You should put them up somewhere, have an exhibition. I bet all your guests would love to see them.'

'That's a good idea.' Joyce handed me the open album. 'Here's a photograph of all the staff, outside the hotel. That woman in the middle with the platinum blonde hair was Mrs McEwan, the hotel owner who first saw the monster in 1933. She divorced her husband, which was quite the scandal back then, and got him to give her the hotel as part of their settlement. It went from being a run-down, quiet place to a booming business.'

'Thanks to Nessie?'

'Partly. She was doing all right before I think, but it was Nessie who put the hotel on the map.' She smiled. 'This one here, with the curly hair, is my mother.'

I looked at the chambermaid she was pointing to, who had sharp eyes and a slightly askew cap.

'And this one' – she pointed to a rather handsome chap in the back row wearing a waistcoat – 'is my father. He worked behind the bar, and did all the odd jobs around the place. He was still mending cupboards and putting up shelves for me well into his eighties.'

'They worked together?' I said in delight. 'Is that how they met?'

'It was. My mother was from Glasgow originally. She had quite a tricky upbringing.'

'They were soulmates,' breathed Bonnie. 'Drawn together.'

I snorted. 'You know I don't believe in soulmates.'

Bonnie gave me a knowing look. 'You will, one day.'

'Maybe knock the Colleen Hoovers on the head and try some

Stephen King,' I joked, as I turned my attention to the photograph. There were about ten young women lined up on the steps outside the hotel, including Joyce's mum, all wearing black dresses, white aprons and little caps and, along with her father, there were a couple of other men either side, also dressed smartly, and Mrs McEwan in the middle looking terribly glamorous and, I thought, rather proud. She should have been proud, I thought. What an achievement to run such a big hotel with so many guests, all on her own.

At the front, one of the maids, with hair tucked behind her ears, had a box hanging from round her neck, like a gas mask. She'd turned away from the photographer at just the wrong moment so I could only see the side and back of her blurry head. I squinted at her, realising the box she held was actually a camera too – though she wasn't taking the picture, obviously.

'There are names on the back, I think,' Joyce said, peeling back the cellophane that held the photo in place in the album and sliding it out carefully. 'Yes, there you are. Perhaps your Hannah is among them.'

On the back of the photograph was a stamp saying *Inverness Herald*, and a list of names. I scanned the names, written in beautiful copperplate handwriting, and my heart leapt as I saw the name Hannah.

'There,' I said in excitement, and Bonnie clapped her hands together with glee. I counted along the names. Hannah was one, two, three, fourth from the left, and I turned the photograph over.

'Which one is she?' Bonnie leaned over to see better, but I was disappointed.

'This one.' Hannah was the one turning away from the camera, her face hidden.

'How annoying that she's not facing the photographer,' Joyce tutted. 'Silly girl.'

I shook my head slowly. 'Clever girl,' I said. 'Clever Hannah.' I jabbed at the photograph. 'Look, she's got her own camera. She must have understood how it worked. She'd have known not to move when the photographer took the shot, but she turned her head anyway.'

'Well why would she do that?' Joyce asked.

Bonnie nudged me. 'Because she didn't want her face in a newspaper?'

'I reckon so.'

'Nice,' said Bonnie admiringly. 'So you think that's our Hannah then?'

I hid my smile at her saying "our Hannah".

'I think so.' I looked at the photograph again. 'I think we've found Hannah Snow.'

Episode one

The Monster in the Loch
Presented by Scarlett Simpson

In 1933, the world was changing. As Britain emerged from the Depression, there was a new president – Franklin D Roosevelt – in America, and a new chancellor – Adolf Hitler – in Germany.

In London, an up-and-coming MP – tipped to be prime minister one day – called Lawrence Wetherby, married his young bride Hannah Snow.

But by the end of their wedding day, Hannah had vanished. And 500 miles north, in the murky waters of Loch Ness, a monster was stirring.

Hannah and Lawrence Wetherby tied the knot in London in March 1933. There's no way of knowing if it was a love match, but we can draw some conclusions from the facts. Hannah was just 19, while Lawrence was almost 35. He stood to inherit his father's fortune on the condition he married before his 35th birthday. So did he love young Hannah or was she just someone who was willing to say "I do"?

We do know that Lawrence's younger brother, Simon, who'd

179

been in line to inherit, never got his hands on the fortune that could have been coming his way if his brother didn't walk down the aisle.

Was he annoyed? We'll come back to that.

Two days after the wedding, there were reports in the newspapers that Hannah had vanished – and that a hunt was being launched for the mysterious bride.

But a few short weeks later, Lawrence was writing off Hannah's disappearance as a "misunderstanding".

Had she returned after a few days away, like famous novelist Agatha Christie?

Had she never been missing at all?

Or was Hannah still missing – and Lawrence lying about her disappearance?

Odd? Undoubtedly. But it's about to get odder. Because Lawrence's brother Simon – who'd missed out on the family fortune – claimed his new sister-in-law's disappearance was not a misunderstanding. He said she had fled to Loch Ness, 600 miles north of their family estate in West Sussex.

And by Lawrence's 35th birthday later that same year, the MP himself had also disappeared. Where was he last seen? Loch Ness.

In 1933, Loch Ness monster mania was gripping the nation. YouTuber Lucas Austen shared the story …

To: SSimpson@britainlive.co.uk
From: RKostas@britainlive.co.uk
OMG, Scarlett! Have you seen social media? Everyone's really engaging with this story – loads of theories to investigate. Also a LOT of love for your YouTuber. He's got a well sexy voice. Send me a pic!

I'm absolutely bloody thrilled with the whole thing, and so are the bigwigs on the fifth floor – you were mentioned

in the daily briefing – and Kevin's totally pissed off. Well done, mate! Send ep 2 when you can.

Rx

@goldielocks7
@scarlett85 *Did Hannah ever really exist? Any proof?*

@FulhamfanDave
@goldielocks7 @scarlett85 *Dude, she literally said there was a photo of her in Loch Ness*

@goldielocks7
@FulhamfanDave @scarlett85 *how do we know it was her?*

@ladymarylovescats
@scarlett85 *when's the next episode?*

@jhbriggs
@scarlett85 *Lawrence was totally gay. Hannah was his beard. They probably did a deal.*

@wilsonalistair
@jhbriggs @scarlett85 *so why did she run off?*

@romcomqueen
@wilsonalistair @jhbriggs @scarlett85 *Maybe Hannah was a bloke, pretending to be a woman so they could be together. #soromantic*

21.32 Monday June 13
Charlie wrote:
Scar, WTF?!?!

21.33 Monday June 13
Charlie wrote:
SCAR? Why didn't you tell me you were doing this?

21.34 Monday June 13
Missed call
Charlie

21.35 Monday June 13
Missed call
Charlie

21.36 Monday June 13
Missed call
Charlie

21.37 Monday June 13
Missed call
Charlie

To: SSimpson@britainlive.co.uk
Cc: KTaylor@britainlive.co.uk
Date: Monday June 13

From: QuentinWetherby@Westminster.gov.uk

Dear Ms Simpson
You will be hearing from my lawyer
Regards

Wetherby

Chapter 21

Hannah

1933

In the car on the way to Inverness, Angus kept me in fits of laughter telling me stories about the people in the *Herald* office. He was doing impressions of the editor, and the sports writers, and he was very funny.

'How can you tell such tall tales and manage to drive at the same time?' I asked, impressed. He grinned at me.

'When I first started on the paper, my news editor was a chap called Fergus who owned a car but who was terrified to drive it. I quite quickly learned that offering to drive him around would get me noticed.'

'A smart move,' I said. 'You're more ruthless than I thought.'

Angus kept his eyes on the road, but I thought he looked pleased.

'Do you drive?' he asked.

'No, I've never learned. There was no call for it in London. If I needed a car I would …' I stopped myself just before I said that I'd often used Lawrie's car and driver when I needed to be somewhere. 'I'd take the bus,' I said weakly. 'Or the tube.'

Angus glanced at me, his expression unreadable. 'Yes.'

'So,' I said brightly, to break the awkward silence that had descended. 'I'm very excited to see the darkroom. Photography just seems like magic to me.'

'Oh it is,' said Angus. 'It's wonderful to watch the images appearing on the paper.'

And it really was. The office was beginning to empty by the time we arrived, with the staff finishing for the day, so there weren't many people around, and no one else wanted to use the room.

'We can take as long as we want,' Angus said, showing me inside.

It wasn't a large room, but it was packed with interesting things. There was so much to look at that I hardly knew where to start.

There were shelves lined with bottles of chemicals, and a sink, and counters with pots and trays stacked up at one end. There was a sort of washing line strung across one end where photographs hung, and the window was painted black and covered in a thick woollen blind. Not one crack of light was sneaking through the edges. Angus put on the electric light in the centre of the room.

'When we actually start work, I'll swap that light for the red one,' he explained. 'Do you have your film?'

Eager to get going, I handed over the film I'd finished taking photos of the monster hunters around the hotel.

'Right then,' said Angus. 'First up, we need to develop the film.'

He reached out and turned off the light and for a moment we were in total darkness. I was suddenly very aware of where he was. I could hear his breathing and feel the warmth coming from his body, in a way that I'd never been aware of Lawrie. Angus felt so real. So present. Lawrie always felt as though he was going dash off. Like a butterfly that had rested for a moment on a bush and then flew away.

'Here,' said Angus. 'Feel.' In the darkness, he felt for my hands and his fingers covered mine. 'Take the ends of the film and hold it in a curve.'

I couldn't see him, of course, but I knew that he was right in front of me, so close I could feel little puffs of breath on my face and smell his cologne. His fingers were warm and I liked how they felt on mine.

'Got it?' Angus said.

I cleared my throat. 'Yes.'

'Right.'

He moved away from me and I felt his absence like a cold draught of air. The red light snapped on and I could see him again. His eyes met mine and I felt a little thrill of anticipation. I liked this man, I thought. I really liked him. Not as I'd liked Lawrie, with a mixture of gratitude and admiration and duty. This was something very different. And oh, it was so complicated. But I liked him.

'Ready?' he said.

I had no idea what he was asking but I nodded with enthusiasm. 'Ready.'

Angus showed me how to rock the loop of film backwards and forwards in the chemicals, and move it from one tray to another, making sure the pictures were developing. I watched, fascinated, soaking in the knowledge.

'Are they dangerous?' I asked. 'These chemicals?'

'I wouldn't drink them,' Angus said. 'Shake it, that's right. Though that first one is just vinegar – you can smell it.'

I sniffed loudly. He was right. 'What now?'

'Now we rinse it out and hang it up to dry.'

'Like washing.'

'Exactly.'

Angus showed me what to do and I followed his instructions. I thought we would drape the film over the washing line at the end of the room, but instead he opened a cupboard and hung it in there instead.

'The airing cupboard?' I joked.

'Pretty much. There's a fan in there so it'll dry faster.'

'How long do we have to wait?'

'Fifteen minutes perhaps? We could go and get a cup of tea if you're bored.' He turned to gesture towards the door.

'No.' I reached out and stopped him with a hand on his arm. 'Let's stay here. Tell me what happens next.'

Angus cleared away the chemicals and then we both hopped up on to the counter, sitting with our legs dangling over the edge and our backs resting against the wall.

'The next bit is the really good bit,' he said.

He began to explain how the negatives were exposed on to metal plates, to get them into the newspaper, but though it was interesting I couldn't concentrate. My hand was next to his on the countertop and our little fingers were almost touching. And then they were touching. Had I moved my hand, or had Angus moved his? I wasn't sure. And now our fingers were entwined. Who had done that? I had no idea, but it was nice.

'And what about prints?' I asked, my voice slightly higher than usual. 'Mrs M wants to put some in a frame.'

'Oh well, making prints is different again ...' Angus began. I felt his thigh against mine and his shoulder touching my shoulder, and I breathed in deeply.

'Angus,' I said, interrupting him. He turned towards me, his face looking sharply defined in the red light. 'I like this. I like being here with you ...'

My words were stopped by him kissing me, suddenly and urgently, and I responded just as urgently. It was astonishing. Every nerve in my body fizzed and sizzled with the joy of it. Somewhere deep inside me I understood, finally, what this was supposed to feel like, and just as suddenly I realised why Lawrie had been so wretched. He must have felt this with Freddie but they weren't allowed to feel this way.

And then just as quickly, I remembered that Lawrie was my husband and there were more things to consider than the way my heart was pounding in my chest, and the way Angus's lips felt on mine.

I pulled away.

'I can't,' I said.

Angus looked appalled. 'I am so sorry,' he said. 'I didn't mean to ...'

'No, don't be sorry, I liked it.' I took his hand. 'I'm just ...' I took a deep breath. 'I'm married.'

Angus slid off the countertop and stood up, looking at me in bewilderment. 'You're married?'

'I am. Well, I was. But for a little while I thought he might be dead. But he's not dead. So I'm still married.'

Angus held his hands out. 'Slow down,' he said. 'I know. At least, I think I know.'

'You know?'

'Lawrence Wetherby?'

I stared at him. 'How did you ...?'

'I'm a journalist, Hannah. We are insatiably curious. And you asked all those questions about him.' He gave a little laugh. 'And your name is Hannah. It didn't exactly need Monsieur Poirot to crack the case.'

'You didn't say anything.'

'I only really put it all together a couple of days ago, when you said you didn't want to be in any photographs.' He frowned. 'Why did you run away? Did he hurt you?'

'No,' I exclaimed. 'Not physically. Humiliated me a little, I suppose. But I really don't think he meant to.'

Angus sat down on the counter again, a little further away from me this time.

'Tell me everything.'

I looked at him through narrowed eyes. 'Can I trust you?'

'Of course.'

'I know we're ...' I paused '... friends. But I have to know this won't go any further. There's too much at stake. And you said yourself, you're insatiably curious.'

'I swear,' said Angus.

And so, all the time wondering if I was losing my mind to tell such a juicy, salacious tale to such an ambitious reporter, I told him about walking in on Angus on our wedding day – but again, mindful of keeping Lawrie safe, I turned Freddie into another woman.

'So you really thought he was dead?'

'I really thought I'd killed him.'

'You didn't check for a pulse?'

I shook my head. 'I was sort of frozen. I didn't know what to do. And erm, Lawrie's, erm lover' – I winced at the word – 'told me he was dead.'

Angus took my hand. I knew I shouldn't let him, but I wanted to. 'None of this is your fault, Hannah.'

'It feels like it's my fault.'

'What I don't understand is why you're still here,' Angus said, just as Davina had when I'd told her. 'Why you've not gone back to London now you know he's alive.'

I shrugged. 'It's complicated.'

'Because you know he's seeing someone else?'

'Because of that and other reasons.' I looked down at his fingers in mine and wished hard that I could stay here, holding his hand, forever. 'There is a lot at stake.'

'Money?'

'Money, reputation.' I sighed. 'The Wetherbys are different from you and me, Angus. When they walk into a room, someone always opens the door for them. Things just happen the way they want them to.' I thought about Lawrie and Freddie and bit my lip. 'Well, not always. Some things are out of their control. But mostly things happen the way they want them to. And Lawrie is a sweet man. He's kind and he's clever and he's funny, but ... Someone once told me he was careless and they were right. He is careless but only because he's never had to be careful, do you see?'

Angus nodded.

'But Lawrie's brother Simon. Oh, Simon is a different kettle of fish. He is bitter and entitled and he will use his privilege to hurt anyone who stands in his way.'

'And you are standing in his way?'

I made a face. 'I am.'

'So why not just go back to London and stand in his way with Lawrie by your side?'

'I can't. It's too late.'

'You're not worried they'll track you down and make you go back?'

'A little. I don't want them to find me.'

Angus was looking at me closely. 'You don't look worried.'

I gave him a little smile. 'It's better for Lawrie if I'm not there. He'll get his inheritance now.'

I thought about mentioning the photographs, then changed my mind. Instead I said: 'I brought something with me. Something Lawrie will want me to keep private. I feel safer knowing I have it.'

'What is it?' Angus's eyes gleamed in the red light. He really was insatiably curious.

But I shook my head. 'It's complicated,' I said again.

Angus looked at me for a long moment. 'You should tell your story,' he said.

'No.'

'Honestly, you should. Get ahead of the news.'

'What does that mean?' I shook my head. 'I don't want anyone to know I'm here.'

'Someone will find you eventually,' he said matter-of-factly. 'Even if you left Drumnadrochit and went elsewhere, someone would track you down and tell your husband. And it's a good story, Hannah. A really good story. People would want to read it. They'd want to know why the bride of Lawrence Wetherby – a man who could be prime minister one day – has been forced to work as a maid in a hotel.'

'I've not been forced to work in a hotel,' I said, prickly with the way his mind was working.

'If you tell the story, then you're in charge,' Angus pointed out. 'You're controlling the narrative.'

'Stop talking this way,' I said, sliding off the countertop and standing up. 'This is my life, Angus. And Lawrie's life too, and you don't understand what's at stake.'

'Then tell me,' he said.

'And have you write it all down and use it to get your fancy job in Edinburgh?' I snapped. 'I don't think so.' I looked at the door. 'I should go.'

He jumped off the counter and took my hand. 'Don't go,' he said. 'I'm really sorry. I got a bit carried away.'

'The story isn't always the most important thing,' I said. But I didn't pull my hand away.

We looked at each other for a moment, and then he smiled. 'You're the bravest woman I've ever met, Hannah Snow.'

'I'm not brave. The first sign of trouble and I ran for my life.'

'That took guts,' Angus said. His expression softened. 'I'm sorry that Lawrence cheated on you and humiliated you on your wedding day.'

'I'm not,' I said. 'I was when it happened but I'm not now.'

'Was it awful?' Angus said.

'That moment when I walked into the room and saw them together was awful. I was shocked and upset and embarrassed.' I felt my cheeks flush as I thought about it and I gave a little shiver. 'But Lawrie ...' I searched for the right words. 'Lawrie didn't mean for it to happen that way.'

Angus looked dubious. 'Really?' he said. 'You're not angry with him?'

I shook my head. 'Honestly, the horror of seeing him on the floor, and thinking I'd killed him. I still have nightmares about it, even though I know he's alive. I can't tell you how guilty I felt.'

Angus was thinking, his brow furrowed. 'Lawrie's inheritance just said he had to be married before his 35th birthday, am I right?'

'Yes.'

'He didn't have to marry you?'

I made a face. 'Goodness, no. I never met his father and from what I've heard about him, I can't imagine he'd think I was a suitable match.'

'So why didn't Lawrie just marry the other woman?'

I looked at him blankly. 'What other woman?'

Angus laughed. 'The one in the hotel room, you goose. The one who Lawrie was cheating with.'

'Oh that one,' I said.

'Yes, why didn't Lawrie marry his lover?'

I rolled my eyes. 'It's complicated,' I said.

Chapter 22

Scarlett

Present day

'Are you worried?' Lucas asked me the next day. 'About the solicitor thing?' We were eating lunch by the side of the loch. Our paths just kept crossing, and we'd both been checking out Joyce's selection of sandwiches at the same time, so Lucas had suggested we eat together, and I'd agreed.

I peeled a bit of tomato out of my wrap and shook my head. 'Not really. What can Quentin Wetherby do? It's not illegal to investigate a mystery from ninety years ago.'

'No, I guess not.' Lucas frowned. 'I just get the impression he's not a very nice person. You should be careful.'

'Really? What do you know about him?'

'Not much. Nothing actually. I just have a vague memory of someone at work talking about him.' We were sitting on a huge boulder by the edge of the water, Lucas a bit lower down than I was. Now he turned his head and looked straight at me. 'Want me to do a bit of digging?'

'No,' I scoffed. 'He's just a rich old man who's not used to anyone saying no to him.'

'If you're sure?'

'Of course I'm sure.'

'What's on the agenda for episode two, tomorrow, then?'

I put the last bit of sandwich into my mouth and leaned back against the smooth boulder. 'Loads of people on social media are speculating that Lawrence was gay, and Quentin mentioned that too, so I thought I'd explore that a bit. It's interesting because Quentin said he didn't want anyone thinking his uncle might have been gay.'

Lucas tutted. 'Dinosaur.'

'That's what I thought, but then I found a photograph of him draped in a rainbow flag at Pride, alongside his son and his son's husband.'

'Interesting,' said Lucas.

'I think it was just an excuse – a fairly weak reason as to why he didn't want us to do a podcast.'

'It's particularly strange when you think that Lawrence being gay would put Hannah in the frame again,' Lucas pointed out. 'If she killed him in a jealous rage after finding out he preferred men.'

'True.' The wind blew my hair across my face and I pushed it out of the way and sat up again. 'I'm not sure how I could ever know for sure that he was gay, mind you. It was illegal in the 1930s, obviously, so he would have hidden it.'

'That's true. Makes things trickier for you.'

I shrugged. The response to the first episode had made me feel more confident about the programme and I knew from experience to follow my gut when it came to investigations. 'It's okay. I've got lots of other things to look at. I want to see if there are any more mentions of Hannah in Joyce's staff records, and I thought I might just go back to basics. See if I can find a death certificate for Lawrence, or one for Hannah.'

'That's a good idea.' Lucas jumped to his feet, brushing crumbs from his lunch onto the ground. 'I'll let you get on with it all, then.'

Today Lucas was wearing a T-shirt that, at first glance, I'd thought bore the classic Ramones logo. When I looked more closely I'd realised it was actually the names of the families from *Game of Thrones* instead of the band members. I didn't want him to go because I needed to ask him something, so I pointed to his shirt.

'Is it your love of dragons that makes you interested in the monster?'

'What?' He looked confused.

'*Game of Thrones*. It's all dragons and stuff, isn't it? Like *Lord of the Rings*?'

He laughed. 'Not just dragons.'

'Really?' I raised an eyebrow. 'I caught a bit of an episode once and believe me there were a lot of dragons.'

'You're not a fan?'

'Of dragons?' I laughed. 'Nope. I much prefer monsters.'

Lucas chuckled.

'Actually, Lucas, I wanted to apologise for being short with you when you offered to help.'

'No need.'

'I was a bit snappy.' I sighed. 'It's not an excuse, but I do my podcast with Charlie. He's my ex. And we just won an award and he accepted it and didn't even mention me, and then he took this job behind my back and told me I was replaceable.'

'He sounds nice,' Lucas said mildly, making me smile.

'And my dad wants to arrange some work experience for me, because he thinks my job is just a hobby, and my boss is a dick ...'

'You've got something to prove, right?'

I grinned. 'Right.'

'I listened to your first episode,' he said. 'It was really good.'

'You listened?' I was chuffed.

'Of course. You need to believe in yourself a bit more.'

I rolled my eyes. 'I know.'

'And you need to carry on with your research, because I want to know what happens next.'

'Ah,' I said. 'I might need a bit of help, there.'

Lucas gave me a glance that could only be described as indulgent. 'Yes?'

'I really need to find out who claimed the inheritance. That's the key to this whole thing. Quentin said the files had been lost or destroyed. But I thought there might be some record elsewhere. Wills are public records, aren't they?'

'They are.' He grinned at me. 'Want me to see what I can find out?'

'Would you?' I made a face. 'I'm really aware that I was rude when you offered help, then used your login for the Met website and now I'm asking for more.'

'It's fine, honestly. Might take me a couple of days, mind you.'

'Are you sure?'

'Totally sure. Stop trying to talk me out of it.'

'I feel bad that you're spending all your time on my investigation and not your own.'

'I've got to be honest, I've lost interest in the monster of Loch Lochy a bit,' he said. 'Your mystery is more appealing.'

'There's nothing you need to be back in Edinburgh for?' I said, casual as anything, not really sure why I was interested. Lucas had told me he lived in the city but hadn't said much more about his life outside accounting and podcasting. 'No one missing you?'

Lucas shrugged. 'Arwen probably hasn't even noticed I've gone,' he said cheerily. 'She's not bothered if I'm there or not.'

Arwen. Who was Arwen? I pictured some willowy Viking-esque goddess and then realised I was actually picturing Astrid and snorted. Quietly.

'My neighbour's feeding her,' Lucas was saying. 'She spends most of her time on her flat roof anyway. She likes it up there because it catches the sun, and she can watch the birds.'

'Arwen's a cat,' I said, suddenly understanding.

'I did have two, but Legolas died last year. I think Arwen likes it better without him, though.'

'I thought you were talking about your girlfriend,' I said. 'I thought it was a bit strange that she needed your neighbour to feed her.'

Lucas gave his hearty laugh. 'No. Though sometimes the disdainful looks she gives me do remind me of my ex-wife.'

'You're divorced?' A tiny bit of me wondered if he'd dropped that into the conversation to let me know he was single. And that tiny bit of me was surprisingly pleased about it. 'Was she a podcaster?'

'No, she was accountant.' Lucas sat back down on the boulder. 'We got married when we'd known each other six months.'

'Whoa, that doesn't sound very accountant-like.'

'Rude,' he said with a smile. 'But you're right. It was ridiculous.'

'Were you soulmates?' I asked, thinking about Bonnie and her belief that her great-grandparents had been drawn together.

'Christ, no. I'm not sure I believe in soulmates.' He gave a little self-conscious laugh. 'I was living in Singapore when I met her. She was British too – had a great job in finance.'

'Clever.'

'So clever. Very ambitious. I liked that about her actually.'

I felt uncomfortable, and not just because the rock I was sitting on was digging into my coccyx. This ex-wife didn't sound like someone I'd be friends with.

'One weekend when we'd been together a few months, we hired a car and went for a drive out to this nature reserve,' Lucas went on. 'It wasn't far – nowhere is very far in Singapore. But I was showing off a bit and I hired a fancy car, to impress her.'

'Right,' I said, not sure where he was going with this story.

'I crashed.'

'Oh shit.' That wasn't what I'd expected. 'Was it your fault?'

He shook his head. 'Actually, no. Someone jumped a red light and smashed into the side of us. But Maya, my wife, she was hurt quite badly. She was in intensive care and she needed an urgent operation to stop her internal bleeding.' He swallowed. 'Everyone thought she was going to die.'

I stared at him in shock. 'She didn't though, did she? She didn't die?'

'No, she survived. Made a full recovery.'

'So what …?'

'Before she had the operation, she asked me to marry her.'

'Oh, Lucas.'

He grimaced. 'We didn't think she'd make it,' he said. 'And I felt so guilty, Scarlett. And you know, I did love her. I just didn't know her very well.'

'So you said yes?'

'Oh I did better than that,' he said with a groan. 'I got a special licence and we got married there and then. Maya in her hospital bed and me in my jeans.'

'Blimey.'

'It was very romantic; everyone said so.'

'Sounds it.'

'We didn't even live together at the time. But it was exciting at first, getting to know each other, setting up home.'

'Most people do that before they tie the knot,' I pointed out.

'I know.'

'So how did it end?'

'We were married for about 18 months, though the first few Maya was still recovering,' he said. 'When she got back to work, back to reality, she started trying to change the way I looked, and the way I dressed.' He snorted. 'She didn't like the films I watched or the TV shows.'

'Not a fan of *Game of Thrones*?' I said.

'She liked shows where smart women walked fast down corridors wearing really high heels. Like *The West Wing* and *The Good Wife*.'

'Ooh I love *The Good Wife*,' I said. 'Sorry, not helpful.'

'And then she met someone else. They were a much better match.' He looked at me. 'She just didn't bother telling me about it until I found them together.' He did that little laugh again. 'Everyone knew about it apparently. Just not me.'

I sat up straighter, outraged on his behalf.

'That's awful,' I said with passion. 'Cheating is unforgivable.'

He looked at me. 'Did Charlie cheat on you?'

'No,' I said. 'He's got lots of faults, but that wasn't one of them. But when I was a teenager, my dad cheated on my mum.' I sighed at the memory. 'I'd bunked off school. God, it was so ridiculous. I'd had a fight with my best friend and I didn't want to see her, so I went into town instead and wandered around a bit, then went to the cinema in Leicester Square.'

'What did you see?'

I winced. 'The Pokémon film,' I said.

Lucas guffawed and I prodded him. 'Oi, I was only 14 and I was in my school uniform. There was no way I'd have got into anything more exciting. Anyway, after the film, I was walking back to the station and I saw my father and this woman coming out of a pub on the Strand. He hailed her a taxi and when she got in, they kissed. It was like something out of a romcom.'

'Shit, that's horrible,' said Lucas. 'Did you tell your mum?'

'Nope. They still don't know I know. But they obviously worked things out, because a few weeks after – in the holidays – I went to stay with my gran for a couple of days. And when I came back my dad worked abroad for ages. And eventually he came home and everything was all right again.' I swallowed. 'But I hate thinking about him being so blatant, you know? And my mum just at work, none the wiser. It's a shitty thing to do.'

Lucas patted my hand gently. 'It is.'

'So what did you do when you found out Maya had done the dirty?'

'I came home, bought my flat, met up with old friends, made new ones, licked my wounds, got on with life,' he said. 'Started a business – Maya would have approved of that, but she wouldn't have liked my YouTube videos. She's still in Singapore, I think. We're not in touch anymore.'

'Brutal,' I said.

'I like to think of it more as a learning experience.'

We looked at one another for a moment and I felt something like understanding pass between us. Then Lucas stood up again. 'Right. I'm off to investigate inheritances. See you later in the bar to catch up?'

'Absolutely,' I said with genuine and fervent enthusiasm. 'See you later.'

I watched him wander off up towards the hotel, then turned my attention back to the water. It was so nice sitting here I wasn't really in a hurry to hit my laptop again, though I knew I should. Instead, I pulled my knees up to my chin and watched one of the Nessie-hunting boats skim across the waves. I could count four of them on the loch at this moment, each stuffed with excited tourists, eager to catch a glimpse of the monster.

'Do you know we had more monster sightings during lock-down than in a normal year?'

I looked round to see Joyce standing next to me, looking out over the water.

'Really?'

'By some way, actually.'

'Maybe Nessie prefers it when it's quiet,' I said. I put my chin back on my knees. 'Before I came here, I thought it was just a story. But now I'm here, I can almost believe it.'

'I know what you mean,' Joyce said. 'There's just so much water.'

'More than all the rivers, lakes and reservoirs in England and Wales put together,' I said. I was proud of that fact, which I'd put into my first episode.

'Apparently, the loch is big enough to hold every person on earth, ten times over,' Joyce added.

'Bloody hell. That is big,' I said. The boats were almost out of

199

sight now, racing down the loch past the ruins of Urquhart Castle further along the shore. 'There could be anything down there. It would almost be more surprising if there wasn't a monster.'

'Perhaps your Hannah drowned?' Joyce said. She looked quite sad at the thought. 'The water is so cold that if she fell in, she'd not have lasted long.'

'I'm going to look up death certificates this afternoon actually. See if they shed any light.'

'I hope she didn't die,' Joyce said. 'Not then. Not like that.'

I smiled. 'She seems a bit more real now I've seen that photograph of her, even though we couldn't see her face. Now we know she was living here and working at the hotel.'

'She does.' Joyce sighed. 'Oh goodness me, I've forgotten the reason I came to find you down here.'

'What's up?'

'Someone called for you. They wanted to know if you were a guest here.'

'Who was it?'

She shrugged. 'He didn't give a name.'

'But it was a man? Was he posh?'

She screwed up her nose. 'Hmm. Maybe. It's hard to tell on the phone isn't it?'

'Did you tell whoever it was that I was here?'

Joyce looked affronted. 'No I did not. I wouldn't give out information like that.'

'Ah it doesn't matter really. Now the first episode's gone out, they know I'm up here anyway.'

'Well, I won't be telling anyone anything – you can be sure of that.'

'Thanks, Joyce,' I said. I slid off the boulder and stretched. 'I guess I'd better get on with looking up these death certificates.'

'Come on into the lounge and I'll make you a cup of tea while you work. Maybe a wee slice of carrot cake?'

'I will,' I said. 'I just need to make a phone call.'

My dad answered straightaway.

'Hello, darling,' he said. 'I was just about to message you.'

'How come?'

'I listened to your thing. Your little programme.'

I was stunned into silence. Dad had never really shown an interest in my work before.

'Scarlett? Are you still there?'

'I'm here,' I said faintly. 'You listened?'

'Yes, well I was at the News Broadcasters' Annual Lunch, you know?'

I didn't know. 'Yes,' I lied.

'And people kept telling me about it. George said it was excellent.'

I had no idea who George was, but I liked the sound of him.

'Thanks, George,' I muttered.

'So, I listened. And he was right.' He paused. 'It was very good, Scarlett. Well done. I'm looking forward to the next episode.'

Inexplicably, I found myself choked with sudden tears. I blinked furiously and tried to swallow the lump in my throat.

'Thank you,' I croaked. 'That means a lot.'

'I'll tell you what you should do,' my father went on. 'You need to get all the legal stuff to hand. Births, deaths, marriages, the whole shebang. Track down this inheritance. That way you'll know what's what. I've got a great chap at work who can help if you like …'

I gave a little laugh. Back to normal then. 'It's fine, Dad. I know what I'm doing. I'm just about to track down all that stuff, funnily enough.'

'Okay, but honestly, he's very good, Scarlett.'

'It's fine.' I said firmly. 'Anyway, Dad. I do have a favour to ask.'

'What's that?'

'This Quentin Wetherby – the MP Charlie called you about?'

'Oh yes?' My father sounded suspiciously offhand.

'I know I asked you not to look into him, but I've changed

my mind. Could you check him out for me?'

'Of course, darling.'

'Have you already started?'

Dad chuckled. 'A little bit. Just put out a few feelers, that's all.'

Feeling warm towards him thanks to his compliments, I simply shook my head, glad he couldn't see me.

'Thanks, Dad,' I said.

*

The carrot cake was excellent; the searching of records was not. I found Hannah's birth certificate – she was born just before the First World War broke out in 1914. And I found Lawrence's too – he was born in 1898, which made the age gap between him and Hannah seem so much more extreme.

I found their wedding certificate, too, from March 1933. And then … nothing. No death certificate for either of them in England. So, I searched the Scottish records. Nothing. On a whim I went back to England to search for Quentin Wetherby and found him – born in 1950 when his father, Simon, was 50, the old dog. Simon must have been married more than once. With nothing better to do, I found the divorce records and searched for Simon Wetherby. He'd been married three times – the final time when he was 75 and his wife – who to my amusement was called Simone – was 40.

'Dirty git,' I said to myself.

With the divorce search page still on my screen, I deleted Simon and typed in Lawrence.

And to my absolute astonishment, there was a divorce record. Hannah Wetherby divorced Lawrence Wetherby in 1938 on the grounds of desertion.

'Oh my goodness,' I said out loud, ignoring the startled glances of the other guests in the lounge. 'Hannah and Lawrence were both alive in 1938. Hannah didn't murder Lawrence.'

Episode two

The Monster in the Loch
Presented by Scarlett Simpson

The response to the first episode of The Monster in the Loch *has been amazing, and I'm really pleased that so many of you are as interested in cracking this mystery as I am.*

In this episode, I'm going to be exploring the theory that many of you have suggested – that Lawrence Wetherby was gay. Some people have suggested that Hannah didn't exist – that she was an imaginary wife to give Lawrence a veneer of respectability in a time when being gay could have got him sent to prison and subjected him to some pretty grim "treatments" aimed at changing his sexuality.

It's a good theory, but we know Hannah was a real person. She was born in 1914, and brought up in England and partly in India where her father worked.

Others have come up with the idea that Hannah and Lawrence's marriage was a sham. That they'd done a deal to marry. Perhaps Hannah too was gay, and they could each protect the other's reputation, claim Lawrence's large inheritance and live separate lives. Again, it's a good theory but why then would Hannah run off on their wedding day? If indeed she did – remember Lawrence claimed that was a misunderstanding. And why would Lawrence then vanish just a few weeks later – before his inheritance was due?

I'll be examining these theories and more, later in the episode.

But first, I want to share some new and exciting information I've discovered.

When we were first made aware of this mystery, we were told that Hannah murdered Lawrence. We were told that though he wasn't declared dead at the time, there was no doubt that Lawrence died in 1933. And that Hannah was to blame.

So of course, I turned to the official records. And I found ... well not much really. I couldn't find death certificates for either Lawrence or Hannah, though they must have passed away by now, clearly.

What I did find, though, was a divorce record. Lawrence and Hannah got divorced – on the grounds of Lawrence's desertion – in 1938. Five years after Lawrence was said to have died at the hands of his wife.

Does that prove Hannah's innocence? I'm pretty convinced. Are you?

From: SSimpson@britainlive.co.uk
To: KTaylor@britainlive.co.uk
Date: Wednesday June 15

Hi Kevin,
Did you hear episode 2? What did you think? Social media is buzzing and Robyn's getting listener data but she said it looks good.

I got your message saying you wanted to talk to me? I'm going to bed now, but give me a call tomorrow.
Scarlett

21.34 Wednesday June 15
Missed call
Charlie

21.35 Wednesday June 15
Charlie wrote:
Pick up, Scar. It's important.

21.40 Wednesday June 15
Charlie wrote:
Scarlett, please. Call me back.

Chapter 23

Hannah

1933

Tuesday May 9, 1933
Darkness in Drumnadrochit
Words and pictures by the Herald's Loch Ness correspondent,
Ann O'Shawn

   The parties and late-night jollity at the Drum Hotel are continuing. The music still plays until the wee small hours. The drink still flows. The excitement and thrills of each day carry on.

   And yet …

   Around the edges of the celebratory atmosphere, a darkness is lurking. The stakes are higher than ever, and suddenly the hunt for the Loch Ness monster seems less like an enormous jape and more like … well, a hunt.

   And what is the cause of this shift? This increasing tension? Money.

   Of course.

Wealthy industrialist Joseph Fox has repeated his challenge. He'll pay £20,000 to the first man – or woman, though to this reporter's weary eyes, there are few women among the hunters – who can prove the existence of the monster.

But there's a catch.

He wants the monster caught and brought to him in London.

That caveat to the challenge meant some of the more creative monster hunters have packed up and gone home. The men who were spotted making footprints on the beach have upped and gone. So too has the chap – a doctor no less – who was rumbled taking a photograph of the top of a child's toy boat as it bobbed about in the water, and making it seem like the neck of a huge beast. It's clear that the staff at the Drum Hotel are sharp-eyed and quick-witted and not much gets past them.

But Joseph Fox's challenge has brought more serious monster hunters to the loch. Big-game hunter Balthazar Webster has been commissioned by the Daily Post in London to track down the beast. And to Mr Webster, the hunt for the Loch Ness monster is not an adventure, or a story to tell his friends in years to come. It's much more important than that.

With so much money at stake, and with men taking to the water each day with harpoons and whaling equipment, instead of cameras and a box of sandwiches, things are getting serious in Loch Ness.

'Davina, have you moved any of my things?' I asked. 'I can't find my notebook.'

Much to my delight, we were moving back into the hotel. With the departure of many of the amateur monster hunters, things were a bit quieter, and Mrs M had allowed us to leave our temporary dormitory behind. Though Davina and I were to share my tiny eaves bedroom now – somehow Mrs M had managed to squeeze another bed in there.

I didn't mind sharing really, but now we were packing our things, I couldn't find everything and that made me unsettled.

'What things?' she said. 'I took your apron that was on the end of your bed to the laundry with mine, but you asked me to.'

'Nothing else?' I was cautious about asking her because Davina tended to get a bit defensive if you pushed her too far.

'Why would I take your things? I don't want any of your rotten things.'

Like that.

'It's just a notebook. I must have left it somewhere,' I said. But I wasn't sure. It was the notebook I'd filled with stories from our Sunday soirées. They'd died a death since the monster hunters arrived so I wasn't completely sure when I'd last seen it.

I felt in the pocket of my apron for my other notebook – the one where I wrote all my Ann O'Shawn stories. It was there, thank goodness. I knew it would be; I didn't let it out of my sight, just in case someone picked it up and realised I was the reporter who was writing all the behind-the-scenes stories. I liked both my jobs and I didn't want to lose either of them.

'Come on,' Davina said, her arms full of her belongings. 'Let's get this back to the main house.'

'Right behind you.'

She headed off out of the dormitory and I started piling up my things. Could I manage them in one trip? I thought, sizing up my pile with a critical eye. Probably. I didn't have much and I could put everything in my overnight bag – the one I'd brought with me from London.

I bent down to pull it out from under the bed but it wasn't there.

'Strange,' I muttered. I definitely remembered it being there this morning because it had been poking out and I'd pushed it back underneath with my foot. Maybe I'd pushed it too far? I got down on to the floor and, lying on my tummy, wriggled a little way under the bed so I could look properly. Because it was only a camp bed, it was low to the ground and quite tricky to manoeuvre myself under but I did it. And to my dismay saw that my bag wasn't there. Brilliant, now I had to get out again. I started to push myself backwards and as I did I felt the floorboards creak as someone came in the building. Davina no doubt, or one of the two other girls who'd been sleeping in the dorm with us.

But from where I lay, wedged under the bed, I saw a man's legs and shiny shoes. Not a monster hunter; that was for sure. They all wore boots and waders. And it wasn't Tobias, because I'd recognise his battered shoes. So I stayed where I was, quietly, waiting to see what the man did.

He paused for a moment by the door, and then started walking along the room. As he reached my bed – where I lay, trying to keep my breathing regular and quiet, he dropped something on to the floor and kicked it underneath the bed. It was my bag. My bloody overnight bag. I gripped the handle with sweaty hands and waited for his footsteps to fade away and the door to the dormitory to swing shut. Then I wriggled out – covered in dust – and ran to the window to see who it was. But there was no one around. Whoever it was must have slipped away into the woods. If he'd gone towards the hotel he'd still be visible.

Confused by what had happened, and with my heart thumping, I went back to my bag and examined it. Inside was my notebook – that's where it was – but I couldn't understand why anyone would have taken the bag, and then returned it. Perhaps it was a mistake? Perhaps it had been a monster hunter after all?

Still, I told myself firmly, no harm done. That faint feeling of misgiving I had wasn't necessary. I put my bag on the bed, and began filling it with my belongings. But as I did, I saw the little embossed luggage tag on the handle. My bag had been a wedding gift from Aunt Beatrice and the label bore my initials – my new initials that was: HW. Would whoever had taken it have seen the letters? No, surely not. And even if they had, no one would make the leap from HW to Hannah Wetherby. No one at all.

Except Lawrence, I thought.

Or Simon.

Who both wore expensive shoes like the pair I'd seen from my hideaway.

'Oh pull yourself together, Hannah,' I said out loud. 'You're being ridiculous.'

With a sudden burst of energy I yanked the luggage label off the handle and shoved it into the pocket of my apron. I'd drop it into the fire when I was next in the lounge. Then I picked up my few belongings and put them into the bag. There was no need for me to be so jumpy. No need at all.

*

Hoisting my bag on to my back, I left the outbuilding and walked along the path towards the hotel.

'Hannah?'

I shrieked in fright.

'Gosh, sorry, I didn't mean to startle you.'

Angus had come up behind me. I turned round to face him, my heart pounding with the shock and, I suspected, the pleasure and squirmy embarrassment of seeing him for the first time since we'd kissed.

'I came to speak to Balthazar Webster,' he said. 'I thought I'd collect your latest film while I was here.'

'Were you in the woods?' I said, glancing at his shoes – which were black and similar to the ones I'd seen in the outbuilding, much to my consternation. Except Angus's were splattered with mud. 'Did you see anyone else in there?'

'No,' he said. 'Just Webster and his crew by the loch.'

'No one wearing smart trousers and shoes?'

'No,' he said again. 'Are you all right, Hannah?'

'I'm fine,' I lied. I took a deep breath, getting myself together, and smiled at him. 'It's good to see you.'

'You too.' He reached out and touched my hand very briefly

with his. 'I'm glad we can still be friends.'

'Me too.'

We stood there for a second, smiling at one another, and I thought how very unfair life was that I'd met Lawrie before I'd met Angus.

'Do you have a film to give me?'

'Oh, yes.' I'd almost forgotten. I put my bag on the ground and began searching through the side pockets for the little canister, taking the chance to have a good look at Angus's shoes, cursing my own nerves as I did so. This was Angus. Why would he take my bag? I looked all the same, though, but one man's shoes were very much like another's, and I still wasn't sure.

When I eventually found the film, I stood up again and handed it to Angus. 'There are a lot of photographs of the new people: Balthazar and his lot. They've got harpoons, have you seen?'

'I have.' Angus shuddered. 'I'm not sure why some folk's first instinct is to kill.'

'Is it fear, do you think? Are they scared of the beast so they want to kill it before it kills them?'

'I think it's arrogance,' Angus said. He looked out in the direction of the water. 'They want to prove they can take on an enormous monster.'

I snorted. 'I met a few men like that in London. Always right, always more knowledgeable, always faster, stronger …'

'More powerful.'

'Exactly.' I sighed. 'When actually they're not even more powerful than the water. Yesterday one of their boats capsized and if it hadn't been for a few men from the village who were out sailing and who rescued them, they'd all have drowned.'

Angus chuckled. 'Aye, sounds about right.'

'I have to go. I need to take my things up to my room and then get the dining room ready for dinner.'

'Me too. Have to get back to Inverness.'

We stood awkwardly for a moment, then I walked away towards

the hotel, expecting Angus to follow – after all, his car must have been parked there. But instead, he went in the opposite direction, back down to the water.

Feeling tired all of a sudden, I dragged myself across the lawn and inside the building, then up the back stairs all the way to the top and my little room. The door was ajar, so I expected to see Davina inside, but when I pushed it open, the room was empty.

Empty and completely turned over.

The bed covers had been pulled back, the mattresses were askew, the tiny bedside table had been tipped over. Even the rug on the floor was crumpled, as though someone had picked it up and put it back down again carelessly. Someone had been rummaging through this room, looking for something.

With a gasp and a horrible feeling of dread, I dashed to the fireplace and felt for the film of Lawrie and Freddie. It was still there, thank goodness. I put it back, with shaking hands, then I sat down on my messy bed. What was happening here?

'What's this? Why is the room like this? Why did you do this?' Davina stood in the doorway, hands on hips, staring at the upheaval.

'This wasn't me, Davina.'

She raised an eyebrow. 'Who else could have done it?'

Bile rose up in my throat and I swallowed. 'I think it might have been Angus.'

Chapter 24

Davina was looking at me like I had two heads.

'You're making no sense,' she said. 'What's going on?'

'Someone did this. Someone's been in the room.'

She made a face. 'And you think it was Angus?'

'Yes.'

'Surely it could have been Tobias and the others when they brought the extra bed up?'

'Really?' I wasn't convinced. 'It's a complete mess.'

'It's a tight squeeze,' she said, looking unconcerned by the chaos. 'They could have just bumped the table and moved the rug.'

'Yes, but …'

'You seriously think Angus is the one who did this?'

'Yes.' I looked up at the ceiling in despair.

'You think that sweet Angus raided our bedroom?'

It did sound a little silly when she put it like that, but I just knew that someone had been in here.

'Why would he do that?' Davina said.

'I think he was looking for … well, for whatever I took from

Lawrie.'

Davina was still frowning. 'The treasure? But how would he know about it?'

'It's not treasure,' I said. Davina gave me a hard stare and I shrugged. 'I told him who I was.'

'Really?'

'Really.' She sat down next to me, and I leaned my head on her shoulder. 'I told him I was married to Lawrie and everything that's gone on.'

'And you told him about the treasure?'

'It's not …' Ah what was the use? It didn't matter anyway. 'Yes, I told him that too.'

'Why?'

'Why did I tell him?' I felt my cheeks flush. 'Because …'

'Because you like him?'

'No,' I said, sitting upright. 'Well, yes. I thought I could trust him.'

Davina looked round the room at the mess. 'But you can't?'

'Apparently not.' I shook my head. 'I'm such an idiot.'

'You're not the first to have your head turned by a pretty face and you won't be the last,' Davina said, sounding much older than her years. 'You really think he did this?'

'He wanted me to tell my story to the newspapers,' I said in a small voice, feeling very young and foolish. 'He said they'd find me eventually – wherever I was – and he wanted me to "get ahead of the news". I said no and he seemed fine with that, but he needs a big story, Davina, to get a new job in Edinburgh. What if I'm that big story?'

'Then he's a terrible person.'

'He's not, he's just … ambitious. He says the story is the most important thing.'

Davina looked unconvinced. 'Right.'

'And it is a good story,' I said. 'MP's missing wife hunting for the Loch Ness monster. I don't blame him, really.'

'Don't you?'

'Yes, I do,' I groaned. 'Damn him.'

'So do you think he found it?' Davina's eyes were flicking from the beds to the floor, to the walls. 'Did he find the treasure?'

I groaned. 'There is no treasure, Davina.'

'That's not what you said.' She sounded sulky. 'You said you'd taken something precious.'

'I did. But it's not treasure.'

She narrowed her eyes. 'So you lied?'

'No.' I shook my head. 'It doesn't matter.'

'It does, if my bedroom is being torn apart by some half-baked reporter looking for treasure that doesn't exist,' Davina said.

'It might not have been him. It mightn't have been anyone. You said that yourself.' I felt prickly, as though we'd been arguing, when we hadn't really.

'We'll never know, will we?'

'Then I'll speak to him,' I said. 'Confront him. Tell him I know what he's up to.'

'So you're sure it was him?'

'Who else could it be?'

'There are photographers and reporters all over this hotel,' Davina said, rolling over so she was on her stomach on the bed. She sounded positively gleeful. 'Any one of them could have recognised you.'

'I cut my hair,' I said weakly. Davina raised an eyebrow. 'And I call myself Snow, not Wetherby.'

'Oh, that will definitely have them stumped,' she said. 'You're a master of disguise.'

'Shut up, Davina,' I wailed. 'A second ago you were saying it was just a mistake, then you were saying it was definitely Angus because he'd sell his own mother for a story, and now you're saying it could have been anyone.'

'Why do you care?'

I stared at her in disbelief. Hadn't she heard anything I'd said?

'Because I'm scared Lawrie will track me down, and I feel stupid for trusting Angus – that's why I care.'

Davina shrugged. 'But if there's no treasure, then there's no risk is there?'

She held my gaze, and I felt she was almost willing me to crack and tell her what I'd taken.

But I didn't.

Instead, I got up and put the bedside table back the right way up.

'Are you going to help?' I asked, rather snappily considering none of this was Davina's fault.

Davina slid off the bed and onto her feet. 'No,' she said. 'I need to be in the dining room.'

And without a backwards glance she disappeared out of the bedroom.

Honestly, she could be so frustrating at times.

My emotions were alternating between being furious with Angus and Davina, or whoever else might have ransacked our bedroom, and being scared that Lawrie would suddenly arrive, or even the police.

Had I done anything illegal? I wasn't sure anymore. I hadn't killed Lawrie but I had hurt him – I'd not imagined him being out cold on the floor, and he himself had said he'd bumped his head. Perhaps I could be arrested for that? Or for running away? My brain frantically whirled through all the options as I started putting the room back in order. I pulled up Davina's bedclothes and my own, and straightened the rug, wondering all the time if I should leave. Should I just pick up my bag and go?

But, a little voice inside me said, it would be better to stay. After all, it was exciting here. It was thrilling to be in the front-row seats for this monster hunt. To watch the reporters and photographers come and go. And of course to have my own writing published too. That simply would never have happened if I'd stayed in London.

And perhaps Angus hadn't been in our room. Perhaps no one had. I gave my bedcover a last twitch, knowing I was being naïve. Someone almost certainly had been here, and I definitely hadn't imagined those feet I'd seen from under my bed in the dorm.

The fact was, though, I wanted to stay. And perhaps that was foolish but so be it.

I just had to take a few precautions.

*

I called the newspaper that afternoon, to give them my latest Ann O'Shawn story, from Mrs McEwan's office as usual. I'd lied and told her I needed to check on my elderly aunt regularly and asked if it would it be all right if I used the phone. She took the cost of the calls out of my wages, but I didn't mind. I was more than covering that expense with the money I was making as Ann.

Like always, I spoke to Joanie, the editor's assistant and read out my story for her to type, her fingers clattering on the keys. But today, when I'd finished dictating my article, she started to say her goodbyes, and I stopped her.

'Joanie?' I asked. 'Do you think I could use the darkroom one day? Maybe tomorrow after work? Or at the weekend?'

'For newspaper pics? I thought Angus dealt with your photographs?'

'No, this is something different. My own thing. I don't want to bother Angus.'

'Hold on, let me check.' I heard her put down the receiver on the desk and I waited impatiently until she came back on the line. 'There's nothing booked in the diary so I don't see why not. It's kept locked but if you come about six o'clock tomorrow, I'll leave the key for you.'

I leaned against Mrs McEwan's desk, relieved.

'Do you know how to use the room?' Joanie asked. 'Angus showed you, didn't he?'

'Yes, I know what to do.'

'Is it a present?'

'Pardon me?'

'Are you giving Angus one of your photographs as a present? You're very sweet, the pair of you. He's smitten. He never stops talking about you.'

I took the receiver from my ear for a second and clasped it against my chest. Angus was smitten? Why then would he have ransacked my bedroom and taken my bag? None of this made sense.

I put the receiver back to my ear again and said: 'He's a nice man.'

'He's a good man. Honest. They're not all like that.'

'Yes,' I said, wondering if that was true.

'But I won't say anything to him,' Joanie said, and I could hear the smile in her voice. 'Oh to be young again. On the hunt for your happily ever after.'

I laughed because she was all of ten years older than me.

'I'm not sure I believe in a happily ever after,' I said.

Joanie tutted. 'You should know better than that.'

I felt a squirm of fear. Did she know my "happily ever after" with Lawrie had ended in disaster? 'What?' I said. 'What do you mean?'

'I mean the Loch Ness monster,' she said. 'You should know that just because you don't believe in something, doesn't mean it's not there.' She laughed again. 'Just because you don't believe in happy endings, doesn't mean there isn't one waiting in the wings for you.'

I chuckled, mostly in relief.

'That's what my friend Davina says.'

'You should listen to your friend Davina, because he's smitten, I tell you,' she said.

'We'll see.'

The following day, which was my day off, I took the precious film canister out of its hiding place and, feeling like I was doing something wrong, even though I wasn't, I took the bus to Inverness. There I sat in a café round the corner from the *Herald* office until I saw Angus walk past, with his battered bag slung over his shoulder like usual. My heart lifted a bit when I saw him, which annoyed me. How could it be that my head said one thing, while my heart said another? Once again I felt a rush of sympathy for Lawrie, whose head had obviously told him to marry me, while his heart yearned for Freddie.

Thinking of Lawrie and Freddie made me spring into action. I left a few coins under my saucer for the waitress and marched off to find the key Joanie had left for me.

Once I was in the darkroom, with the door locked and the film in my hand, I began to doubt myself. Maybe it would be better for everyone if I destroyed these photographs, I thought. Maybe I should pull the film out, turn on the light, and ruin them forever.

But I'd meant it when I'd told Angus they would keep me safe. And perhaps it hadn't been Angus who'd gone through my things. Perhaps Lawrie was still none the wiser about where I was. But I felt, deep down, that I needed these pictures more than ever.

Just in case.

I'd been worried that I wouldn't remember what to do once I got to the darkroom, or that I'd ruin the film accidentally, but luckily everything went smoothly.

And by ten o'clock, I was on the last bus back to Drumnadrochit, bumping along the road with my bag on my lap.

Back at the hotel, I checked to see that Davina was busy in the dining room, then darted upstairs to our bedroom. I shut the door and rolled the rug up and wedged it under the frame, to stop anyone coming in, and then I pulled the photographs out of my bag. There were quite a lot of them. Some of them were blurred or out of focus but there were a couple that were shockingly candid. Lawrie and Freddie's faces were both soft with love, though perhaps just because I knew Lawrie, I could see pain and worry in his eyes, too.

As the photographs had appeared in the developing fluid, I'd been struck again by how beautiful the men were. And how intimate. There was no mistaking the situation they were in for anything other than what it was. It made me feel guilty and angry and a little embarrassed all at the same time. Most of all, though, I just felt so very, very sad for Lawrie. He was a good man. He was kind and he was clever and he was stuck in an impossible circumstance because the law said he couldn't love who he wanted to love.

A few months ago I'd have said that the law was right, because that was all I'd ever been taught – that two men loving each other was wrong. But now I saw that Lawrie and Freddie were just like any other couple. And I may have still been furious with Freddie for his lies and manipulation, but I forgave them both.

Well, not quite. But I was definitely on my way to forgiving them.

First of all, I put the envelope with the negatives in the fireplace again. I put it on the little jutting-out shelf and weighed it down with a pot of rouge that I never used.

Then I took the larger envelope and I went outside in the dark, having taken the lamp from beside the back door. I hurried along the path to the outbuilding where we'd been sleeping and went inside. The beds were all gone now, back inside the hotel and squeezed into bedrooms to increase their capacity, and the room was bare. Where my bed had been, I knew there was a loose floorboard – I'd felt it wobble when I was hiding from the man who'd taken my bag.

I took the lamp and the envelope and trod over the boards until I found the loose one. Then I put the lamp on the floor, got on my knees and prised the board out. I dropped the envelope inside the gap and put it back. Then I got up, brushing the dust from my skirt, and headed back outside into the dark garden.

As I walked along the path, back towards the bright lights of the hotel, I thought I heard footsteps behind me.

I turned, holding the lamp up to light the darkness. But there was no one there.

'Hello?' I called, my voice a little shaky.

No one answered. So, with the hairs on the back of my neck prickling, and my hand tight on the lamp's handle, I dashed back to the safety of the hotel.

Chapter 25

Scarlett

Present day

Kevin wasn't a punctual man as a rule. He was never at his desk before 10 a.m. He started meetings late. He kept us waiting for announcements and appraisals and even for cups of tea on the rare occasions he offered to make them.

But at 8.59 the day after episode two was aired, my phone rang.

I drained my coffee to give me a boost, and answered with a cheery "good morning". Surely I'd finally have impressed him? Loch Ness was trending on Twitter after the show went out – he couldn't argue with that.

'Scarlett,' Kevin said.

'Hi, Kevin. How are you? Did you hear episode two?'

There was a pause. 'I did.'

That wasn't the enthusiastic congratulations I'd been expecting. My confidence wavered a little. 'What did you think?'

There was another pause and if my confidence wavered before, now it plummeted. 'I'm pulling the show.'

I laughed. 'Pulling it?' I was bewildered. 'I'm not following. Pulling it where?'

'Cancelling it,' Kevin said bluntly. 'It's cancelled.'

'What? No, you can't. Why would you? Look at the analytics, Kevin. Listener numbers are great, and the podcast's been downloaded thousands of times already. Did you check the socials last night? Everyone was talking about it …'

'It's out of my hands, Scarlett,' Kevin said. 'I'm sorry.'

'You don't sound sorry,' I pointed out. He really didn't. He sounded, well, *pleased* was the word that sprang to mind.

'I really don't have a choice,' he said in a way that told me he absolutely did have a choice.

'You're in charge. Of course you have a choice.' I was annoyed that my voice sounded shrill and upset. Any second now he'd tell me to …

'Calm down, Scarlett. You know how these things work. Something else came up and you've been bumped. It's just bad luck.'

'Bumped from the schedule?' My heart lifted a little. 'That's fine, I can still do the podcast though? Upload the episodes instead? I can do them more frequently, if you like? Get a bit of momentum going. We could do a listen-along on social media. They're always fun.'

''Fraid not,' Kevin said. 'No podcast. No space on the schedule. I'm pulling the plug.'

'This is bonkers.'

'It's show business,' he said, so animated that I could almost see him doing jazz hands.

'Oh, bog off, Kevin,' I said.

'May I remind you, Scarlett, that I am your manager. The show is over. I need you back at your desk on Monday. I've put you on the *Breakfast Show* rota.'

'Fine,' I said, even though it was anything but.

'I'm going to get that work experience lad to book you a return

222

train ticket. I'll make sure he emails it to you.'

'Fine,' I said again.

'Good,' Kevin said. 'All right, then, Scarlett. I'll see you on …'

Without waiting to hear him say goodbye, I ended the call and threw my phone down in fury. What on earth was he thinking? The mystery of Hannah Snow's disappearance had really captured people's interest. Our *Cold Cases with Burns* podcast had really good listener numbers – excellent, in fact. We were often in the top twenty charts on release day, though we didn't always stay there. But Hannah's story had propelled me into the top ten for the first time. What part of "trending on Twitter" didn't he understand? I had to call Robyn and find out what was going on.

'You look absolutely fuming.' Bonnie slid on to the chair opposite me where I sat in the hotel lounge. 'What's got you so angry?'

'My boss.'

'Same,' she said, tilting her head in Joyce's direction.

I gave a half-hearted chuckle. 'What's she done?'

'Nothing,' Bonnie said. 'I just wanted to make you laugh.'

She was so sweet. I gave her hand a squeeze. 'Thank you.'

'I listened to episode two,' she said. 'It's amazing. I'm so pleased Hannah's innocent. But I knew she would be.'

'You did?' I smiled. 'I wasn't always sure.'

'Yes, because I like her.'

'I like her too.'

'When's episode three?'

'Urgh,' I groaned. 'Never.'

'What?' Bonnie looked horrified. I opened my mouth to explain just as my phone rang. It was Robyn.

'Rob, what the absolute …'

'I know, Scarlett, I'm so sorry.'

'What's happened? Why has Kevin stopped the show?'

'No one knows. Kevin just keeps saying it's one of those things.'

'No explanation? Have you spoken to anyone else?'

'I went to see Malc.' Malc was Kevin's boss, the head of news

223

and current affairs.

'And?'

'Malc said Kevin's decision was final.'

'This is awful, Robyn. It was going so well.'

'I'm bloody furious.'

'And there's really nothing you can think of? No reason? What's replaced it? Something that's time-sensitive?'

'Urgh.' Robyn sounded despairing. 'A repeat of *The Tunes that Made Me.*'

'A repeat of our knock-off version of *Desert Island Discs*?'

'You got it.'

'This makes no sense.'

'None at all.' Robyn sighed. 'Kevin had a meeting yesterday afternoon. And when he came back he said he was pulling the show. No discussion.'

'Who did he meet? Was it to do with that?'

'I don't know. Maybe? He went out somewhere though. It wasn't anyone in the company.'

'Great,' I said. 'Probably sodding Quentin Wetherby has bribed him to take me off the air.'

Robyn laughed for a second then she stopped. 'Oh my God, what if Quentin Wetherby bribed him to take you off the air?'

'That's crazy, Rob.' I thought for a second. 'Though, is it crazy?'

'I have no idea – you're the one who met him. Would he do something like that?'

'He did send me a fairly threatening email,' I said.

'And you're only mentioning this now, because …?'

'Because it was rubbish. He said I'd be hearing from his lawyers, but as if doing a podcast about a 90-year-old mystery is a crime.'

'Well, perhaps that's what his lawyers told him, so he's gone down a different road and got you cancelled.'

'Charlie rang me about four times last night – maybe that's what it was about.'

'Call him,' Robyn said. 'Then call me back.'

'Okay.'

I ended the call and looked at Bonnie who was staring at me.

'What's happened?' she asked.

'My radio show's been cancelled.'

'The show about Hannah? Why would they cancel it?'

'I don't know.'

'Are you leaving? Before you've found out what happened to her?'

'Looks like it.' I picked up my phone and scrolled to Charlie's number.

'You can't leave.' Bonnie looked distraught. 'All my friends at school are desperate to know what happened to Hannah and Lawrence. Daisy Philpott thinks Lawrence murdered Hannah and then did a runner to the Costa del Sol.' She looked round in a shifty fashion then leaned forward like she was telling me a secret. 'Daisy's dad lives in the Costa del Sol. She knows about that stuff.'

I looked at Charlie's number and thought about calling it, but I couldn't bear to speak to him and hear him being all smug. So instead, I sent a voice note.

'Charlie, Kevin has cancelled my show and I think Quentin Wetherby might be responsible. What do you know?'

Charlie hated voice notes, which gave me a small amount of satisfaction.

'Is that Charlie who you did your podcast with?' Bonnie asked. 'Your ex?'

'That's him.'

'But that's different from the show you've been doing about Hannah, right?'

'Yes.'

'Is it easy to do a podcast?'

I smiled. 'Possibly a bit too easy,' I said, nodding my head in the direction of a group of young men standing outside the window recording each other.

Bonnie rolled her eyes. 'Thought it was. So why not do another podcast. Like the one you did with Charlie, but just you. Do Hannah's story yourself. Loads of people are interested. Did you see Loch Ness was trending on Twitter?'

'I did see,' I said. 'But I can't, Bonnie. I need to go back to work.'

'But you don't like your job.'

'Who told you that?'

'You did.'

'No I didn't.'

She sighed. 'Body language, isn't it? When you talk about it, your shoulders hunch up like this …' she showed me '… and you look really sad. But when you talk about Hannah's story, you're all perky and eager.'

'Perky and eager?' I said dubiously. 'Really?'

'Totally.'

I groaned. 'I don't like my job much. Well, I like the actual job and I did like being at work until Kevin became my boss. Now it's pretty much unbearable.'

'Don't do it then.'

'I've got rent to pay, and other bills, Bonnie. I can't just leave.'

'Being a grown-up really sucks.'

'It does.'

My phone rang and I groaned to see Dad's name on the screen. 'As if my day could get worse,' I said. 'Hi, Dad.'

'Scarlett.' He sounded sharp and business-like, which was unusual.

'Is everything okay? Is Mum okay?'

'Your mother's fine. Everyone's fine. It's you I'm worried about.'

'Me? Why?'

'I asked around about that Quentin Wetherby chap. Had a drink at lunchtime with Chris Neilson. Remember him?'

'No.'

'Oh, Scarlett, of course you do. Economics editor for years. Then he went to Sky, I think. Or was it Channel 4? No, it was Sky. Pretty sure it was. He did the lunchtime business news, with

226

that woman with the short hair.'

'Dad,' I said, sounding faintly desperate. 'Dad, tell me.'

'He said Wetherby is a nasty piece of work. Friendships with Russian oligarchs, which have all fallen apart now. Being investigated by parliamentary standards. Offshore accounts. Murky tax arrangements. He could even owe thousands to HMRC apparently, but he's like Teflon. They just can't make anything stick.'

'He told me things weren't great financially,' I said. 'He blamed Brexit.' Out of the corner of my eye, I saw Bonnie slide off her chair and go over to see Lucas who'd just wandered into the lounge. Today he was wearing a *Star Wars* T-shirt with his jeans. He'd tied his hair back and trimmed his beard. He looked, I couldn't help but notice, like he was trying to impress someone. He waved at me and I waved back.

'Scarlett, are you still there?' My dad sounded cross.

'Sorry, Dad, I think the signal just dropped out for a second,' I lied. 'What were you saying?'

'I was saying it could be Brexit, or it could be Ukraine, the pandemic – all sorts,' Dad said. 'But the fact is, he's up to his eyeballs in debt, and he's aligned with some rather unsavoury people. I really don't want you having anything to do with him.'

I sat up a bit straighter. 'Well that's not your decision.'

'Scarlett, you're the one who asked me to check him out.'

He had a point. 'I don't like being told what to do,' I said, sulkily. 'Anyway, who cares if he's in debt? He's not paying me anyway.'

'He's in a very bad position, financially and professionally,' Dad said.

'So?'

'So, he's desperate, Scarlett. And desperate people do desperate things.'

'Well, it doesn't matter now anyway,' I began, then stopped as I thought about how pleased Dad would be if I told him I was going back to London.

'Why doesn't it matter?'

'It … another … podcast …' I said, holding the phone away from my mouth so it sounded like the signal was going.

'You're breaking up, Scarlett,' Dad said. 'I'll call you back.'

'Nope,' I muttered. I ended the call and turned my phone off, dropping it down onto the table with a thud.

'Hi,' said Lucas, appearing next to where I sat.

'Hi,' I said, feeling my spirits rise at the closeness of him.

'Tense?' He nodded at my discarded phone.

'Dad.'

He made a face. 'Bonnie said they've cancelled your programme?'

I put my head on the table in dramatic fashion. 'They have.'

'That sucks.'

'It does.'

There was a pause as we both considered how much it sucked.

'I had a bit of a nose into Quentin Wetherby,' Lucas said. 'He's way overstretched financially and he's on his knees. Brexit's been the nail in the coffin, but he's been chancing his luck for years. The standards people in parliament are sniffing round, too.'

'My dad says he owes a lot of money.'

'Word is he's about to get a huge tax bill. It'll finish him off and if he doesn't pay up, I reckon he could be looking at prison.'

'Shit,' I breathed. 'So he needs the inheritance to pay for it?'

'I reckon. And if you were to prove Hannah didn't steal it, then he won't have a claim and he'll lose everything.'

'That's not my problem.' I shrugged. 'I'm not proving anything anyway, now.'

'No,' Lucas said. 'And to be honest, it's probably for the best. From what I've heard, Wetherby isn't the sort of person you want to get on the wrong side of. He could make your life very difficult.'

'Like getting my radio show cancelled?'

'You think he's behind that?'

'Possibly.'

'You know how men like him are, Scarlett. I don't think he's evil or even bad. He's just … entitled. He wants things to happen a certain way and he'll pull every string and exploit every contact to make it happen.'

'Well he's got his way with this,' I said. I put my face into my hands and rubbed my eyes. 'It's over.'

'There will be other programmes,' Lucas said. 'I bet once you get back to work, opportunities will come flooding in. You've more than proved yourself.'

The thought of being back at my desk, while Kevin micromanaged me, felt like a weight on my shoulders. I leaned my head against the back of the booth we were sitting in and closed my eyes.

'It doesn't matter now, but I do have some news,' Lucas said.

I opened one eye. 'What news?'

'I've been digging into the inheritance like you asked me to.'

'And?'

'Lawrence inherited the estate.'

'Lawrence did?' I opened both eyes and sat up straighter.

'That's what it says.'

'Not Hannah?'

'Nope. She wasn't a beneficiary – the will was written before she and Lawrence married. Though obviously she'd have inherited once Lawrence died, if they'd stayed married.'

'What did Lawrence get?'

'Everything. The money, the country house, the shares, the whole lot.'

'What about Simon?'

'He got a trust fund. He was hardly left destitute.'

'But Hannah didn't get anything?'

'Not nothing. She got some money in the divorce settlement and Lawrence actually left her something in his will, too. And there's an interesting clause in it.'

'In Lawrence's will?' My heart was beating faster with the thrill of getting somewhere. 'What is it?'

'Hold on.' Lucas took out his phone and found the notes. 'Yes, it says "to be paid to Hannah Wetherby, nee Snow, or whatever name she is known by".'

'Whatever name she is known by?'

'That's right.'

'She changed her name?'

'Sounds like it.'

'This is brilliant,' I said. 'Every tiny piece makes the jigsaw even more interesting. I could mention this in the episode ...' With a crash, I remembered that I had no episode to record. No podcast to promote. It was done.

'I need to go and pack,' I said, rubbing my head. 'Thanks for doing all that work, even though I can't use it.'

Bonnie, who'd been sitting talking to Joyce the whole time Lucas and I were chatting, darted across the room as I got up and barred my way.

'Don't go,' she said.

'I need to pack my stuff.'

'Don't go back to London.'

'I told you, Bonnie, if I don't go, I'll lose my job.'

'And you told me you don't like your job.'

'That doesn't mean I don't need it.'

'Do you though?'

'Yes.'

'No, but do you actually? Because Hannah's story was in the top ten podcasts, right? Loch Ness was trending on Twitter. Literally everyone in my school is talking about it.'

'Everyone?'

'Well, a few people. Loads of people reckon it would make a brilliant Netflix show. You know like a true-crime thing?'

'That's flattering but it doesn't pay my rent.'

'It does. Not the Netflix thing – that's just dreaming, right? But the top ten bit does.'

'It doesn't pay me, though, the ad revenue goes to Britain Live.'

Bonnie gave an overdramatic sigh, like I was being completely stupid.

'I told you – you should do the podcast yourself,' she said. 'Then you'll get the money and it won't matter if you lose your job. You can totally find another job later. A better job.'

I stared at her. 'Bonnie, I don't think …'

'She's right.' Lucas stood up behind me. 'You should do this yourself. Do a *Cold Cases* job on it.'

'Without Burns.'

'Definitely without Burns. Come on, Scarlett. Didn't I say you should have more faith in yourself?'

I chuckled, thinking about how annoyed Charlie would be. But then I shook my head. 'It's a lovely idea, but I can't.'

'Really?'

'It's too risky,' I said. 'I've already lost everything when Charlie and I broke up and my job changed. I can't handle the thought of losing everything again, even if everything is a shitty flat-share and an even shittier job.'

'I'm sorry to hear that.'

I was quite pleased with how sorry Lucas sounded. But he wasn't half as sorry as I was.

'I'm going to pack,' I said, swerving round Bonnie and heading for the door before either of them saw the tears in my eyes. 'I'll see you both later.'

Chapter 26

Hannah

1933

Friday May 12, 1933
Bright days and dark nights
Words and pictures by Ann O'Shawn

Daytime at the Drum Hotel is a hoot. We've been blessed with temperate weather for the time of year, and so each day parties of monster hunters, always accompanied by my fellow reporters of course, make the short trip to the shores of the loch.

Once there, they clamber into boats and set out across the water. Often so many boats cast off at once it is like a flotilla setting off to war. Which, in a way, I suppose it is.

Sometimes the men trudge the path at the edge of the waves, binoculars firmly fixed to their eyes.

They break frequently for tea, for cakes and a slap-up picnic lunch, provided by the willing staff at the hotel who traipse down to the loch carrying platters and folding tables every day. The parade of waitresses picking their way across the *lawn and down to the edge of the water is quite a sight to see.*

In the afternoon it's hip flasks that are passed around. The atmosphere becomes more jovial. Shouts and laughter fill the air. It's as though they've taken their camaraderie off the golf course and transplanted it into a boat on the loch.

As for Mr Balthazar Webster, the big-game hunter. Well, he ploughs his own furrow. He and his team keep slightly apart for most of the day, dressed in safari get-ups and large hats that must do a marvellous job of keeping off the African sun, but are less suited to a stiff Highland wind. Chasing Mr Webster's hat has become something of a sport.

It's all top fun and games.

During the day.

At night, the atmosphere shifts. This reporter, dear reader, is skittish and jumpy. Startling at strange noises and scared of her own shadow.

More than one member of the hotel staff has told of a feeling of being watched as they walk from the hotel to the loch in the evening as the day is ending and the trees are creating odd shadows on the ground.

Tempers fray in the hotel bar as monster hunters taunt one another, rubbishing their sightings and mocking their evidence, while hotly defending their own.

Perhaps it's not the monster we should fear?

Meanwhile, in London, Mr Joseph Fox – he of the £20,000 challenge – sits back, assured his money is safe. For now, at least.

The jazz still plays into the early hours. But for how much longer can this carry on?

I put down the newspaper and sighed, worried I'd over-egged it. I'd let my own nervousness seep out on to the page and I wasn't sure that was how real journalists wrote. All the reporting I'd read, all the accounts of parliamentary sessions and meetings with foreign dignitaries, were factual and, I had to admit, rather dry. But wasn't that how it was supposed to be? I was pleased to see that not much of my article had been changed though. Perhaps, the editor liked what I was doing.

I wasn't sure Mrs M would, though. Business was still booming but perhaps all this talk of shadows lurking would put people off. Once again I thanked my lucky stars she didn't know that Hannah Snow and Ann O'Shawn were one and the same.

'Hannah?' Mrs McEwan bellowed from the dining room. 'Hannah!'

I froze, standing beside the reception desk. What did she want? Had she worked it all out?

Slowly, with a feeling of genuine dread, I folded the newspaper up and walked towards the dining room.

'Oh Hannah, thank goodness.' Mrs M was trying to move a table, shoving it with her backside. She was a bit red in the face and more than a little sweaty. 'We need to squeeze another table in here.'

'Another one?' I looked round at the cramped dining room, that was already full to the brim with tables.

'Aye, we're booked up again.'

'We are?'

'Yes, come and help me move this.'

I went to where she was standing, braced my legs, and together we pushed the table with our bottoms over to the side of the room.

'That'll do,' she said. We stood up and she surveyed the space with satisfaction. 'We can get another six-seater in there. That'll do for now.'

'There are more guests coming?'

Mrs McEwan grinned. 'Ghost hunters.'

'Ghosts? Heavens.'

'Oh I know, it's completely ridiculous but these chaps want to investigate something or other they read in the newspaper about strange noises and whatnot.'

I laughed out loud. 'I think those are metaphorical ghosts, not actual spooks.'

Mrs McEwan gave me a conspiratorial nudge. 'Right enough, but who am I to turn down more guests, eh?'

I couldn't argue with that. 'Where will they sleep?'

'Tobias has distempered the outbuilding, fixed all the broken floorboards and put down some rugs, and they're going in there.'

'He fixed the floor?' I thought about the photographs I'd hidden underneath the boards.

'Yes, some of them were very wobbly, he said. But they're all secure now. He said he's put that many nails in them, he's more likely to start wobbling than they are.'

So I'd not be getting my hands on the photographs any time soon, I thought. Still at least I knew no one else would come across them either.

'I'm charging a reduced rate for that room as it's more of a dormitory,' Mrs M continued. 'They think they're getting a bargain, and I have ten guests I wouldn't otherwise have.'

'You are a very clever businesswoman, Mrs M,' I said with genuine admiration.

'I know.' She looked pleased with herself. 'Actually, Hannah, that reminds me. Do you know who this reporter is? The one who's writing all these articles? Ann someone or other?'

'Ann O'Shawn.'

'That's the one. Who is she?' Mrs McEwan frowned. 'Because there isn't a woman among the journalists staying here and I asked your friend Angus …'

'He's not my friend,' I muttered and Mrs M gave me a quizzical look but she didn't question me further.

'I asked Angus and he said he didn't know her. Even though she writes for the same newspaper.'

I shrugged, not quite meeting her eye. 'No idea,' I said.

'Well, I hope I get to meet her because I'd like to shake her by the hand,' she said.

'Me too,' I said honestly.

'That Ann O'Shawn doesn't work at the newspaper,' Davina said, appearing behind us. 'Do you need a hand with those tables?'

'No, we're all done now, dear,' Mrs M said. 'What's that about Ann O'Shawn?'

All this chatter about my alter-ego was making me nervous. 'Anything else you need us to do, Mrs M?'

'I phoned the newspaper and asked to speak to her, and they said she didn't work there,' Davina said.

'Why did you want to speak to her?' I stared at her, feeling sweat prickle on my brow. 'What did you want with her?'

Davina's eyes widened, looking startled at my interest. She rubbed her nose. 'Nothing important,' she muttered. 'Just something about those men with the umbrella stand, making the footprints.'

'Right,' I said. We looked straight at each other and I thought, for a confusing moment, that my mistrust of her was reflected back at me in her eyes.

'Hannah, could you go and check how Tobias is getting on with the outbuilding?' Mrs McEwan said, breaking the tension between Davina and me.

'Sure,' I said.

I straightened my apron and walked away, but when I glanced back over my shoulder, Davina was watching me.

Unsettled I headed off down the path towards the outbuilding. I'd just got about halfway – close enough to hear Tobias and the other men shouting to one another as they worked – when I heard footsteps behind me.

I turned, expecting to see Davina. But there, looking oddly out of place in his waistcoat and suit, was Simon Wetherby.

'Hello, Hannah. Fancy seeing you here.'

I stepped back, wanting to be further away from his self-satisfied smile and glanced down at his smart, shiny shoes. Shoes I'd seen before.

'It was you,' I said, suddenly understanding. 'You took my bag, and ransacked my bedroom?'

'Oh so many accusations,' Simon said, sticking his bottom lip out like a sulky toddler. 'That's not a very nice way to greet your favourite brother-in-law.'

'What are you doing here?'

He looked me up and down. 'I think the real question is what are you doing here?' he said, sounding amused. 'Are you ...' his voice dripped with disdain '... a maid?'

I lifted my chin. 'I'm a chambermaid and a waitress, and I work on reception,' I said. 'We all chip in here. We're like a family.' I tilted my head in mock sympathy. 'Not your family, obviously. We all like each other here.'

'Do you?' He sounded smug and I didn't like it. 'It doesn't seem like that to me.'

'What do you want, Simon?' I asked, trying to sound much less frightened than I felt. 'I'm very busy and I don't have time for your games.' I clasped my hands behind my back so he wouldn't see them shaking.

'I want whatever you stole from my brother,' he said. 'Maybe he's all right with you stealing from our family and running away to the ends of the earth, but I'm not.'

'I didn't steal anything,' I said honestly.

Simon's face was growing redder. 'You're a liar,' he said, pointing towards me vigorously. 'You're both bloody liars, you and my brother.' He stepped closer to me, stumbling a little as he did. I could see the broken veins on his cheeks and smell alcohol on his breath and I realised he was drunk. That scared me even more. Lawrie had told me stories about what an awful drunk his brother was.

'I don't know what you're talking about,' I said, trying desperately to stop things escalating. I wondered if Tobias would hear if I shouted for help. But then I'd have to explain what was going on and that would be a disaster. 'Listen, why don't we go and sit

237

down by the loch and have a chat?'

Simon reached out and grabbed my wrist. 'I'm not going anywhere until you give me what you took.'

I yanked my arm away. 'Stop it,' I hissed at him. 'Stop.'

'I know you took something. Something precious. And as you and my brother have cheated me out of my inheritance, I deserve this.'

'We didn't cheat you out of anything, Simon,' I said, my fear replaced by irritation now. 'I wanted to give you some of the inheritance, but Lawrie said you'd drink it, or gamble it away because you'd already done that with your trust fund.'

'Is it any wonder I drink, with a brother like mine?' Simon said in disgust. 'He owes me.'

'He owes you nothing.'

Simon ran his fingers through his hair, visibly gathering his thoughts. 'Why are you here?' he said. 'Lawrie's told everyone you're in Sussex.'

I wasn't sure what to say. I glanced round hoping someone would be coming, but the path was empty.

'What are you hiding?' Simon said.

'Nothing,' I said but I sounded weak and I knew he wouldn't believe me.

'You've got twenty-four hours,' he said. He pulled out his pocket watch – one I recognised as belonging to Lawrie and which Simon must have swiped – and he checked the time. 'Meet me here tomorrow at eleven o'clock and bring the treasure.'

'The treasure?' I blinked at him. 'There is no treasure, Simon.'

He shrugged. 'I know you took something precious from Lawrie when you ran away. Either you give it to me tomorrow at eleven, or I'll call the papers and tell them where you are.' He laughed. It was a horrible laugh, full of malice. 'Imagine if all these monster hunters found the missing MP's wife instead of the beast. What fun.'

'You're a pig,' I said.

Simon grinned. 'I want the treasure.'

Defeated I sat down on a tree stump next to the path. 'There isn't any treasure,' I said again, feeling weary.

'But I know you took something.'

I looked up at him. 'Is that what Angus told you?'

'Who's Angus?' Simon looked genuinely confused.

'Angus Reid?' I said. 'The man who told you I was here.'

Simon screwed his nose up. 'It wasn't a man. It was a young woman: Davina Campbell. I had to get my assistant to speak to her at first. Couldn't understand a word she was saying.'

'Davina?' I said, feeling the betrayal like a sharp pain in my heart. 'Davina told you I was here?'

'She said you'd taken something from Lawrie and if I gave her one hundred pounds, she'd tell me where you were.'

'One hundred pounds?' I repeated. 'I thought you were on your uppers. Did you even have one hundred pounds?'

'You have to speculate to accumulate, Hannah,' Simon said. 'She assured me whatever you'd taken was worth much more.'

'Did she?' I shook my head. Davina was a master of manipulation; that was for sure.

'Tomorrow at eleven,' Simon said again. 'Or I'll go to the papers and tell them the wife of the man tipped to be PM one day is scrubbing floors in a hotel.'

My mind was racing. 'Fine,' I said. 'Tomorrow at eleven o'clock.'

'How do I know you won't run again?' he said, narrowing his eyes. 'You've done it before.'

That was exactly what I'd been planning to do. I shrugged. 'You don't.'

'Where is Davina?' he said. 'I'll speak to her. She can keep an eye on you.'

'Seriously?'

He loomed over me where I sat, his face twisted with annoyance. I turned away from his boozy breath. 'Don't play me for a fool, Hannah Snow. Tell me where she is.'

'She's in the dining room,' I said.

'Then I'll see you tomorrow.' Slightly unsteadily, he turned and lurched off along the path towards the hotel.

I got to my feet, feeling slightly unsteady myself, though from the shock rather than any alcohol. I had to find Angus, and I had to find him before Davina found me.

In a rather unladylike fashion, I hitched my skirt up and took to my heels, running over the lawn, then through the trees and down to the loch.

Angus was on the shore, speaking to some of Balthazar's men. He looked earnest but happy. He was covering this story as a commission for a national newspaper and he was putting a lot of effort into it. In fact, I suddenly thought, he was making this work instead of telling my story. He was doing this for me.

'He's a clever chap.' I turned to see Balthazar himself standing beside me, his safari hat flapping gently in the breeze.

'Angus?'

'I've done a fair few interviews in my time,' Balthazar said thoughtfully. 'But he's been the best. He really listens. I found myself telling him things I'd not mentioned in previous interviews. I trust him.'

I glanced over at Angus again. 'That's good to hear,' I said.

'Now tell me,' said Balthazar. 'Was that Simon Wetherby I just saw you talking to?'

I took a step backwards, so surprised was I to hear him say Simon's name. 'Simon? Erm … yes. How do you know Simon Wetherby?'

'We were at school together. Here on holiday is he?'

'Holiday?' I sounded stupid to my own ears. 'Yes, holiday.'

'Well, let's hope he stays out of my way,' Balthazar said. He was holding one of his large fishing spears and now he gestured with it, as though he was hunting the monster. 'Would be a shame if I accidentally hooked him, eh?'

'You don't like him?'

'He's a bloody idiot,' Balthazar said cheerfully. 'Only interested in the things that can benefit him in some way. No integrity, you know? Strange, really, because I knew his brother too and he was a nice chap.'

I shut my mouth and nodded, not wanting to give myself away.

'And a cruel streak,' Balthazar said, looking away from me, across the loch. I thought he was talking to himself more than talking to me. 'So cruel. I always thought he got pleasure out of making the other boys' lives a misery.'

'Was he cruel to you?' I said, feeling sorry for him.

'Oh yes,' said Balthazar. 'Simon seemed to hate everyone, but he was especially cruel to me.'

'I'm sorry,' I said.

'No need to be.' He straightened up a bit. 'I did all right in the end.'

'You did.'

'But if I come across him while he's up here, then perhaps I'll take the opportunity to give him a piece of my mind.'

'You should.'

He smiled at me. 'I believe Mr Reid is finished with my men for now.'

Sure enough, Angus was closing his notebook and shaking the men's hands. I caught his eye and gave him a little wave, and he came over.

'Hannah? You look worried. Is something wrong?'

I wanted to throw myself into his arms and apologise for ever doubting him, but as he didn't know I'd doubted him, I managed to stop myself.

Instead, I led him away into the trees and said: 'Simon Wetherby's here.'

'Here?' He looked confused.

'Here in Drumnadrochit.'

'Good Lord,' he said. The mild exclamation made me want to hug him even more.

'Davina told him I was here. He paid her £100.'

This time his exclamation wasn't so mild.

'Davina lives on her wits,' I said, with a shrug. 'She's not had it easy. Don't be too hard on her.'

Angus looked doubtful but he didn't argue. 'What does he want?'

'Remember I told you I'd taken something from Lawrie?'

'Something precious?'

'That's what Simon wants.'

'Are you going to give it to him?'

I took a deep breath. 'I'm not.'

'And will he accept that?'

'I very much doubt it. He says he'll go to the papers.'

With a frown, Angus said: 'It's a good story, to be fair.'

I thought it was even better than he could possibly imagine, so I gave him a nudge that was perhaps a little harder than it should have been. 'That's not helpful, Angus.' I swallowed. 'There's more at stake than my independence. If people start digging into Lawrie's personal life …'

Angus's eyes gleamed. 'What?'

'I will tell you,' I said honestly. 'Just not right now.'

He looked like he was going to try to persuade me then thought better of it. 'So, what are you going to do?'

I groaned. 'I've got no idea.'

A shout from the loch made us both jump. We looked through the trees to see men running towards the water, binoculars in hand.

'Maybe they've found the monster, and no one will be interested in me,' I said hopefully.

'They think they've found the monster at least twice a day,' Angus pointed out.

I leaned against a tree. 'I don't know what to do, Angus. Simon's going to cause trouble for Lawrie whatever happens.'

Angus leaned against a tree opposite me and looked at me.

'Why are you so worried about Lawrie? I know he's your husband, but he cheated on you on your wedding day. He treated you horribly. Why do you care?'

I thought about Balthazar saying that he could trust Angus. I thought he was right. Despite his ambition and his conviction that the story was the most important thing.

'If I tell you, you have to promise not to breathe a word,' I said. 'I mean it. It's too risky.'

Angus's eyes widened and he nodded. 'Is it dangerous?'

'Not for me,' I said. I paused, trying to find the right words.

'For Lawrence?'

'It could be.'

Angus looked straight at me. 'Hannah, I give you my word. You can trust me not to tell another soul.'

I nodded, thinking about the right way to say this. 'When I walked in on Lawrence on our wedding night, he wasn't with another woman.'

'Right, but you said …'

I held my hand up to stop him talking. 'He was with a man,' I said. 'Freddie.'

'With a man?' Angus looked confused and then his face changed as the penny dropped. 'Oh, you mean *with* a man?'

I nodded. 'I do.'

'He's homosexual?'

'He is.'

'Right.' Angus didn't look disgusted, which I was pleased about. Just concerned.

'He can't help it,' I said, strangely wanting to defend Lawrence despite the heartache he'd caused me. 'It's just how he is.'

'And the rest of it – him falling and hitting his head?'

'All true,' I said. 'Except Freddie was there, too. He was the one who told me Lawrie was dead even though I thought I'd seen Lawrie moving. Freddie was very convincing. I think he just wanted shot of me.'

'And the precious thing?'

I sighed. 'Photographs,' I said. 'I had my camera with me and I took photographs of them together.'

'Oh, Hannah.' Angus sounded almost admiring. 'You really are a journalist.'

'I didn't really think – I just started snapping away,' I said, pleased with his praise. 'But now I have them and I thought they'd keep me safe, but actually they're causing more trouble.'

'Joanie said you'd been in the darkroom. Was that what you were developing?'

'It was. They're hidden.'

Again, Angus looked impressed. 'You've thought it all through, haven't you?'

'No,' I said. 'I've messed everything up. Because Simon won't take no for an answer, and even if I destroy the pictures, he's bound to think I'm lying.'

'I think there's only one thing for you to do,' Angus said.

I winced, because I knew what he was going to say, and I absolutely didn't want to do it.

'I think you're going to have to contact your husband.'

Chapter 27

Scarlett

Present day

I checked out of the hostel early the next morning. I was booked on the 8 a.m. train from Inverness to London and due back in work at an ungodly hour on Monday because Kevin had put me on the *Breakfast Show.*

My train was so early that I hadn't been able to have a proper send-off, even though Lucas had offered to take me for dinner at the pub. Instead, I'd gone to bed feeling disgruntled and resentful.

I dropped my rucksack onto the floor in reception with a thump. My bag wasn't heavy, but my heart was. I felt like I was leaving unfinished business, with the podcast and – if I was being completely honest – also with Lucas.

'I'm sorry to see you go,' Joyce said, taking my key. 'Maybe you'll come back again soon and find out what really happened to Hannah?'

'Maybe,' I said, though deep down I was fairly sure Charlie would be on his way to Inverness right this very moment, ready to reveal spurious evidence that Hannah killed Lawrence. Even though they were both alive years after this murder took place and she was totally innocent. Probably I'd see him as our trains whizzed past each other somewhere near the border. He'd be in first class, no doubt.

'Are you all right, Scarlett?' Joyce looked concerned.

'I'm fine.'

'You looked very cross there for a second.'

'I don't want to leave,' I admitted.

Joyce raised an eyebrow. 'Don't want to leave Drumnadrochit or don't want to leave lovely Lucas?'

I flushed. 'Bit of both.'

She reached out and patted my hand. 'I've got a feeling you'll keep in touch.'

'Perhaps,' I said. 'But long-distance relationships are difficult at the best of times, let alone when you don't even have a relationship yet.'

'Never say never,' she said, as the clock in the hallway chimed seven o'clock.

'I'd better go.' I picked up my bag. 'Thanks for everything.'

'See you,' Joyce said.

'Soon I hope,' I added.

I trudged down the steps at the front of the hostel and there – to my delight – was Lucas. He was wearing his *Red Dwarf* T-shirt and holding two takeaway cups of coffee.

'Thought you might like some company to Inverness,' he said.

'Don't be nice to me,' I said, walking past him but holding out my hand for the coffee. 'Because I will cry, and you'll be sorry.'

'Not a pretty crier, eh?' He gave me the cup and walked along with me.

'Oh I'm the worst,' I said cheerfully, my mood lifting considerably because Lucas was by my side. 'Snot. Puffy eyes. Sometimes a bit of dribble.'

'Nice.'

I laughed. 'Trust me, it's not something you want to see.'

We reached the bus stop – deserted at this hour of the day – and I leaned against the wall to drink my coffee. Lucas leaned next to me and we both stared straight ahead, across the road towards the loch.

'Thanks for coming,' I said, looking down at the plastic lid of my cup.

'I wanted to …' Lucas paused and I glanced round at him. He was looking uncharacteristically serious. 'I wanted to say goodbye properly.'

'That's nice.'

He nudged me with his shoulder. 'Can we keep in touch?' he said.

'Yes please.'

'Good.'

I took another mouthful of coffee. Along the road in the distance, I could see the little single-decker bus trundling towards us. I wanted to tell Lucas that I liked him, and I wanted to do more than keep in touch, but I couldn't find the words, or the courage to voice my feelings. And the bus was coming, and it was all too late and too bloody rubbish.

'Got everything?' he said. 'Got your ticket?'

I pulled my phone out of my pocket. 'On here, Grandad,' I said. I unlocked my screen to show him.

'Hold on,' he said, taking my phone and peering at it. 'Today is the 17th, right?'

I looked at my watch. 'Right.'

'This ticket is for the 24th. It's a week out.'

'What?' I snatched my phone back. 'Oh my God, this is for next Friday.'

'I know!' Lucas looked delighted. 'So you can't go, right?'

'Ha. Yeah right. Kevin will just book me a new ticket.' I checked my watch. 'Though he won't be in the office for ages, so it'll be a few hours. We could go for breakfast?'

247

'A few hours is better than nothing,' Lucas said as the bus approached. He waved it on and it rumbled past. 'We could get sausage and egg rolls at the café? They open early.'

'Sounds good,' I said. I hoicked my bag up my back and typed a message to Robyn as we walked, explaining what had happened. Immediately, my phone rang.

'Stay there,' she said when I answered. I stopped walking, then realised that wasn't what she meant when Lucas turned round and looked at me quizzically.

'Hello, Robyn,' I said. 'What?'

'Stay in bloody Loch Ness,' she said. 'This is a sign, Scarlett.'

'It's a sign that Kev's work experience student is rubbish.'

'No, that's not what I meant,' Robyn said. She sounded tearful.

'Are you okay, Rob?'

She sniffed. 'I'm fine. I'm just a bit hormonal.'

'At least now I'm coming home I can see you and your bump.'

'I don't want you to come home,' she screeched.

'Robyn, bloody hell …'

'Kevin's not in the office today,' she said, her words falling over themselves as she hurried to get them out. 'He's off on Monday, too – he's going on some shitty stag weekend. And remember the other week when he told me off for signing off Rick's expenses? He was very clear I wasn't supposed to, even though it's totally in my job description. So …'

'So no one can sign off my train ticket,' I finished for her. I looked at Lucas who was watching me hopefully. 'No one can buy me a new ticket until next week? And I can't possibly be expected to fork out for it myself.' That wasn't even an exaggeration as I suspected putting a very expensive, last-minute train ticket on my credit card would take me over my limit.

'Exactly,' Robyn said, triumphant. 'You're stuck in Loch Ness. For a few days at least. And I'm pretty much done for the day already, because I'm on the *Breakfast Show*, so if you wanted any help editing anything …'

'Robyn, are you saying I should do my own programme?'

'That's exactly what I'm saying. This is so good, Scarlett. Loch Ness was trending—'

'On Twitter, I know.'

'Do it. You have to do it. We'll put it on all the Britain Live socials to spread the word. Kev never looks at those.'

'What about Quentin Wetherby? My dad says he knows unsavoury people.'

Lucas was nodding frantically. 'I'll find them,' he hissed at me. 'I'll find something we can use against him. There's always something.'

'Really?' I looked at him, half impressed, half alarmed.

'Totally.'

'I might lose my job.' I looked up at the morning sky. 'I'll almost definitely lose my job.'

'So, you'll get another one. A better one. Or you'll go freelance. Everyone will want you after this, I reckon.'

I felt a little shiver of excitement. 'I could go freelance,' I said. 'That might be fun.'

'What do you say?' Robyn asked.

I looked at Lucas who was jiggling about on his army-boot-clad feet and I sighed.

'Fine. I'll see what else I can find out. But it might not make an episode – I'm not promising anything.'

'But what will we call it?' said Robyn. She sounded teary again. 'We can't call it *Cold Cases with Burns*. We've got no name.'

'We'll think of something,' I said, amused by her mood swings. 'Rob, go home and have a lie-down when the show's finished, will you? I'll call you later.'

'Okay,' she said with a sniff. 'Good luck.'

I ended the call and turned to Lucas. 'When do you need to be back in Edinburgh?'

'Monday.' He scratched his beard. 'Afternoon.'

'Want to help me make a podcast?'

He gave his big, hearty laugh. 'Well of course I do.'

I threw my arms around him and then without me even knowing how it had happened or who made the first move, we were kissing. His beard felt scratchy against my face, but in a nice way and he smelled of lemons and the coffee he'd just been drinking.

Eventually we broke apart, smiling at each other. 'I wasn't planning on doing that,' he said.

'Me neither, but I'm glad it happened.'

We stood there for a second, until a group of schoolgirls, who'd clearly been waiting for us to move away from the bus stop for a while, came and sat down on the wall next to where we were standing. They all looked up at us expectantly.

'Carry on,' one of them said, while the rest giggled and got out their phones.

Feeling horribly self-conscious suddenly and fearing we were about to end up as a TikTok video, I said: 'Shall we go back to the hostel? Hopefully Joyce hasn't given my room to another guest yet.'

Lucas took my hand. 'I'm slightly hoping she has.'

I felt a bit giddy with excitement and happiness. I'd not felt like that for a long time and it was nice.

As we strolled along the road, hand in hand, he said: 'It's erm, been a while for me.'

'Dating?'

'Yep, I've been on my own for a long time. Since my divorce. I'm a bit …'

'Nervous?' I said. 'Me too. Charlie didn't cheat but the speed with which he replaced me didn't do a whole lot of good for my self-esteem.'

'I promise not to replace you with unseemly haste,' Lucas said. 'It's five years since Maya and I split. I'm more of a taking it slow kind of guy.'

'Not too slow, I hope,' I said, squeezing his hand. He squeezed back, making me shiver with anticipation. 'And I promise not to snog anyone else.'

'Sounds like a good start,' he said. 'A good start to something good.'

I beamed up at him, my cheeks aching from smiling.

Lucas tugged my arm gently to bring me closer to him. 'Things always work out in the end, don't they?'

We'd reached the hostel. 'I hope they worked out for Hannah.'

'Well that's what you need to find out.'

'We,' I said, alarmed. 'That's what WE need to find out, surely?'

'Of course,' Lucas said. 'But I need to find some dirt on Quentin Wetherby first and I really need to do that this morning because if I know my colleagues – and I do – they'll be clocking off early as it's Friday.'

'Oh thank goodness,' I said, standing on my tiptoes to give him a kiss. 'I thought you were leaving me to it already.'

'Well, I am. But only for a while.'

'Meet you in the lounge at lunchtime for a debrief?'

'Perfect.'

He sauntered off and I watched him go, fairly sure he had a bounce in his step that hadn't been there before. Then I bounced my way into the hostel to find Joyce and ask for my room back.

*

Thankfully, though Joyce had allocated my room to another guest, they'd not checked in yet, so with a bit of frowning at the computer and a lot of me assuring her I'd be fine in a different room and her telling me how the Wi-Fi wasn't up to scratch if I was going to do my podcast, and I really needed to be at the top of the building, she moved things around and my room key was back in my hand and I was heading back upstairs feeling the weight of her expectation. And more than a little nervous about what I was going to do. Maybe this story wouldn't make another episode. Maybe I'd never be able to find out exactly what happened to Hannah, but Robyn was right. This was good. And I needed to try.

I unpacked all my notes, my recorder and my laptop and laid them out on the bed.

'Right then,' I said, wondering where to start. 'What first?'

On the top of my pile of notes was a printout of one of Ann O'Shawn's stories from the *Herald*. They were so good – very well written and evocative. I'd especially liked this one about a darkness lurking underneath the fun of the monster hunt, so I'd asked Joyce to print it out for me. Perhaps that was a good place to start. After all, murder was dark. Even if no murder had actually taken place.

I sat down on the bed, arranged the pillows behind my back, and picked up my notebook to plan the episode. I needed to write down what I already knew, what I still needed to find out, and what the story of the episode would be.

At the top of the page I wrote, *Hannah Snow is innocent*, and underlined it.

I'd start with reading some of Ann O'Shawn's story, I thought. So I wrote Ann O'Shawn and underlined that too. And then I underlined it again. Because something had just clicked in my head.

I crossed out the A in Ann and then in Hannah. Then the Ns, then the other letters. And there it was. Ann O'Shawn was an anagram – almost, I had an H left over, but no one was perfect – of Hannah Snow.

'You bloody marvellous woman,' I muttered. 'You bloody brilliant, marvellous woman.'

Because hadn't Lawrence's divorce papers mentioned Hannah – *or whatever name she was going by*? And hadn't she had a camera slung around her neck in the only photograph I had of her working at the hotel?

Hannah had come to Drumnadrochit, she'd changed her name, and she'd been hiding in plain sight all along, reporting on the monster hunt that had swept this sleepy village all those years before. She was amazing.

At least I thought she was amazing.

I still wasn't entirely sure why she'd run away in the first place, especially given how she and Lawrence seemed to be amicable by the time they divorced. But somehow, I knew she'd had her reasons.

I leaned back against the pillows, holding my notebook up and squinting at it.

Maybe, I thought, it had something to do with Quentin Wetherby's father. The one who'd been profiled in that feature Bonnie had found. If he was half as mean as Quentin was, he'd have definitely been a nasty piece of work.

Now I just had to find out what happened to Ann O'Shawn.

@BritainLive wrote:
Fans of The Monster in the Loch will want to keep an eye on our socials for some exciting news about a bonus episode coming soon. Don't miss it! #hannahsnow

Friday June 17
Missed call
Charlie

Friday June 17
Charlie wrote:
Scarlett, what are you doing? Call me.

Chapter 28

Hannah

1933

Angus and I went to the Post Office in Drumnadrochit and sent the same telegram to Lawrie at his London flat, the Commons, and the house in West Sussex because I didn't know where he was. I winced at the expense, crossed my fingers and hoped he wasn't abroad somewhere.

In Drumnadrochit. Simon here. Please come. Send travel arrangements, I sent, watching the postmistress tap the message out on her telegraph machine.

We waited for a reply, me pacing up and down the pavement outside, Angus leaning against the wall, his foot tapping.

'And he'll definitely know what you mean?' he asked for the fiftieth time.

'He'll understand,' I said, hoping I was right. But Lawrie was clever and he had an office full of staff who would make arrangements for him to get here. I really hoped he'd come quickly – I didn't think I could handle Simon on my own.

254

After what seemed like an age, the postmistress put her head round the door.

'Got your reply,' she said.

We both turned and looked at her. 'What does he say?' I asked.

'Coming on early sleeper.'

'Thank goodness,' I said. I looked at the clock outside the post office and sighed. 'Will he get here before I have to meet Simon?'

'He might be cutting it fine, but he should do.'

'I'm working this evening, so that will be a good distraction.'

'Gosh, me too,' said Angus. 'I need to get back to Inverness and write this profile of Balthazar.'

'Oh my goodness,' I said, suddenly remembering Balthazar's candour about his schooldays. 'I forgot to tell you that Balthazar knows Simon. He said he has a cruel streak. They were at school together.'

'Well, that's true enough,' Angus said. 'Balthazar told me he had quite a rotten time of it at school.'

'Because of Simon, I think.'

'He really doesn't have any redeeming features, does he?'

'Not as far as I can see.'

'Maybe I'll do a profile of him next,' he said, with a wink. He gave me a slightly awkward hug with us both turning our heads away from each other. 'I'll come back tomorrow morning.'

'See you then.' I gave him a small smile and he squeezed my hand.

'It'll be all right. You'll see.'

*

But it wasn't.

I woke up the next morning – late because I'd been on the evening shift and I hadn't got to bed until after midnight – to see Davina sitting on her bed opposite mine, looking at me in a very odd way.

'What is it?' I said, scrambling to sit up and blinking the sleep from my eyes. 'What's happened?'

'First of all,' Davina said, speaking quite slowly and carefully, 'I want you to know that I never meant for any of this to happen.'

'Right,' I said, understanding suddenly. 'You told Simon Wetherby I was here, and you never meant for him to come and find me? What did you think he was going to do?'

Davina pinched her lips together. 'I didn't think,' she muttered.

Very aware that I was wearing a nightgown that reduced my fierceness somewhat, I scowled at her. 'No.'

To her credit, Davina looked sheepish. 'I thought about the money,' she said. 'I thought about how having one hundred pounds would make me feel.'

'Guilty?' I said. 'Ashamed of betraying a friend?'

Davina rubbed her nose. 'Safe.'

I pulled my knees up to my chin, feeling an unwelcome wave of sympathy for her. 'You've got a job,' I said. 'And a place to live.'

'But things can change in a heartbeat. I know that. I told you that.' She looked cross suddenly. 'Your parents died. You know.'

'I do know.' I sighed. 'I understand, Davina, but I'm still upset.'

'You might be more upset when I tell you the rest.'

With dread, I looked at her. 'The rest?'

'I was on the lunchtime shift yesterday, you know. And Mr Wetherby came to find me. He was in a bit of a state.'

I nodded, grim-faced. 'I saw him too.'

'He wasn't how I'd expected him to be,' Davina said. 'He was much scruffier. Looked like he'd been sleeping in a hedge. And he was drunk.'

'He was.'

'And he came to tell me to keep an eye on you.'

'Yes.'

Davina dropped her face into her hands for a second, then she looked up. 'He was loud,' she said. 'And people noticed him.'

I had a horrible feeling I knew where this was going, but I

asked her anyway. 'What people?'

'That chap from the *Daily Mirror*. Matthew Clayton?'

I closed my eyes. 'Yes.'

'He knew who Mr Wetherby was.' Davina was talking faster now. Sounding more desperate. 'And I tried to take him – Mr Wetherby – outside but he was sort of shouting, about how no member of his family should be reduced to working as a maid, and I swear to you, Hannah, when he said that you could have heard a pin drop in that lounge. Every man in there, all the reporters, they all had their ears virtually out on stalks. And then Mr Clayton, he whipped out his notebook and started asking Mr Wetherby questions, and buying him drinks. Not even an hour later, I heard him asking Mrs M if he could use the telephone. And—' She broke off, looking like she was about to cry.

'And what?' I hissed. 'What?'

'This.'

From behind her back, she produced the *Daily Mirror*. And there, on the front was the headline: MP's "missing" wife forced to work as a maid.

I looked from the newspaper to Davina in horror. 'What does the story say?'

'I can't … Tobias read it for me.'

'Tobias knows?'

Davina swallowed. 'He told me not to tell Mr Wetherby.'

'Give me the newspaper.'

Davina held it out and I grabbed it, scanning the story. It was pretty thin, all based on Simon's drunken ramblings. There were no photographs, obviously. But it was bad enough.

'Mrs M said the phone's been ringing off the hook. People wanting rooms. She said first it was the monster hunters, now it's the Hannah hunters.'

'Great,' I groaned. 'So everyone knows?'

'Yes.'

Davina ran her fingers through her hair. 'But, Mrs McEwan is

257

telling all the reporters calling that we're full. She says it's none of their business what you do and if anyone asks her anything, she'll say nothing.'

'She said that?'

'She's furious about it. I thought she was going to sack me, but Tobias stuck up for me. He said I was just like she was when she was young, and she laughed and said if I put another foot out of line, I'll be out.'

'Seems fair.'

Davina nodded. 'What will you do, Hannah? Will you give Mr Wetherby what he wants?'

'I can't.' I sighed. 'It's not mine to give away really.'

'I think you're really brave, sticking to your guns like that.'

I sighed. 'It's not really about me. It's Lawrie I'm worried about.'

'Why do you care? He cheated on you.'

'He did. But it's complicated. And I'm afraid this newspaper story makes it even more complicated. I'm frightened for him. People might start digging about in his life, and then things could just fall apart.'

A tear rolled down Davina's cheek. 'I really am sorry,' she said.

'I know.'

'What are you going to do?'

'I'm going to get dressed, and then I'm going to find Simon,' I said.

'Want me to come with you?'

'Would you?'

'Course. Bet Mrs M would too, if we asked her. And Tobias.'

'Angus is coming as well.'

'He'll have to take us all on.' Davina grinned. 'I don't fancy his chances.'

'Lawrie's on his way,' I said, getting out of bed and taking a clean dress out of the tiny wardrobe.

'To Drum?'

'Yes.'

'Does he know about the story?'

'Depends if he sees the newspapers on the train.'

'They sometimes bring them on at Edinburgh.'

'Then yes, he'll know,' I said.

'Will he be angry?'

I thought about it as I buttoned my dress. 'No, I don't think so. Scared, perhaps.'

'Has he done something wrong?'

'I thought so, at first. But now I think not.'

Davina shrugged. 'Are you ready?'

'Yes, almost.' I ran a brush through my hair quickly. 'Done.'

'Shall we go?'

I took a deep breath. 'I suppose so.'

*

Mrs McEwan and Tobias were waiting at the bottom of the stairs for us, like a receiving line at a wedding. Mrs M put her hand on my shoulder as I got close to her and gave it a gentle squeeze and the little show of affection made tears spring into my eyes.

'What's the plan?' said Tobias. 'We need to show this Wetherby that he can't just throw his weight around like this.'

I looked at them all, gazing at me with expectation, and I shrugged. 'I don't have a plan.'

'But you're going to meet him?' Tobias said.

'I suppose so. But what can he do to me now?' I gestured to the newspaper that Davina was clutching with a snort. 'That story was his threat and it's gone now. That Clayton chap's done me a favour in a way.'

'We need to give the reporters something else to talk about,' said Angus, coming through the hotel's main doors into the foyer where we were huddled. I was so pleased to see him that once more I almost threw myself into his arms, but once more I resisted. He was carrying a copy of the *Mirror* under his arm.

'I saw the story,' he said. 'Changes things a bit, I think.'

'A lot,' said Tobias, who seemed to be filled with fervour. 'But I still think we should challenge Wetherby.'

'Giving the reporters something else to talk about isn't a bad idea,' I said thoughtfully, ignoring Tobias who was bouncing on his toes like a boxer. 'What about if someone saw the monster? But no, that's just going to bring everyone down to the loch and I'm meeting Simon down there.'

'What about Loch Lochy?' said Davina in excitement. She gripped Tobias's arm and I couldn't help noticing he looked rather pleased about it. 'There are stories about a beast in that loch, too. What if someone saw it? They could tell the tale and keep the reporters and the hunters up here at the hotel.'

'That's clever,' said Angus in approval and I stood up a bit straighter under the glow of his attention. 'Someone trustworthy. Believable.' He turned to Tobias. 'You.'

'What?'

'Where are the reporters?'

Mrs M tipped her head towards the lounge. 'Most of them are in there.'

Angus nodded. 'Tobias, you go outside then give us five minutes and come rushing in saying you've just come from Loch Lochy and you thought you saw a beast. That'll keep them busy for a while.'

I chuckled, despite the nerves I felt in my stomach.

'Will they go for it? What if they all go charging off there instead? Mrs M won't like that, will you?'

Mrs McEwan shrugged. 'It's too far,' she said, looking unconcerned. 'I don't think anyone will bother.'

'I'll tell the story and then backtrack a bit so it's not worth their while going off to check,' said Tobias. 'Trust me.'

'All right,' I said. 'Angus, can you wait outside for Lawrie and fill him in when he arrives? Then you'll need to bring him round the side of the hotel. We don't want any of the reporters to spot him.' I took a deep breath. 'And I'll go and meet Simon.'

'I don't know, Hannah,' said Angus. 'I don't really want you going alone. He's desperate and he's a drunk, and that's a dangerous combination.'

'I'll go with her,' Davina said.

'Really?' I was doubtful.

Davina looked affronted. 'Course. Told you I was sorry, didn't I? Let me prove it.'

I couldn't deny I would welcome the support. 'All right then.'

Angus looked at his watch. 'Lawrie should be on his way from Inverness already,' he said. 'Was Simon staying up there overnight? Let's hope there isn't a brothers' reunion on the bus.'

'Lawrie won't take the bus,' I said. 'I don't think he even knows how to take a bus.'

Tobias snorted. 'How can he represent our interests, if he doesn't know how we live ...' he began.

To my relief, Mrs McEwan jumped in. 'Simon isn't in Inverness,' she said. 'At least I'm assuming he's the chap I found passed out under a hedge in the front garden last night. Tobias helped me put him in the outbuilding to sleep it off.'

'That was Wetherby?' Tobias said. He looked disappointed. 'Not what I expected. He's a bit pathetic, actually.'

'He's disappointed with life,' I said. I straightened my cap and my apron. 'I'm going to find him.'

Angus reached out and touched my fingers lightly. 'Be careful,' he said.

'Bring Lawrie when he arrives.'

'I will.'

'And, Tobias? Really ham up the monster sighting, will you?'

'I'll help with that,' said Mrs M with a wink.

'Right then,' I said. 'Come on, Davina. Let's go.'

Chapter 29

Davina and I hurried down the path to the outbuilding. I knocked on the door before we went in, not wanting to disturb anyone in any state of undress, but thankfully when we went inside, there was only Simon there.

He was sitting on the side of his bed, his shirt creased and his tie undone. His hair was a mess and his face was ruddy. He looked much older than he was. Older and sort of broken.

'Good morning,' I said.

He looked up at me and groaned. 'I don't have the energy for your games today, Hannah. Just hand over whatever you took, and I'll go.'

'I can't,' I said.

Simon put his hands on his knees and with what seemed to be supreme effort, he stood up.

'Then I'm afraid I'll have to go to the papers.' He pushed his hair back off his forehead and gave me a wolfish smile. 'I did warn you.'

'It's too late,' I said. I held my hand out and Davina, who

was standing a little behind me, gave me the newspaper. 'They already know everything.' I threw him the *Mirror* and he caught it. I watched his face as he read the story.

'You did this?' he spat at Davina. 'You bitch.'

I shrank back in the face of his anger, but Davina was defiant. 'You did this,' she said cheerfully. 'You were singing like a canary in the bar last night.'

'I need fresh air,' Simon said. He lurched past us and out into the garden. Davina and I exchanged a look and followed.

We found Simon leaning against a tree, a little way from the path, looking rather green around the gills.

'I just want what's mine,' he said as we approached. 'Lawrie's going to get everything, while I get nothing.'

'Your father had his reasons,' I told him. Out of the corner of my eye, I saw Tobias saunter towards the hotel and I was glad he'd distract the journalists for a while.

'It's not fair,' Simon whined like a sulky schoolboy. 'And you're a thief.'

'I didn't take anything that belonged to you.'

'That's what Lawrie says, when it's clear he took half of my inheritance.' He straightened up away from the tree. 'He's a thief and so are you. You deserve one another.'

'Lawrie's a good man,' I said. 'You'd do well to remember that.'

'You'd better hope he's a good man, if you want him to forgive you for running out on him the way you did.' Simon gave me a look of pure disgust.

'Forgive Hannah?' Davina had been hovering at my side, silently, but now she stepped forward. 'Are you serious? It's Hannah who needs to forgive Lawrie. He was the one who cheated on her, after all.'

'Davina, there's no need to go over all that,' I said, not wanting Simon to hear all the details. But he was looking at me through narrowed eyes.

'He cheated on you?' he said. 'Well, well, well. That's not

something I'd have expected of Lawrence. He never seemed very interested in women. Frankly I was surprised when he announced his engagement ...' He trailed off and I watched the cogs whirring in his brain.

'Simon,' I said, desperately trying to keep him from putting everything together. 'Let's see if there's a way to convince Lawrie to give you some of his inheritance, shall we?'

But he wasn't listening. 'He's homosexual, isn't he? Lawrence likes men.'

Beside me, Davina gasped.

'Simon, let's not discuss this now ...'

'There were always rumours,' he said. 'Whispers. But Lawrence is very strait-laced. I thought those rumours were being spread by political rivals to keep him from parliament. But it's true?'

I didn't speak. I didn't want to say anything that might make things worse.

'So that's why my father wanted him wed.' He laughed loudly and without humour. 'Poor old Dad, knowing he could either leave his estate to a drunk or a poof.'

His face twisted suddenly and I wondered if he might cry. 'And he chose Lawrence all the same,' he said. 'Not me.'

He pulled a hip flask from his pocket and shook it.

'Full,' he said, pleased. 'Seems I did some things right last night.'

He took off the lid and drank the contents, wiping his mouth as he finished. 'He chose Lawrence,' he said again.

'I didn't ask him to.'

Davina and I turned to see Lawrie and Angus standing behind us.

'Oh, Lawrie,' I said, absurdly pleased to see him there, and not out cold on the hotel carpet where I'd left him. I went to him, and he opened his arms to hug me and I let him. Because whatever had happened between us, I did feel for him, and we'd been happy for a while. Or at least, we'd almost been happy for a while.

Over his shoulder I saw another man, standing slightly back

from us.

'You brought Freddie?' I said in disbelief. 'Really, Lawrie?'

'I wanted to come,' Freddie said. 'To say sorry.'

'We both need to say sorry,' said Lawrie firmly. He looked at me. 'I thought I was doing the right thing, Hannah, and I apologise.'

I stared back at him, feeling the humiliation and the horror of our wedding night all over again. 'Thank you,' I said, stopping short of adding my forgiveness.

'Is this the boyfriend?' Simon said with glee, adopting a mocking tone. 'Oh how fabulous. Welcome to the family, darling.'

Simon was getting louder, and across the lawn an elderly couple – who'd turned up for their annual stay at the hotel and been taken aback by the monster hunters taking up the lounge each evening – looked round at us.

'We can't talk here,' said Lawrence. 'Is there somewhere more private we can go? Into the hotel, perhaps?'

'No!' Angus, Davina and I all shouted at once.

'It's full of reporters,' I said. 'Covering the hunt for the Loch Ness monster.'

Angus pointed towards the shore. 'How about the loch?' he said. 'Can you row, Lawrence?'

'I was a Blue at Oxford,' Lawrie said.

Angus rolled his eyes, and so did Freddie, which made me smile inwardly.

'You won't be overheard if you're out on the water,' said Angus. 'Let's go.'

No one argued, so we all trooped down through the trees and out onto the shore of the loch, where a line of rowing boats sat. Anyone local with any sort of boat had brought them to hire out to monster hunters – it wasn't just Mrs M who was bringing in more money thanks to the beast. They were chained to iron fastenings on the rocks – the fastenings were new too. There had never been call for security like that before. There were a few people out on the water, but it was quiet, no doubt thanks to

Tobias telling his tall tale to anyone who'd listen, up at the hotel.

A little further along, Balthazar Webster's boat – a large vessel with sails – was bobbing in the shallows. I could see Balthazar on board, lounging at one end, his hat over his face as he dozed in the weak spring sunshine.

'That one,' said Simon, making for Balthazar's boat, obviously not recognising his old nemesis from school.

'No,' Angus said, pulling him back. 'This one.' He pointed to a small rowing boat with bench seats. 'I've used it before. The owner won't mind us borrowing it. I know the combination for the padlock.'

Swiftly, he unlocked the boat and together he and Lawrence dragged it across the sandy shore to the water's edge.

Lawrence jumped aboard and, unsteadily, Simon clambered in too.

'Hannah?' Simon said. 'You need to come. Explain yourself to your husband.' He spat out the word and, behind him, Lawrie winced.

'I don't think so.'

'You need to tell him what you stole,' Simon taunted. 'Or does he know?'

'Hannah?' Lawrence looked puzzled. 'What's he talking about?'

From up at the hotel, I heard voices and we all glanced round.

'I think people are coming,' Angus said. 'You should go before anyone gets here.'

'Oh for heaven's sake.' Annoyed, I tramped down to the boat and let Lawrie help me aboard, as he pushed off.

Lawrie was strong and we were soon speeding across the water, out into the middle of the loch.

'You look well,' he said, pulling through the water.

'I am well.' I folded my arms, looking away from him. I didn't want to make small talk.

It was quiet, the further we got away from the shore, and still. Lawrence stopped rowing, pulling the oars in the boat, and we stayed barely moving.

'You can believe there's a monster here, can't you?' he said, gazing in wonder at the scenery just as I'd done all those weeks before when I'd first arrived in the Highlands. 'It's extraordinary.'

'You're the monster,' Simon said. He'd been sitting in the bow of the boat, sulking silently as Lawrie rowed. 'You disgust me.'

'Oh shut up, Simon,' I said.

'You're no better. Pretending to be worried about him when you've stolen from him. From our family.'

His eyes gleamed as he caught sight of something under the seat in front of him and reached for it. It was a bottle of beer. He expertly knocked the top off on the side of the boat and glugged.

I looked at Lawrie. 'I didn't steal anything,' I said. 'I told Davina I'd taken something precious but it was …'

'I know,' he said. 'The photographs.'

'You took photographs?' Simon said, his lip curling. 'Why would they be precious? Unless they were naughty pictures. Is that what they were?' He grinned. 'Naughty pictures of you, were they?'

He shifted over onto the seat in front, so he was closer to me. 'You're a nice-looking woman, Hannah,' he said. 'But you're not going to get anywhere with Lawrence. Bit too ladylike for him, aren't you?'

'That's enough, Simon,' Lawrie said. 'They weren't photographs of Hannah. They were photographs of me.' He swallowed. 'With a man.'

'Ohhh,' Simon breathed. He took another swig of his beer. 'Even better. They'll be worth a bob or two, won't they?'

'I destroyed them,' I lied. 'I pulled the film out of the camera and exposed it. They're gone.'

'Then why did you tell Davina you had something precious?'

'Showing off?' I said, shrugging. 'Trying to impress her?'

'You're lying,' Simon said.

'I'm not lying.'

'I'll shake it out of you, you bitch,' he roared. And before I knew it, he'd launched himself at me, clambering over the bench seats and the oars, and past Lawrie to reach me.

His weight sent me flying backwards into the recess at the back of the boat, with a thump, hurting my back and winding me.

I lay there for a second, looking up at the sky, and then Simon loomed over me once more and I shrieked, curling myself up protectively, as his punch made contact with the side of my face and stars exploded in my eye.

'Get off her!' Lawrie shouted. I saw him make a grab for Simon, who swung round with a clenched fist and landed a punch on his brother's jaw.

Lawrie, who'd not only rowed at university but had also boxed, picked Simon up by the front of his shirt and hit him back, sending him sprawling across the seats and knocking one of the oars into the water.

'Lawrie, don't!' I screamed, scrambling to get up but I was uncomfortably wedged under the bench seat, my leg caught under me.

We were rocking now, swaying from side to side as the men scuffled. Simon gave Lawrie a heavy jab to the ribs, and Lawrie stumbled. Simon saw his chance and reared up, grabbing Lawrie round the neck.

'Stop it,' I shrieked. 'You're going to kill him. Stop it!'

And then there was one enormous swell of the waves, as though the boat had been lifted up, the whole vessel tipped and Simon lost his balance and began tumbling towards the water, releasing his grip on Lawrie. With a yelp of fear Simon slid along the slippery deck, making a grab for anything to hang on to in order to save himself.

From where I was safely stuck under the bench, I watched in horror as Simon gripped Lawrie's foot, pulling him into the water too, and the pair of them sank down into the depths.

'Lawrie,' I shrieked. With a yank, I pulled myself free out of the bottom of the boat, and crawled to the side where the men had gone over. 'Lawrie?'

I could see Balthazar Webster's boat skimming over the water towards us, with Angus at the front, and I waved frantically.

'Help!' I shouted. 'Help!'

'Hannah?' A spluttering cry from the other side of the boat caught my attention and I turned to see Simon, holding on to the oar, and doing an undignified doggie paddle towards me. 'Help me, Hannah.'

Did I think for a second that I could leave him to his fate there, in the icy water? Possibly. But after just a tiny pause, I leaned over. 'Hold out the oar,' I said. 'I'll pull you in.'

With a bit of effort, Simon managed to manoeuvre the oar round so I could grab the end and with my arms screaming at the exertion, I yanked him towards the boat and helped half drag, half lift him over the side.

He lay face down across the seat, still clutching the oar, and wheezing and spluttering. 'Lawrie,' he gasped. 'Where's Lawrie? I didn't mean to push him over the edge. I didn't mean it.'

I was beginning to cry. 'I don't know.' I went back to the side of the boat, desperately scanning the water for any sign of him. My eye was swelling shut and it was hard to see. 'It's too cold,' I sobbed. 'It's too cold to be in the water for long.'

Simon was shivering now, as if to prove my point, and in that moment I hated him more than I'd ever hated anyone.

Desperately I turned to look the other way, and to my amazement, I saw Balthazar and Angus dragging Lawrie into the sailing boat. They were still quite far from where we were drifting, and I was surprised Lawrie had made it all that way in the cold water. But it didn't matter how he'd got there. He was safe. Weak with relief I sank down on to the bench.

'Lawrie?' Simon said through chattering teeth. 'Can you see him?'

I squinted at him through my good eye, and decided I'd make him suffer a little longer. 'I can't see him,' I said, bleakly but honestly, because Lawrie had vanished from view and Balthazar was turning his boat around and heading for shore. 'I need to get you back to land.'

Simon's lips were turning blue and he was shaking violently as the cold seeped into his skin. I searched under the seats for a blanket, but had no luck. Instead, I found a sou'wester and hat that must have belonged to the boat's owner. I threw them at Simon. 'Take off your wet clothes and put these on,' I said.

'Don't … be … ridiculous.' His breath was raspy.

'Well, then freeze,' I snapped. I tugged one oar from his grip, picked up the other and slotted them into the edge of the boat. 'I don't much care either way.'

Slowly, Simon began unbuttoning his shirt with shaky hands, while I started to row. It took me a while to make it back to shore, but the current was in my favour and the waves seemed to carry us along. As we approached the edge of the water, Angus and Freddie appeared and waded out into the shallows to pull the boat into shore.

'What happened?' Angus said, putting his arms around me to support me out of the boat. I sank into his embrace and let him help me. 'Did you hit your head? We should get your eye checked out. Gosh it looks awful.'

'Simon punched me,' I said bluntly. My back and my head were aching too much for me to sugar-coat this. 'And he pushed Lawrie and they both fell into the water.'

Simon, wearing the sou'wester and hat, with his skinny bare legs on display, scrambled out of the boat in an ungainly fashion.

Angus turned on him. 'What did you do?' he growled. 'What were you thinking? We need to call the police.'

Simon began to cry like a little boy, standing on the rocky shore in his underpants, sobbing. Freddie gave him a look that dripped with disdain.

'You're pathetic,' he hissed. 'Your father was right to disinherit you.'

270

Simon winced but I didn't feel remotely sympathetic. 'Where's Lawrie?' he wailed.

Angus tipped his head towards Balthazar's boat, where I could see Balthazar's safari hat bobbing as he crouched over someone on the deck. He gave me a small nod, telling me Lawrie was all right.

'We need to find my brother,' Simon was sobbing. 'I didn't mean to push him. I didn't mean it. You have to believe me. I'm sorry. I'm so sorry.'

I looked at Freddie, and he looked back at me, and a moment of understanding passed between us.

Freddie gave me the tiniest of winks, then he took a deep breath. 'Lawrie's gone,' he said with such convincing, hollow desperation that I almost believed him myself.

Again.

'Lawrie's gone, Simon, and it's all your fault.'

Chapter 30

Scarlett

Present day

With time an issue – I knew I had to get the episode edited and put out as quickly as I could before anyone got wind of what I was doing and tried to stop me – I decided to record what I knew as I was going along and then put it all together at the end.

I'd start by reading some of Ann's article about the darkness, and then add an introduction to the episode, explaining that I knew for sure that Hannah didn't murder Lawrence in 1933, because Lawrence was still alive in 1938. And I'd record a quick teaser about Hannah being Ann O'Shawn.

And then … well, I'd do some digging into Ann. See if I could find out what happened to her.

I wrote a quick script – just a few paragraphs – and set up my equipment. And as I got ready, the heavens opened and the rain started bucketing down. Because my room was right up in the roof of the hotel, the raindrops overhead were very loud and I quickly realised I couldn't record anything while it was still raining. So I decided to go and find Joyce, to see if she knew anything about Ann O'Shawn. Perhaps she'd even stayed local. Maybe Joyce's mother had known her – she must have known Hannah, after all. Perhaps I could even meet her. I did some sums in my head. No, that wasn't possible. But maybe she had children? Grandchildren?

Excited at the idea, I gathered up all my bits again, and headed downstairs.

And there, standing in reception, looking very bedraggled from the rain and more than a little sorry for themselves, were Quentin Wetherby and Charlie.

I stopped with a jolt on the bottom step and dropped all my papers, which scattered across the tiled floor and ruined all my hopes of sneaking back upstairs before either of them noticed me.

'Scarlett,' Charlie said without warmth, bending down and picking up the printout of Ann's article. 'Hello.'

I bent down and collected the rest of my papers. Quentin stood there, not moving and not even pretending to help, as I scrabbled round his feet. Then I retreated to the bottom step again.

'There is no one working here,' Quentin said, with a tut. He leaned over the reception desk and dinged the bell several times. 'We've been waiting five minutes already. This is disgraceful.'

'You're not staying here.' I stared at them in horror.

Quentin looked round at me. 'That was the plan, but now I've seen it, I rather think we'll be better in the Marriott at the airport. I'll get my assistant to book it.'

He put his phone to his ear and turned away from us.

'Why are you here?' I hissed at Charlie, as Quentin barked instructions.

'I have been calling you and calling you,' he said. 'It's all gone tits up, Scarlett.'

'Because of him,' I said in a low voice, nodding towards Quentin. 'He's the one who bloody got the programme pulled.'

'No, because of you.' Charlie was glowering at me. 'Astrid and

273

I had found a house and we had to pull out because the money from Quentin was going to cover the deposit.'

'Oh, have a word with yourself,' I said. 'He's bloody skint. He would never have coughed up even if we'd done as he asked.'

'Well, he'd have had the inheritance, wouldn't he?' Charlie said sulkily. 'But now he won't, thanks to you.'

'It's not his. His father didn't inherit because Lawrence didn't die.'

'So you say.'

'Can I help you?'

Our whispered argument was interrupted by Joyce.

'I think these people have decided to stay in Inverness instead,' I said pointedly.

Joyce frowned. 'Are you all right, Scarlett?'

'Right as rain,' I lied. 'Absolutely fine.'

'The car's coming back to get us,' Quentin said. 'But he said the traffic is bad, so he might be a while. Can we get a drink while we wait?'

'We have a lounge,' Joyce said, spreading her arm out in the direction of the doorway. 'Follow me.'

'That'll have to do.' Quentin picked up his bags, and strode off.

'Come on,' he snapped at Charlie, who ran after him like a devoted puppy.

'And you,' he said, pausing to look at me.

'Me?'

'There's no one else here, is there?'

'I'm busy.'

'I suggest you do as I say.'

I thought about arguing but he was quite intimidating and, actually, I had some questions I wanted to ask. So I nodded and followed him and Charlie into the lounge, where Joyce was already serving drinks.

'Scarlett?' she said.

'Bit early for me.' I wanted to keep a clear head. 'Just a Coke, please.'

We sat down at the biggest table in the lounge, which pleased me because I didn't want to be too close to Charlie.

Quentin took a mouthful of his beer. 'I won't beat around the bush, Miss Simpson. I simply ask that you put an end to this ridiculous podcast. Tell your followers that you were wrong, shut up and go home.'

I bristled. Who was he to make such demands?

'Was it you who stopped the programme from being broadcast? How did you get Kevin to agree?'

'Everyone has a price,' Quentin said. He gave a small, unattractive smile. 'His was surprisingly low.'

'And Charlie's was fifty grand,' I muttered. Charlie scowled.

'I'm afraid there is too much at stake for this line of enquiry to continue,' Quentin said. 'As I explained to you and Charles, I am owed this inheritance. I need this inheritance.'

'I've heard it's a bit late for that.'

We all whipped round to see Lucas standing at the door of the lounge, looking pleased with himself.

'Too many fingers in too many pies,' he said. 'And every pie is slightly murkier than the one before.'

Quentin's face was red and he looked absolutely furious. 'You're talking nonsense.'

'I'm not,' said Lucas mildly. He began counting on his fingers. 'There's the HMRC investigation, which is not looking like it's going in your favour. I believe parliamentary standards want to talk to you about the Battersea property deal. And there's a very large question mark over some of your expenses.' He frowned. 'What was it exactly your decorator did to your constituency office to deserve his £200,000 payment?'

'How dare you?' spluttered Quentin. 'More to the point, who are you? Some conspiracy theorist, I bet?'

'Lucas Austen,' said Lucas, coming over to where we sat. 'Austen Ingleby Accountants.'

That meant nothing to me, but I was impressed that Lucas seemed to be in charge at the company where he worked, and both Charlie and Quentin sat up a bit straighter.

'We use you guys at work,' Charlie said, sticking his hand out for Lucas to shake. 'I'm DC Burns.'

Lucas barely glanced in Charlie's direction. 'Pleased to meet you,' he said, without shaking his outstretched hand. 'Shall we have a chat, Mr Wetherby?'

Quentin pulled a chair out from under the table. 'Sit.'

Lucas sat down next to me instead, and nudged my knee with his. I felt the warmth of him spreading through me and put my clasped hands over my mouth in a thoughtful gesture so I could hide my goofy smile.

Quentin fixed me with a steely stare. 'Charles warned me you were trouble.'

'I'm just getting started,' I said, feeling bold as anything with Lucas by my side. 'Hannah didn't kill Lawrence. I know that for a fact because they were both alive in 1938 when they got divorced. And he left money to her in his will.'

It was quite satisfying to see Quentin's jaw drop.

'Did you know this?' he said to Charlie.

Charlie shrugged. 'Only when I heard the show,' he said.

'You didn't find it out in your own research?'

'Well, erm, I'm sure it would have come up …' Charlie blustered. I knew he wouldn't have done any of his own research. Delegation was much more his style.

Quentin was still looking entirely bewildered. He rubbed his head. 'How is this possible?'

I leaned over the table. 'Why were you so convinced that Lawrence had died in 1933 and that Hannah had claimed the money?'

He took another mouthful of his beer. His mobile phone was ringing and he declined the call before he spoke.

'Because,' he said, 'my father told me he'd killed him.'

It was hard to guess which of us looked most shocked. Me, I suspected, but Lucas and Charlie both looked pretty taken aback, too.

'He told me when he was dying,' said Quentin. 'Though my stepmother was there when he spilled the beans and she didn't seem shocked, so I don't think I was the only person he told. She said he was talking rubbish.'

'But you believed him?'

'He was very convincing.'

I opened my notebook. Quentin gave it a pointed glance but I ignored it. 'Tell us about your father,' I said. 'You said he was a businessman?'

For a minute I thought he was going to tell me to get stuffed, but he didn't.

'He was 50 when I was born,' Quentin said. 'So he was more like a grandfather than a father really. He wasn't a very nice man. He was … disgruntled.'

Like father, like son, I thought.

'He felt like he'd been hard done by?' I said.

'I suppose so. He'd been a big drinker in his youth, apparently. And he always had a fondness for the horses. My mother always said he'd bet on two flies crawling up a wall. But he told me he was hurt when his father left everything to Lawrence instead of him – with this condition that he be married by his 35th birthday.'

'Your father – Simon – thought he was about to get his hands on the money, when Lawrence rocked up with a wife just before his birthday and foiled his plans,' I said.

'Yes.'

'So he killed Lawrence – in the hope he'd inherit instead?' said Charlie, in a policeman-like manner. 'If Lawrence was dead, then Simon was next in line?'

'No,' Quentin almost shouted and Charlie winced. 'No, he said it was an accident. A fight – out in the middle of Loch Ness.'

'How dramatic,' I said, drily. 'Did he throw poor Lawrence overboard then?'

Quentin shrugged. 'I don't know the details.'

'Simon chucked his brother in the loch, but when he went to claim the inheritance, someone had beaten him to it?'

'The money had been claimed, and the house had been sold,' Quentin agreed. 'And because Simon "knew" he'd killed his brother, he thought that if someone had claimed the inheritance that he believed should be his, it had to be Hannah.'

'Simon got a lump sum from the sale of the house, though?' Lucas spoke for the first time. 'I found evidence of that.'

'He did. He used it to start the business.'

'So he wasn't that hard done by,' I pointed out. 'And he could hardly report the inheritance as being fraudulently claimed without admitting to murder.'

Quentin nodded. 'Caught between a rock and a hard place.'

'Of his own making,' I said. 'If he'd ditched the gambling and, you know, not murdered his brother, his life might have been a bit easier.'

'Except,' said Quentin, leaning over the table. 'He didn't murder Lawrence did he? You've proved that. So he spent his days feeling guilty for doing something he didn't do.'

'Well, excuse me if I don't feel much sympathy for him,' I said.

Quentin's phone buzzed and he glanced at it. 'The car's here,' he said to Charlie. 'Are you coming back to Inverness?'

Charlie shifted in his chair. 'Could I just have a quick word with Scarlett?' he said.

I looked at him. 'What?'

'In private.'

I rolled my eyes. 'Fine. Five minutes. No longer.'

'Make it three,' said Quentin.

I got up and followed Charlie into the foyer, where I leaned against the reception desk and folded my arms.

'What is it?'

'It's good to see you, Scar,' he said.

'Oh, sod off.'

He laughed. 'Same old Scar.' Then, serious again, he reached out and touched my arm. 'I'm sorry about all this. I blame myself for this whole mess.'

'Well, that's because it's your fault,' I said. 'If you'd been honest and not taken this ridiculous job without me, then none of this would have happened. You're a bloody idiot. Are you in trouble at work?'

He looked down at his feet. 'Nope, seem to have got away with it.'

'God, you always come up smelling of roses, don't you? You even found yourself a better girlfriend when I dumped you.'

'She's not better,' he said, moving a bit closer to me. 'She's just … different.'

'Oh, come on.'

He laughed again and then he kissed me. For the tiniest fraction of a second and really just because it felt familiar and comforting, I kissed him back. Then I came to my senses and pulled away.

And over his shoulder I saw Lucas, watching us. His face was unreadable but I knew what he was thinking – he was thinking that I was just the same as Maya, when I'd promised him I wasn't.

'Lucas,' I said.

'God, sorry, mate, I didn't realise you two …' said Charlie.

Lucas shook his head, still looking at me. 'I'm leaving.'

'No, please,' I begged. 'Stay. Let's talk about all this.'

But he turned and went upstairs. I made to go after him, but Quentin appeared in front of me.

'So, we're agreed then?' he said. 'You're going to stop this podcast.'

'What? No! We didn't agree that.'

'It's the only thing that makes sense.'

'For you.' I was furious. 'But the genie's out of the bottle now, and everyone knows Lawrence was still alive in 1938. I'm going to finish this sodding podcast if it's the last thing I do.'

'It may well be,' said Quentin darkly but I jabbed him with my finger.

'Oh, enough of your stupid threats,' I said. 'I hate to do this, but do you know who my dad is?'

'He's not some two-bit policeman as well, is he?' Quentin said.

'Oi!' Charlie looked affronted.

'He's not in the police, no,' I said. 'He's Michael Newton, and I reckon he and his mates at the BBC would be very interested in your financial dealings.'

'Not to mention that woman you keep visiting in Bloomsbury,' Charlie said. 'Though perhaps your wife would be more interested in that bit.'

I looked at him in surprise.

'What?' he said. 'I did some research.'

It wasn't an exaggeration to say the colour drained from Quentin's face.

'Perhaps I'll just leave it,' he said.

'I think that's for the best.' I smiled at him sweetly. 'Have a safe trip home.'

He headed for the door without looking back, and I turned to Charlie. 'You too,' I said.

'But Scar ...'

'Sod off, Charlie.'

He was still watching me, open-mouthed, as I climbed the stairs and went to find Lucas.

Chapter 31

Hannah

1933

Simon was drunk, and freezing cold, and emotional, and Freddie was worryingly convincing, and those things combined meant it wasn't hard to convince him – and everyone who was gathering at the edge of the water – that Lawrie had plunged to a watery death.

The monster hunters, who were pumping with adrenaline anyway after Tobias had told them of his "sighting", and the reporters, all jumped into the boats and headed out into the loch, searching for any sign of Lawrence.

I felt bad for them, knowing as I did that Lawrie was safe and well on the deck of Balthazar Webster's sailing boat.

Angus, though, shrugged. 'They've spent these last weeks looking for something that isn't there,' he pointed out. 'This is no different.'

Mrs McEwan took Simon up to the hotel to get warm and dry. As they passed me, her arm around Simon's sou'wester-clad shoulder, I heard her say: 'And you're absolutely sure your brother was on the boat with you?'

Freddie grinned. 'She's a clever one.'

'What do you mean?'

'If we add a bit of doubt into whether Lawrie was on the water at all, it makes things easier.'

I sat down on a rock, feeling weak and dizzy suddenly. My head was pounding and my eye was so swollen I couldn't see very well.

'I'm going to call the doctor,' Angus said, looking at me with concern.

'In a minute. What things? Easier how?' I said.

'Don't you see?' Freddie said. 'We're free now.'

I didn't see. He wasn't making any sense.

'If everyone thinks Lawrie is dead, then we can start again.' He sighed happily. 'We can be together.'

'Everyone will be looking for him,' I said sharply. 'And homosexuality is still illegal.'

Freddie nodded. 'I know. But it gives us a chance, doesn't it?'

'I suppose so.'

He came over to where I sat and, crouching down next to me, he took my hand in his. 'I know you probably hate me, Hannah, but I am sorry.'

I looked at his beautiful face and his eyes full of genuine regret and I smiled as best I could with my swollen cheek. 'I don't hate you,' I said. 'But you did something really awful to me. Finding you both together was enough of a shock but then to let me believe I'd killed Lawrence …'

Freddie groaned. 'I know. I was horrible and I have no excuse, except to say my heart was broken when Lawrie married you, and I was hurting, and I wanted you to feel as bad as I did.'

'Well, you managed that all right,' I said.

'I do really love him you know.'

'I know.'

'And he might not have loved you, in that way, but he adores you. You know that too, don't you?'

'I think so.'

Freddie leaned forward so his mouth was close to my ear. 'What's the story with you and the handsome Scot?'

'Angus? Nothing.'

'But you'd like there to be something?'

'Maybe.'

'So Lawrie disappearing would do you a favour too?' He sat back on his haunches again. 'And not just in the romance department, I'm guessing? You'd be free to do as you pleased.'

'I suppose so.'

I swayed a little on the rock and Angus darted forward to support me. 'Let's go,' he said. 'You need to rest.'

He picked me up – actually scooped me into his arms. Over his shoulder, I saw Freddie nodding in approval, but my head was hurting so I rested it on Angus's chest and closed my good eye.

And when I woke up, it was two hours later, and I was on a couch in the lounge, with Davina sitting next to me, looking anxious.

'Oh thank goodness,' she said, as I stirred. 'I was so worried.'

I put my fingers to my puffy eye and winced. 'Ouch.'

'It looks awful,' Davina said cheerfully. 'It's purple.'

'Nice.'

I tried to sit up too quickly and made my head swim. So I tried again more slowly this time, and managed to get myself upright.

'Where is everyone?'

Davina grinned. 'Who do you want me to start with?'

'Lawrie. No, start with Simon.'

'Simon's away back to Inverness. Mrs McEwan's driving him. He is …' she looked up at the ceiling, feeling for the right word '… confused.'

'How so?'

'He was convinced that he'd been on the boat with Lawrie, but we kept asking if he was sure, and either he couldn't remember or he realised that it was much better for him if he wasn't the last person to see his brother, so now he's playing dumb.' She chuckled. 'Angus took a photograph of him on the shore in his sou'wester, with his wee hairy legs sticking out the bottom. He's sold it to three newspapers already and they've not even seen it yet.'

'Where's Lawrie?'

'In Tobias's room, with that Freddie. No one knows they're there, don't worry. Balthazar gave Lawrie a jacket and hat that belong to one of his men and he just blended in with the big-game hunters.'

'But the reporters?' I said, pushing my hair away from my face carefully without touching my eye. 'Surely, they're asking questions?'

'Balthazar said he saw the boat Simon was on – he didn't mention you or Lawrie being there of course – rise up out of the water, like it was being pushed by a gigantic creature,' she said. Her eyes were gleaming with excitement. 'And then he said that there was no way the boat could have got back to shore so fast unless it had been pushed. He told the reporters he was sure as he could be that there is a monster in the loch – and that it saved Simon's life. They're all fighting over the telephone to get in touch with their offices in London. Half of them are writing about Lawrie going missing and the other half are claiming to have seen the beast themselves.'

'That was kind of Balthazar to distract them all,' I said. 'Ooh, my head really does hurt.'

'I've got some aspirin for you.' Davina handed me a glass of water and two tablets wrapped in foil. Then she reached behind me and moved the cushion so it was supporting my back. 'Balthazar wasn't just being kind, you know? He really believes he saw something out there. He said Lawrie would never have made it all the way to his boat so fast without help.'

I laughed and then regretted it because it hurt. I swallowed the pills with a wince and hoped they would work quickly. 'Do you believe him?'

Davina shrugged. 'I've heard stranger stories,' she said. 'Lawrie wants to see you, if you're up to it?'

'I think so.'

'I'll go and fetch him.'

'No, don't. I'll go to him. He can't roam around the hotel if he's pretending to be missing, even in disguise.'

'I suppose so.'

'Where's Angus?' I asked.

'He's with all the reporters. He said his editor would kill him if he missed this story after being here for so long.'

I felt a flicker of envy that Angus was off being a journalist, and I wasn't. Wouldn't the editor also be expecting something from Ann O'Shawn? I'd have to put an article together later.

'He's right.'

'I'm surprised you're not out there, taking photos,' Davina said.

I thought, suddenly, of the pictures of Lawrie and Freddie, hidden under the floorboards in the outbuilding and I rubbed my nose. 'I'll go and find Lawrie,' I said getting to my feet slowly.

'Are you all right? Shall I come too?'

'No, I'm fine. Why don't you go and see what the reporters are up to?'

Davina looked concerned but to my relief, she let me wander off alone. I hauled myself up to our bedroom and found the negatives in the fireplace. I didn't have the energy to try to get the photographs hidden under the floor, but I thought they'd be safe. Tobias had fixed the wobbly boards and no one would look there now.

With the negatives safely in my hands, I went over to the far side of the hotel where Tobias's room was and knocked on the door.

'It's Hannah,' I called softly.

Freddie opened the door a tiny bit and peered out. 'Lord, you look dreadful,' he said.

'Thanks.'

He stood back to let me in, then locked the door behind me.

Lawrie was at the window, his shirt unbuttoned with its sleeves rolled up to his elbows, and looking more relaxed than I'd ever seen him. He was watching the reporters on the shore of the loch. 'This is extraordinary,' he said, kissing my cheek. 'How are you feeling?'

'Bruised and battered but fine. How are you?'

'I was only in the water for seconds,' he said. 'That Balthazar fellow was very quick to pull me out. I remember him vaguely from school.'

'He remembers you, too,' I said. 'I just hope he doesn't tell anyone what he did.'

'He won't,' said Lawrie with the confident air of a man who knew how to make things happen.

I smiled at him. 'Apparently, Balthazar thinks the monster pushed you to the boat, because you couldn't possibly have swum so fast.'

'I'm a very good swimmer,' said Lawrie indignantly. 'But the current was in my favour, admittedly.'

I rolled my eyes.

'What are you going to do? You can't stay in Tobias's room forever.'

'Thank goodness,' said Freddie, with a disdainful glance at Tobias's dirty laundry basket, which was overflowing.

'We're leaving,' Lawrie said. 'Going abroad.'

'Where?'

'Tangier.'

'Morocco? Why there?'

'It's an international zone,' Lawrie said, sounding like an MP again for a second. 'It's administered by several countries.'

'Which means really it's not administered at all,' Freddie added. 'I've got friends who have visited.'

'Is it safe?' I asked.

'Safer than staying in England.' Freddie sounded bitter and I couldn't blame him really.

'How will you get there?'

'I've arranged a boat.' Lawrie gave me a little smile. 'Not everyone thinks we're terrible people. We have friends who will help. And money, of course. That helps, too.'

'You're not terrible,' I said. 'None of this is your fault, not really.'

'Thanks, sweetheart,' said Freddie.

I glared at him, only half joking. 'I wasn't talking to you, Freddie. It's absolutely all your fault.'

Not bothered, he threw himself on to the bed and gazed up at me. 'Darling, I did you both a favour really. You'll thank me one day.'

'Maybe,' I said. I pulled the envelope out of my apron and handed them to Lawrie. 'These are the negatives of the photographs. I hid the pictures under a loose floorboard, which has now been nailed down and I can't get to them anymore.'

'Is it secure?' Lawrie frowned.

'Tobias did it, and he's never one to shirk on a job. I'd reckon on the whole outbuilding falling down before that floorboard coming loose again.'

'Then that's good enough for me. Thank you.'

We smiled at one another and then Lawrie squeezed my hand. 'I'll have to come back to England sometimes. Will you keep in touch?'

I was surprised to find that I liked the idea of that. 'I will,' I said.

Chapter 32

Scarlett

Present day

Lucas wasn't in his room. Or at least, he wasn't answering when I knocked.

I went back down to the lounge but there was no sign of him. I even went outside and walked down to the shores of the loch, hoping to see him in among the people filming and taking selfies, but he was nowhere to be seen.

I rang him but it went straight to voicemail, so I left a message asking him to call me back. Then I sent the same message by text. But when I checked, it had stayed unread.

I felt awful about him seeing me kiss Charlie. Just as I thought we might have had something, I'd gone and ruined it all. And he'd been so honest with me, too, telling me all that stuff about Maya. I was such an idiot.

Feeling wretched, I walked back up to the hostel, and when my phone buzzed with a message, I grabbed it out of my pocket so fast I fumbled it and dropped it onto the grass. When I eventually picked it up I was disappointed – unfairly – to see it was Robyn and not Lucas.

How are you getting on? she'd written. *On track to get me something this evening?*

'Oh shit,' I breathed. I'd been dealing with sodding Charlie and horrible Quentin, and now looking for Lucas, and I was running out of time to get this podcast done.

Absolutely! I typed to Robyn, hoping that writing it would make it true. Then I hurried back inside, heading for the lounge, where I'd abandoned all my papers and my laptop, and hoping they were still there.

Fortunately, I found Bonnie in the lounge, surrounded by all my notes, reading Ann O'Shawn's articles.

'This is brilliant,' she said as I sat down next to her. 'It must have been so exciting to work here back then.'

'Know what's even more brilliant?' I said. She looked up at me, intrigued. 'I think this Ann O'Shawn was our Hannah Snow.'

Bonnie looked delighted. 'OMG the names are an anagram,' she said.

'Did you literally just work that out by looking?' I was impressed. 'I had to write it down and cross the letters off.'

She shrugged. 'I like crosswords.'

'Geek,' I said and she beamed at me.

'Look at this,' she said. 'In one of her first articles, she says everyone is talking about whether or not they believe in the monster and she says that just because you don't believe in something, that doesn't mean it doesn't exist. That's what my great-granny always said. Maybe Hannah got it from her?'

'They're wise words.'

'I don't believe in ghosts,' Bonnie said. 'But maybe they're all around us now. Maybe Hannah's watching us right this minute, getting annoyed with us trying to figure out her happy ending.'

'Maybe.' I laughed. 'But I don't believe in happy endings either.'

Bonnie gave me a fierce look. 'Well, you should.' Then she

grinned. 'Just because you don't believe in something doesn't mean it doesn't exist.'

I whacked her with a cushion.

'I've got a lot of work to do, getting this podcast done before my boss comes back from his weekend away.'

'Is Lucas helping?'

I felt a flash of guilt. 'I don't know where Lucas is,' I admitted. 'We had a bit of a … falling-out.'

'I wondered why he went early.' Joyce came into the lounge, carrying a crate of bottles, and Bonnie jumped up to help her. 'He said something had come up, but I got the impression he was fibbing.'

'Lucas has gone?' I said. 'Gone where?'

'Back to Edinburgh.' Joyce started taking bottles out of the crate and putting them into the fridge.

'He's gone, gone?'

Bonnie looked at me. 'You didn't know?'

I wanted to cry. 'No.'

'What happened?' Joyce asked. 'I thought you two were made for each other.'

'We were. Nothing happened.' I was defensive but Bonnie was looking at me sceptically and I folded. 'Charlie kissed me, and Lucas saw.'

'Awks,' she said.

Joyce paused in her bottle filling. 'We all make mistakes, Scarlett. Just apologise and I'm sure it'll be fine.'

'He's not answering his phone. And my messages aren't being read.'

'Burn,' said Bonnie. 'Has he blocked you?'

'Oh God, do you think he's blocked me?'

Bonnie, looking more gleeful than was necessary, nodded. 'Looks like it. Don't blame him. His heart's probably shattered.'

'You'll have to write him a letter,' Joyce said. 'Like we did back in the day. Send him a proper message instead of all this texting nonsense. He can't block a letter like he can an email.'

'I don't have his address,' I said. My mind was racing. 'But I could send him a message in another way.'

'You could hire a plane and get it to write "I love you, Lucas" in the sky,' said Bonnie.

'Or,' I said, glaring at her, 'I could send him a message in the podcast.'

'Would he listen, though?' said Bonnie. 'I wouldn't.'

'He might.'

'S'pose.'

I pointed at her. 'Just because you don't believe in something, doesn't mean it doesn't exist.'

'Riiiight.'

'Lucas doesn't believe in soulmates,' I said. 'We had a whole conversation about it. But maybe he's mine and I'm his.'

Bonnie threw herself back onto the cushions, the back of her hand to her forehead. 'Ohmygod, this is the most romantic thing I've ever heard.'

I faltered. 'Well, maybe not soulmates, but my point is, how will we know if we don't try?'

'Are you going to say that in your podcast?' Joyce said, her brow furrowed. 'Because I'm not sure your listeners will be interested in your love life.'

'I am,' said Bonnie.

'I'll work it in somehow,' I said, hoping inspiration would strike. 'I need to try at least. And I know he'll want to know how the story ends.'

'Can I help?' said Bonnie. 'I want to know too.'

'I could definitely use some help.'

She sat up looking eager.

Joyce put the last bottle in the fridge and leaned over the counter. 'What's the story so far?'

'So, we know that Hannah and Lawrence got married in March 1933, and then for some reason Hannah ran away and ended up here, working at the hotel with your mum … What was her name?'

'Davina,' said Joyce. 'And my father was Tobias.'

'She was working with Davina and Tobias, and writing stories for the newspaper about the hunt for the Loch Ness monster, under the pen name Ann O'Shawn.'

'That's an anagram of Hannah Snow,' Bonnie told her grand-mother, who looked impressed.

'In May 1933, Lawrence disappeared. We know the police in Inverness were involved in looking for him, but we also know there was a bit of confusion about where he was last seen. Quentin said his father Simon, who was Lawrence's younger brother, told him he'd killed Lawrence here at Loch Ness.'

'Goodness,' said Joyce.

'We know Lawrence didn't die though, so Simon was wrong about that. I don't understand why he'd lie about murdering someone, mind you.'

'Maybe he thought he had murdered him. Or, maybe Lawrence was like that canoe man,' Bonnie said. 'Remember, Gran? We watched the drama about him. Everyone thought he was dead but he wasn't.'

I stared at her. 'Bonnie, you might be on to something there. Perhaps Lawrence faked his own death.'

'Why though?' asked Joyce. 'Canoe man did it for the life insur-ance. If Lawrence did fake his death, it couldn't have been for the money because he was about to inherit everything anyway.'

'Perhaps he was fed up with his old life and wanted a new start,' said Bonnie. 'Maybe he wanted to go off grid and live in the woods eating grubs.'

'Instead of living in a beautiful house with a beautiful wife? I don't think so.' Joyce shook her head.

'Although, Quentin said there were rumours at the time that Lawrence was gay,' I explained. 'If he was gay, he probably wouldn't have wanted a wife, no matter how beautiful she was.'

'Lots of people on social media suggested he might have been gay,' Bonnie pointed out.

'Perhaps he wanted to start again and just be his real self?' I said. But I frowned. 'Was there anywhere he could have been out and proud though, back then? It was illegal in England. Was it illegal in Scotland?'

'Gosh, yes,' said Joyce. 'I believe we were a bit behind England in legalising same-sex relationships, though it pains me to admit it.'

I chuckled.

'Maybe abroad then? Europe perhaps? Or South America?'

'We did an assembly thing for LGBTQ+ history month at school,' said Bonnie. 'I'll find it online and see if there's any info in that.'

'Blimey, school assemblies have changed since my day,' I muttered, feeling old. 'But thank you.'

Joyce was frowning, looking like she was thinking hard.

'I've got something,' she said. 'Something that might help.'

She came out from behind the counter and disappeared off out of the room.

'What's she up to?' I asked Bonnie. She made a face.

'Could be anything, knowing Gran.'

Joyce came back into the lounge holding a folder. 'Look at these.'

She handed me the folder, and I opened it. Inside were a series of black-and-white photographs. I slid them out. They were beautiful shots of two men lying on a bed, each very handsome in his own way. They were both naked, though they were covered by sheets and the contours of their bodies and faces were highlighted in the light from the window next to the bed.

The photographs were artistic and intimate and quite erotic. I felt a little like I was watching something I shouldn't be seeing. The men weren't touching, but they were close to one another. Looking at each other with love.

'Is that Lawrence?' I said in wonder. 'Oh my goodness, it is

– that's Lawrence.' I looked at Joyce. 'Where did you get these?'

'When we made the glamping site a couple of years ago, we knocked down an old outbuilding and we found them under the floorboards,' she said. 'I was going to throw them away but I rather liked them so I kept them.'

'Gran's quite arty,' said Bonnie, looking at the photographs over my shoulder. 'Look at that man's six-pack.'

'Well done, Lawrence,' I said, impressed. 'Mind you, he's quite a catch himself isn't he? Look at those shoulders.'

'What I don't know is why they were under my floorboards,' Joyce said. 'My father did all the maintenance round the hotel for years, but I don't think he'd have had anything to do with hiding these photos.'

I pointed to the man who wasn't Lawrence.

'That's not your dad, is it?'

Joyce laughed loudly. 'Goodness me, no,' she said. 'My father was a sweetheart and my mother adored him, but he was definitely not model material.'

'Perhaps Hannah took these pictures?' I mused. 'Though they seem more candid than posed. Ooh, maybe she spied on Lawrence and this man together and took the pictures. She was a journalist, after all. Perhaps she saw an opportunity.' I frowned. 'It doesn't sound like her, though, from what we know of her.'

'I suppose we'll never know,' said Joyce. 'Just like we'll never know who the other man is.'

Bonnie was practically drooling. 'You should put these up somewhere, Gran,' she said. 'They're lovely.'

'I don't think so,' Joyce said. She took the pictures from me and slid them back inside the folder. 'I think they're private.'

I nodded. 'I agree. It feels a bit unfair to show off photos of Lawrence that he can't agree to. We don't even know anything about the other man.'

Bonnie looked disappointed. 'I guess.' She sighed. 'So if Lawrence faked his own death and went off somewhere to live a fabulous gay life with his hottie boyfriend, then what's next?'

'I think there's only one question left to answer,' I said.

'What happened to Hannah?'

'Indeed,' I said. 'But I have a feeling she might have called herself Ann O'Shawn after all the business with Lawrence.'

'Would she be allowed to do that?'

'I think so,' I said. 'We did another podcast where someone had changed their name and it seemed pretty straightforward to do.'

I opened my laptop and found the Scottish register of births, marriages and deaths. Then I typed in Ann O'Shawn. I set the dates from 1930 to 1990, and pressed return.

Up came the results – just one. Under births, marriages and deaths. Holding my breath, I clicked on it.

Ann O'Shawn married Angus Reid, in St Giles, Edinburgh, January 1939.

'She got married again?' Bonnie said.

'Just after her divorce from Lawrence went through,' I said.

Bonnie frowned. 'So who's Angus?'

'I've seen that name somewhere.' I leafed through my notes and found the printout of the story about the first sighting of the monster by the woman who ran the hotel. 'Bingo!'

'He was another journalist?' Bonnie said. 'They must have met because of the monster hunt.' She clasped her hands to her chest. 'I wonder if they thanked the Loch Ness monster for bringing them together in the wedding speech?'

Laughing I typed Angus's name into the search engine and found a census that told me he and Ann had three children – Laura, right at the beginning of the war, and then James and Robert after the war – and lived in Edinburgh.

'She named her daughter after her ex-husband,' I said. 'How very civilised.'

'She got her happy ending,' Bonnie said with satisfaction.

'Looks that way,' I agreed. I clicked off the register site and instead turned to Google, typing in Ann O'Shawn, journalist,

Edinburgh. It brought up hundreds of results. Hannah – Ann – had been a reporter for several newspapers, all the way through the Second World War, and well into the 1950s and 60s. She'd even written two books about women in journalism. She'd died, aged 80, in 1994.

'Ohh,' I breathed. 'She did have her happy ending.'

Joyce waved the folder containing the photos at me. 'Hannah got her happy ending, Lawrence got his, so now you know what you have to do?'

'What's that?'

'You have to go and get yours.'

Chapter 33

Episode 3

The Monster in the Loch

There you have it. Lawrence Wetherby didn't die in 1933 when he went missing from the shores of Loch Ness. I think he shrugged off the shackles of public life in England and went abroad with his lover, chasing a happy ending. I don't know where they went or if they did live happily ever after, but I like to think so, don't you?

And as for Hannah, she too found a way to escape from society's expectations. She was released from a marriage that I don't think would have ever made her happy. She had the freedom to pursue a career she loved and was clearly very good at. And she found happiness with another man – she and Angus were married until he died just eighteen months before she did, after more than half a century together.

The only mystery that remains is whether there really is a monster lurking in the depths of Loch Ness.

And, let's be honest, it's possible. As Hannah – writing

as Ann O'Shawn – said: 'Just because you don't believe in something, doesn't mean it doesn't exist.'

She was talking about the monster, of course, but as I've been investigating her story, I've realised it can refer to so much more.

I never believed in happy endings, but now – thanks to Hannah, Lawrence, and a very special person I've met along the way called Lucas – I think, perhaps, I've changed my mind.

Thanks for listening.

Sunday June 19
From Dad:
Well done, darling. Great listen. Shall I have a word with the chaps on the Today programme for you?

Sunday June 19
From Charlie:
Good one, Scar.

Sunday June 19
From Robyn:
Check Twitter! Loch Ness is trending again! So is Hannah Snow. Well done, mate.

From HR@ BritainLive.co.uk
CC: Kevin@ BritainLive.co.uk
To: SSimpson@BritainLive.co.uk
Date: Sunday June 19

RE: URGENT breach of contract

Dear Scarlett
We've been informed that you've been working on a direct competitor's broadcast while employed by Britain Live.

This is in contravention of the terms of your contract, and therefore, your employment is terminated with immediate effect. Please see the attached information regarding a financial settlement.

Yours etc,

From: recruitment@goldmanproductions.co.uk
To: Scarlett85@readmail.co.uk
Date: Sunday June 20

RE: Potential opportunity to work together

Dear Scarlett
We're putting together a team to work on a series of investigations for Channel 4. I've been avidly listening to your report on the Hannah Snow mystery and I'd love you to join us. Can we meet for a coffee and have a chat?

My phone was buzzing with so many messages that it kept falling off the table. There was a party atmosphere in the lounge bar. We'd done a live listen-along to the podcast when it dropped early on Sunday evening, with me Tweeting comments and frantically answering people's questions as they arrived.

Joyce, bless her, had put on drinks and nibbles for all the hostel's guests, who all got really involved in the whole thing and reacted to each revelation in the podcast with "ooh"s and "aah"s that made it way more dramatic than podcasts usually were.

I could have gone back to London when I'd finished recording. I probably should have really, as my life was about to implode – already had imploded, considering my email from HR. But I wanted to listen to the podcast with Joyce and Bonnie in the place where all the action took place.

Robyn was sending me endless voice notes, which were making

me laugh.

'My mum says can you do a follow-up show about what happened to Simon?' she sent.

'No,' I sent back. 'Tell your mum he's a git.'

I scrolled through my notifications listlessly, tuning out the hubbub of excited voices. I knew I should be happy about the attention Hannah's story was getting, but I felt flat and miserable. Even the prospect of a new job wasn't enough to make me smile.

Because the only person who I wanted to hear from hadn't got in touch.

'Can you record a message for the girls at school?' Bonnie said sliding into the seat next to me. 'They're all totally obsessed with Hannah Snow. Lucy Anderson says she's going to cut her hair like Hannah's.'

'How does Lucy Anderson know what Hannah's hair was like? We've literally got one photograph of her and it's blurred.'

Bonnie grinned. 'She's just googled 1930s hairstyles I think.'

'Very enterprising.'

'So, like, can you record the message now?'

'Go on then. What do you want me to say?'

'Just that we're friends and that I was really helpful?' Bonnie held her phone up and then put it down again. 'Actually, we can do this later.'

She jumped up from her chair and I turned to see what had changed her mind. And there, standing in the doorway to the lounge, wearing his *Red Dwarf* T-shirt, was Lucas.

Even though the room was full of chattering podcasters and bloggers, it felt like they all faded away.

'Hi,' I said, getting up and going over to where he stood.

'Hi.'

'Did you hear the episode?'

'I did.'

'Do you believe in happy endings?'

'I'm starting to.'

I couldn't stop myself grinning. 'Charlie kissed me, you know. And I did kiss him back for a second, but that was just … muscle memory.'

'Muscle memory?' Was there a hint of a smile at the corners of Lucas's mouth?

'That's a thing.' I reached out and touched his arm lightly. 'But I'm sorry.'

'I'm sorry too,' he said. 'I over-reacted. You're the first person I've really liked since Maya, and it just all came back. I was embarrassed, but I misjudged you.'

I took a little step towards him. 'Ah yes, the mistake you made was thinking I was a Lannister, when it's quite clear to everyone who knows me that I'm more of a Stark.'

'Scarlett Simpson, have you been watching *Game of Thrones*?' he said, his eyes dancing with amusement. 'I thought you hated stuff with dragons?'

'No, not all stuff with dragons,' I lied. 'I watched the first few episodes. The first episode. I watched the first episode.'

'Did you like it?'

'God no,' I said, as his arms circled my waist and he pulled me close for a kiss. 'Absolutely hated it.'

'Sorry to interrupt,' said Joyce, tapping me on the shoulder. 'But this lady has come to see you.'

Reluctantly, I untangled myself from Lucas's arms. Standing with Joyce was a smart, older woman with dark grey hair, wearing glasses with bright red frames, and a colourful long beaded necklace.'

'Hello,' I said. 'I'm Scarlett Simpson.'

She gave me a firm handshake. 'It's lovely to meet you,' she said. 'My name's Laura Nicholas.'

'Nice to meet you, Laura,' I said, beginning to understand who she was. I glanced at Lucas who was looking confused. 'Did you come from Edinburgh?'

She gave me a broad smile, nodding. 'I did. I've been listening to your programme and I so wanted to meet you,' she said. She took a breath. 'My father was Angus Reid and my mother was Hannah Snow, except we all knew her as Ann.'

I did a little bounce on my toes. 'You're Hannah's daughter,' I told her in excitement, even though she knew. 'I'm so pleased you're here.'

We sat down, Lucas and I next to one another, our legs touching, and Laura opposite, and Joyce went off to get us more coffee.

'My brothers and I have all been listening to your podcasts,' Laura said.

I put a hand to my mouth as a thought occurred to me. 'Did you know? Did you know who your mother was?'

'Oh yes,' Laura said and I let out my breath. 'She never kept it a secret really. She just said she liked the name Ann better. When we were a bit older, she told us about Lawrence. It was when Lord Lucan went missing and there were lots of stories about Lawrence's disappearance. She said she'd named me after him.'

'Did you meet him? Lawrence?'

'Just once. When I was about 15, we went on holiday to Morocco. He lived in Tangier with his partner Freddie, and Mum took us to visit. He was nice. He and Mum always kept in touch, I think. He died in the late Seventies and Freddie moved to the south of France. He died a few years after my mum.'

'That's lovely,' I said. 'I'm glad they were happy.'

'I think they were,' Laura said.

'And your mum? Was she happy?'

'My mother was very independent,' Laura said carefully. 'She didn't always like being a parent, and she often went off travelling following stories. She wasn't a conventional mother.' She leaned forward across the table and lowered her voice. 'But I have to say, she was more exciting for it.'

'She sounds brilliant,' I said.

Laura opened her large handbag and took out some sheets of

302

photocopied paper. 'Mum kept diaries her whole life,' she said. 'When she died, there were shelves and shelves of them in her study. All in order. I copied these pages from 1933. I thought you might like to see them. Find out what happened.'

'Her happy ending?' I said.

'Oh I'm not sure Mum really believed in happy endings,' said Laura.

I smiled and under the table, I felt Lucas lace his fingers through mine.

'Just because you don't believe in something, doesn't mean it doesn't exist,' I said.

Chapter 34

Extract from Hannah Snow's diary

May 1933

Lawrence and Freddie have gone. Lawrie says they've got tickets for a ship sailing to Tangier in Morocco. It sounds terribly bohemian, which is probably the perfect place for Freddie, though I'm not sure how Lawrie will deal with it. Perhaps he'll surprise us all.

After they'd left the hotel, very early the day after Lawrie "disappeared", Davina came and told me Angus was at the hotel and he was looking for me.

I went to find him, positive that he wanted to tell me his interview with Balthazar had paid off and he was going to say goodbye before he left for a new life in Edinburgh.

But he surprised me too.

He was sitting in the hotel garden, looking out towards the loch when I found him.

'How's your eye?' he said, as I got closer.

'Sore.'

I sat down on the bench next to him.

'So I guess you're off to Edinburgh then? The big job?'

'I am. Balthazar's interview swung it for me.'

'Good for you,' I said honestly, with only the briefest, tiniest glimmer of envy.

Angus took my hand. 'Lawrie came to see me,' he said.

I bristled. I did not like the idea of men talking about me without me being present. Angus obviously realised because he quickly added: 'He told me that I shouldn't let you go.' He smiled. 'And he said he wasn't going to tell me to look after you, because you could look after yourself.'

'That's true,' I said. I liked how his fingers felt in mine. 'But you're going to Edinburgh, Angus. It's too late.'

'Except it isn't.'

I rolled my eyes at him. 'Of course it is.'

'The editor at the News saw Ann O'Shawn's articles. All of them. They've got a vacancy for a columnist, and they wondered if Ann might want the job.'

'How did he see Ann's work?'

'Everyone's seen it, Hannah,' Angus said with a sigh. 'The Herald's circulation has increased since you started writing it.'

'That's because everyone wants to know about the monster.'

'That's some of it.'

I looked down at my feet. 'There's a job for me in Edinburgh?'

'If you want it?'

'I'll have to make sure Mrs McEwan can do without me.'

'Davina will cover. She and Tobias are virtually running the place anyway, now Mrs M's busy with her interviews.'

'True.'

'So, what do you say, Ann O'Shawn?'

I took his face in my hands and planted a kiss on his lips.

'Let's go,' I said.

A Letter from Kerry Barrett

Thank you so much for choosing to read *The Missing Wife*. I hope you enjoyed it! If you did and would like to be the first to know about my new releases, you can follow me on Twitter and Instagram @kerrybean73, and on Facebook at https://www.facebook.com/kerrybarrettwrites. Or have a look at my website kerrybarrett.co.uk.

In that strange pause between lockdowns in summer 2020, my family and I were lucky enough to take a trip to the Scottish Highlands. My younger son, who was 10 at the time, was obsessed with the Loch Ness monster and was desperate to visit. So we spent a day at the visitor centre in Drumnadrochit learning all about the hunt for Nessie – and this story was born.

As part of my research, I listened to many, many podcasts about the Loch Ness monster. And a strange thing happened. I went from being someone who was faintly amused by everyone who believed in such a ridiculous tale, to someone who now thinks it's totally plausible!

Apparently, Nessie sightings were at an all-time high during 2020, which makes sense to me. After all, if you were the monster wouldn't you be more likely to stick your head out of the water when the fleets of Nessie-hunting boats were all stuck on shore?

Sadly, we didn't see any sign of her when we visited, but Loch Ness is such a magical and strange place that, like Scarlett says in the story, once you're there, the idea of a monster living in the depths of the loch suddenly seems possible.

I'd love to know what you all believe. Are you convinced that Nessie exists or do you think it's all nonsense? Let me know!

I hope you loved *The Missing Wife* and if you did, I would be so grateful if you would leave a review. I always love to hear what readers thought, and it helps new readers discover my books too.

Thanks,
Kerry x

www.facebook.com/kerrybarrettwrites
www.twitter.com/kerrybean73
www.instagram.com/kerrybean73/
www.kerrybarrett.co.uk

The Secrets of Thistle Cottage

The truth can be dangerous in the wrong hands …

1661, North Berwick, Scotland

One stormy night, healer Honor Seton and her daughter Alice are summoned to save the town lord's wife – but they're too late. A vengeful crusade against the Seton women leads to whispers of witchcraft all over town. Honor hopes her connections can protect them from unproven rumours and dangerous accusations – but is the truth finally catching up with them?

Present day, North Berwick, Scotland

After an explosive scandal lands her husband in prison, Tess Blyth flees Edinburgh to start afresh in Thistle Cottage. As she hides from the media's unforgiving glare, Tess is intrigued by the shadowy stories of witchcraft surrounding the women who lived in the cottage centuries ago. But she quickly discovers modern-day witch hunts can be just as vicious: someone in town knows her secret – and they won't let Tess forget it …

The Smuggler's Daughter

Only she knows the truth. Only she can save them.

1799

Emily Moon lives with her mother in an inn on a clifftop
in the darkest reaches of Cornwall. After her father mysteri-
ously disappears, her mother finds solace at the bottom of a
bottle, and the only way to keep afloat is to turn a blind eye to
the smugglers who send signals from the clifftops. But Emily
knows that the smugglers killed her father to ensure his silence,
and she will not let his murder go unpunished …

Present day

After a case ends in tragedy, police officer Phoebe Bellingham
flees to Cornwall for a summer of respite. But rather than the
sunny Cornwall of her dreams, she finds herself on storm-beaten
cliffs, surrounded by stories of ghosts and smugglers – and the
mysterious Emily Moon, who vanished without a trace over two
centuries ago. As rain lashes down around her, Phoebe deter-
mines to find the truth behind the rumours – but what she
uncovers will put her in danger too …

The Book of Last Letters

Inspired by an incredible true story, this is an unforgettable novel about love, loss and one impossible choice …

London, 1940

When nurse Elsie offers to send a reassuring letter to the family of a patient, she has an idea. She begins a book of last letters: messages to be sent on to wounded soldiers' loved ones should the very worst come to pass, so that no one is left without a final goodbye.

But one message will change Elsie's life forever. When a patient makes a devastating request, can Elsie find the strength to do the unthinkable?

London, present day

Stephanie has a lot of people she'd like to speak to: her estranged brother, to whom her last words were in anger; her nan, whose dementia means she is only occasionally lucid enough to talk.

When she discovers a book of wartime letters, Stephanie realises the importance of our final words – and uncovers the story of a secret love, a desperate choice, and the unimaginable courage of the woman behind it all …

Acknowledgements

There is a wealth of information out there about the Loch Ness monster and it's almost all brilliantly entertaining – and, much to my surprise – pretty convincing! If you're ever in Drumnadrochit, I recommend visiting the Loch Ness Centre and Exhibition. It's a really fun place to visit. It's in what was once the Drumnadrochit Hotel – it was a real place and the hotelier did indeed spark the monster-hunting fervour of the 1930s. Mrs McEwan in my story, though, is fictional.

When it comes to broadcasting and podcasting, I had help from the radio and television presenter Kevin O'Sullivan who talked me through how to make a radio show. And the fabulous Danny Robins spared an hour of his extremely busy time to explain how to make a podcast. If you're after a spooky listen, check out his shows *The Battersea Poltergeist* and *Uncanny*, which are both on BBC Sounds.

Thanks as ever to my fabulous editor Abi Fenton, my former agent Felicity Trew, and my new agent Amanda Preston. And of course to you, my readers. Thank you all for reading this one! I hope you enjoy it.

Dear Reader,

We hope you enjoyed reading this book. If you did, we'd be so appreciative if you left a review. It really helps us and the author to bring more books like this to you.

Here at HQ Digital we are dedicated to publishing fiction that will keep you turning the pages into the early hours. Don't want to miss a thing? To find out more about our books, promotions, discover exclusive content and enter competitions you can keep in touch in the following ways:

JOIN OUR COMMUNITY:

Sign up to our new email newsletter:
http://smarturl.it/SignUpHQ

Read our new blog www.hqstories.co.uk

🐦 https://twitter.com/HQStories

📘 www.facebook.com/HQStories

BUDDING WRITER?

We're also looking for authors to join the HQ Digital family!
Find out more here:

https://www.hqstories.co.uk/want-to-write-for-us/

Thanks for reading, from the HQ Digital team